Ameri

The Los Angeles Cauldron

Elizabeth Harris

DEDICATION

For Dodd

In 1984, everything changed

DISCLAIMER

The information in American Bruja about Native American cultural practices as relates to the spirit world are entirely imagined on the part of the author. The selling of ceremony is an abhorrent practice and the author has never, nor ever will write about any actual sacred Native American tradition. Becoming a Bruja requires practice and persistence, not unlike choosing the rocky, twisting path that winds along the rock formation known locally in the Simi Hills as the Twelve Apostles.

ACKNOWLEDGMENTS

Character Illustrations by Joshua Hurwitz

Symbolic Illustrations (Section Headings) by Cameo Lussier-Lawrence

Photography by John Luker

Chantico, Goddess of Fire Dia de los Muertes (Day of the Dead) Face Painting
by Carlos Nietos

www.AmericanBruja.com

Table of Contents

House on Lizard Hill

Divine beings are we

PROLOGUE

Suddenly, Amber McBride broke through the overgrowth and onto a tiny clearing atop a rock outcropping. Brush tottered above, indicating that her pursuers were not far behind.

The ridiculousness of this predicament was not lost on Amber: a jealous senior wanted to kick her ass because the older girl's boyfriend had allegedly taken an interest in Amber. Was Lourdes Navarro delusional? Amber was just a skinny, gawky, redheaded ninth grader.

The whole thing was so stupid, but the older girl wouldn't listen and had brought three tough, tattooed friends with her. It didn't help that today had been christened *Kick a Ginger Day*.

Something scaly brushed Amber's leg. Yelping with surprise, she leapt aside. Gaping, she watched a rattlesnake slither obliviously past.

Angry shouts reached her ears, forcing Amber to swallow her fear. Readying to bolt past the rattler, she was stopped yet again by a furry wave of small rodents. Bushy-tailed tree squirrels and thin-tailed ground squirrels moved in unison with their sworn enemies, voles and weasels. Tiny field mice scampered astride bulky gophers. Unbelieving, she saw more snakes join the fray, as predator and prey descended side-by-side.

Desperate, Amber spied a ledge along the canyon side, higher than the rutted trail. Leaping up, she stumbled precariously through brush while trying to keep her balance. Trying hard not to look down into the deep chasm, Amber made her way down to a gully. The streambed was deep, requiring her to scramble on all fours up the banks.

The entire hillside erupted in a cacophony. Quickly turning, she faced the path and simultaneously had to duck down low as a screeching flock of quail stormed over, grazing her as they went.

Before she could lift her head, a clowder of bobcats stampeded past with unearthly screeches. Whatever pursued the creatures had reduced them to blind terror, despite their fearsome pit bull size and Goblin ears.

Before she could stand, deer bounded down the hill and leapt over the streambed. One nearly kicked her in the head with its hind legs. The herd kept on going as if the devil himself was in pursuit.

Amber's nose twitched with the scent. Raising her head, she saw what was *really* coming for her.

A tidal wave of fire cascaded down the hill, engulfing the path she'd taken only moments earlier.

Panic threatened to overwhelm her senses. Through resounding *booms* from nearby laurel sumac exploding, three words pierced her consciousness:

Burn the witch

I

TRANSFORMATION

Be patient. You will know when it is time to wake up and move ahead – Ram Dass

AMBER McBRIDE

CHAPTER 1

CHANGE

August 2011

Amber McBride fidgeted restlessly in her seat, thinking about the terrible turn of events her young life had taken: uprooted from the only home she had ever known in Seattle to be ridiculously played out against the otherworldly terrain of the Simi Hills. This strange, shadowy place her father now drove through was nothing like her glamorous, palm-lined vision of Los Angeles!

Even more infuriating was the fact that her mother Michelle sent Amber packing while she stayed behind in Seattle. She had managed to put off joining them with excuses of Amber's Aunt Cathy needing help to get through some personal crisis. Until now, Amber's mother had devoted her life to *family*. Intuitively, Amber understood there was far more behind her mother's action than she would admit to. For all intents and purposes, it was beginning to appear as if Amber had been abandoned.

Kibbles, the family dog slept contentedly in the backseat of the car. Pointy ears twitched above a husky nose as his long-furred yellow chest rose and fell rhythmically with every breath. Kibbles was the product of a mutt gene pool collision that managed to produce a very fetching pup. Only the occasional, barely noticeable wheeze in his throat betrayed old age.

Usually at some point when trapped within the confines of a car with her father, Amber would mentally reach out and check in to see what Kibbles had been up to lately. However, rage enveloped all thought, feeling and purpose, leaving no room for curious exploration. If Amber had used her unique and secret talent, she would have seen the butthole of an attractive Great Dane her dog had checked out earlier that day. The scent, although intoxicatingly romantic for a canine, would have made Amber want to gag.

A recurring thought haunted Amber: perhaps her mother had *never* really been there for her, at least not in the ways that were most important. She had been useless when Amber was six years old and connected mentally with an animal for the first time.

Nose hair

The first image Amber plucked from an animal's mind was nose hair. A larger-than life close-up of hairy nostrils flooded little Amber's mind when she threw her arms around the neck of the then-homeless Kibbles. The vision overwhelmed the actual sights and sounds in front of her, as if she had suddenly been transported to the front row of a movie theatre.

Releasing her grip, Amber had backed away from the dog but the image remained. Retreating as a camera would, the view widened to reveal an elderly man, prone upon the floor. Amber didn't understand it at the time, but she was seeing Kibbles' previous owner from the dog's vantage point. Six-year old Amber's vision zoomed in to hover right above the elder's face as a pink tongue darted out, licking his checks. The old man didn't move, nor did he appear to be breathing.

Terrified about the fate of the elder, Amber had immediately informed her mother about what she'd seen. Instead of taking her seriously, Mrs. McBride patted Amber's head like she were a dog and told her to stop making up wild stories. Her mother never considered the possibility that what Amber experienced was real. First-grade student Amber McBride was left to make sense of a confusing, frightening experience on her own. Without guidance, she'd come to a conclusion any child would: there was something *wrong* with her.

Maybe her mother thought she was a freak and, despite her valiant efforts over the years to be the perfect mother by staying home and putting family first, Mrs. McBride was ready to give up on her only child.

Stomach churning as the reality of her abandonment settled in, Amber realized that her mother probably used her dislike of the house as a convenient excuse. Although never enthusiastic about the move, Mrs. McBride became uncharacteristically withdrawn as soon as her father showed them the online photos of the rambling old home. She'd retreated to the master bedroom, refusing to speak to anyone. When Mrs. McBride emerged later that night, her parents had the worst argument Amber could ever remember.

Strange also was the cryptic collection of online pictures: the few available depicted odd, cavernous rooms filled with a strange assortment of broken-down furniture and junk. What did Amber's father see in the house? Amber doubted even a ghost would want to live there!

Attempting to make conversation, Dr. Christopher McBride cut into Amber's unhappy musings. Gesturing toward the side of the road where a young man walked, her father remarked cheerily, "Maybe they're filming a movie. That guy looks like a Spanish cowboy!"

Glancing out, Amber spotted an oddly dressed mustachioed Latino walking toward town. Wearing a wide-brimmed hat, stiffly formal jacket with double caps upon the shoulders and a vibrant red neck scarf, his manner of dress appeared to be from the late 1800's.

Exhaling heavily, Dr. McBride didn't show his disappointment over his daughter's refusal to respond as he slowed the car to a crawl. Ancient oaks lined the road on both sides of a narrow choke point ahead. Broad branches intertwined overhead into a natural arbor as they passed a sign that read, 'Lake Manor: 15 MPH.' In an attempt to diffuse some of the tension, he turned on the radio.

Looking around in absolute disbelief as her father pulled into town, the first building Amber's widening eyes processed on route to her rapidly panicking brain was a rustic log cabin with an 8-foot carving of Buddha in front. Although Buddha's arms were uplifted and his smile welcoming, Amber's growing sense of alarm was fueled when she spotted a sign advertising 'a helluva time' at a local bar called the Hillbilly Haven. To the north was a narrow street lined with densely packed, tiny one-story cottages upon a hillside so steep she had no idea how anyone could get to them without a four-wheel drive.

Piling on was Led Zeppelin singing from the radio about *Going To California*. Robert Plant seemed to purposefully challenge Amber as he invited others to join in the search for the meaning of life, suggesting that the Golden State held the answer.

"This is Los Angeles?" Amber gasped in horror. "We moved from Seattle to this?" Glaring at her father, Amber seethed and bristled as the terrible reality of her new surroundings began to sink in.

Dr. McBride swallowed hard as he guiltily glanced over at his daughter, her face so red it nearly matched her hair and eyebrows. He'd learned from hard fought experience that arguing with an Irish redhead was a losing proposition. Whether she be Amber or his wife Michelle, the feminine of the fire-haired always had to have the last word. Stubborn nature drove the McBride women to continue any argument well past the point of fatigue, long after the original issue was even relevant.

"Wait until you see the house," Dr. McBride said quietly.

"I know why mom didn't come with us! She doesn't want to be here anymore than I do!" Amber retorted angrily. Letting out a strangled cry of frustration, she sat so heavily into her seat that Kibbles was unfairly jostled.

Amber's life was circling the drain. A delicate balance had been reached and maintained over the years in the McBride household, until her mother began complaining to her father about not having enough money. Dr. McBride, problem-solver that he was, responded by searching for a new job. Offers abounded, including within the company he currently worked for, Boeing's Aerospace Division.

As a rocket scientist, the way up meant accepting the promotion offered by Boeing. In the corporate world, the raise in pay and stature came with strings attached: moving from the Seattle Boeing plant to the Santa Susana Field Lab. Where the plum job and pay raise solved the money problems, Hicksville must've totally turned her mother off. No wonder Mrs. McBride was delaying moving to what must have appeared to be a dramatic step-down compared with the caffeinated edge of urbane Seattle.

Therefore, her parents were right back where they started. Her mother was unhappy. When Amber thought about it, *she* wasn't the only one being rejected. Every time her father tried to touch her mother, her body language betrayed an impulse to retreat before accepting the contact. Was it contempt Amber glimpsed periodically in her mother's face? Was there any way to bridge the growing chasm if her mother simply didn't want to be around them anymore?

The rising tide of anxiety didn't abate when her father stopped to turn. Amber couldn't see the house from the street entrance as they pulled up to a massive flagstone wall featuring an imposing iron gate harshly illuminated by intricately wrought antique streetlights. Her father punched in numbers on a keypad and the gate swung inward, hinges creaking in protest.

The driveway wound around a gently sloping hill. Nothing that lay ahead was revealed.

Dr. McBride slowly drove around the backside of the incline towards a vast nature preserve as the iron barrier rattled shut behind them. When the street was no longer visible and Lake Manor had vanished from sight, he pulled the car to a stop.

"I hate it here!" Amber growled.

Kibbles jumped out of the car after her and barely missed having his long, fluffy yellow tail slammed in her wake.

From the motor court, the McBride's new home didn't offer much of a first impression. It had clearly not been designed in the age of curb appeal. A single-story California ranch-style structure, the house was adorned simply with vertically arrayed sandstone-colored wooden slats. A brick staircase led to what Amber presumed, in the growing pinks and grays of sunset, was the front door. The uneven bricks, peeling paint and sagging rain gutters were testimony that the house was in desperate need of freshening up.

They began walking up the long flight of stairs to the quiet, unassuming house upon the hill. As they drew closer to the top, Amber felt a discomforting squirmy sensation, like an electrical pulse running across her skull. The knowledge that a creature was near *always* happened in the form of an image that appeared in her head, reflecting what the animal or bird was seeing, or had recently seen. The experience was passive and a lot like checking out the latest YouTube video.

This sensation was unpleasantly *different* from anything she'd ever experienced because it felt like something was kicking down the door in forcible entry. Whirling about, she spied the perpetrator: an enormous black bird with a featherless blood-red colored head perched upon the branch of a dead oak out beyond the motor court. Seeing she'd noticed, he caught her gaze and held it fast.

When their eyes met, chaparral and sagebrush faded away, revealing the shadowy form of a man. With the image flowed knowledge that overwhelmed her senses:

Lose your way and Shadow Man will claim you

"You coming, Amber?"

The turkey vulture unfolded his wings, a span of six feet from tip to tip, and whirled away.

Amber repeated the vulture's warning in her head. What did it mean? Her mind was racing because she was now stuck in the horrid situation of not knowing what was going to happen next and no way to communicate with the vulture so she could ask him questions. Seeing head pictures of what animals and birds experience had been at first frightening and then interesting, but despite her best efforts, Amber had yet to find a way to mentally speak to them. She wanted to stomp her feet and scream in frustration!

"Amber! Are you okay?" Dr. McBride gently touched her shoulder.

"Did you see that *thing*?"

"See what?"

Groaning inwardly because her clueless father never noticed all of the wildlife that followed her around, Amber hastened through the heavy double-doors, anxious to be away from whatever Shadow Man was lurking around outside.

Just inside the entrance, she stopped as she felt a strong sensation of being embraced, like when her father used to sweep her up into her arms when she was small and in need of comfort.

It's the house, she realized. First, the warning from the turkey vulture, then a *house* sending out warm fuzzy greetings like a friggin' welcome party? She tried mightily to be annoyed but found her rage draining away, despite her best efforts.

She had to speak to her best friend Shelby as soon as possible, to help her make sense of this freak show! However, seeking counsel with Shelby would have to wait because the house demanded her full attention. Despite her attempt to remain sullen, Amber looked in wonder at this western-equivalent of a fairy-tale castle, five times larger than what she'd initially surmised.

Surrounding her on three sides was a graceful hacienda-style home shaped like a U around a courtyard, every room with a door that opened into the 'U.' Overwhelmed, Amber couldn't figure out which was the main one. Did the house even have a front door? The bottom of the house's U shape and the curves extending into each arm were decoratively covered in flagstone, each piece uniquely cut to a special pattern and inset into the wall to create the illusion of the Simi Hills. Directly in front of Amber was a burbling stone fountain with two ducks spouting water from their mouths, surrounded by delicate, fern-like plants. In the center of the lawn squatted an ancient, gnarled tree surrounded by a fragrant herb garden.

A large swimming pool in the long, rectangular mosaic-style of old

Hollywood stretched out beyond the other end of the courtyard to jut out into the skyline, producing the visual effect of disappearing into the preserve. The same antique streetlights that Amber saw at the entrance gate were silhouetted in twilight at the far end of the pool.

"Wow," she leaned into her father, who had comfortably placed his hands on her shoulders, lightly massaging them, triumphant that the house had won her over as he'd predicted.

"It was built in 1939. Old Hollywood used to come out here to vacation, but this place looks like it was more than a weekend retreat." He pointed to the pool area, explaining, "Those lights at the end are from Hollywood Boulevard in the 1930's. So are the two at the front gate. But there's so much more! Come and see inside."

Amber placed her hand on her father's arm, stopping him before the tour began to ask the most important question, "Which one of these is my room?"

Gazing fondly at his daughter, Dr. McBride gestured Amber down three brick steps leading to the pool area. "Your room? I thought you were gonna die if we lived here?"

They followed their brick road in between the pool and lawn to an identical set of three brick steps leading to the rooms at the far corner of the house. Her father pointed to a French door that opened out onto its own little brick patio as Kibbles came padding up behind Amber, nuzzling her leg for a pat on the head.

Stepping inside her new room, she turned on the lights to get a better look as the dog walked inside, claws clicking on the wooden floor. The closet jutted out into the room, separating the hall entrance from her bed. Though the closet was small, this normally fatal flaw was compensated by the presence of an old-fashioned wardrobe in which to hang even more clothes. Pointing to the large armoire, she asked, "Did this come with the house?"

"It was here when I bought it, yes. If you look at it closely, it's actually built into the wall and floor. You definitely don't have to worry about it falling on top of you if there's an earthquake."

"Earthquake? I have to worry about earthquakes?" Amber's voice raised an octave as annoyance resurfaced.

"We had a couple in Seattle too, if you recall. At least this house has withstood some big ones, without so much as a crack. Her foundation is built into solid rock underneath and the framing was done in 3x6s instead of the normal 2x4s. The realtor told me there's nothing like it anywhere in the area."

Amber nodded absentmindedly. Her thoughts tended to drift whenever a Dr. McBride lecture ensued.

Seeing he was losing Amber's attention, Dr. McBride removed her room key from his pocket and handed it to her. "This is a big responsibility, but you're a responsible girl. You get good grades, you have nice friends…" His voice trailed off as he guiltily looked away.

She moved to jump on her bed, but seeing the expectant look on his face, turned back and gave him a big hug. The house had the effect of taking all the fight out of her, returning Amber to herself.

Patting her shoulder, Dr. McBride said, "I'm going to make us a little dessert to celebrate our homecoming. I'll call you when it's ready."

Her father stopped at the door, chin tilted upward, recalling, "Oh yeah, I forgot to show you this." He pointed to a box on the wall near her light switch. "Old school, but it does the trick. Push to talk, let up to listen. An intercom system, probably from the '70's."

"You could just learn to text, you know," Amber retorted.

"Cell service is hit-and-miss up here," Dr. McBride informed his daughter.

As soon as her father left the room, Amber tried to reach her best friend Shelby but had no luck, so she instead used her laptop to search Wikipedia for a more information about the turkey vulture that had met her at the door. Small creatures and birds had been drawn to Amber her entire life, so his appearance in and of itself was not unusual. What unnerved her was that he'd purposefully sought her out and warned her of impending danger. That was completely unexpected.

Fascinated, she read about the vulture's preference for rural settings, which explained why she'd never seen one around urban Seattle. A scavenger, Cathartes Aura, as he was formally known, had a keen sense of sight and uncanny ability to detect gas emitted from decaying corpses.

Cathartes was the Latin word for *purifier.*

Feeling spooked, Amber closed her laptop and busied herself unpacking some of her things. Despite her odd encounter with the turkey vulture, she had to admit that she really liked her room. The house made it clear she was welcome and this room was meant for her. It was like a cocoon tucked away from the rest of the world.

"Amber," crackled her father's voice through the intercom, "dessert is ready."

Pressing the intercom button down as instructed, she asked, "Where is the kitchen?"

"Walk out your door into the hallway and go through the den and living room. Follow the yummy smells and you'll end up at the kitchen."

Amber opened the door and looked down the long hallway to the family room. Beyond the den, she could see partway down another hallway that presumably wound up in the living room, but then a bend where the house formed its U shape blocked the remainder of the passageway from her view.

As Amber was about to leave her room, she heard a crackling noise coming from the intercom. Fiddling with the buttons and knobs of the vintage device, she tried to raise her father in the other part of the house. Listening to the static for familiar sounds and pressing the *Speak* button, she called, "Dad? Can you hear me?"

The intercom hissed sharply before a tinny, faraway-sounding voice broke through, calling, "Daniela?" It was a young woman.

Another teenage girl wearily responded, "Yes, I'm here."

This time the teenager who'd initiated the conversation came through loud and clear. She snapped, "He was right, *she came back*."

Depressing the button, Amber tried to break in with, "Hey! Can you two hear me?"

A static whine was her answer before the device fell silent.

Figuring the ancient technology had somehow picked up on a cell phone conversation; Amber gave up and turned the switch off.

The hallway led to the family room with a high, rustic beamed ceiling. At the north end of the room was an elaborate Art Deco bar replete with a shiny maple counter, stainless steel doors and drawers and an apothecary display of spirits and bottles backlit in warm yellow. The bar had a tilt-up pass through that could be raised in order to allow a bartender to enter and make drinks. The whole setup was around a bumped out panoramic picture window with a mountain view. Despite her initial angst and misgivings, Amber had to admit that this was indeed a pretty cool party house.

Next was the living room, also with high, wood-beamed ceilings. There were built in bookcases, a large fireplace with a slate bench running all the way from the corner of the room to the door and a grand piano nook. Like most of the rooms in the house, the living room contained a door that opened out onto the courtyard, allowing the occupants to enter and exit the home through virtually any room they pleased.

"Hacienda-style," her father had explained earlier.

The setting sun momentarily brought light into the room at an odd angle, illuminating the fireplace, yet abandoning the corner to creeping grey shadows.

Amber shivered. Despite the oppressive heat outside, the living room was markedly chillier than the rest of the house. Formal lines, dramatic angles and a sweeping view of the nature preserve, the flow was in keeping with the rest of the hacienda and yet the chill betrayed the fact that this room was *not right*.

Amber felt a prickling sensation at the back of her neck.

Slowly she turned, realizing that the living room had now been completely claimed by shadows.

Across the room, sunlight glinted against the glass covering the fireplace. Amber caught the slightest indication of movement *inside*. Heart racing, she focused, willing her eyes to see through the shadows. Stepping forward, Amber caught her reflection against the glass and simultaneously registered someone else. Behind her right shoulder materialized the faint silhouette of a blond teenage girl.

"Amber? Your treat's ready, c'mon."

"Wait!" Amber begged as the image disappeared. Frustrated that her father scared the teenager away, Amber's mind raced. She and Shelby had always faced ghosts *together*. Neither had ever gone solo when helping those that were lost find their way home. Yet she'd been in town less than three hours and one of the lost had already found her! Amber needed to seek counsel with the elders, ASAP.

"Amber, are you okay?"

Going on the offensive, she asked, "Why is this room so friggin' cold?"; curious as to whether her father had experienced any spectral encounters in this room since moving in.

"Maybe because of the basement underneath," her father shrugged.

Amber wondered how it was possible that her father never noticed any of the spectral children that were drawn to her over the years. She was beginning to suspect there was a reason the house had welcomed her so warmly, and sensed that it would take some digging to get to the bottom of what was really happening here. However, one thing was clear; the house didn't want her bolting for the door at the first sign of a ghost.

Amber realized that there was something very different about the teenager she'd glimpsed briefly in the reflected glass: every ghost drawn to Amber, up until now, had been Amber's age or younger. This girl was older. She appeared to be at least 18.

The sweet scent of melted chocolate permeated the air as Amber brought spoons and paper napkins over to their old dining table. It looked humorously small and overwhelmed in the center of a dance hall sized room. Although the style of the kitchen and dining room was from a far older era, the rooms appeared fresh and new.

"It didn't look like this at all in the pictures!" Amber insisted.

"You're right. It was pretty dilapidated when we bought it. The previous owners, the Blanks, I don't think they changed anything in the house since the 1980s. I had these rooms remodeled first. Eating is a priority!"

Amber grinned. Her trim, fit Irish father loved to cook.

"The den and living room just needed a good cleaning and a paint job. As for the rest of the house, well, we'll get to it when we get to it." Dr. McBride smiled broadly, eyes lighting up with excitement about the prospect of a large project to work on.

The art deco chandelier dangling over the table illuminated buttercup yellow walls, suggesting to Amber that the dining room was making a bold attempt at being cheery, perhaps to stand in stark contrast to the bloodless living room next door.

"Call Kibbles on the intercom."

"How do I know to make it go to the room he's in?"

"It isn't that sophisticated. It goes to all of the rooms."

The dog appeared shortly after his mistress' summons and they all sat down to eat an inaugural snack of sundaes for the humans and meaty treats for the canine.

When they finished dessert, Dr. McBride asked Amber to clean up so he could call her mother. Perking up her ears, Amber listened closely. Quickly moving past the small talk as he paced across the room, Dr. McBride struggled to keep a level tone for his daughter's sake.

"And you're telling me this *now*?" Her father attempted to draw away from Amber, but she intended to hear everything and shadowed him into an alcove where she could hear his side of the conversation.

"You belong here with *us*," Dr. McBride admonished. Spying his daughter trailing behind, he closed a door in between, shutting her out.

Kitchen cleaning was something that Amber and her father regularly did together and was their way of casually connecting. Although chores were not something she liked, she didn't mind spending after-dinner time with her dad because there was never any pressure. He simply allowed her to be. If she didn't feel like talking, he was comfortable with silence. When Amber had stories to tell, he was a wonderful listener and often offered interesting observations and insight that she'd not considered.

Tonight, Amber was alone in the kitchen of their new home.

Finishing up, she heard the muffled highs and lows of the argument coming from her father's phone call. Amber wondered why they had to move. If her parents were just going to fight, why not stay in Seattle and do it there? They could just as easily have their problems back home, without uprooting her and plunking her into the middle of Hillbilly Heaven.

She made her way into the chilled living room as Kibbles continued on down the hallway toward what he now considered his bedroom, tuckered out from the day's events. Without meaning to, Amber glanced back out the windows overlooking a vast nature preserve and froze, her image reflected in the multi-paneled glass. Something was outside underneath the bay window and it wasn't one of the birds. It had touched her mind only briefly before retracting stealthily.

Moving forward, Amber stopped herself as she realized that the light inside the living room would impede her ability to see outside. With her heart beating quickly, Amber slid her sweaty palms down her shirt to dry them off and took a deep breath to calm down.

She had a choice to make: cut and run back to her room, or take a look and see what was lurking around. Bailing seemed very attractive and definitely presented an easier path. Amber pictured herself running back to her room. Then what? She would cower, waiting for something to come and *get* her?

Anger simmered up from a primal place within and with purpose she shut out the lights and strode toward the windows in darkness. Seeing nothing and feeling silly, she crouched down on the floor and rested her arms on the window seat. Cupping her chin in her hands, she contemplated the return to her room.

As Amber lifted her gaze, her eyes met an exotic visage of black diamonds surrounded by sea-foam green. Holding her breath for a moment, she mentally reached out and briefly touched the wild, foreign consciousness of the mountain lioness before her. She experienced a rush of wind and the sensation of speed from when the big cat ran across the open meadow earlier that day to bring down a mule deer. This thrilling sensation was followed by slow, deep inhalation and exhalation as the lioness purred contentedly in the present moment. Exhilarated, Amber stared at the mountain lioness nonchalantly watching her through the little square panes of glass, her globular eyes glistening in reflected moonlight. Her broad, flat nose sniffed the air delicately in what appeared like mild interest, or perhaps even amusement.

Amber was amazed to realize that the lioness had sensed her and specifically come to check her out in order to determine if she was a threat. She'd assessed Amber and didn't find her to be an enemy. It was the first time she'd discerned anything so complex from an animal! Typical was awareness of basic needs such as hunger and the need to take flight or fight, and whatever images came along with what the animal was experiencing in response.

The lioness sat back on her muscular haunches and lazily licked a front paw, yet beneath the familiar white, fuzzy cat's muzzle were long, pointy fangs, capable of tearing apart a mule deer in minutes. Leisurely, she finished cleaning her toes and gently placed the paw upon the grass. Ears twitching as she slightly inclined her massive head in Amber's direction, the lioness then turned and flicked her tail as she sauntered off into the brush.

Mesmerized, Amber stayed at the windows, wondering where the mountain lioness had gone. The lonely call of a night owl gently parted the heavy, warm air. In Amber McBride's fourteen years on the planet, the mountain lioness was the largest creature to seek her out. She'd grown used to the curiosity of the smaller animals and birds over the years, but a mountain lion? What did its sudden appearance mean, and so close on the heels of the mysterious turkey vulture?

Touching the mind of the mountain lioness had been amazing. Amber felt dangerous, grownup and best of all, no longer helpless.

When the lioness did not return, Amber eventually gave up waiting and walked dreamily into the den. Her thoughts strayed again to her mother abandoning them to go stay with Amber's Aunt Cathy. On the one hand, she couldn't blame her mother for wanting to stay in Seattle.

But weren't you supposed to stay with the one you love, through thick and thin, 'till death do us part and all that? Was this the first step down the road to a formal separation with an eventual end in divorce?

Yet even if her mother was willing to let Amber come home, the thought of living alone with her was frankly intolerable. Amber's father brought much-needed balance, what he called homeostasis, to their relationship. Two strong-willed redheads constantly at each other's throats wasn't how she wanted to spend the rest of her youth.

Amber trudged to her new, unfamiliar room, where she opened her laptop and again tried to reach her best friend Shelby Pierce. Shelby was an Urban Indian, which means her family was Native American but had chosen to live in a city instead of on their Tribe's Reservation. Shelby and Amber had known each other since preschool and were inseparable. The two girls presented a striking pair. Shelby was quick and strong, with high cheek bones, an aquiline nose and long, thick dark hair that fell to her waist. Amber hadn't quite grown into her angular form and stood four inches taller than Shelby.

As her oldest friend's cheerful face appeared onscreen, Shelby asked, "Hey Red, how's my rez[1] dog doing?"

Kibbles lay comfortably curled up on a throw rug behind Amber's desk chair.

After putting the laptop camera right in Kibbles' face so Shelby could see for herself how the old dog was faring, she told her best friend about everything that had happened, including the turkey vulture, ghostly teenager and the mountain lioness. Amber even walked the laptop around so Shelby could get a good look at her new bedroom.

Sticking a flashlight under her chin, Shelby intoned spookily, "Ooh, you just met your animal spirit guide. Gotta admit, a mountain lion's more badass than the loser squirrels and skunks that usually hang around you!"

"I don't get an animal guide, like you never stop reminding me! Besides, it was a *real mountain lion*, not a spirit animal," Amber menaced.

Many Native Americans view the spirit world as natural part of the grand continuum of life, so seeing one's relatives after death was not considered extraordinary. Growing up with Shelby Pierce as her best friend and the number of misadventures they'd had over the years, encountering a ghost didn't frighten Amber in the slightest. The two had come to learn through personal experience that, without a body and lacking the ability to inflict physical pain, the worst thing a spectral encounter would leave you with was a cold clammy feeling.

---

[1] 'Rez' is slang for 'Reservation.'

15

Getting serious again, Amber asked, "You haven't seen any ghosts since I left, have you?"

"No," Shelby responded, "you're right, it's weird that your ghost is older than us. I don't know what it means. But my aunts will know what to do."

After speaking with Shelby for an hour, Amber was ready to call it a night. She was about to sign off when Shelby asked, "I can tell, you're thinking about *Bedelia* again, aren't you?"

Nodding, Amber bade Shelby goodnight.

Shelby's reference to the first ghost they'd ever encountered, little Bedelia Bredell, was spot on. Amber tried not to think about Bedelia because it made her feel so sad, but this evening's ghostly encounter stirred the memory.

Amber and Shelby were eight years old that summer. Shelby's mother had invited Amber's family to come with them to the Reservation for a powwow. Amber's father had to work, so just Amber and her mother joined the Pierce family for the trip. During the vacation, they went on a chokecherry picking expedition on the old Bredell property near the river. As their mothers picked the bright red berries, the girls took a break and ran around in an adjacent field. Amber had been chasing Shelby when she hollered at her to *watch out!*

Shelby skidded to a stop, nearly colliding with a small Native American girl that sprang up from a hiding place in the middle of the field.

"I'm Bedelia. May I join you?" the child with long, thick, dark braids asked.

"Sure, but you'll never catch me!" Shelby teased as she took off again.

Shrieking and laughing, the three ran around in the tall grass, spinning in circles until they grew dizzy and fell to the ground.

"Girls! Time to go!" Mrs. McBride called out.

Bedelia's narrow face grew taut with these words.

"May I see you again?" she asked in an oddly formal manner.

"I don't think so, we go home tomorrow," Amber explained.

Bedelia stood alone in the middle of the field, unmoving, watching them as their car drove away.

Around midnight, Shelby shook Amber awake.

"You're not gonna believe this!" she whispered, taking care not to awaken her younger cousin whose room they were presently sharing. Beckoning her to the window of second story home, Shelby pointed down.

Moonlight streamed down over Bedelia. However, the full moon illuminated a *different* version of Bedelia: one in an old-fashioned white hospital gown, wasted by disease, lustrous locks now thin and straggly.

Exchanging a quick glance, Shelby and Amber ran down the hallway to alert their mothers.

At the living room window, the four stared outside.

"You've been dreaming, dear, there's no one there," Amber's mother stroked her daughter's hair as she led her back upstairs.

When Shelby rejoined her shortly, she confirmed that her mother Susan had no trouble seeing Bedelia, and so began 'The Ghostly Adventures of Shelby and Amber.'

With the help of Shelby's aunts, the girls came to understand that ghosts didn't know they were dead. Bedelia Bredell was one of these poor souls, stuck at the time of their death without knowing they'd passed on. They were harmless. For some reason, those that died in childhood were attracted to Amber and Shelby.

Amber and Shelby also learned that the goal was to dispatch the ghost onward. This was the tricky part because if the ghost suspected change was in the works, she or he would flee and you may not see them again. Amber and Shelby were particularly helpful in this regard, because neither knew, nor understood how to propel a ghost onward. They were innocents, perfect foils for what Amber now realized was a Shaggy-Scooby Doo routine. Amber and Shelby provided the set-up that allowed the elders to then step in and do the heavy lifting. For the process of transition was considered a solemn, sacred duty. Only an experienced elder was allowed to shepherd a lost soul beyond the earthly realm due to the danger involved.

This sacred task had *never* been entrusted to Amber and Shelby because they were too young. Shelby's aunts would never risk the girls' lives by putting them in such peril. As well-intentioned as the aunties were in shielding the girls from the sacred duty, Amber was now facing a situation in which a teenage ghost needed to move on, and she had *no* clue as to how to help her.

Amber re-examined her memories of the following summer, when they'd returned to the Reservation with their mothers for the annual powwow. At twilight on the first evening, Bedelia Bredell returned, creeping to the edge of Shelby's Aunt Merri's yard to shyly wave "hello." Not unnoticed by Amber and Shelby, Aunt Merri took counsel with her sisters while Shelby's mother Susan Pierce kept Mrs. McBride preoccupied.

Late that night, Amber and Shelby snuck downstairs and spied on Aunt Merri and her sisters.

Shelby's aunts Fawn and Flora and her mother Susan stood in a circle around Merri. One by one, each woman solemnly came forward to embrace her. Returning to the circle, the women bowed their heads in prayer.

Aunt Merri's form shivered slightly and became hazy around the edges. Wispy mists gathered around her heart, and then took shape into a young Native American girl that strongly resembled Aunt Merri. The little image appeared superimposed over Aunt Merri's stout figure before the elder vanished into the haze surrounding the ghost child. Nodding to the sisters, the small newcomer exited the house alone.

There was no way to follow without being found out, so Amber and Shelby silently returned to the house and spied out an upstairs window. They observed the little Native American girl that was Aunt Merri walk slowly to the edge of the yard and greet Bedelia. The ghost's lip quivered; she burst out crying and threw her arms around Aunt Merri's neck.

"Eleanor!" Bedelia cried, "I missed you so much! Where have you been?"

"Do you trust me?" Eleanor/Aunt Merri asked.

"Yes, yes!" Bedelia answered emphatically.

"Then I'll take you to your mother," Eleanor/Aunt Merri reassured Bedelia as she grasped her hand.

Beaming, Bedelia kissed her friend on the cheek, and the two began walking away from the house.

Shelby cried out in alarm as the elder Aunt Merri slumped to the ground. The little girl that was Eleanor continued walking with Bedelia Bredell until they were no longer visible. Heedless to being found out, Shelby and Amber raced down the stairs and out the door. Aunt Merri's sisters had already reached the prone woman and were helping her to her feet. She was dazed, but otherwise appeared unhurt.

"You okay?" Shelby asked.

"She's fine, you little spy," Shelby's mother admonished her.

"Where'd they go? Who's Eleanor?" Amber asked.

Aunt Flora reassured the children, "Bedelia moved on, thanks to the help of our grandmother. She was Bedelia's childhood friend. We asked for her help, and she gave it. Everything's going to be fine now."

Amber's fatigue overwhelmed the sad recollection. The wild yipping of a lone coyote in the preserve barely registered. She was sound asleep by the time others joined in. Yapping morphed into mournful howling that came to a climax of banshee wails when the prey they'd been stalking was brought down.

AΩ

A lone coyote drank deeply from the pond inside the Chatsworth Nature Preserve. When his thirst was slaked, he silently moved off to rejoin the pack. To the southwest, the coyote spied a large rocky hill. More darkly sinister than the rest, he instinctually knew to avoid it.

Suddenly, the night sky was ablaze. Frozen in place, the coyote stared helplessly into fiery depths. From the hilltop rose the shadowy form of a man. Untouched by the flames, he beckoned to the coyote to come forward.

Coyote had no choice. His kind had always answered when called.

∞

The Los Angeles Police Department (LAPD) pilots saw the orange plume from miles away as they soared in the airspace over nearby Canoga Park. It immediately registered in their brains as fire, flaring beyond the constant glow of city lights amidst the darkness of the preserve.

The sky cops' training kicked in and they performed the standard procedures as they called in the details to the Los Angeles Fire Department (LAFD) and their ground team. As they flew in, queries and chatter were fielded from the groundlings. Moving closer, the lead pilot, Officer Johnson, noticed that the helicopter was surprisingly stable. Normally fires create a lot of choppy air.

Within a matter of seconds, the LAPD helicopter was directly over the source of the blaze. In the midst of calling in coordinates and landmarks, the pilots were instantaneously plunged into complete darkness as their instruments flickered and the rotor hiccupped. Attention and actions automatically changed to shifting levers and gears as crucial seconds passed, followed by the roar of re-ignition.

The pilots breathed a sigh of gratitude that a stall and subsequent crash was averted.

The sigh became a collective gasp because the fire popped and then simply disappeared.

Staring at each other in disbelief, Officer Johnson cleared his throat before soberly observing, "Those flames had to have been over fifty feet high." Running a hand over his shaved head, he turned the chopper's searchlight on, harshly illuminating the hilltop.

Nothing: not a person, animal, or even a fire pit. There were no signs of disturbance on the ground.

His junior ranking officer and partner, Gutiérrez, remarked to the dispatcher, "Cancel that last call."

Dispatch insisted, "Repeat please, Air Four."

Glancing to Johnson, Gutiérrez repeated, "Yeah, we're not looking at any incendiary activity here, please cancel all units and LAFD."

A now incredulous Dispatch repeated, "Please advise: THERE IS NO FIRE?"

"Yes, we have no fire, please cancel all response."

Johnson's round face appeared pale in the unnatural electrical illumination. Ever curious as to his methods, asked in a singsong voice, "Yes, we have no fire?"

Gutiérrez frowned, his dark eyebrows nearly touching in grim concentration under the regulation LAPD trim haircut, "Put a sock in it, cabron."[2]

Suddenly, darkness enveloped the pilots.

"I said shut up, not shut out the lights!" Gutiérrez grumbled.

_____

[2] Spanish for 'jerk.'

"That wasn't me," Johnson responded. Swearing under his breath when the blazing lamp failed to turn back on, Officer Johnson gritted his teeth and flicked the switch a couple more times. When it was clear the searchlight was out, Johnson reached around to his gear bag and produced a large flashlight. Shrugging, he showed it to his partner as Officer Gutiérrez gently lowered the helicopter even closer to the ground. As Gutiérrez stabilized the helicopter in the air, Johnson angled the beam of the flashlight out the window.

The faint artificial light barely illuminated dark, round stones below, but the LAPD officers were able to see that they were arrayed in a perfect circle, like a druidic temple.

Movement around one of the stones caught their attention. Directing the flashlight, the beam illuminated dust kicked up by the chopper. "Wait, do you remember them being like this before?" Officer Johnson asked.

Shrugging, Officer Gutiérrez remarked, "I looking for the source of the fire, not Machu Picchu." Figuring that their efforts had come to naught, Gutiérrez shifted gears on the helicopter and began to pull away from the strange altar.

A piercing shriek echoed against the inner walls of the chopper and startled Officer Johnson so badly that he swung the Maglite in self-defense, accidentally smacking a critical lever out of place.

The chopper began spiraling out of control, toward the craggy peak. As it whirled uncontrollably, Johnson's head slumped forward into unconsciousness.

SHELBY PIERCE

CHAPTER 2

EXPLORATION

Officer Gutiérrez marshaled his years of training on the force and bore down, bringing every one of his senses to focus on taking the helicopter out of a death spin.

It was nearly impossible to see as the chopper spiraled dangerously close to the circular stone formation. The whirling blades were creating a vortex that threatened to suck them right into the center, swallowing men and machine into a twisted jumble of wreckage. Dirt and small fragments of rock rose from the hilltop, churning into the funnel and whistling through the helicopter's ventilation system, causing Gutiérrez to cough and choke.

For the briefest moment, the debris field was swiped clear and the hilltop itself filled Gutiérrez' entire field of vision. In that instant, the helicopter searchlights inexplicably switched on, clearly illuminating the unnatural rocky ring atop the hill.

Dust coalesced at the west end of the hilltop and then swirled around one of the round stones in a twister formation before collapsing.

Bizarrely, Officer Gutiérrez remembered training with his mentor Commander Jose Rodriguez, one of the first Latinos on the force. Gutiérrez had experienced a crisis of confidence when they were called to quell a skirmish that had broken out in downtown's Macarthur Park. LAPD ground forces needed assistance in containing a group of immigrants protesting roundups and deportations. The protestors, men and women who may as well have been his mother, father, and grandparents looked in particular contempt at the Latinos on the force as they threw up rude gestures at the officers in the helicopter.

Where his initial instinct was to turn and leave in shame, he watched his mentor operate in unison with his LAPD brothers and sisters. Commander Jose Rodriguez was a professional to the core, taking no offense at the actions of the protestors and only serving to maintain order and uphold the rule of law.

After the melee was over, Commander Rodriguez informed Officer Gutiérrez privately, "Get used to it, man. *We* are the new LAPD."

In the split second before Gutiérrez lost control of the helicopter, the stone shifted. A cloaked figure unfolded and ancient yellow eyes locked on Gutiérrez's.

"You have no claim to him," Commander Rodriguez ordered in Spanish. His voice echoed eerily over the sound of the rotors. Rodriguez sat at Officer Johnson's controls, hands working quickly and automatically to steady the helicopter.

Johnson was nowhere in sight.

"Jose! How…"

A sibilant hiss resonated throughout the chopper before the cloaked figure collapsed into the stone atop the hill.

Rodriguez gently placed the palm of his hand on Gutiérrez' forehead and said, "Be well, my old friend."

Dreamlike, Officer Gutiérrez opened his eyes. He was automatically operating his controls, flying steadily away from the misshapen hill and the nature preserve. Officer Johnson was unconscious, but breathing steadily, head slumped against the seat occupied moments earlier by Commander Rodriguez. His teeth were chattering, despite the still-oppressive heat.

Gutiérrez spotted cold condensation on the outer surface of the windows. The tiny water droplets dribbled thin rivulets.

His mentor Rodriguez had died in his mid-forties of a heart attack, more than three years ago.

Although it was morning, the San Inferno Valley stayed true to its nickname by quickly heating up. Amber changed into her swimsuit and stepped into the pool. When the water reached her thighs, she shivered uncontrollably. The temperature was frigid! Instead of feeling refreshing, it chilled her.

Grumbling, Amber got out of the water and moved to a shady spot near the deep end. The pool jutted out into the skyline, producing the visual effect of disappearing into the preserve. Spreading her towel upon the brick, she knelt down and reached in to splash a few drops over her skin. In between dappled sunlight upon the water, Amber thought she spotted wavy movement at the bottom. Patchwork paint made it hard to see, so she squinted as she leaned forward to get a better look.

The pool floor appeared to *bulge*, as if something was trying to break through from the women's changing room.

As a burst of bubbles scattered from the drain, Amber was finally able to see clearly.

Long blond hair floated up from someone crawling from underneath the pool.

Amber leapt to her feet, knowing full well that this *someone* was no longer living.

"Hey!" a young male voice called out to her from the nature preserve, causing her to recoil with surprise.

Amber raced down semi-circular steps alongside the pool. She paused as she spotted a dark opening inset into the concrete wall, ivy vines hanging down in dark green tendrils over the entrance. Out of the corner of her eye, Amber simultaneously spotted a teenage boy beyond her fence line. His freckled face broke into a broad grin as soon as their eyes met.

"Sorry, didn't mean to sneak up on you."

"Did you see anyone go in here?" she asked.

"Nah, didn't see anyone," the boy answered nonchalantly.

Trying to act casual, Amber quickly poked her head into the darkened underside of the pool, but the blond was nowhere in sight. She spied a filthy shower built into the back wall, and a long vanity with oversized light bulbs lining the top of a streaked, cracked mirror.

"Hold on a sec," Amber shouted, as sunlight glinted off something on the floor. She picked up a small, muck-encrusted object.

Exiting the dank room, she introduced herself as the boy asked, "What did you find?"

"Here," Amber handed him the tiny box through the chain link fence.

"Weird," he observed as he handed it back to Amber, "I think it was used to hold matches." Changing the subject, he introduced himself, "I'm Seth."

She motioned to the nature preserve, and asked, "How do I get in there?"

Seth's brown eyes lit up mischievously at the prospect of another partner in crime. "You have a gate to cut the grass by your property because of the wildfires. But that's it. Otherwise you're not supposed to be in here."

"You're in there."

"I like to bike in here. And I don't get caught."

"Where's the gate?"

Seth walked along the fence line until he came to a chain link gate fastened into place by a padlock. Grinning saucily, he produced a key ring, opened the lock and sauntered through.

Amber sized him up as Seth looked over her shoulder, calling out, "Hey Dr. McBride, I've got your keys." He casually tossed the ring high over Amber's head and Dr. McBride deftly caught the jangling bunch in one fist.

"Hi Seth, thanks for bringing them back."

Amber stared at her father. "Um, you two know each other?"

"Seth's been keeping an eye on things since I bought the house. He's been opening the front gate for workmen who needed to get in. Been a huge help."

"How'd you guys meet?" Amber asked.

"My mom's a realtor," Seth chimed in. "My services came highly recommended."

Dr. McBride informed his daughter, "You and Seth will be in the same grade at Castle Peak High School this fall."

The two teenagers appraised each other anew, in light of this information.

"Want me to show you around?" Seth asked.

"Sure. Okay with you?" Amber asked her father.

Dr. McBride tossed his daughter a can of sunscreen, instructing, "Spray before you go."

"Back in a sec," Amber informed her new friend as she went to her room to change out of her swimsuit.

Kibbles stared up at Amber, tail wagging expectantly with the understanding that some adventure was about to be undertaken.

Patting his head, she explained, "It's too much walking for you, old buddy. You stay here with daddy."

Understanding the tone of voice that always accompanied being left behind, the dog sadly hung his head as she departed.

Δ

Dr. McBride watched Amber and Seth's forms receding into a tangle of sagebrush. Seth was a good kid, plus Amber was nearly six inches taller. These two facts made him a fine boy for her to hang out with.

As the two teenagers disappeared from view into a grove of ancient oak trees, Dr. McBride took a deep breath and surveyed the rugged, undeveloped terrain. He had grown up watching old Westerns on Saturday mornings and now he stood overlooking the very location where most of them had been filmed. The land looked much the same as it did back when the famous singing cowboy Roy Rogers rode his horse Trigger through the foothills of his Double R Ranch. Dr. McBride now owned a slice of old west heaven.

Why couldn't his wife see that he had worked hard all these years to deliver her to the paradise in which he now stood?

As the sun had nearly reached its zenith, Amber and Seth stuck to the oaks that lined the edge of the nature preserve. Hot rays tried to burn their way through the mighty boughs, but the youths were protected in the shade. The canopy of each Valley Oak spread out like a giant umbrella, underneath which the airspace was appreciably cooler.

Seth gestured above his head to tiny leaves flintily shimmering from the bits of sunshine that managed to seep in. "Like my shortcut? Taking the road means baking in the sun."

"You know all the trails around here?" Amber asked.

"Yea, we bike all over. Some of the best trails are up on the mountain. Our favorite trail is on the *Salvia* property. There's a cabin up there where an old TV series was shot, and a really steep track that runs down the side of the Twelve Apostles. It has great jumps all the way down."

"The Twelve Apostles?"

Seth pointed through the trees to a formation directly overlooking Lake Manor.

Looking to the mountains, Amber's vision came to rest on a gigantic row of stone columns aligned next to one another. The exact number was difficult to discern because it was hard to tell where one ended and another began. A couple appeared to have been split asunder, perhaps in one of Southern California's legendary earthquakes. The Twelve Apostles were strange citadels in a land of sunburnt stone.

Amber tried to envision Seth and his friends riding mountain bikes, hurtling headlong down the side of the sheer rock formation. "Do you ride with the Salvias?"

Seth sputtered out the water he had just taken a sip of, snorting some out his nose in the process. When he recovered himself, he explained, "They're psychotic bullies! Think Darth Vader meets the Terminator!"

Amber stopped and appraised Seth, wondering about how much of an adrenaline junky he was. "Why do you go up there?"

Seth shrugged, answering, "Their property has the best trails. C'mon and I'll introduce you."

"Not to the *Salvias*, I hope?"

Seth just laughed as he resumed walking and multitasked by texting his friends to meet up at his place. "I gotta admit though, their senior stunts took some friggin' sack to pull off!"

Curious, Amber asked, "What'd they do?"

"I'll show you my personal favorite of the three - Martin Salvia's. He's had a rattlesnake tattooed on his hand since he was twelve! Watch this."

What May or May Not Be the Legendary (and Allegedly) Salvia Senior Stunt: Part III

The screen revealed Castle Peak High on a school day during lunchtime. The courtyard is full of laughing, gossiping teens. The camera pans up to the base of the Simi Hills, where the aptly named Castle Peak is the prominent landmark because it's in the shape of a turret. Grey boulders litter the mountainside spanning out into a steep, brushy expanse. In the foreground of the peak and behind the main school buildings stands an ancient, vandalized, thirty-foot high water tank.

Seth chimed in with some narration, "See that tank there? It was left over from the fire corps before they had water mains out here. It's been empty for years. The Salvia's diverted a hose from a *fire hydrant* and filled it up over a weekend. They rigged a panel with explosives so it would drain instantly."

Amber's eyes narrowed as her nose crinkled, trying to figure out if Seth was teasing her, accusing, "You've got to be kidding me."

Seth just shook his head, "Wait for it, wait for it"

The camera zoomed to the gap between the two buildings where a young man wearing a ski mask nonchalantly walks towards the courtyard carrying a kayak and a paddle. A mysterious sound system begins to play:

the opening salvo from *When the Levee Breaks* by Led Zeppelin. The crowd takes notice of him as he drops the kayak on the concrete and climbs in. Chuckles and giggles are heard as he puts a helmet over his ski-masked head and readies his paddle. The lunching students experience a wave of realization that they may now be in harm's way and, slowly at first, and then with more urgency, begin to part and scatter as a nervous wave of anticipation sets in and they break for higher ground.

On cue, an epic explosion of sparks and magnesium erupt from the top and sides of the water tower. The camera zooms in to reveal a yard-wide hole erupting from the base of the tank, instantaneously sending the entire contents of an Olympic sized pool cascading down the hillside behind the school. The deluge hits the erstwhile boater, who immediately paddles and bobs expertly as he is swept up and rides the wave to the horizon where he drops off into the terraced parking lot of the school. Almost as soon as the water stops flowing, the crowd furiously hoots and erupts in awed adulation.

Amber stared at Seth's cell phone for a few seconds, not quite able to believe what she'd seen. Finally, she asked, "Did he get arrested? Kicked out of school?"

"No, totally got away with it. They couldn't prove it was him! That's part of the stunt, they have to get away with it."

Admittedly, Amber's curiously about the Salvia brothers was piqued. Watching the way Seth spoke admiringly about the death-defying stunts, she wondered whether he secretly harbored other reasons for trespassing on their property. Perhaps preferring to push the envelope of danger right to the edge to satisfy his need for thrills?

"So everyone's wondering what George Salvia's going to do. He's the youngest brother, and a senior, so this is the year," her new friend concluded.

Emerging from the arboreal shadows, Seth led Amber to a spot in the fence that bordered a yard containing a funky, eclectic collection of iron sculptures and wooden carvings. A house with a low-slung roof and a Hobbit-like round door in the center sat to one side.

Seth pulled on the fence with no visible gate and the chain-link easily opened. He gallantly motioned for Amber to step through and pulled the fence back into place behind them, hiding any evidence of a breach.

A tall, thin man with long, flowing grey hair, a hawk nose and a black top hat strode toward them from one of the outbuildings.

"Hey Mr. Baccharis," Seth greeted him. "Meet my new friend Amber. She just moved into the house on Lizard Hill."

Mr. Baccharis raised a hand to Seth in greeting as sharp eyes curiously examined the newcomer. "Lizard Hill, you don't say. Oh, wait, I think I see something here."

He reached behind Amber's ear and produced a quarter. "Funny place for you to keep your money. Most girls carry purses." He winked at her. "But then again, you aren't like most girls, are you?" Flipping her the coin without waiting for an answer, he turned to Seth and asked, "Come to see that thing we've been working on?" Baccharis raised a bushy grey eyebrow, to which Seth nodded conspiratorially in response.

"Excuse us just a moment. La Luz will keep you company."

Amber felt something brush against her leg and discovered an enormous creamsicle striped cat waiting expectantly for her tribute.

"You're a cute kitty." Amber bent and scratched behind the cat's ears. La Luz purred in approval. Briefly touching the cat's mind, Amber was jarred by the image of the feline biting the head off a large pigeon she'd caught earlier that morning. Disgusted, Amber quickly withdrew.

Examining the closed door of the outbuilding into which Seth and Mr. Baccharis had gone, she wondered what it was they were plotting. Although Mr. Baccharis was most definitely odd with his funky yard and top hat, she liked his easy manner and sense of humor.

After a while the two emerged, laughing as Seth secretively stashed something in his pack. La Luz left Amber's side and nonchalantly strolled over to Mr. Baccharis.

"Thanks, this should work," Seth said.

"Nice to meet you, Amber." Mr. Baccharis scratched La Luz's neck as she rubbed against his leg as affectionately as a feline can muster.

As the two teens left Mr. Baccharis' place, Amber began her inquisition with, "What an interesting guy! Is he an inventor?"

Crossing Lake Manor's main street, they headed uphill in between quaint cottages and quirky cabins.

Seth cautiously answered, "He's retired."

Deciding on a direct approach, Amber grilled her new friend, "C'mon! What're you two working on?"

"Top Secret, Burn After Reading. You get my point?"

Amber moved to punch him in the arm, but Seth was too quick and darted in front of her. When he reached the end of the street where it met another country lane in a T, Seth waited. The enigmatic Twelve Apostles framed his short figure.

Amber was panting by the time she met Seth at the top. Yet, to her irritation, he'd not even broken a sweat.

"You think it's this hot in hell?" she quipped.

"You'll get used to it. I have cold drinks at my house. It's just around the corner."

Seth led Amber past a yard protected by a tall, severe stone fence topped by razor wire and marked with a sign for good measure, in case anyone didn't quite understand the owner's preference for privacy: *Hell's*

Angels – STAY OUT 13! After passing less threatening abodes, they reached a charming, simple, one-story cottage at the end of the street. Seth and Amber climbed aging flagstone steps and followed a rustic path that wound around to a backyard shaded by giant oaks, where three boys were lounging on rusty metal chairs. She thought she heard one of the guys whisper, "He wasn't kidding, it really *is* a girl!"

The new arrival brought the afternoon to life, inspiring the boys to sit up straight and introduce themselves. Amber blushed when she realized, to her embarrassment, that one stocky Latino boy was actually gawking, while a pale, shy Asian boy appeared to be struggling mightily hard *not* to stare at her.

A tall, slender black boy named Jonah Abernathy was the first to make her acquaintance. His mannerisms were graceful and fluid, reigniting Amber's ongoing desire that she could grow comfortable in her lanky form and move like a swan. Jonah looked vaguely familiar to her, but she couldn't figure out how she could possibly know him. Before she had the opportunity to inquire, Jonah kicked at his companions and nudged them forward.

The next boy introduced himself as James Toshima. His manner was very reserved and his eyes never met hers. James was short, like Seth, and moved like a phantom. Amber had the sense that he could enter a room and no one would notice he was there.

The final teen, Luis Garcia, finally found his words and said, "Welcome to Los Angeles." He deliberately over-exaggerated the Spanish pronunciation of "Angeles," so that it sounded like "Anheles." The chubby Latino grinned widely and extended his arms out to his sides, as if he were greeting her on behalf of the entire city.

Amber relaxed and received this welcome in good humor.

"Let's go inside," Seth motioned to everyone to follow him in through the back screen door. Once in the house, Seth retrieved some sodas out of the refrigerator and everyone settled in front of his gaming system in the living room. Despite the cottage lacking central air, the oak shelter and rotating fans kept a pleasantly cool temperature. The youths proceeded to battle it out in the virtual world, taking turns fighting zombies, opposing armies and other foes as the heat of the day wore on.

Amber had no issues keeping up with the boys. As an only child, she often had time on her hands, which she had no problems filling with gaming.

She saved Jonah Abernathy from being eaten from a zombie for the fifth time, this time by beheading the evil dead with one fell swoop of her sword. As her character chopped and blasted the remainder of the walking bag of bones into oblivion, Jonah checked the time on his cell phone and said, "Thanks, but we gotta bounce. We're going mountain biking now that

29

it's cooled down."

"Yeah, it's too rough where we're going. Wouldn't want to mess up your mani-pedi!" Luis Garcia teased.

Glancing at her unpolished nails, Amber snapped back, "I bet I've been mountain biking longer than you! I'm from Seattle! You know, Mount Rainier?"

"Mount Reindeer?" Luis goaded, then ducked as Amber hefted a throw pillow at his head.

"I guess I owe you," Jonah decided. "I'll have Max bring an extra mountain bike for you when mine gets dropped off."

"Oooooh," Luis teased, "I wish I had a manservant to haul my bike around."

Jonah jumped up, dove onto Luis and punched him in retribution, challenging, "How's about you tell Max that to his face when he gets here? You live just a couple of blocks from here! I live, like, five miles away and it was one hundred degrees this morning!"

Despite the height difference, Luis easily threw off his attacker, protesting, "Abernathy, I was just kidding."

Studying Jonah's face closely, dawning awareness took hold as Amber stated, "I know why you look so familiar. You look like the actor, Marcus Abernathy."

Luis laughed heartily, "You mean he looks like his dad, Marcus Abernathy."

Jonah was sending a text message and barely looked up from his phone in response to this startling revelation.

Luis smiled at Amber, revealing, "He doesn't like to be reminded about it."

Amber shook her head. Boys were so weird! If her father were a completely cool action hero instead of a nerdy scientist, she would want everyone to know about it!

"So you go to school with Seth and the rest of these guys?" she asked Jonah.

"I wish," Jonah replied longingly. "I go to a private school with a bunch of stuck up assholes." His face suddenly lit up as he appraised his posse, now increased by one. "You'll help me think of something. It has to be really creative. But it can't land me in jail, or be so bad that the public schools won't take me. It has to be perfect." His gaze rested on Amber to ensure that the point had been made.

She cleared her throat and looked to the others for rescue, but as they quickly glanced away, she had the sinking feeling that the guys had tried this route before and now Jonah Abernathy was looking to her for the ultimate solution.

Jonah's cell clanged to indicate an incoming message. Looking down at

30

his IPhone, he announced, "We're on. Max says to meet him in the church parking lot."

"Max is Jonah's manny," Seth called out over his shoulder as he simultaneously ran for the door.

Jonah darted out after him as everyone else piled out behind. Seth was already on his bike and speeding down the hill by the time the others vacated the premises. Luis and James hopped on their bikes and followed, leaving Amber and Jonah to walk down to the bottom.

"Max is not my…." Jonah glanced over at Amber and explained, "he helps us out, like if I need a ride somewhere, or mom needs her dry cleaning picked up, you know."

"You mean like a personal assistant?"

Jonah brightened, "Yea, except he's not my personal assistant, he's my mom's. And since she's usually busy, he's the one who ends up giving me rides." He sighed, "I wish I was old enough to drive."

"True that. I hate asking my mom every time I want to go somewhere." Amber wondered how things would change now that her mom may not be coming back. In Seattle, her mother had tried to be a helicopter parent, involved in every aspect of Amber's life. Mrs. McBride was room parent every year of elementary school and eventually became PTA president. Yet to Amber, something about her actions always felt forced, as if she were acting like she thought a good mother was supposed to behave. As a result, Amber felt as if she had no privacy and her mother's interference was the source of constant battles between them.

Now her mother had done a complete turnaround.

Her thoughts were interrupted by a shiny black SUV pulling into the church's dirt parking lot. In under a minute, the other boys were loading their bikes onto the lowered tailgate at the back. A tall, broad-shouldered, muscular, dark-haired man with neatly trimmed facial hair was assisting them.

"Max!" Jonah enthusiastically waved as he and Amber reached the bottom of the hill. Jonah picked up his pace and jogged across the dusty swath. Amber strolled casually behind, not in any way motivated to break into a run under the tyranny of oppressive heat.

"Amber, meet Max," Jonah introduced the two when Amber caught up to the group.

Max inclined his handsome face in Amber's direction, greeting her with impeccable politeness, "A pleasure to meet you." His voice was deep and heavily accented, which Amber placed as Russian. He added, "Rizhii eval nikogda ne syshestvoval."

"What does that mean?" Amber asked.

"It's an old Russian saying: There was never a saint with red hair"

Amber's face turned the color of her hair as she mumbled, "Thanks, I guess…" hearing the boys snickering.

Max gave them a sharp glance and they immediately fell silent. "Now we make leave," Max waved them into the truck.

Jonah sat up in front, while Amber and the rest of her male companions clambered into the back. The interior smelled new, with seats of soft buttery leather; it was immaculately clean.

Amber poked Seth and whispered, "Won't he mind the bikes getting the back dirty? And what about our feet?" Examining the bottom of her shoes self-consciously, Amber was fearful that she might have accidentally stepped in coyote scat somewhere during the morning's trek across the preserve.

"Nah, he'll probably just get it washed later. We do this all the time," Seth whispered back reassuringly.

They drove through Lake Manor, past the entrance to Amber's driveway, which Seth pointed out for everyone's benefit and on towards a stop sign at the end of town. Here the road forked. To the left, it widened; bearing right was a narrow track at a strangling width meant more for Model T's. Max turned right and the road twisted around hairpin turns. They passed strangely shaped houses built right into the cliffs. Narrow driveways wound off the road at various intervals and vanished over and around eerie bends to places unseen.

Max steered the SUV like a test-driver in a car commercial by zooming around turns and yet managing to hug the road, his speed never varying. Amber half-expected the SUV to come up onto two wheels when rounding corners at the rate they were traveling. Max's considerable skills notwithstanding, Amber found herself digging her nails into her legs involuntarily each time another vehicle passed on the opposite side of the narrow roadway.

They rocketed past a huge, carved face. Looking back to try and catch a glimpse of the stone sculpture, she was surprised to see how far up they had come in such a short time. The entire valley opened up in a broad panorama before her eyes, with her house a tiny U in the diorama far, far below. She was only able to pick it out because it stood alone on Lizard Hill, right at the edge of the readily identifiable expanse of the preserve.

The view and sunlight suddenly disappeared as they rounded another sharp turn and entered into a narrow canyon lined with cabins and towering oaks. Max abruptly made a sharp right onto a primitive dirt road between two of the little structures, bouncing the teens up off their seats as he shot across a dry creek bed.

Lurching over potholes and around fallen branches for several minutes before emerging into brilliant sunshine, the cabins and trees quickly receded until disappearing completely after the SUV crested a large hill and then plummeted down the backside. Roaring along the primitive dirt road absent any sign of habitation, the valley now looked indistinct and distant from their vantage point atop one of the mountain plateaus.

Crossing a broad meadow, prairie grass burnt brown and brittle by the merciless sun, they headed towards towering cliffs of stacked sandstone. The rich, vibrant color reminded Amber of caramel candy and she almost giggled when she thought about her new friends in their own private Big Thunder Mountain Railroad.

Her view of the rock formation was interrupted when the SUV made a sharp turn in front of the cliff, onto a dirt road not visible until they were upon it. They careened up a narrow track barely wide enough for one vehicle. Amber swallowed hard when she spotted the steep descent, no railing or barrier of course, ending in a rocky ravine hundreds of feet below, all clearly visible in Technicolor out her passenger window.

It was impossible to see anything out the left side because they were so close to the cliff and passing it by at a speed she considered beyond the limits of any sensible person. Like a subway train rushing past the inner tunnel walls, the view was a complete blur.

The SUV burst over the top of a ridgeline in an airborne jump. It sailed through the open air for breathtaking moments, before landing heavily and subsequently bouncing up again.

The guys were clearly expecting this because they let out whoops and hollers the likes of, "That's sick, man!"

"We have AIR!"

When Amber recovered her stomach, she smiled weakly at the boys and hoped her face wasn't paler than normal.

Debris skidded off the tires as Max slid to a stop behind an enormous stand of laurel sumac. The thick brush sported thin, folded Crayola green leaves the length of one's index finger. The laurel's limbs, like the Simi Hills in which they had taken root, changed in color chameleon-style, depending upon the angle at which they were viewed. Extended as they currently were over the top of the vehicle, they appeared a dull grey. Yet Amber caught a flash of silver, even ox-blood red here and there as birds within the stand rustled about, searching for seeds.

Assuming they'd arrived at their intended location, Amber moved to hop out of the SUV. She longed to fling herself upon the earth and kiss the ground in gratitude that she'd arrived in one piece. But the boys remained seated. No one moved. They simply looked smug with their raised noses and impish grins.

Jonah Abernathy was intrigued by the redheaded newcomer, but not in any romantic way. His lack of amorous interest had nothing to do with her being white; Jonah just wasn't into girls. But he was a practical sort and therefore of the mind to tackle one major issue at a time. Right now, priority number one was getting out of the hated private school.

Coming out was challenging for any teenager, but for Jonah it would be announced in the tabloids because of his movie star father. The entire world would share the experience when Jonah revealed to his family and friends that he was gay. No doubt the black community would make a big deal about it as well. The inevitable contrast would be drawn between Marcus Abernathy's two sons: the world's most sought-after, highly paid action hero with one son in his image and the other his mirror opposite. Jonah's eldest brother Jeremy was everything his father wanted: a highly sought after prep starter playing on UCLA's basketball team. Jonah had only been a disappointment.

With such weighty matters on his mind, why had this redheaded girl captured his attention?

Within a few minutes, Amber heard an engine's revving. Completely shielded behind the thick clumps of sumac, she couldn't see how many vehicles were approaching, or how close they were.

Everyone within the car remained still, patiently waiting, while Amber tapped her fingernails impatiently upon the hem of her shorts. After what seemed to her an agonizing wait, she heard what sounded like a military bomber whoosh by, the sounds defying the mechanical age of the vehicle.

"Right on schedule," Max tapped the clock inset into the SUV's dashboard: 6:00.

Amber was about to ask what he meant, but Max was already out of the SUV in one fluid motion, the teenagers following and helping unload the bikes out the back, without being asked.

Max handed Jonah and Amber helmets. "Wear these." Staring pointedly at Jonah, dark eyes dancing at the edge of menacing, Max ordered, "You know how your mother feels about this."

Without putting up a fight, Jonah held out his hand to accept a hated object on par with being asked to wear a diaper and half-heartedly motioned to Amber to do the same.

Glaring at Jonah, she crossed her arms.

"Is there problem, young lady?" Max crossed his muscular arms as well. Before she could open her mouth, he added, "We go if you refuse."

Glancing to Jonah in desperation, he shook his head slightly as the others watched nervously, uncertain as to whether Amber would ruin the adventure before it even started, just to make a point.

Pouting, Amber stuck out her palm for the helmet, resulting in relieved exhalations from her compatriots.

"Head injury cause death, so say CDC," Max advised as he slipped into the SUV. Not a speck of the reddish dirt marred his dark suit. As the pricey gas-guzzler drove away, spewing a cloud of dust as it departed, Jonah made a big show of putting on his helmet. Shrugging, he bade Amber to do likewise.

As soon as Max was out of sight, they promptly took off their constraints and strapped them to the back of their bikes. Amber pulled a band off her wrist and twisted her long red hair into a ponytail. She asked, "What was that about the cars leaving at 6:00?"

The group followed Seth as he leisurely pedaled out from behind the brush and onto the dirt road. "The Salvia brothers," he called back over his shoulder. "They like to hang out at the Hillbilly Haven with their dirt bag friends. We like to wait until they leave before we ride on their property."

"How convenient," Amber quipped. "So we don't have to worry about getting shot at?"

Luis laughed heartily, "No, but with that hair, maybe you *should* wear a helmet! If George sees you, he'll for sure recognize you at school!"

Putting on a burst of speed, Seth turned off onto the narrowest trail of three available, a little deer path that Amber had spied moments earlier. In his best *Max* impersonation, Seth admonished the slowpokes, "My dust, you will make hearty meal of it!"

Only one bike at a time could fit on the chosen route, so the others were forced to fall, single file, behind Seth. Amber would have chosen to bring up the rear, but James Toshima slid in as the voluntary group sweep and urged her forward with a polite hand gesture.

Her face would have burned red with embarrassment at the mere thought that she needed babysitting, if all her concentration were not needed just to keep the mountain bike moving and upright at the same time. It quickly became quite annoying how her companions rode so easily. Amber worked hard just to go around the rocks and washouts without being thrown over them as she soldiered on, determined to keep up.

By the time they skidded to a halt in front of an old dilapidated cabin, her face and neck glistened with sweat.

"Zorro's cabin," Seth announced as each youth took a hearty swig from the water bottles attached to their bikes. "It was an old Disney show that my grandma used to watch, way before even my mom was born, about some superhero."

"A *Mexican* superhero," Luis added enthusiastically. "He was a badass, always in black and carving a Z into the flesh of his enemies."

"That was on TV back in the day?" Amber asked skeptically.

Luis looked sheepish as he kicked at the dirt, admitting, "Well, maybe I read about the flesh-carving. But the rest is true! He was La Raza, and wicked with a blade."

Making a point of rolling the *r* in Raza with relish, Luis made grand sword-fighting motions, and swash buckled off to join his companions climbing atop boulders.

Amber raised an amused eyebrow at Luis before turning her attention to the rotting movie set, flanked by two ancient oaks presently in the process of dying after two hundred years of vigorous growth. Crumbling adobe shingles valiantly tried to protect the roof from the elements, but the collapsed chimney suggested that the conclusion was forgone. Internal exploration was out of the question: thick metal grates barred the windows and a heavy padlock blocked entry through the front door.

"No one films here anymore, do they?" Amber called up to Seth.

From atop a boulder aligned perfectly behind Zorro's humble abode, Seth pretended to walk an imaginary tightrope across the roofline as he nonchalantly answered, "No, but I bet things would be different if they'd put Disneyland here in Chatsworth, instead of in Anaheim. My mom told me old man Disney really thought about it!"

Seth made a melodramatic show of losing his balance and vanished from the rooftop.

Unimpressed, she asked, "The Salvias don't live in there?"

Seth's hearty, frog-like laughter echoed up from behind the forlorn outpost, "They may as well. Their shack looks just about as bad as this sorry place!"

"So what's with this *George*? He hangs out in bars and he's in high school?"

"We're just messing with you. They serve food at the Hillbilly Haven so anyone can go in. There are pool tables so a lot of guys like to hang out there. You have to be twenty-one to go into the bar." Seth reappeared near the front door looking positively professorial. He motioned for her to follow as, to Amber's envy, the boys effortlessly saddled upon their bikes when she was forced to slowly lift a strained and sore leg and swing it over the other side.

"I wish we were riding horses," Amber sighed.

"You've gotta meet my sister, Marisol," Luis volunteered. "We have horses and she loves to ride!"

The youths rode their mountain bikes around the south side of Zorro's cabin, where giant boulders blocked further progress.

"This way," Seth called as he wound his way in between a narrow crevice, invisible to the uninitiated, unless one stood directly in front of the seam.

Amber followed, the sound of the wind rustling through the decaying oaks as it started to pick up with the approach of evening.

Once inside what was, in reality, a maze of boulders, Seth disappeared in its myriad twists and turns and she could only see the rider directly in front of her. As they progressed, the stone sarcophagus pressed and loomed in, forcing her to quench a strong desire to scuttle the bike and flee out the way she'd come.

"Watch out for rattlesnakes!" Seth's voice floated back.

"Wait...what?!!" Amber stammered.

"They like to come out on the rocks when it cools down," James's soft voice spoke up behind her. "Don't worry, they don't want any trouble. They just want to be left alone."

When she thought she could take no more of this torture, the sky opened up in a vast, brilliant blue expanse. High winds assailed them from all sides, blowing away even the memory of any heat-induced funk. Amber emerged from the boulder maze to find the entire community of Lake Manor on display below, a tiny town resembling a model village.

Seth drove his bike right to the edge of the cliff, stones skittering off into the abyss as the tip of his front tire dangled precariously over the edge. The others followed, though none strayed as close to the open air as where Seth was. He appeared indifferent to the fact that one misplaced foot would send him plummeting to certain impalement upon sharply angled rocks far below.

"We're standing right on top of the Twelve Apostles," he announced for Amber's enlightenment.

Amber hesitated only briefly before following Seth's bold lead to the edge. Stepping off the mountain bike, she stood at the precipice, her toes hanging out and over into the open air upon the stone shelf she'd glimpsed earlier that day from her home. Inhaling deeply, she bravely looked down and took in the long stone column unfolding before her eyes.

The wind buffeted them mercilessly now that they were out in the open. Despite the tears that stung her eyes from the onslaught, Amber raised her head into the full force of the blast.

Her house was easily identifiable, in vivid, stark detail. She flushed slightly when she realized that anyone standing at that very spot had a direct line of sight to her pool. With a pair of binoculars, one could probably peer right into her bedroom!

To the northeast, Amber saw the sloping hills of the Santa Susana Mountains, the range ringing the northern part of the San Fernando Valley. As Amber followed the Santa Susana Mountains' ridgeline east, she found forbidding, grey granite peaks belonging to the San Gabriel Mountain range. To the southeast was Griffith Park's lone peak, flanked by Burbank in the San Fernando Valley and iconic Hollywood in what locals referred to as 'the west side.' Following her line of sight west, she found the verdant green Santa Monica Mountains and tracked them as they circled around and connected up with the rocky bones of the Simi Hills until linking with the very ridgeline upon which she stood.

"Uh, guys…." the obvious concern in James's voice caused them to all sharply turn in his direction. His index finger pointed to the top of a high peak to the northeast, where a topless Ford Bronco was winding its way down a twisting dirt road.

MARISOL GARCIA

CHAPTER 3

QUESTIONS

"I thought they all left...." Amber didn't have time to finish her sentence before the boys were barreling on their bikes across the top of the Twelve Apostles, in the opposite direction from where the car was coming. Despite aching muscles, she managed to jump on her bike and follow, brain quickly registering that James had again slipped in behind her.

There was no time to argue as they furiously pedaled away.

Hearing the truck screech to a stop, she badly wanted to look back to see if the Salvias had gotten out, or if any heavy weaponry was aimed at their retreating forms, but she couldn't risk it due to their precarious position along the edge of the towering rock formation. There was no question of survival for anyone who went over the cliff to drop several stories.

Seth disappeared in front of her over a ridge. Amber gulped as her bike crested the hill and began descending a barely-discernible shard-strewn path running down the northwest side of the Twelve Apostles formation.

The pace slowed because the angle was nearly vertical, but hazards appeared much too quickly for Amber to properly process, forcing her to constantly react. The guys expertly maneuvered around and over rocks, making the entire endeavor look easy. Her bike shook and rattled as if it would fall apart over every bump, her bones jarring each time the wheels struck a deep pit in the trail. Making her way down the side of the Twelve Apostles was a painstaking effort. Amber's arms ached from the effort of gripping the handlebars to maneuver around the rocks that blocked the barely navigable trail. Her calf muscles protested over constantly being put to use to assist in braking and pushing off turns. Scratched and scraped skin began to burn as sweat and dirt seeped into wounds.

Amber's head started to ache and sweat ran down her forehead, only to be blasted back by wind blowing so hard it made her eyes sting. She fleetingly wondered if the laurel sumac, coyote bush and scrub oaks clinging to the side of the cliff trail somehow shielded them from view because no shots rang out over their heads. Or maybe she just couldn't hear them being fired upon because of the howling wind?

Refocusing, she continued on, determined to make it without tumbling off the mountain bike and taking anyone else down with her.

After fifteen minutes, the ground leveled and Seth again disappeared, this time around a corner, followed by each rider in progression. When Amber rounded the bottom of the cliff, she realized with no small measure of relief that they had miraculously descended the steep formation in one piece. Seth now led them on a path away from the Twelve Apostles and danger, continuing west towards the promise of home and safety.

The guys put on a burst of adrenaline-induced speed as they drew away from Amber.

Pedaling faster, she was halfway past a low foothill when, to her alarm, Amber heard gruff shouts of, "There they are! Get those little...."

The wind carried away the rest of the sentence, but she was sure that whatever was at the end of it was a rough expletive. Adding one of her own under her breath, she mustered her internal strength and picked up the pace. The voices had come from her left, from behind the hill she'd just passed! If she could only go *faster*, she might escape them.

Her companions had already disappeared from view in the dimming twilight when a renewed round of angry threats reached her ears, much closer now, driven on by urgency as they closed in on their quarry.

Just when she realized that the Salvias' braying shouts had distracted her from the trail, her bike struck a rock and she torpedoed over the handlebars.

Amber desperately tried to stop herself mid-air by grasping for the bike. Although this effort slowed her flight, it flipped her completely over, her head the last to hit, with a painful *thud.*

Lying in the middle of the trail, she was unable to move.

Three youths sat silently within the dark folds of a hideout known locally as "The Bat Cave." Tucked away within Castle Peak, the cave's mouth was set up into the hillside. Given the climbing required, the area had cleared out with the oncoming darkness.

A needle passed between the three, bringing temporary relief.

Lulled into that dreamlike state that is not sleep nor quite yet death, each youth drifted away into formless nothingness.

Whispering

Shane had no idea how long he'd been floating on his heroin high, but the insistent whispering nudged him to semi-wakefulness. Opening his eyes, he tried to find the source of the sound.

Using the walls for leverage, he stood and inched his way to the back of the cave.

Unsteady on his feet, Shane leaned against a rock for support, and inhaled sharply as the back wall of the cave slid open.

Dreamlike, Shane walked into the secret cavern as the wall slid shut behind him.

A tall, darkly clothed figure spoke in a language he'd never heard before, "Why waste your time with these fools, chasing something illusive? You use filthy tools and put poison in your body."

"Who are you?" Shane demanded.

"I exist only to serve the gods that walk in human form upon this earth. You are one such king, and your body is a temple. Why pay for poison, when I offer you something beyond your imagination?"

Intrigued, Shane looked to where the figure pointed: a clear liquid pool within a stone basin. As Shane watched, the water rippled slightly and a vision appeared. Shane saw an older version of himself: arrogant, healthy, handsome and strong. The vision then shifted, and revealed Shane's darkest desires.

Smiling, Shane cupped his hands and drank from the basin.

In a flash, someone had Amber by the hands, dragging her limp form under a thick stand of nearby laurel sumac. James Toshima's dark form was barely visible in the dimming light as he moved back onto the trail like a wraith. He returned momentarily with the bikes, quickly stowing them out of sight under the low-hanging boughs of the ample grove. Crawling in combat-style as dead, rusty leaves crackled under his weight, James settled in next to Amber.

Heart pounding so loudly she could hear her pulse in her ears, Amber tried to shake her aching head to clear her blurry vision. Why weren't the Salvias upon them at this very moment?

The persistent wind picked up, blowing into the brush, infusing the air with the overwhelming fragrance of sage and green apples. Breathing in the strong elixir oddly brought a strange sense of quiet calm, clearing her mind of all thoughts. Amber became an empty vessel, at one with the silvered limbs surrounding her and the rocky hills overhead.

They waited for telltale heavy breathing, leaves rustling, boots stomping and the dire threats that would be cast their way.

Amber subconsciously took James's hand. He stared at her in surprise, but Amber's face remained impassive and impenetrable as her breathing took on a rhythm that matched the quiet pulse of the mountain itself.

Heavy footsteps clumped along the path and gruff voices grew louder with each step. Scraping sounds from a tree limb being drawn along the cliff side lent a surreal quality to their approach. Noise of shoes scuffing along the trail grew louder until a gravelly voice right at the edge of the chaparral that James believed to be Ken quipped, "Where did those pendejos[3] get a *girl?*"

"Yeah, she looked ok, too," another voice drawled. *Martin,* James thought. Despite the danger, James' pride puffed at Martin's compliment about the company he was presently keeping. The seriousness of the

---

[3] Spanish for 'idiot'

situation quickly returned, however, when a cold voice silenced the others. It caused a chill to run up his spine because it was completely devoid of *any* emotion.

"Hold up. We're not done here."

The speaker was Ben Salvia, the oldest of the brothers.

A strangely detached Amber heard him sniff the air in a feral-like manner before he turned toward the sumac in response to a rustling sound. Setting the tree branch aside, Ben Salvia bent at the knees and squatted down on his haunches. Looking back at his brothers to make sure they were paying attention, he returned to the brush and lifted up the bottom layer.

Using the opening he created, Ben moved forward a few inches.

When Amber inhaled, shadows gathered. A dark, misty veil swirled closely around the two teenagers, separating them from Ben Salvia. Amber had only a fraction of a second to take in his features: dark, shaggy hair with no discernable part and a pair of intense brown eyes that nearly caught her impassive gaze before the curtain of shadows enveloped her. Surprisingly, Ben's unlined face was cherubic.

Moments passed as Ben stared into the leaves and branches with a strange expression, listening carefully, ignoring the queries from his brothers asking what he was seeing. The shadows were now still, a dark screen separating Ben Salvia from the two teenagers. Yet Amber sensed *others* in the sumac, dozens of them.

"C'mon man, let's go!" Martin entreated from outside the brush.

Ben turned and dropped the brush he was holding. Standing, he motioned for silence.

Suddenly, Ben knelt and swept the tree branch off the trail in one fluid motion. Eyes fierce, he poked the sharp tip of the woody limb straight at Amber.

Breathing out in one long, slow exhalation, she felt as if the contents of her head were emptying in a most unsettling manner. Amber's otherworldly exhalation concluded with a flock of small birds that burst out in a screech from under the brush. They flew straight into Ben's face, sending him backward into a startled sprawl on the trail. The tiny winged creatures swooped across his body and a few even had the courtesy to drop little presents on their flight over.

Sputtering, he leapt up and set about striking his brothers, who had collapsed into barking laughter on the trail.

"For real, dude, you're going to meet a lot of chicks with bird poop on your head!"

"That your new cologne? What do you call that? Essence of bird shit?"

"A little *birdie* told me you won't be hooking up tonight..."

The sound of bird poop jokes, punches, shoving and shouting could be heard as the brothers left the stand of laurel sumac and went back the way they had come.

After a few minutes, James gently removed his hand from Amber's, studying her intently.

"He was only inches away from us and he didn't see us," James observed, and then waited for an explanation.

Amber blinked hard.

The bottom layer of brush in front of Amber and James slowly lifted, causing them both to gasp and shrink back into the center of the laurel sumac.

Seth stuck his head into their hideaway, smiling from ear-to-ear. "Yee haw!" he mocked the Salvias in their retreat. "Mr. Baccharis' shadow bomb worked! That was so sick, man! I can't believe it!"

Seth extracted himself from the native chaparral and pumped his fist into the air in triumph, adding in an exhilarated jig to burn off the jumpiness that comes with very nearly taking a beating.

"What just happened?" Amber's mind was swirling. She remembered being propelled over the bike. Everything afterward was a total blank.

James continued to stare at her with an odd expression on his face as he crawled out from under the brush. Noticing her wobbly state, he extended an arm to Amber, insisting she take it to steady herself. "Amber? Amber!" James snapped a finger in front of her face, trying to get her attention. Following her dazed stare, he spied an enormous black bird circling overhead.

With a shriek, the turkey vulture flew away and Amber shook her head as she accepted James' offer of assistance.

"I think she has a concussion," James quietly informed Seth.

The blond boy joked, "I'm no doctor, but I'll have a look!" earning a scowl and headshake from James. Seth promptly got serious and retrieved the bikes out from under the laurel sumac.

"It's too dark, I can't see shit!" Seth called over his shoulder to Amber, where James had propped her up, sitting against a smooth, flat, waist-high sandstone.

"Bro, you know I'm not one to criticize," Seth commented to James as they walked the bikes over to Amber, "but what was the deal with shaking the brush like that? Did you *want* to get your ass kicked?"

James responded flatly, "That wasn't me."

"So if it wasn't you, then…" Hearing no response from James, Seth added, "No judgment here, Jimbo…"

"I know. It's just that, there's more. Glancing about to make sure no one overheard what he was about to say next, James asked, "Did you hear *something strange* under the brush?"

The corner of Seth's mouth twitched into a crooked smile. "Dude! I thought that was you breathing so heavy, maybe because you were alone with Amber."

"For reals!" James admonished his friend. "This'll sound crazy, but I felt like she made the birds attack him."

"No shit?" Seth exhaled heavily, "What is she, the *bird whisperer*?"

"Let's keep this to ourselves for now," James requested.

"True that, or we'll all wind up in a shrink's office!" Seth agreed.

Reaching Amber, James gently helped her to stand. He insisted upon walking her bike, despite her protestations.

"Where are the others?" she asked, head pounding from the simple act of speaking.

Seth pointed to another low foothill ahead, its dark shape rendering it indistinguishable from the rest of the shadows in the gloom. He called out with a bird whistle and within moments, two human head-like shapes tentatively peeked around the southern edge of the slope. Sensing freedom, Jonah and Luis high-fived each other and walked out with the bikes, distinctly swaggering from having once again outwitted their nemeses.

The simultaneous pummeling of questions caused Amber's head to throb.

"Give it a rest!" James ordered. "She took a pretty good bonk on the head back there!" He anxiously examined Amber's face, devoid of all color and glistening with a slick sheen of sweat.

The other boys stopped jabbering as James commanded, "We've got to get her back. We'll talk on the way."

Instead of the usual embarrassed reaction, Amber simply felt bewildered as Seth and James related the tale of their narrow escape. Nothing in the narrative sparked any memories.

Seth explained that when he realized Amber and James were no longer behind him, he had sent Jonah and Luis up ahead to scout out the path and they picked a rendezvous point. Seth then doubled back, making sure to stay off the trail and retain the advantage of surprise.

By the time he reached James and Amber, they were hiding under the laurel sumac. He figured it out because of the scrum of agitated Salvias gathered around the bush.

Seth explained that he had then snuck up behind the large stand of chaparral. Taking one of the special effects that Mr. Baccharis had provided earlier in the day, he described it like a grenade, complete with a pin to be pulled when ready to explode. Seth quietly pulled the pin out and, when the Salvias were arguing, tossed it into the center of the laurel sumac bush.

"It worked even better than I expected! Instead of looking like that fake fog you see in the movies, it looked like a dark shadow! It covered Amber and James and that butt munch couldn't even see them, even though he was inches away!" Seth paused for air, then continued, "The shadow bomb must have scared some birds in the bush, because they came screaming out, right into Ben Salvia's face! It was sweet, man!"

"No way! Really?" Amber spoke up for the first time since the tale began.

Everyone stared at her.

"Maybe I do have a concussion," she added, "I don't remember anything, except the smell of sage and green apples."

"The sumac," James confirmed. "The blooms smell like apples."

'George must've stayed home and called his brothers in the bar. They walked up to us from Lake Manor," Jonah realized as he smacked his forehead with his palm. "I should've thought of that!"

"We are *so* lucky they don't know our names, or where we live. That maniac Ben would hunt us down for sure!" Luis shook his head.

"Do you think they saw our faces?" Amber asked nervously.

"I don't think they saw nada[4] in the dark," Luis answered.

"We totally dodged a bullet that time!" Seth joked.

"Dude, I figured you must've sharted yourself!" Luis teased James.

"The only crap came out of the birds. They shit all over asshole Salvia when they flew out!" Seth laughed with his hearty, froglike croak.

Perhaps it was a result of so much tension built up and the need for release. Or maybe it was the thought of Ben Salvia getting pooped on that started the teenagers tittering, and then outright guffawing. The guffaws turned into hysterical laughter that didn't stop for several minutes as they walked on in the darkness.

After carefully picking their way for about a quarter hour along what was now a dirt road, the welcome lights of houses beckoned ahead. Seth veered off to the left and cut across a stubbly field. Eventually they emerged out of another oak forest and into Seth's homey backyard.

After another round of backslapping over their narrow escape, Amber's cell phone rang. Examining her phone, she saw that her father had called no fewer than ten times. How had she not heard it?

Gulping, she answered.

"Where – are – you?" her father asked in a slow, staccato voice.

"Um, I'm still with Seth. We went mountain biking."

"In the dark?" her father asked incredulously.

"No," Amber recovered quickly. "We got back a little while ago and now we're hanging out at his house. I'm really sorry. I'll be right home."

"No you won't. I'm picking you up."

"Your dad?" Jonah asked.

"Yep," Amber said. "I have to tell him about hitting my head because I

---

[4] Spanish for 'nothing'

might have a concussion, but I don't want him to tell me I can't go out with you guys again."

"Tell him you hit your head after we were done riding!" Seth suggested.

The group conspired briefly and decided the story would be that Amber had tripped walking the bike back to the house in the dark.

Within minutes, Dr. McBride's car pulled in front of the house. Before Amber could object, Seth was out the door and down by the vehicle, attempting to explain the situation to Amber's father.

As Amber emerged out the front door, her father was already at the top of the stairs to meet her. Dr. McBride's face was lined with obvious concern as he fretted, "C'mon. We're going to get you checked out."

"See you guys later," Amber called back into the cottage, "sorry for the trouble."

"Hey, no trouble," Seth responded. He added earnestly, "We had a *great* time."

When Amber reached the car, Luis shouted from the front porch, "Stay fine, Red!"

Amber was helped by her father into the front seat and grinned weakly as the guys waved goodbye from the porch when she drove away.

"The hospital's not far from here," her father informed her.

"Sorry dad," Amber apologized.

Patting her leg affectionately, Dr. McBride gently admonished his daughter, "No more riding around at night, okay?"

"I didn't know that it gets darker here earlier than in Seattle. It was dark before I knew it."

"Of course!" her father smacked the steering wheel with his palm a little too hard. Amber wondered if his relief was because she hadn't purposefully rebelled.

"We're closer to the equator now that we're in Los Angeles," Dr. McBride realized.

Exhaling with relief because her ruse was going to hold up, Amber cradled her throbbing skull between her palms and closed her eyes.

They spent the next couple of hours at the local hospital emergency room. Amber was bored out of her mind as she underwent scans, had flashlights shown in her eyes and answered questions under the harsh glare of the hospital's florescent lights.

The end result, to her great surprise, was that she had *not* suffered a concussion. But if she wasn't brain damaged, why couldn't she remember what had happened?

The appearance of a Bobcat excavator at the House on Lizard Hill put the Salvia brothers distinctly on edge. Though nowhere near their property atop the Twelve Apostles, any digging in Lake Manor was cause for alarm. Drawing straws, eighteen-year-old George Salvia found himself at the short end of the stick. He was designated as the one who'd investigate.

Before he left the modest Salvia home that night, his brother Kendrick handed him a brown paper bag, instructing, "My best Mexican flap steak yet! This oughta keep that dog busy while you check the place out."

Standing beneath the skyline pool, George surveyed the partially finished work undertaken by the Bobcat and exhaled with relief. A contractor was fixing the sewer line. Mission complete, he could return home.

Turning to leave, George caught a whiff of perfume. Transfixed, he stopped and inhaled deeply. The logical part of his brain warned him to get out of there as soon as possible. He'd avoided rousing the dog and, as a college bound senior, shouldn't be risking a breaking and entering charge.

Yet, there it was, his dead mother's favorite perfume, overwhelming his senses. George dropped the bag with the competing scent of steak.

Dreamlike, he followed his mother's scent and was compelled to walk around the pool to a dark opening in the underside. He stopped at the entrance.

Creaaaaaak

The door opening from somewhere inside that dank hole sounded as if it was separating from its hinges under extreme protest.

Bewitched, he stepped inside the women's changing room.

Furious barking erupted from the pool overhead.

Instantly roused from the spell, George was out the doorway and over the nature preserve fence by the time the elderly Kibbles made his way down to investigate.

He never noticed the teenaged Latina that peered out from the women's changing room. Her intense, dark eyes watched the young man with familiar interest as he retreated.

Amber bolted upright in bed. Tearing off the covers, she jumped out of bed with cell phone in hand and stepped on a soggy brown paper bag in the middle of her floor.

"Ewww, Kibbles!" she admonished, "Did you raid the trash again?"

Scooping up the mess and throwing it in the trash, Amber ran down the hall to find her dad. Halfway across the living room, she skidded across the wooden floor in her Hello Kitty socks when she remembered he was at work.

Glancing down at her cell, she found a post-it note from her father asking her to call him. Amber was amazed that her father, the brilliant aerospace engineer, refused to learn how to text. She dialed and Dr.

McBride picked up immediately.

Voices in the background asking for Dr. McBride interrupted the conversation, "Honey, I need to go. We're working on something here. Sure you're ok?"

Bidding her father goodbye, Amber trudged on to the kitchen to scrounge for food. As she ate her breakfast, Amber thought about the girl she believed was haunting the house. The poufy hair was a dead giveaway as to the time period, totally '80's…

Shaking her head, she resumed eating and recalled a photo of her father with his 80's haircut. She wracked her brain to remember the name, *a mullet?* Her father protested when her mother made him cut that mullet. His mantra was, *"business up front and party in back!"*

Amber laughed to herself. *How did people ever look so weird? What were they thinking?* She chuckled to herself when she pictured her father with that flowing red mullet, wearing a puffy pirate shirt and dancing to 80's music around the pool….

A text message from Luis Garcia interrupted her thoughts. He invited Amber to come hang with his older sister for the day. He'd made good on his promise to hook Amber up for some horseback riding. Dumping her cereal bowl in the sink, she raced off to her room to get ready and take advantage of this unexpected turn of events.

She quickly put on mascara and felt her lighthearted mood start to dissipate when she noticed that her eyes were her mother's.

Amber realized that she hadn't heard from her yesterday. She had *never* gone an entire day in her whole life without speaking to her. Calling her was briefly considered then rapidly dismissed. *Mother* was the one who had chosen to not to join them, so the onus was now on her to reach out.

Deliberately setting thoughts of her mother aside, she finished getting ready, stuffed some cash into the pocket of her jeans and made a mental note to buy some sunglasses. It was so bright in Southern California it was nearly unbearable to go outside without shielding her eyes. Sunglasses were strictly for attitude and not something she'd thought about for practical purposes when living in the gloomy Pacific Northwest.

Jangling in her pocket indicated another incoming message and a photo of Luis' sister Marisol appeared next to a text notifying Amber that she and her mother were nearly there. Feeling too guilty today to even attempt an excuse for the poor waiting Kibbles, Amber darted out of her room and ran across the courtyard, bounding out the tall double wooden doors before the dog could give chase. She sprinted down the stairs and driveway, reaching the country road before Marisol and her mother arrived.

Studying the picture on her phone, she found that Marisol's big, brown eyes belied an uncommon earnestness. She did not wear the bored, jaded look that so many teenagers affected. Amber thought she looked kind, innocent even.

A small car silently approached and Amber was pleased to see Marisol and her mother inside instead of some random stranger. Introductions were made as she slipped into their air-conditioned Prius. To her delight, Amber learned that Marisol was an incoming sophomore at Castle Peak High School. Marisol's mother, Mrs. Susanna Garcia, was elegantly dressed in a conservative business suit with matching shoes.

"Mom's an accountant," Marisol informed Amber.

Mrs. Garcia passed the nature preserve, turned left onto one of the residential streets leading into a funky horse neighborhood and headed north, following the rocky ridgeline of the Simi Hills. Amber and Marisol clicked immediately and chattered happily about Marisol's horses.

Eventually, the pavement gave way to a ranch road. Mrs. Garcia turned abruptly to the right and into the gravel driveway of one ranch marked with a wooden entrance sign reading Hacienda Hernandez.[5]

"My maiden name," Mrs. Garcia explained as she parked the car. "We Hernandez' have been in Chatsworth even before it was founded in 1888."

The house, set far back from the road, was built in the one-story Spanish Adobe-style. A quaint wooden door with an opening at the top covered with wrought-iron bars was inset into the center of the home, behind which was an adobe chimney. Metal-latticed windows were adorned with colorful planter boxes. The entire roof was covered in hand-made clay tiles of muted orange-red.

Even the two-story barn was built in the Spanish style. The first floor had four semi-circular doors. Above them was centered a single hay door. A horse-training ring was situated in front of the barn, within which a trainer walked a spirited Appaloosa.

One of the barn doors opened and Luis emerged, dusting off hay and raising a hand in greeting to the girls.

Bidding her mother goodbye, Marisol led Amber into the barn where the peaty smell of hay and sweat wafted out from the stalls. Marisol stopped when she reached a tall, red quarter horse. "This is Lady. Would you like to ride her?"

Nodding, Amber reached out and gently touched her nose. Lady bowed her head and whinnied, snuffing about Amber's palm for a carrot.

Marisol grinned, opened the paddock and placed a halter over Lady's head to lead her out.

Stomping, huffing and pawing sounds erupted from another stall.

"All right, all right, I'm coming!" She handed the bridle to Amber and walked over to another stall where a gorgeous buckskin-colored Paint was now banging the stall gate with her hoof. Marisol hugged the large head and

---

[5] Spanish for 'House of Hernandez'

introduced Amber to Catarina, "She gets pretty excited about going out."

Amber eyed Catarina, who looked as if she would burst out of the gate the moment it was opened.

Giggling, Marisol bridled her horse and Catarina pushed open the paddock gate, anxious to be off. Catarina nudged Lady in greeting as the four made their way out of the barn and into a staging area.

Marisol showed Amber the currying combs and brushes and explained how to care for the horses before putting on all of the gear. Patting Lady's back, Amber watched a cloud of dust float off the thick horsehair.

The equines clearly knew the routine, as they stood contentedly while being brushed and pampered. Luis stopped by and offered the horses small carrots from his pocket and asked, "Where're you two going?"

"Into the state park," Marisol responded.

Amber patted Lady on the nose, eyes narrowing in Luis' direction as she asked, "Is that anywhere near the Twelve Apostles?"

Luis snorted, "The state park is on the other side of the Simi Hills. *Not* where we were yesterday. Don't worry, Amber."

Marisol raised her eyebrows, but said nothing in response to her brother's provocation.

After the horses were curried, the girls placed thick Mexican blankets over their backs, followed by leather western saddles. Amber was surprised at how difficult it was to tighten the saddle around the horse's belly. Marisol was slight of build, but expertly fastened the saddle onto each horse so that it sat comfortably on the animal without slipping.

"A lot of the girls around here ride in the fancy dressage style. Not my thing, too uncomfortable," Marisol explained. She stepped into a stirrup with her left tennis shoe and easily swung her right leg over Catarina.

"You don't wear cowboy boots," Amber observed.

"I said I like to ride Western, doesn't mean I'm a hick! Now you," Marisol motioned for Amber to hop on her horse. "You've ridden before, right?"

"Yea, yea," Amber left out the minor detail that she had been a mere child at the time, figuring it wasn't important. She loved riding because it had felt so natural to her. Imitating Marisol's graceful movements to mount her horse, Amber swung her leg easily over the top of Lady's back and into the stirrup and assessed her new friend from atop her mount. Although shorter in stature, Marisol's face was at the same level as Amber due to the height of Catarina. Marisol sat easily in her saddle, straw hat upon her head to shield her from the sun. Amber was already starting to sweat and was grateful for the lightweight straw cowboy hat Marisol had lent her.

Clicking sounds from Marisol indicated to Catarina she was free to depart. The horses ambled out of the yard, turned left at the dirt road and headed out for their destination.

"So, what happened yesterday with my brother?"

"Swear you won't tell?"

After Amber extracted promises, she related the events of the preceding day to Luis' sister.

Mari was so aghast upon hearing Amber's story, she didn't pay attention to where the horses were going. Luckily, Catarina and Lady needed no guidance for the familiar route. They passed rambling horse ranches that eventually gave way to suburban homes and then a sprawling complex named the 'Rockridge Condominiums.'

"They *can't* go up there again! It's too dangerous!" Marisol's jaw was tight and her eyes glassy as she imagined the horrible things that could've happened had the Salvia's caught the trespassers. "I'm going to tell my brother if he goes there again, I'm going to narc him out."

Amber glared at Marisol, but quickly softened her gaze when she realized her new friend was right. It was way too risky to go up there again. If she had a brother, she wouldn't want him in harm's way.

"My brother and his Zorro fixation! He wants to be a cowboy movie star!"

"I understand. You think he'll listen to you?"

"Uh-huh, the only thing Luis truly fears is our father."

Mari led the way through the condo maze to a place where a chain link fence broke up the monotony of *sameness*. A small opening lay in between a sandstone block wall and yet another row of condos. Beyond the chain link fence, a gravel road stretched away into a small meadow covered in sunburnt mustard. Jumbled rocks lay piled along the road to the right, growing progressively higher until peaking upon a hill. A small brown sign read: Santa Susana Pass State Historic Park. Amber viewed the narrow passageway out of suburbia into the wilderness as Marisol gave her a quick smile, clicked her heels against her mount and proceeded onward. Lady and Amber followed through the narrow opening in the fence, grateful to leave the pavement behind.

Once inside the park, the gravel road was wide enough to accommodate the two horses side by side. They had only ridden five hundred feet when Marisol turned to the right toward a large rock formation, leading her up and around the backside to the stone ledge on top.

From this vantage point, high upon their horses, meadows and low hills lay at their feet. Off in the hazy distance, the Simi Hills were arrayed before them in burnt-brown splendor, dark green chaparral vibrantly abundant, wedged in and amongst the rocks in defiance of the withering heat. No one else was within sight on the trails that snaked throughout the park.

Clucking at her mount, Marisol led Amber and Lady along a sage-lined trail from the top of the rock formation and along a boulder-strewn ridgeline. The gentle *clop-clop* of the horses' hooves combined with the swaying motion of the saddle produced a hypnotic effect.

The trail narrowed upon the descent, requiring the horses to walk single file. Catarina insisted upon taking the lead, resulting in a whickered disapproval from Lady.

A gentle breeze stirred and with it came the jarring sound of bones rattling.

The girls shook their heads in response to the sound and tried to clear the heat-induced funk. Surveying the scenery around her, a broad expanse of white high in the hills far to the north caught Amber's attention. "What's that?"

"Stoner's Jump."

Amber sharpened her focus to find a huge rock formation stuck out from a cliff, over which someone had taken gallons of white paint and dumped it over the side. Although far away, Stoner's Jump was clearly visible because of the white paint emblazoning it.

"What is it with you guys and stoners? Stoney Point, Stoner's Jump…." Amber giggled.

Marisol's face remained serious as she soberly informed Amber, "I don't like Stoner's Jump. Every year there are weirdoes who come there because of Charles Manson. They call it the *Manson Caves*."

"Who?" Amber hated to ask because she had a feeling she was supposed to know who Marisol was talking about.

"Charles Manson was this psycho cult leader in the 1960's. He had this gang of teenage girls over at Spahn Ranch, an old movie studio. There," she pointed north of Stoner's Jump, "on the other side. It's part of the state park now."

"So, what, he was just some loser dude? What's the big deal?" Amber was mystified at Mari's reaction to this *Manson* character.

Marisol took a deep breath and said, "I guess it's hard for you to understand because you didn't grow up here. When it happened, my parents say everyone who lived here was totally freaked out. They won't even talk about it, not even now."

"Talk about what?"

"The *murders*. He got his followers to kill people! These teenage girls, not much older than you and me!"

Amber asked, "Dude, really?"

"They got caught and they're all in jail now, but some people think that there are bodies that were never found, over on that," she pointed north, "side of the park. That's why I stay away from Stoner's Jump. That place is muy malo."[6]

---

[6] Spanish for 'very bad'

Amber had already whipped her cell phone out to Google Charles Manson. A photo materialized onscreen, depicting a young, longhaired, bearded man whose crazed look and beady, intense eyes certainly fit her expectation of *creepy cult leader*. She quickly read the Wikipedia synopsis of his exploits. "No shit, you weren't kidding. This guy's a total nut sack!"

Mari giggled, despite herself, "You kill me, Amber. I've never heard anyone called a nut sack before."

"Well, Google the definition and I bet you find a photo of Charles Manson," Amber sniped. "So we're not going that way?"

Mari nodded and tugged at the halter to turn Catarina away from the hulking overhang that was Stoner's Jump.

A prickly sensation at the base of Amber's skull caused her to cautiously turn back toward the formation. The forbidding white cliff jutted out in awkward, pale contrast to the golden hills and the vivid blue skyline. Amidst a jumble of stone and brush to the northwest, Amber spied a darkly clothed, hooded man. He appeared to be doubled over because she could only describe his next move as *unfolding*.

"Mari!" Amber hissed. Hearing no response, she turned to see where her new friend had gone, only to find that Catarina had turned off onto a hilly trail leading up into the foothills to the west.

Snapping her head back in the direction of the oddity, Amber thought she caught a glimpse of darkness retreating into the brush. Digging her heels into Lady's sides, she stirred the mare forward to catch up with Marisol as she ascended towards a sheer cliff face rising hundreds of feet above the hillcrest.

"I just saw some creeper back there!"

"Where?" Marisol asked.

"Up off another trail. He looked *totally* freaky."

"Probably another Manson follower headed to Stoner's Jump." Marisol sounded surprisingly dismissive about the possibility of an attacker lurking about the park.

"Where are we going?" Amber inquired with increasing urgency.

"My favorite place to chill," Mari called back over her shoulder. "Don't worry, it's a special place. Nothing bad ever happens there. I've even seen horses that come down from the other side of the hills to graze sometimes. Even they feel protected from coyotes and mountain lions when they're there."

"Are they wild?" Amber asked, cowgirl visions dancing before her eyes.

"No, they're broken in. They live over at a summer camp but just like to roam around. My dad knows the camp manager. He says they always come home by night."

The San Fernando Valley slowly emerged into view with every hoof beat, a giant leviathan creeping out of the depths of what was once an ancient, primeval sea. Amber marveled that millions of people in Los Angeles were going about their day, just outside of the state park. Yet within mere miles, the two teenagers rode like pioneers on horseback through a silent, wild landscape devoid of all humanity.

Catarina entered a blocky stone passageway and the city disappeared from view. Both horses lifted their heads and picked up their pace to a slow trot. They would have burst from the corridor like stones sent out of a sling shot, had Mari not brought Catarina to a halt.

"Oh...my..." was all Amber could manage.

A broad, natural rock amphitheater opened up in front of them, with rows of smooth, grey stones arrayed in a semi-circular formation. Sheltered by towering cliffs on three sides, Amber noticed that there were narrow slits and round holes in the rock and even a small cave high up in the face of the northernmost cliff. Oddly shaped sandstone boulders lay scattered about the bowl-like formation, dropped during the evolutionary ascent from under the primeval sea.

Marisol clucked gently to Catarina, indicating the mare was now free to descend the low slope and enter the amphitheater. Lady obediently followed and Amber prudently leaned back in her saddle, grasping the horn to avoid pitching forward.

"This place is called the grotto," Mari informed Amber. "A lot of people just call it the waterfall."

"Where..." Amber asked.

"Only in winter, after it rains," Mari stopped her before she could continue, raising her index finger to indicate an indentation mid-point between the high cliff walls. Dark watermarks splayed out from the edge of the cliff, trailing down to end in a rocky jumble of brush far below. Periodic waterfall over thousands of years etched a reminder of the pathetic rainy season that Southern California experiences as winter.

Dismounting, Marisol led Catarina around the basin where a small pool forms after winter rains, picked her way around the rocks strewn about the ground and came to stand underneath a strangely shaped oak growing out from under the bottom of a cottage-sized boulder. The trunk split into two large branches like fingers forming the Hawaiian *hang loose* symbol. The thumb branch pointed back at a forty-five-degree angle toward the hill from where they'd descended.

Marisol tied Catarina's reins to the thumb branch. After Amber had safely secured Lady under the shade canopy, they turned in surprise as someone hailed them from the basin.

"Fancy seeing someone from the old country here," an older man wearing dark glasses and a patch over his left eye addressed Amber in particular from the underside of a ledge that jutted over the broad, flat floor of the dry creek bed.

The girls peered down at the frail old fellow dressed in a manner more suited to sailing than hiking. The rock overhang under which he stood was an odd space because the layered grey stones tapered down into an upside-down pyramid shape, yet held up the massive structure in a delicate balance.

"We made so many brilliant films, here in these hills," the old man remarked.

Amber examined him quizzically before asking, "What movies?"

"So, so many. *Grapes of Wrath* and *Wee Willie Winkie* were but two of them."

Turning to Marisol, Amber remarked, "My dad has pictures for both of those movies in his office!"

Looking back to the stone overhang, the old man was nowhere in sight.

"Where'd he go?" Amber asked.

"I've met lots of weird people up here," Marisol answered with surprising nonchalance as she made her way down to the streambed. "They're harmless."

Amber wondered for a moment if they'd encountered another ghost, but if this was the case, this fellow was *nothing* like the ghosts she'd encountered over the years. With her years of experience, Amber now knew what to look for and a couple of the things shown in old movies are true: the space becomes markedly colder and if you look closely enough, you can see through them.

Neither of these truisms applied to the elderly gentleman they'd just met, so Amber wrote him off as a harmless old crackpot.

The two teens took respite on a fallen limb underneath the oak and ate a light lunch Mari had packed.

Full, they leaned back against the grand trunk. As a heat-induced mirage of water began to seep across the stone floor of the amphitheater, eyes fluttered shut, after-lunch-sleepiness taking hold.

Thrum-thrum-thrum. A deep, pulsating rhythm emanated from the ground and ran the length of the oak. Mari and Amber sat bolt upright and stared at each other, simultaneously placing their palms against the tree.

"She told me about this, but I've never felt it, until now!" Marisol marveled.

Simultaneously annoyed at being out of the loop again on local folklore and grateful for making a new friend that would fill in any crucial gaps before school started, Amber tried to blunt the sharpness in her tone as she asked, "Who told you about what? What's going on?"

Gentle vibrations continued to pulsate through their palms, soothing sensations that reminded Amber of a beating heart.

"My grandmother. This oak, this is…was…her favorite place. She told me that you feel the oak drinking water from deep underneath the ground. She said the oaks and rocks are the *First Peoples*, living things just like you and me." Marisol's eyes grew moist as she concluded, "She died about a year ago. I miss her a lot."

Amber put her arm comfortingly around Marisol's shoulder and reassured, "I get why you like this place. I'm glad you brought me here."

Marisol sniffed, "I have to learn to talk about her without crying." She looked up at Amber and smiled. "We have a photo of her at home when she's my age, taken right here! I always remember her being old. Crazy, huh?"

"Let's take the same picture of you!" Amber suggested.

Marisol stood still upon a fallen bough underneath the oak tree. No staged poses, flashy hand-signs, or duck faces were made. Looking directly at Amber, she smiled shyly.

Positioning herself far enough away in order to capture the image of both tree and girl, Amber snapped a few photos on her cell phone.

"Here!" she proudly showed Mari her work.

Marisol examined the photo thoughtfully, "I look a *lot* like grandma."

As the girls turned back towards the grotto to mount up, Marisol grasped Amber's arm. The amphitheater had fallen completely silent. Squirrels and rabbits lined the natural stone seats. Red-tailed hawks wheeled gracefully down to rest atop higher perches, strangely uninterested in the abundant prey arrayed beneath them.

At least one hundred animals and birds had joined the two teenagers in the grotto.

NOELLE MERTENS

CHAPTER 4

FORGOTTEN

Glancing at Amber's face, Mari found it flushed with embarrassment.

"Amber," she whispered, "what *is* this?"

"I don't know," Amber admitted, blushing even more deeply, "but it happens to me *a lot*, just not so many of them…"

"Madre Maria!"[7] Marisol exhaled before asking, "What next?"

"We watch each other for a while, sometimes they come over and then they leave. My best friend Shelby calls me Snow White."

A loud clash of cymbals rang out from Marisol's phone, causing both girls to jump.

"Damn Luis! I told you to stop messing with my ring tone!" she scolded her brother as she answered her cell phone.

Amber could hear his hearty laughter through the phone, even as she saw the animals scatter and the birds take flight.

"You're an asshole!" Marisol hung up on her brother as she informed Amber, "The last time he changed my ring tone, it made a farting noise!"

Despite her desire to be angry at Luis along with Marisol, Amber giggled at the idea of a flatulating phone.

"So can you make the birds do your chores for you like Snow White did in the movie?" Marisol asked.

"I wish! I can only sense them. I know when they're around. I don't know how to *talk* to them or anything like that."

Grinning broadly, Amber was inwardly appreciative that Marisol thoughtfully took this in stride and didn't run in terror or make fun of her as being some sort of freak. She chose not reveal that she could also see through their eyes, at least for now. After all, she and Marisol had only just met.

Shaking slightly, Marisol asked, "You know that strange old man we saw earlier? Google *John Ford*."

Eying Mari somewhat suspiciously, Amber did as she was bid and found herself staring at a photo of a famous Hollywood director with many westerns among his credits and the iconic *Grapes of Wrath*.

It was the same old fellow, and he'd died in 1973.

"Sorry I didn't tell you before," Mari apologized. "But I thought you'd think I was loco.[8] I've never been with another person when I've seen them; ghosts, I mean."

---

[7] Spanish for 'Mother Mary'
[8] Spanish for 'crazy'

"I've seen them too," Amber revealed, "but the SoCal spooks have their own set of rules!" Amber quickly explained ghost rules as she and Shelby understood them.

Mari actually cracked a smile, "We have to do things different down here! But it's pretty much like you said, I mean, they don't have a body so they can't do anything, but it never feels cold around them. Maybe cuz it's so warm here? I dunno…"

"Then how come they don't look like ghosts? Shelby and I could *always* see through them if we looked at them long enough…"

Mounting up, the girls headed back for the ranch and continued to debate 'ghost rules', with neither reaching any satisfying conclusion as to why SoCal spooks were so decidedly different from their Pacific Northwest counterparts.

When they reached the trail crossing where Amber first spotted Stoner's Jump, Marisol brought Catarina to a halt as she stared down at something on the trail. Handing the reins to Amber, she dismounted and scooped up a shiny round river stone from the path.

Shuddering, she examined the object before handing it to Amber.

In crude, childlike scrawl was written:

Shadow man is in your house

"What the hell?" Amber muttered, "This wasn't here before!"

Taking the stone, she threw it away from the two as far as she could send it, hearing it ping off faraway rocks when it landed.

The mares recognized familiar sights close to home and picked up their pace to a slow trot. Upon seeing the ranch gates, they broke into a canter[9] until they gracefully rounded the corner into the yard.

After hosing off the horses, removing the water with specially rounded squeegees and putting away their gear, the two girls trudged into the kitchen for some lemonade.

"I feel so disgusting. I definitely need a shower," Amber remarked.

"Mom should be home soon. She can drop you off at La Casa de Cabesa Roja."

Amber raised one red eyebrow in inquiry.

"House of the Redhead!" Mari giggled.

Mrs. Garcia entered the kitchen within a few minutes and Mari pounced with, "Mom, can you take Amber home?"

"Hello to you too, mijita.[10] I just walked in the door. Let me relax a bit and then I will be happy to drive Amber home." Mrs. Garcia sat down

---

[9] Cantering is somewhere in between galloping and walking
[10] Spanish term of endearment, which means 'my little girl'

upon a wooden stool at the brightly colored Mexican-tiled kitchen counter and asked, "So, did you girls have a good time today?"

Amber politely thanked her hostess and remembered the picture she took of Mari, "You have to see this!" She whipped out her smart phone with the photo and placed it directly under Mrs. Garcia's nose.

Mrs. Garcia's face immediately went blank as her features smoothed unnaturally and then turned deathly pale. Her hands fluttered subconsciously to her throat. "Excuse me," she mumbled as she stood up and quickly left the room.

"Mom?" an alarmed Marisol cried out as she ran after her.

Hearing a door click definitively shut, Marisol soon came back, somberly shaking her head.

Minutes passed as the girls sat at the kitchen counter, conjecturing as to what had upset Mari's mother. Neither had the faintest idea as to what had rattled her so badly.

After a while, the bedroom door opened and a composed-looking Mrs. Garcia emerged. Her face wore the professional mask of detachment, practiced over years of delivering not always welcome income tax news to clients.

"Look at the two photos together," Mrs. Garcia carefully placed an old-fashioned black and white framed photograph on the counter. A teenager with long, thick brown hair gazed intensely from the frame, a faint smile upon her lips. The teenager could have been Marisol, only sixty years earlier.

"Wow," Amber marveled. She placed her smart phone with Mari's photo right next to the picture of Marisol's grandmother.

"Yes," Mrs. Garcia agreed. "The resemblance is uncanny." Smiling a little too quickly at Amber, she added, "C'mon then, I'll take you home now."

Over dinner, Amber listened as her father described his first day at work. Dr. McBride gestured exuberantly as he spoke about his employment at the Santa Susana Field Lab. He explained to Amber that the site was the location for the very first moon rocket launch tests and that the old test stands were still there on the company property. Her father added that the property encompassed two ancient Native American sacred sites in which the Summer and Winter Solstices were observed.

Dr. McBride marveled, "How amazing is it that the Simi Hills are *the* place for people seeking the stars? From the Native Americans thousands of years ago, right up to today!"

Amber was quite pleased to see that the worried, worn look fell away from his face when talking about a topic near and dear to his heart. She thought about what her mother might be doing at that moment. Anger briefly flared until she decided that she didn't care what her mother was up to on this particular evening.

Not one to linger after having made a decision to move on, Amber brought up something that had been bothering her all day, "So what's the deal with this *Charles Manson*? It should be ancient history by now. Why are people still obsessed with him?"

Blanching, Dr. McBride stammered, searching for the correct words in which to speak about the unspeakable.

"I mean, I get how horrible it was to murder people. But this was, like, forever ago and he didn't kill anybody here in Chatsworth. Well, at least anybody anyone knows about. So…why the big deal even now?"

Having taken the opportunity for composure during her opening questions, Dr. McBride now attempted to explain, "Amber, it wasn't the murders per se that shocked everyone, although, granted, they were horrendous. It was the fact that he got normal teenage girls to commit them."

She thought about this and quickly conducted internet research via her smart phone. Other than Squeaky Fromme, whose name alone christened her as a lunatic, the surprisingly wholesome, bright young faces rattled Amber.

Leslie Van Houton.

Susan Atkins.

Patricia Krenwinkel.

Mary Brunner.

"So, these girls were nuts, right? Crazy? That's how he got them to kill."

Her father soberly explained, "Amber, I wish it were that simple, but no, the girls weren't crazy. They allowed him to control them. They joined his group willingly. They were looking for something and whatever they were missing, he provided. They wanted to do those terrible things for him. They would have done whatever he asked. It's the power he had over them. That's why it's still such a big deal today."

"Then they were weak. I would *never* let someone have power over me like that. I wouldn't *want* anyone controlling me!" Amber felt bile rising in her throat at the appalling idea.

She read with grim satisfaction that Patricia Krenwinkel is currently the longest-serving female inmate in the California penal system and that Susan Atkins died of brain cancer in 2009. Amber's fist clenched in anger when she read that whack job Squeaky Lynette Fromme was released on parole in 2009. Her partner-in-crime Atkins had died in prison, yet she roamed free.

As far as Amber was concerned, they all deserved to rot in jail.

Hailing Shelby online, Amber informed her about encountering a ghost who'd displayed none of the usual signs.

"He looked like some harmless old dude! The only thing that tipped me off was, he wasn't dressed for hiking. He looked like was about to go sailing! But other than that, nothing!"

"Maybe it's so hot in Los Angeles that even a ghost can't make you feel cold," Shelby retorted.

"Then why'd it get cold when I saw the girl in my house?" Amber shot back. "I know it's hard to believe, but I'm telling you *he looked alive*. I knew blondie was a ghost the second I saw her! So why's this guy different?"

"I dunno, I'm surprised my aunties never talked about this. I'll have to ask them." Shelby's brow was furrowed into a rare display of worry as she listened patiently to the remainder of Amber's wild story of what had happened during the past two days. Amber concluded the tale with, "...and it happened again, with the animals and birds, except there were a hundred of them this time."

Shelby's expression hadn't changed from a fretful grimace that didn't suit her at all.

"Shelby? So, what do you think? Why can't I remember anything?"

"I don't know, but you think maybe you called the birds when the Salvias were after you and they helped you out? Maybe you finally figured out how to get the animals to do stuff for you."

"Oh," was all Amber could manage. With virtually no memory of the encounter, this was not a possibility she'd considered.

"Aren't you going to let me get a word in?" an older woman's voice sounded from behind Shelby.

Shelby scooted out of her chair and bid the woman sit.

"Hey Auntie Fawn," Amber greeted Shelby's relation warmly, relieved about the possibility of getting some answers.

"Shelby says you're spoiling our rez dog out there in Hollywood. Better watch it, maybe more of them will show up at your place," Aunt Fawn warned with mock-seriousness.

Anxious to get down to ghost business, Amber forced herself to politely ask about how Shelby's aunt and her family were doing; knowing that Auntie Fawn would not tolerate rudeness. After moving past the pleasantries, Amber ventured, "Um, I met an old man today who was a ghost."

Shelby's Aunt Fawn didn't respond immediately. After what felt like agonizing minutes, she turned her head and called her niece over, "Sit down, dear, there's something you both need to know."

Shelby pulled up a chair next to her aunt and waited.

Taking her time, and speaking slowly and deliberately in the manner characteristic of many Native Americans, Aunt Fawn began, "There was no reason to tell you two sooner because you were so young. Only lost children were drawn to you, so we left it there." Pausing momentarily, Aunt Fawn searched for the right words before resuming, "There are three kinds of ghosts, not just one."

"Three?" Shelby interrupted, earning a stern look from her aunt.

"The lost are harmless, and so are the second kind. I think this old fellow is one of them. They *choose* to stick around because of their devotion to a sacred place. They know they're dead and they don't care. They're happy right where they're at. We call them the *Guardians*."

"If they're harmless, why are they called Guardians?" Amber asked.

"They battle *the third kind*," Shelby's Aunt Fawn answered, her face growing solemn with the task of delivering unwelcome news.

Amber and Shelby shifted uneasily in their chairs as Aunt Fawn resumed, "Unfortunately, you don't find one without the other. The third kind are those that, in life, were nasty, bitter, horrible people. Think about the meanest person you know. That's who clings to life and becomes the third kind of ghost. They blame everything and everyone for their unhappiness. They also know they're dead, but they hang around out of spite."

Aunt Fawn paused again as she looked at her hands, preparing to deliver the worst, "After some time, usually one hundred years or so, they forget who they were. All that's left is hate and rage. They are what popular culture refers to as *demons*."

Amber slid back from her computer involuntarily, unsure of how to respond. If she'd been back in Seattle, she'd feel much better equipped to deal with this. But she was alone in a foreign place.

Aunt Fawn said you don't find one without the other, which meant that where the elderly gentleman hung out, demons lurked.

"What do we do?" Shelby asked.

"Tell me about the place where you saw the old man," Aunt Fawn asked Amber.

Amber related what she observed, and what had happened with the grotto oak and the gathering of the animals and birds.

Aunt Fawn smiled slightly as she exhaled in relief, "I really wish we could help, Amber, but what works for us won't work for the Irish. That grotto sounds like a powerful place, though. I'd look for answers there."

After saying goodbye, Amber immediately called Marisol Garcia and shared what she had learned. Marisol said nothing for several moments, prompting Amber to ask if she was still there.

Sighing heavily, Marisol answered, "I wish my grandmother was still alive. She was *Bruja*."

"What's a Bruja?" Amber asked.

"A witch. But not like how it is in the movies. A healer; someone with great respect in the community. That is *Bruja*."

"Wow. So, are you a Bruja, too?"

"That's the problem! I don't know! My mom wouldn't let grandma teach me anything. She says we need to be modern, forget all that witchy stuff. Now that grandma's gone, she freaks if I even mention it!"

Amber considered their mutual predicaments: with Mrs. Garcia disavowing anything to do with her Bruja heritage, she exhibited denial on par with Mrs. McBride's, when confronted with the animals attracted to Amber. "You're not alone," Amber revealed, and shared with Marisol her ability to see through the eyes of birds and animals, along with her mother's refusal to believe that any of what Amber experienced was real.

Although neither girl found the answers to their problems, shared pain forged a closer bond of friendship.

Amber flopped down upon her bed. Her head was spinning from the confusing jumble of events that had unfolded earlier and she thought she'd never fall asleep. Was her mother even thinking about her? The more Amber dwelled upon her mother's absence, the sadder she became. From the time she'd confided in her mother about what she'd seen through Kibbles' eyes, her mother refused to believe any of it and tried to force normality on Amber. Maybe she'd decided she'd had enough of her psycho daughter and a husband she no longer cared for.

Tears streamed down Amber's face and she wished the earth would open up and swallow her. Anything to erase the excruciating pain and loss she felt in this moment.

✝

That night, the bad dream that tormented Marisol and Luis' mother since she was a young girl returned. The players changed over the years, but the theme was always the same.

She stood in the barn tending to the horses when she realized night had fallen. Brushing off her pants, Mrs. Susanna Garcia exited the stalls to find herself awash in cool darkness. Casting about, she searched for her family as fear took root in her gut.

When she was a child she sought her father and older brothers. As a mother, Mrs. Garcia now called out for her children, Marisol and Luis. At first her tonal quality was sharply annoyed, until she received no reply.

As Mrs. Susanna Garcia strode closer to the door of her home, the house appeared to pull further away from her until she was forced to run. Panting for air, she reached the heavy front door and pulled upon the iron latch to open it.

The door wouldn't budge.

Inside, the children began screaming.

Susanna Garcia pounded on the hot door, yelling at them to open up and let her in. When the door didn't open she picked up a nearby ax and heaved it at one of the windows.

It bounced off harmlessly, a useless implement against whatever was inside and harming her children.

Frantic, she beat her fists against the glass and screamed as her skin seared from the heat.

The curtains fluttered aside momentarily as a charred thing pressed against the window, mouth burnt open and agape in silent approximation of a scream.

Terrified, Susanna Hernandez Garcia awoke awash in sweat. Temporarily immobile, she didn't recognize the strange man looming over her.

Limbs released from sleep paralysis as she came fully awake, Susanna bolted from the bed, but Jorge Garcia grabbed her. Screaming, she punched and kicked at her husband as he sought to bring her back to reality.

Because the August heat was unbearable, the teens had planned to spend the day at Zuma Beach. Amber learned that, for a dollar, a summer beach bus left from the nearby mall every morning. The beach bus shuttled mostly unlicensed teens or a handful of drivers who rejected freeway traffic, expensive parking and gas, to and from the Pacific Ocean.

After being dropped off in the Zuma Beach parking lot, the group made their way across the searing sand. Newbies like Amber prematurely removed their footwear and rewarded their shod friends with the burning foot dance as they made their way to Zuma Beach Lifeguard Tower Number 7. Old #7 had been the haunt of Castle Peak kids for decades. No one knew when or why this meme came to be, but even some grandparents remember Zuma 7 as the cool spot to hang. Outsiders from other schools were treated with disdain by Castle Peak jocks from staking out a spot in the Zuma 7 zone, unless they were extremely attractive girls.

One of Marisol's friends, a lovely, compact black girl named Noelle, informed Amber, "I'm in the film program at school. Even though you're a freshman, if you have good grades, you should be able to get in."

"Thanks, I'd like that," Amber responded, pleased at the prospect of a shared class with her new sophomore friend.

Gesturing towards the boys, Noelle joked, "Then you won't be stuck with these scrubs."

The teenagers relaxed on the beach for the rest of the afternoon, soaking up the Southern California sun. The more moderate temperatures at the beach infused everyone with good cheer, a general mood that persisted during the bus ride home.

A pretty, quintessential California blond in front of Amber turned around in her seat, sized up the redheaded stranger, and asked, "You go to Calabasas?"

"No, I just moved here from Seattle. I'll be a freshman at Castle Peak in…" Amber paused. Was school really starting so soon?

"You mean next Monday. Yeah, me too. I'm a freshman, Slone. Slone Summers."

"Amber McBride. These are my friends Marisol and Noelle. You know the guys?" She motioned across the aisle to the four boys.

"Whassup?" Luis nodded his head.

"I don't know him, but he looks kind of familiar." She pointed a finger at Jonah and asked Noelle, "Is he your boyfriend?"

"Why, because we're both black?" Noelle shot back, causing Slone to blanch. Breaking into a wide grin, Noelle punched Slone lightly in the arm, teasing, "I'm just messing with you! No, he's NOT my boyfriend." Grinning conspiratorially at Jonah, she introduced him to Slone by first name only, without any mention of his famous action hero father.

The teenagers bantered on the ride home, exchanging views and gossip on clothes, bands, movies, people they knew and stuff from the Web.

"So I'll look for you at school," Slone called over her shoulder to Amber as she disembarked the Beach Bus when it reached the shopping mall.

Waving goodbye, Amber walked with the youths across the mall parking lot over to Max, waiting in the black SUV.

"I can't believe school is starting so soon," a dejected Jonah said. "I still don't have a plan to get kicked out."

"Maybe it won't be so bad this year," Amber said.

Jonah looked up at her with the long face of a man going to the gallows.

"We'll think of something," Amber quickly squeezed his arm in a gesture of reassurance as everyone piled into the SUV.

When Max reached Amber's driveway, she hopped out and punched in the security code to open the creaky gate.

She passed through as it slowly swung shut behind her, locking into place with loud clicking sound. The ongoing cricket chorus was interrupted by jangling inside Amber's pocket. Pulling out her cell, she saw her mother's number onscreen. Dreading the conversation to come, she answered the phone with, " 'sup?"

"Is that how you answer when your mother calls?"

"How would you like me to answer, *mother*?"

"Don't be a smart-ass. How are you?"

"Ok. What exactly are you doing, mom?"

"Amber, is everything ok there?"

"What do you think? What are you doing?"

"Taking a break."

These three words confirmed what Amber had suspected all along. If her mother was taking a break, it meant she also needed time away from her daughter. It's one thing to be a teenager and feel like you dislike your parents at times, but she'd never really wanted to believe that her mother didn't want to be around her either.

Feeling like her mother just stuck a knife in her back, Amber lashed out, "From what, exactly? Your life is so terrible? It's not like you work or anything."

"You're just being cruel. I'm going to go, but you need to let me know if you're not okay, if anything happens to you."

Amber hung up on her mother. *WTH?* First her mom says she needs a break, but then tells Amber to call if something happens to her? Was Mrs. McBride going to try to rule her life from afar so she wouldn't have to actually interact with Amber in person?

Mrs. Michelle McBride stared at her cell phone, sick to her stomach. This mess was entirely her fault. She'd gotten too comfortable hiding under the camouflage of her marriage; she'd neglected to remain on guard. If she'd been content to play the role of the 'good wife and mother,' perhaps her family could avoid what now felt inevitable.

Tossing her phone aside, she paced fretfully back and forth across her older sister's kitchen. To be fair, she was fond of Dr. Christopher McBride and loved her daughter dearly. Indeed, Mrs. McBride valued Amber's life above her own. Mrs. McBride's unhappiness began to fester when she realized Amber was becoming a young woman and would soon no longer need her. Just as her Aunt Ester O'Donnell foretold, the time was soon at hand when Amber would come into her own as a powerful member of the O'Donnell family sisterhood.

Feeling rudderless, Mrs. McBride began to complain and the dutiful Dr. McBride tried to fix it.

She figured he'd change jobs, make more money and they'd remain in the Pacific Northwest.

Mrs. McBride never considered the possibility of her husband uprooting the McBride household from Seattle to relocate in Southern California. Indeed, Dr. McBride had been lukewarm about the Santa Susana Field Lab position, until he found the House on Lizard Hill.

Clenching her fists, Mrs. McBride shuddered involuntarily at the thought of that horrid house and how it ensnared her spouse. For when she'd replayed the events in her head, she realized the house *found him.* After the House on Lizard Hill got its hooks into Dr. McBride, he'd become a man possessed, unwilling to consider any other job offers.

Mrs. McBride had no intention of allowing her daughter Amber to leave Seattle. She'd planned on filing for formal separation from her husband and Amber would remain with her. Mrs. McBride prepared to make her announcement to her husband when her cell phone rang. The call was from Donegal County, Ireland.

"Well, well, the chickens have come home to roost," an old woman with a thick Irish accent clucked.

"What do you want?" Mrs. McBride demanded as she moved into a room and shut the door so her family wouldn't overhear. Under ordinary circumstances, one would ask how Aunt Ester O'Donnell knew about the family's business, but the elderly relation had an uncanny ability of knowing everything and anything about the McBride household.

"We've respected your wishes and left you alone, but there are greater forces at work here now. You're being pulled to the house for a reason."

Mrs. McBride had freaked out at this pronouncement and unloaded on her aunt about the dangers of allowing Amber into that house because of its long, sorrowful history, "It's a dead place! You can't be serious!" she shrieked into the phone, now oblivious to being overheard.

Aunt Ester countered, "You can't force a path for Amber. She must find her own way. By the looks of things, you'll all end up there whether you like it or not. Do you remember your vow?"

At that point Mrs. McBride had no choice but to agree. Her sister Cathy fled Ireland for Vancouver and never looked back. Cathy was nineteen and Michelle but a baby. They'd had no contact with their parents since leaving. Indeed, only Aunt Ester and her sisters knew that Cathy O'Donnell and Michelle O'Donnell McBride were alive. Further, the debt extended to Amber: she owed her life to Aunt Ester and her sisters.

Mrs. McBride felt trapped and helpless. Things were rapidly spiraling out of control and she battled inwardly. What would her presence at the House on Lizard Hill mean for Amber? Would it help her daughter, or make things worse?

Storming down the driveway and up the stairs to the large wooden barn doors leading into the compound, Amber was about to kick them open when she saw canine nose leather pressed up against the gap and the soft brown eye of a waiting Kibbles looking for his mistresses' arrival. Opening the door gently, she crossed the courtyard to the dining room and found it empty. No enticing aromas wafted out, because no dinner was cooking. Even the dog dish was empty, something that must have distressed Kib, evident by the lack of wag in his tail and the posture of a dog who thinks he's being punished. She walked through her father's study to his bedroom door and knocked, but there was no answer.

Retrieving her cell phone, she dialed up her father on his work line.

"Amber? Oh! I didn't realize how late it is. We were working on a problem here… I'm so sorry, I'm leaving now."

The phone dropped down in her hand to her side as she sat down in his study chair, spun around and patted Kibbles on the head with each rotation. The day had been picture perfect on Southern California sands and her mother had gone and ruined it. To top it all off, no dinner when she got home!

Amber slowly rose, passed through the cheerily painted yet mostly empty dining room and into the kitchen, where she opened a can of dog food, mixed it and served it up to Kibbles.

At least one of us gets to eat.

Alone and dejected, Amber was determined to have a bitch session with someone about her mother. Shelby would oblige and the two girls spent the next half hour talking in the virtual world about her awful abandonment. Shelby pointed out that her parents were still together, despite the fact that they had some terrific fights and her mother had even gone to stay with her sisters from time to time.

"Hey Amber," another of Shelby's aunties scooted her friend aside. Amber grinned at the sight of Auntie Merri. Shelby's three favorite aunts were unflappable. A zombie horde could attack and the aunties would remain completely unruffled as they rolled up their sleeves and dispatched the invaders with garden spades.

After moving past the pleasantries, Amber questioned, "Can demons move things?"

"No, dear. Those rules stay the same, no matter what type of ghost. No body, no way!"

"How will I know if I see one?" Amber pressed, "What do they look like?"

Aunt Merri's face grew somber as she informed Amber, "Don't rely on your eyes because demons can take whatever appearance they want. Sometimes they appear in the guise of someone you love and trust. How you *feel* around them gives it away. You feel…wrong. That's the best way I can describe it. You'll know, Amber, you're intuitive."

After the call concluded, Amber wondered how she would recognize a demon. As she considered her predicament, in came a message from Slone that truly alarmed Amber.

What are you wearing the 1st day of school?

OMG! Is there a dress code?

No dude, whatever. Shorts & tanks.

Amber quickly considered her Pacific-Northwest inspired wardrobe, which consisted mainly of long-sleeved shirts and jeans. She owned nothing even remotely along the lines of daisy dukes and tops that bared her shoulders.

After making plans to go to the mall the next day, Amber saw her father rush through the double front doors and decided to pounce. Before he could get a word of apology out, she begged, "Dad! I have to go to the mall and get clothes! I don't have anything to wear when school starts next week!"

"Wait, didn't we just unpack boxes full of clothes?" Dr. McBride protested.

She persisted, "Mom used to always take me shopping before the first day of school. *Mom* said she would be here to take me. Do you see her here?"

Defeated, he half-smiled as he responded, "Okay, I'll give you money when we go inside. Just don't go crazy, ok?"

Amber threw her arms around his neck, kissed his cheek and accompanied him to the kitchen to rustle up dinner together.

The tiny closet in Amber's room was already crammed full of clothes, so she opened the corner wardrobe for inspection. Wooden rods lined both sides, providing room to hang up pieces of the new school collection she'd bring home tomorrow. Above each rod sat a narrow shelf, presumably to put jewelry and other small personal treasures.

Shutting the heavy wardrobe, Amber turned away when she heard a jangling sound. Turning around, she found Kibbles standing before the wooden unit, wagging his tail happily.

"You're not scared?" she asked the dog. He simply looked at her, then turned his muzzle to the door, tail never losing its upbeat.

Hand quivering, she placed it upon the knob and hesitated as ghastly images alternated in her imagination: skeletons, rotting bodies and dismembered corpses…all the terrible images she could think of that a *demon* might use to throw her off balance.

Every possible curse word Amber could think of floated into her brain at that moment, along with the urge to turn and run out of the room. But if her reservation dog wasn't turning tail to flee, or minimally growling at some hidden menace, then she had to butch up! Horrid images were swept aside as Amber firmly pulled the wardrobe door open.

The hangers upon the poles underneath the shelves were swinging back and forth wildly.

Amber slowly backed away from the wardrobe. Had she accidentally bumped it?

Suddenly, the hangers stopped moving and a small square in the bottom of the wardrobe retracted with a click.

SLONE SOMMERS

CHAPTER 5

INVESTIGATION

Taking one step toward the wardrobe, Amber cautiously leaned forward and saw a secret 2x2 compartment. Shaking so much she could barely close her fingers around the object at the bottom, Amber quickly reached in and pulled out a faded cutout from an old newspaper.

Forcing her hands to be still, Amber's eyes widened as she recognized the thick, luxurious, California-blond hair framing grainy features in aging newsprint. A young woman's face stared blankly outward, from an old article dated 1982:

LAPD SEARCHES FOR MISSING TEEN

Amber quickly scanned the article. The girl's name was Lucy Carpenter, age eighteen. She had lived off a nearby street and had disappeared from a party at place locally known as The House on Lizard Hill.

Gulping, Amber continued reading: Unnamed sources were quoted as seeing the teen leave with a young man on a motorcycle. She hadn't been seen since.

Gently smoothing out the newspaper on her desk, Amber quickly searched the internet, but found nothing useful. Carpenter was a common name and nothing further had been published online about the disappearance.

Frustrated, Amber slammed her laptop shut, knocking the tiny matchbox off her desk in the process. Snatching it up off the floor, she raced to her bathroom. Taking the brush she normally used to cleanse her nails, she soaped up the back of the heavily tarnished metal matchbox and scrubbed.

Amber held the somewhat-clean rectangular match holder up to the light and read the now-visible inscription on the back:

Robert

Turning the box around, she examined the lid. Etching in enamel revealed a partially cloaked form: feminine, skeletal, with outstretched bony hands, palms upward and expectant.

Jangling from her phone caused Amber to nearly drop the matchbox. Catching it just in time, she clenched the box in one fist and answered her phone deftly with the other hand.

"See you tomorrow at the mall, McBride!" Slone's cheerful voice confirmed their shopping date.

"Yeah, see you then," Amber agreed absentmindedly.

Hanging up, she returned to her room and placed the eerie matchbox inside the secret compartment. No other treasures were concealed within. Figuring she must have triggered it somehow when she opened the armoire door, Amber conducted a careful search and was gratified to find a tiny latch underneath.

Reopening her laptop, Amber tried to reach Shelby, but to her frustration, her best friend didn't answer.

Quickly conducting an online search about the strange matchbox image, vivid drawings surfaced onscreen, all bearing the same name:

Santa Muerte: Saint Death, the Lady of Shadows

Did the mysterious, skeletal image have anything to do with the nefarious Shadow Man? What did any of this have to do with the missing Lucy Carpenter? Lucy had to be the blond teenager who'd sought out Amber since she'd arrived at the House on Lizard Hill. The question was, *why?*

Did Lucy Carpenter want Amber's help? In Amber and Shelby's experience, no ghost had ever asked for help!

If this were true, not only had ghost rules been upended, Amber was totally flying blind.

Amber collapsed into her desk chair with shopping bags of clothes upon her arms. The critical mission of school clothes shopping had been accomplished, but Slone's presence at the mall was a source of frustration because Amber decided at some point during the day that she desperately wanted to talk to Marisol Garcia about what she'd learned about Lucy Carpenter.

Slone had chattered away about this person and that person and introduced Amber to a number of kids at the mall. Although Amber was happy to have made such a popular new friend in her grade, the possibility of living in a house with the ghost of a long-missing teen was troubling, weighing on her as she made small talk with less preoccupied minds. Marisol had witnessed the animal gathering at the grotto without fleeing in terror from Amber, making it likely she was a friend Amber could count on to help her handle the whacky whirlwind she'd experienced in the brief time since relocating to Los Angeles.

Laying the shopping bags aside as Kibbles sniffed them in order to determine if she'd been keeping company with any competitive canines, Amber tried to reach Marisol Garcia.

No answer.

She texted Luis and a short reply came back:
We're at dinner with our parents. Mari'll text you later
Amber recalled the conversation with Seth, the day they met:
"My mom's a realtor..."
Fingers flew at near light-speed over her phone's keypad as a message was typed out to Seth. Could she meet him and his mom tomorrow to ask a few questions about the former occupants of the House on Lizard Hill?

Seth's reply buzzed through shortly. They would meet at his house tomorrow.

Lip curled up beneath her nose for a moment in contemplation, she flipped open her laptop and finally reached Shelby. In a rush, Amber spilled out the news about the latest bizarre happenings. "So, do you think my ghost is Lucy Carpenter?"

"I dunno. If she was really kidnapped, why would she be hanging around your house? You'd think she'd show up at her parents."

"If she's asking for help, she knows she dead," Amber reflected. "Maybe she's that Guardian kind of ghost your aunt talked about, the one that decides to hang around. Maybe she's trying to warn us about something!"

Shelby's cell phone rang, immediately capturing her attention as she smiled shyly, "Hey, gotta go, talk to you later."

Amber reviewed what she'd learned so far about Lucy Carpenter, and was dismayed to realize that all she knew was that Lucy wanted Amber to know she'd disappeared from the House on Lizard Hill.

Maybe she knew she was dead, but was still lost and didn't know how to move on?

But if that were true, then why hadn't Lucy gotten directly to the point and asked Amber for help?

Groaning, Amber recalled that she had not a clue as to how to help Lucy Carpenter move on. For all intents and purposes, Amber was as lost as Lucy.

Looking at the article, she thought about the lovely young woman and considered the two of them in their mutual predicaments: Lost Lucy, frozen in space and time, and Amber, hiding her true self from the rest of the world so that no one learns the truth about the carnival freak she believes she is.

Amber rolled her desk chair into the center of the room and spun around to make sure she was alone before stating somewhat shakily, "I want to help, Lucy. I promise, I'm going to find out what happened to you."

Sighing from the wardrobe brought Amber out of her chair in a flash. She threw open the armoire door and depressed the release button to the secret compartment with her big toe.

The wooden lid lifted up to reveal a long, thin strip of paper. Grasping it with one hand while keeping a keen eye on the wardrobe, Amber brought it up to her face for closer inspection.

It was a commercial black and white photo booth strip with four pictures.

Lucy Carpenter, even more gorgeous than the newspaper article revealed, was framed in the center of each photo. She was alone in one photo, smiling out as if she knew Amber would be studying her nearly thirty years later. In another frame, Lucy leaned comfortably into a good-looking young man who appeared to be in his early twenties. Something about the close physicality between Lucy and the young man suggested intimacy. The third photo showed Lucy leaning forward and two young people clowning around, trying to form a triangle behind her, but they moved up too high in the frame. Only their torsos were captured. Clothing matched the young man, but it was impossible to tell who the third person might be. The fourth photo, judging by the clothing, also contained the mystery third person, another young woman, but she turned her head aside as the flash went off. Only Lucy's smiling face was visible.

Amber's cell phone rang as Marisol called. Picking up, Amber spilled out the story of seeing a blond teenager on her first night in the House on Lizard Hill, and what she'd learned since about Lucy Carpenter's disappearance. She concluded with, "I'm meeting Seth's mom tomorrow at his place, to see what she can find out about the people that used to own this house."

Mari insisted, "I'll meet you there. I want to help."

That night as Amber slept, she dreamt that something underneath her house scratched and clawed through dirt and stone as it tried to make its way to her.

After showering and getting ready, Amber headed to her father's study, where Kibbles sat on the floor beside him. Smothering Dr. McBride with kisses to thank him for the shopping spree, Amber asked his permission to meet up with Seth.

Her father appraised her request skeptically, brows beginning to furrow, "After what happened last time?"

"We aren't going mountain biking, just hanging out at his house."

Recalling that Seth lived at the edge of Chatsworth Oaks Park where local dogs liked to romp, Dr. McBride offered a compromise.

"You can go if you take Kibbles. The dog park is right next to Seth's place. He'd enjoy an outing."

Hearing his name, the dog scrambled to his feet with near youthful enthusiasm, tail wagging expectantly.

"Fine," she agreed as she snapped the leash onto his collar.

"Be back by dinner. Tomorrow's your first day of school."

"Thank you Captain Obvious," Amber grumbled. Opening the sliding door to go outside was like entering a blast furnace and the contrast from cool to hot was so severe, it made her sneeze. Wiping her nose on her arm, she inwardly heard her mother scold her for such unladylike behavior. Hastily dismissing her mother from her head, Amber and Kibbles headed off across dry, stubbly grass that cracked under her feet. The sun blazed hot overhead, producing a sweltering layer of heat just like the day prior. Amber glanced over at the lumpy hill across from her house, standing apart from the others in the preserve.

Atop the hill stood a tall man in heavy dark clothing, stifling for such a summer's day. Unmoving, Amber was unsure in the sun's glare if he was real or perhaps a visual trick made by the heat? The distance made it difficult to tell.

Kibbles stopped short, the fur along his back raised as he growled.

Nearly tripping as her foot landed in a ground squirrel hole, Amber regained her balance. She glanced back toward the lumpy hill.

Shadow Man had vanished.

Upon entering the shelter of the tree line, Amber breathed in the much-cooler air as she sought to slow her racing heart, noticing that outside noises were muffled under the giant oaks, as if the boughs effectively screened out sound as well as heat.

Yet on this day, no ground squirrels popped out of holes and the birds kept their distance.

Before venturing out of the tree line, Amber peered cautiously around to make sure that no DWP minions were working out in the nature preserve, or any nosey busy-bodies were out on the street where they would see her when she and Kibbles emerged. When she was sure she was in the clear, she sauntered out from in between the gap in the fence, walking like she belonged there in case anyone emerged to challenge her. No snoopy adults waylaid her, thus Amber proceeded undisturbed to Seth's house.

A zaftig thirty-something woman answered the door. "You must be Amber, I'm Tammy Lobata," Seth's mother greeted Amber warmly as she ushered her inside.

Amber couldn't help but notice that Seth's mother was very pretty, with shoulder-length blond hair and really white teeth. Amber towered over her.

"You have the most gorgeous hair, girl!" Ms. Tammy Lobata reached out and touched Amber's red locks, causing the teenager to flush deeply.

"Thanks," she mumbled, wondering if she would ever get used to being complimented about her mane.

"Amber wants to know what you know about that old bat that used to own her house," Seth interjected.

"What old bat?" Luis Garcia emerged from the living room and into the kitchen, where Ms. Lobata had led Amber.

"Sorry Amber," Marisol apologized. "When he found out I was coming here, he followed me."

"Luis is welcome here any time," Ms. Lobata said. "Maybe Kibbles would like a bowl of water first?" Ms. Lobata gently reminded Seth.

Seth complied, and put out a bowl of water in the kitchen for the elderly canine.

Ms. Lobata explained, "The Blanks owned the house since 1987. The husband passed sometime in the '90's. When Mrs. Blank died, their son sold the house to your family."

"And?" Seth asked.

Ms. Lobata placed her hands on her ample hips and asked the youths, "What else do you want to know?"

"Did they have any children?" Amber was grasping at straws. The newspaper article had clearly stated that Lucy attended a party at her house but lived nearby.

"Just one son, his lawyer handled the estate after his mom passed. I don't think he ever lived there. He's in his sixties, so he would have been an adult when his parents bought that house."

Ms. Lobata noticed the dejected look on Amber's face and asked with genuine concern, "What is it, hon? What are you trying to find out?"

Amber revealed, "I found some strange stuff."

Ms. Lobata and Seth looked at each other and an unspoken conversation took place. Amber had a sneaking suspicion, based upon Seth's sudden fidgeting, that they wouldn't be surprised to hear about strange happenings at the House on Lizard Hill. Taking a deep breath, Amber decided to go for it. She pulled a plastic Ziploc bag out of her backpack containing the clipping about Lucy, the matchbox and the photo booth strip.

Ms. Lobata took the article and studied it closely, her face brightening as she read the contents, remarking, "Just like CSI!"

"What about CSI?" Jonah asked as he, James and Max walked in the back door.

"I swear, it's Grand Central Station around here today!" Ms. Lobata clucked good-naturedly.

While Luis brought the new arrivals up to speed on what had happened, Amber asked Seth's mother, "Do you know anything about her disappearance?"

"Sorry honey, I was just a kid in the 80's. This Lucy has a good ten years on me." Ms. Lobata thought for a moment, tapping her chin, before offering, "You know, let me see if her parents are still in the same house." She opened her laptop and excitedly typed, but energy fizzled just as quickly as she pushed the laptop back and sadly informed the teenagers, "Looks like they died a few years ago. It says they didn't leave any heirs. Donated the proceeds of their estate to the Missing Children's Fund."

"That's so sad," Marisol remarked.

"Mom, c'mon! There must be something else we can find out?" Seth demanded.

Mrs. Lobata pulled a protesting Seth in close for a hug as she concluded, "I don't have access to LAPD records, so I can't tell you if the case is still open or not. But judging from her parents' final gesture, I'd say she's still missing." Frowning, she considered their dwindling options before offering, "Lucy obviously knew the previous owners, the ones before the Blanks. Hold on a sec." Ms. Lobata typed on her keyboard, studied the screen, and announced, "Someone named Robert Hugo Franklin sold the house to the Blanks in 1986. Before that, a woman named Grace Graymer deeded the house to Franklin, in 1976."

"Deeded?" Amber asked, as she typed the names and dates into her cell phone for future reference.

"That means she left it to him in her will." Ms. Lobata explained.

"May I," Max asked, gesturing for the Ziploc bag and its contents.

Amber thanked Seth's mother as she handed the information about Lucy Carpenter over to Max.

"I give back later," he informed Amber.

Amber was grateful to hang out at Seth's house for the rest of the afternoon. Despite her prevailing sadness about the beautiful blond girl who had unexplainably disappeared, she definitely didn't relish the prospect of being alone in the house with Lucy all day. Sometimes it got too intense inside Amber's head when she dwelled upon how different she was from everyone else. Distraction was welcome.

The youths hung out for the better part of the afternoon at Seth's house, waiting for the heat to abate. Kibbles sniffed around the cottage, then flopped down on a throw rug as the teens engaged in virtual battle on Seth's gaming system.

When the heat slacked off a bit, they ventured out. Seth led the way, on a trail from his backyard into a broad open meadow marking the start of Chatsworth Oaks Park. The group skirted around the edge of the stubbly prairie grass and descended a low hill before entering the picnic area where dogs romped and played. Seeing Kibbles' springy joy, Amber unhooked his leash and allowed him to join the others racing around a large sandstone boulder in the center of the lawn.

Sitting on a nearby swing, Amber spotted an overlarge house sporting a stone turret jutting from a cliff high above the dog park. Seth informed Amber it was officially called the Rock Tower as Jonah snickered.

"What's so funny?" Amber asked.

James Toshima flushed and looked away as Jonah Abernathy explained, "That place has been used for about a thousand porn movies, or so I've heard."

"Now I get why you guys wanted to ride up here!" Amber kidded them. Glancing back to the grassy area, she searched for Kibbles and saw no sign of the yellow-furred mutt. Standing up from the swing, Amber called out, "Kibbles?"

"Uh, he's up there," James pointed to the northern end of the park where a yellowish form was barely discernable as it wound its way up the hill.

"Kibbles!" Amber roared as she took off at a run, the guys close behind.

Perking up his ears, the elderly dog stopped, looked back at her, then turned and picked up his pace before disappearing behind a large sandstone formation. Cursing beneath her breath, Amber led the way as she sprinted up a narrow, dusty trail, recalling all the times he'd pulled the escape routine back in Seattle, but those parks had been fenced.

When the group reached the top of the hill, they crossed a narrow asphalt road and spotted two separate trails winding off and down into the state park on the other side.

There was no sign of Kibbles.

The teens stood on a ridgeline formed in a semi-circle, sandstone towers stacked upon their sides and tilted southward toward the sea. Peering down, they saw an ancient dried-up bay, now a vast meadow garlanded by a caramel-colored trail.

Fear began to well up inside Amber. What if she couldn't find Kibbles? She imagined her old dog surrounded by coyotes, his hackles raised before lunging in for the fight of his life…

"Does this fella belong with you?" an elder's voice spoke.

From behind a large stand of laurel sumac stepped a cowboy carrying a guitar, Kibbles walking nonchalantly by his side. The old man's hat had an upturned brim that failed to shade his leathery, weather-beaten face.

Amber threw her arms around Kibbles' neck and snapped the leash back on as she thanked the stranger.

"Hey, Joe, how goes it?" Seth greeted him warmly.

Cowboy Joe's eyes twinkled when he met Amber; he said, "I recollect having a dog like this down in Tampico when we shot *Treasure of the Sierra Madre*. Who's this young lady?"

Amber waved a friendly 'hello' and introduced herself.

"She just moved into that old house on Lizard Hill," Seth explained.

"Did she, now?" Cowboy Joe appraised her. "How are you liking it here?"

Amber assured him that she liked the area just fine.

Cowboy Joe offered, "It's nice to get out for some fresh air when it cools down. Good time to make music."

Buzzing erupted from Amber's pocket. Checking her phone, she saw a text from her dad that she had a half hour to get home in time for dinner. "Uh, guys, sorry, but I have to go. I promised my dad."

Bidding her farewell, Cowboy Joe's brown, weathered face beamed a toothy grin, "You take care now, Amber. I'll see you young folks around."

As the youths walked away, Amber heard Cowboy Joe's soulful strumming receding into the distance. The song was mournful, like so many old country songs. She only caught a few lines about lost souls realizing they were condemned to hell. Strangely, the damned appealed to the stony mountains for deliverance…

Shuddering, Amber recalled the song's name: *The Great Judgment Morning*, by Hank Williams. She'd heard it performed by a cowboy cover band during happier times, at the famed Puyallup Fairgrounds.

Seth led the contingency single file through a sage-lined corridor along the eastern end of the park. Traversing a minor decline, the teenagers emerged from the brush to find the western hills shrouded in hazy purple shadow as the sun continued its evening retreat.

When Kibbles spotted the green expanse of grass and the happy retinue of hounds and human companions, he acted as if he'd not gone on a walkabout and was still due time on the course. Irked, Amber ignored his expectant tail wagging and readied to leave.

"I have something for you," Max announced as Amber walked Kibbles past the black SUV in the parking lot. He reached into the SUV and handed Amber a slip of paper, along with her Ziploc bag containing the article and photos of Lucy Carpenter.

Marisol quickly crowded in as she and Amber eagerly reviewed the paper's contents. It was a print out of a newspaper article titled:

CHATSWORTH RESIDENT ARRESTED: "DOCTOR" IS A FRAUD

The article described a colorful, mysterious man who lived in a mansion atop what was locally known as Lizard Hill.

Amber and Marisol looked at each other in surprise and then back at the article. The man, Dr. Robert Hugo Franklin, was known in Los Angeles for his elaborate parties, often attended by the Hollywood elite. He had grown wealthy from successful medical practices in Beverly Hills and Encino.

However, the wife of a patient had complained to the California Medical Board after her severely ill husband died while under Dr. Franklin's care. Following an investigation, the California Medical Board turned the case over to the District Attorney, as it wasn't a case of malpractice, it was a case of quackery: Robert Hugo Franklin had never been licensed as a medical doctor. Indeed, he'd never been to medical school.

Within days, the DA issued a warrant and LAPD arrested Robert Hugo Franklin. He was in jail at the time the article was written, and looked to be there for a long time.

"What's up?" Seth asked as Amber handed the article to him.

"How'd you find this?" she asked Max.

"Los Angeles Times Archives. Much historical information is there."

"Thanks! Do you know what happened to him? Is he still in jail? Are there more articles? Did…"

Max held up his hand for silence. "No more articles." He saw Amber's mood turn from excitement into dour and added, "I checked other sources and learned he did eight years after he struck plea deal. He sold house to pay for legal expenses. Disappeared after jail."

"Wow, thanks, Max, really! But what does that mean? He's in hiding? Is he dead?" Amber asked, considering the options.

"No record." Max snapped his fingers, concluding, "He make vanish."

"How old would he be now?" Marisol asked.

"Fifty-four," Max responded.

Amber was impressed with the speed and thoroughness of his investigation and appreciated his thoughtfulness in helping her out. Why had he taken the time to do so? Why did he care about any of this? "So, was Grace Graymer his mother? Is that why she left him the house?" Amber asked.

"No."

The youths briefly exchanged confused looks.

"So, like, she was his aunt or something, a relative?" Luis asked.

"She was no relation. He was twenty when he inherit house," Max explained.

Imitating thumping bass and accompanying beat box, Luis joked, "Dude! I bet the party never stopped at your place!"

Ignoring Luis, Amber assumed the worst when she asked, "So, how'd she die?"

"She was in her ninties's, nothing suspicious. Graymer left house to Franklin. She had no children, but her relatives contested. Franklin won."

Wrinkling his nose in disgust, Luis mused, "Man, I wonder what he had to do to get the old lady to leave him everything?"

"Enough!" Max's sharp rebuke erased the saucy look right off Luis' face.

"Did you find a picture?" James asked.

Max's right hand deftly reached into his suit pocket and produced a photo. The teenagers crowded in for a look. The face staring back at them was taken when Robert Hugo Franklin was arrested and it was the *same face* as the young man in the camera booth picture, next to Lucy.

Amber wondered how on earth Max was able to obtain all of the information he had amassed *and* a booking photo. He was like one of those henchmen the super-hero or villain has in the movies, much more than a driver and bodyguard. Why did Jonah's family need someone with such skills?

Turning her attention back to the photo, she took in his features, finding Robert Hugo Franklin very handsome, in an '80's sort of way. High cheekbones, full lips, clear skin and a straight, Roman nose. His blond hair was swept up onto his head and cascaded down over his forehead into a V-shape, leaving only one eye visible.

"Check that hair!" Jonah laughed.

"Jealous?" Luis teased, "You can't ever get your hair to look like that."

"Like I would *ever* want my hair to look like that," Jonah retorted. "You, though, I can totally see you with that club boy hair. That's what this dude looks like! Who knew they were wearing their hair like that, back in the day?"

Normally Amber would have joined in the laughter over his ridiculous hair, but the depth of his despair came through his photograph so clearly, he may as well have been standing next to her.

Amber looked over at Marisol. Her brow was furrowed.

"Put it away," Marisol said quietly. "I can't look at his face anymore."

Amber bid her friends goodbye and headed out from the dog park toward Lake Manor's main drag. She reached the road without breaking a sweat thanks to twilight's reprieve and waited for the cars to pass.

A rumbling sound reached her ears before she saw a strange, door-less vehicle round the corner from the east. Just as she remembered where she'd heard that jet bomber noise before, the jacked-up truck slid to a stop, hood vibrating with every pulse from the powerful engine.

The Salvia's drove what once had been an Orange 1970 or so Ford Bronco. Over the years many parts and panels had been haphazardly replaced with little regard to their aesthetic value. The engine and mechanical components were another story: the Salvia's had an eye for quality. On more than one occasion some wealthy off-road enthusiast would come back from a night at the movies to find some expensive part of his four-wheel drive vehicle missing. Sometimes the vehicle disappeared entirely, only to later be found stripped and left for dead in a ravine. The locals named the Salvia truck FrankenBronco in reference to both the vehicle and the men who drove it. The term was never used to their faces.

Amber felt vulnerable and exposed on foot. A tingling sensation started at her toes and shot painfully up to her neck as she stood still, uncertain.

She risked a quick glance over at the vehicle.

All four Salvias were in the Bronco.

Ben Salvia sat at the steering wheel, his expression impassive, casual. If he recognized her from when she'd trespassed on his property at the Twelve Apostles, he gave no outward indication. He simply waved his hand, indicating she should cross the street.

His startling, intense eyes met hers for a moment. Inwardly squirming, she quickly averted her gaze. Amber tried to act nonchalant and quickly cross at the same time.

Ben suddenly shifted gears, causing the Bronco to lurch forward with a loud *vroooom*. In response, Kibbles stopped short and savagely snarled. Amber narrowly missed tumbling headlong over her dog.

"Hey ginger! Need some help?"

Without thinking about the impulsiveness of her action, Amber turned to the brothers and fumed, "Don't call me ginger! Only a ginger can call another ginger, *ginger!*"

A darkly handsome brother whom she took to be George, in the backseat on the driver's side, laughed good-naturedly at the feisty redhead standing her ground. Although Ben's face remained expressionless, his piercing eyes regarded her in a manner suggestive of knowing her secret weaknesses. Unnerved by Ben's icy stare, she sprinted across as she heard another brother snort, "So that's the girl those dweebs talked into mountain biking?"

Heart feeling as if it would burst out of her chest, she and Kibbles reached the other side and darted behind a nearby house. Amber leaned back against the wall and exhaled deeply when she heard the rumble of the engine fade away. After a moment, she risked a look around the corner and found the street empty again.

Amber grimly acknowledged that the unstable and dangerous Salvia brothers knew who she was.

That night, Seth's mother Tammy Lobata had trouble falling asleep as she recalled how bizarre the listing of the House on Lizard Hill had been. Like everyone else in Lake Manor, she'd heard stories of the wild Hollywood parties during the 80's, before the Blanks moved in. Seth's mother was naturally curious about the old home, particularly because none of her peers had ever been allowed to set foot on the property.

In a manner truly befitting their name, the Blanks were completely forgettable. They never entertained, kept to themselves and they'd not even opened the gates for trick-or-treaters on Halloween.

When Mrs. Blank died, Ms. Lobata attempted to get the listing, only to be rebuffed. Mrs. Blank had promised the listing to her manicurist, a part-time realtor who'd barely passed the exam, a license she'd obtained for the sole purpose of representing the House on Lizard Hill.

Mystified, Ms. Lobata expected the manicurist would send in a cleaning crew after Blank Jr. cleared out his parents' belongings, then she'd take marvelous photos and the house would quickly sell for the $1.2 million asking price.

All standard operating procedures when selling a home, and none of them set in motion.

She heard snickering among her colleagues that the incompetent manicurist had gotten lost putting out signs and ended up at the Salvia property atop the Twelve Apostles. Depending upon which realtor told the story, the manicurist/wanna-be-realtor either succumbed to the legendary Salvia charm and didn't come back until the next morning, or she was chased off the property. Either option disgusted Seth's mother.

Ms. Lobata was aghast at the online photos because they may as well have been taken at a homeless encampment. In addition, the wrong high school was listed. Instead of the very attractive Castle Peak High, the incompetent boob put down the far less desirable Canoga Park High School, conjuring up images of street violence at the hands of Canoga Park's notorious Alabama gang.

Acting as an agent, Ms. Tammy Lobata was contacted by the owner of a popular cantina in the adjacent affluent community of Calabasas who'd attended one of the infamous 80's parties. He informed Tammy that he'd had to beg the manicurist on bended knee for an appointment just to see the home and she'd only relented after he finally called Blank Jr. himself. Sounding almost giddy, he'd spoken excitedly about restoring the house to its former glory.

It was clear that he'd love the house and do it proud. He was even willing to pay the full asking price.

Midway through escrow, the Cantina owner was diagnosed with pancreatic cancer and withdrew the offer. He was dead within three months.

The house languished for six more months without any interest, until one Charles Graymer contacted Ms. Lobata, choosing to do business with what he termed "a **real** realtor, not that nincompoop the Blanks hired."

Though she was inclined to agree with him, just thinking about that horrid man brought a nasty taste to Ms. Lobata's mouth. Nary a pleasant word crossed his lips. He was singularly focused on obtaining the House on Lizard Hill and dispensed with any pleasantries in his efforts to seal the deal as quickly as possible.

Ms. Lobata found it odd that a man of his advanced years wanted the house, sight unseen no less! When she inquired politely about his interest, he'd said something that she never forgot, not so much because of his explanation, but because of what happened *after*.

"It's time to finally set things to right after my cousin Grace left it in her will to some outsider."

The papers were prepared and Ms. Lobata headed over to Graymer's place to get his signature.

When knocking on the front door brought no response, Ms. Lobata walked around the back of his slime green house with puke yellow trim. She was confident he'd be there because his nondescript car was in the driveway.

Peering in through the sliding glass door, Ms. Lobata stepped back involuntarily when she spied his prone form upon the floor.

Sighing, Ms. Lobata fought the urge to give into pity, tempting though it was to think the universe was aligning against her at every opportunity when it came to the sale of the House on Lizard Hill. Retrieving her mobile phone, she called 9-1-1 to report Graymer's death.

Over seventy years of age, his passing was not unusual.

That night when Seth's mother returned home she found her son uncharacteristically pensive and silent. Given that his nature was much like hers, easy-going and optimistic, she was immediately concerned.

"Hon, what's wrong?"

"You finally sell that house?" Seth answered her question with another question.

"Sit down, Seth," Ms. Lobata gestured to the kitchen table. "What's going on?"

"Did anything strange ever happen when you were at the house?" he asked, still refusing to answer her initial question.

Ms. Lobata joined her son at the table, tapping her fingers over the surface before responding slowly, "Well, you know about the first guy getting cancer. Today, when I went to Graymer's house to have him sign the offer papers, I found him…dead."

Seth's tanned face grew so pale his freckles stood out in stark contrast.

Knowing her son's tendency to flout the rules and go anywhere and everywhere he pleased in Lake Manor, Ms. Lobata gently grasped her son's shoulder and said, "You went to the house. It's okay, tell me what happened."

Taking a deep breath, Seth looked away as he began, "I'd been over there a couple times already. I never thought about it until the third time I went, but it always felt like someone was watching me. So the last time I was there, I heard 80's music coming from Amber's room. It was coming from an old intercom like we used to have in our camper. I went in, pressed the button and asked if anyone's there, but I only heard the music. Then…." Seth shivered as he recalled what happened next, "I saw a shadow on the wall. *Someone* was coming up behind me. I turned around to see who it was."

Ms. Lobata's mouth grew dry as she clasped his hands.

Seth quickly continued, "I looked outside and saw some dark-haired chick crying, going down around the pool, so I ran after her. When I got to the top of the stairs, I saw her go into that dark hole *under* the pool, so I followed. When I got inside, Mom, no one was there. I wasn't scared, it didn't feel like she was trying to hurt me, but I've never felt that bad before…" He stopped speaking, struggling to find the right words.

"*Abandon all hope ye who enter here*," Ms. Lobata whispered as Seth's eyes flashed. "Sorry, it's Dante, from a book called *The Inferno*."

"That's it," Seth confirmed, "like she sucked all the happiness out of me. Maybe how you'd feel if you wanted to die. I got out of there fast."

Ms. Lobata fielded some inquiries over the next few weeks about the house, but the manicurist's incompetence made the overall experience too frustrating for most potential buyers. The simple act of making a viewing appointment at a time that suited the amateur's schedule was next to impossible.

Then Ms. Lobata received a call from the LA Coroner's Office. The City's normal standard operating procedure when someone of advanced years dies in a secured home with no signs of a struggle is to label the deceased as having died of natural causes.

But a young intern at the Medical Examiner's office observed some swelling and a minuscule puncture wound on the neck of Graymer's corpse. She brought this to her supervisor's attention and the ensuing autopsy revealed something no one at the coroner's office could recall *ever* seeing before: Graymer died of a scorpion bite, behind his ear. Even odder was the fact that the deadly poison came from a Mexican scorpion, not indigenous to Southern California. Despite their fearsome reputation, the arthropods of Los Angeles deliver venom on par with a bee sting.

Morbidly curious, Ms. Lobata attended Graymer's funeral, hoping to ask a relation about his fixation with the House on Lizard Hill.

She was the only person to attend the service, other than the chaplain.

No one else inquired about the House on Lizard Hill until Dr. McBride.

Shane stood atop Castle Peak and examined the strange native plant at his feet. Listening carefully to the sorcerer's instructions, he removed the necessary parts and prepared the ingredients. When all was ready, night had fallen.

"Only the most worthy are able to partake of this plant. Ingesting it brings power from the other side, and you will no longer be a mortal man," the voice whispered in Shane's ear.

"I am ready," Shane affirmed. Sprinkling the potion on his tongue, he closed his eyes briefly, then immediately opened them as the universe spread out before him. Simultaneously, Shane perceived the minutiae of a speck of dust on his clothing to the unending, expanding cosmos. Men like Shane had come before and would come again because they brought order to the chaos. And where men like Shane had come, enemies followed to try and cut them down.

The names and faces of his foes became clear to Shane in the vision. The most dangerous had to be destroyed first, a witch:

Amber McBride.

JONAH ABERNATHY

CHAPTER 6

AWAKENING

Dr. McBride sat at the desk in his study, chin resting in his hands, computer on, but he paid no attention to the onscreen images. His mind wandered back to the night he met his wife Michelle. They were both college students at the University of Washington in Seattle.

At a party with his fraternity brothers, Chris McBride noticed the striking redhead amidst a sea of blonds and brunettes. He smiled involuntarily at the memory. It was impossible *not* to notice her.

Chris McBride watched his buddies crash and burn, one by one, as each tried to get her attention. She swatted them away like troublesome flies. The future Dr. McBride bided his time until she looked completely bored and ready to leave. Then he made his move, crossing the room to her as Tears for Fears' *Working Hour* kicked off, lending courage to his noble effort.

In his most outrageous Leprechaun accent, he introduced himself, "Oh, fancy meeting a fellow clanswoman from across the pond, here at a party in Washington State! Are ye from Louth, Cork or Donegal?"

Stone-faced, she appraised him and then burst out laughing at this brazen stranger. Shaking her head, she admitted, "Donegal, but how'd you know?"

Returning to his normal voice, he revealed, "My family's from Donegal too."

They spent most of that night engrossed in conversation.

Many formal and informal dates followed and before long, Chris and Michelle were officially a couple. While his friends wanted to bag as many girls as possible, he was content with his girl. They married immediately after college and until the past year, he believed they were genuinely happy together.

Initially, he looked at his wife's waning affection as a scientist posed with a problem. He examined his behavior: had he changed? Did he alienate her through indifference? Had he become unattractive to her? He combed the Internet looking for guidance; he secretly bought and read many books on the subject of love and marriage. His eagerness to discuss and explore the problem was met by resistance from his wife. He went to counseling alone; he tried to give her space and understanding. He was willing to do whatever was needed to keep her. In his mind, she was the only woman for him. In his frustration, he began to secretly loathe married couples for their happiness and he wondered to himself: why he was so unlucky? If he had had more experiences with women, he may have had his heart broken at a younger age and would have entered this love with a slight hesitation and the protection of romantic cynicism. However, he dove in with no reservations, no holding back.

It works great in the movies, but in real life, you can be burned.

There is an old saying: How do you tell if a man's had his heart broken? Answer: He's a man.

Unfortunately for Dr. McBride, he was in the process of being burned by the one true love of his life.

He looked up from his hands and out the window, seeing only his reflected image in the glass.

What the hell could he do about it?

He'd thought that the promise of making more money would make her happy.

It didn't.

By the time he showed her the online photos of The House on Lizard Hill, her withdrawal accelerated. She'd stated, "*I need a little time right now.*"

Her words echoed painfully in his memory. What sort of bullshit was that? It was the equivalent of appearing to say something without really saying anything.

If Dr. McBride were a religious man, he'd have gotten down on his knees and prayed for her return. However, he could not pray to a God he neither believed in, nor expected to intervene on his behalf. His problems and his pain were his own.

Other than hanging out with her new friends, the first day of school was the same old bore it had been back in Seattle. The day was spent shifting uncomfortably in institutional seats and trying to stay awake. Luckily for Amber, a few thousand students attended Castle Peak High and she didn't run into George Salvia.

That night Amber checked in via video chat with Jonah Abernathy to see if the first day portended another dreadful school year. The strained expression upon his face and downcast eyes provided the answer without asking. Desperate to change the subject, Amber inquired about something she'd been curious about: "How'd your mom find Max? Do they advertise for henchmen?"

Recovering some of his good humor over her attempt at levity, Jonah explained, "She told me she and dad were at a nightclub in Miami before my brother was born. My dad was rolling with a posse of big guys that liked to flash their pieces....What?"

Amber was laughing hysterically, informing Jonah in between snorts, "It so doesn't work when you try and talk street! You sound like a professor giving a lecture!"

"Well excuse me! Do you want to hear the story or not?" Glaring at

Amber, he waited until the giggling subsided and a forced look of serenity settled twitchily over her features.

"As I was saying, it was before we were born. My dad had some crazy-ass stalker at the time back in LA. No way did they think he'd follow them to Miami when dad was filming *Dead to Rights*. Max was the doorman at the club and he was the only one who spotted this nut. Before he could even get a shot off, Max had him against the wall and got the gun away. Mom said he moved like a ghost. Dad was so impressed, he hired him on the spot."

"Wait, you said your dad hired him, so how come he works for your mom now?"

"My dad's a romantic; he cares more about mom's safety than he does his own. But Max is in charge of screening and hiring all security for us."

Because of school, the week passed quickly. Amber's desire to spend time investigating Lucy Carpenter's disappearance was supplanted by mountains of homework. But mostly, Amber's distraction was due to her increasing concern about her father. The first alarm bell went off when he stopped cooking at some point early in the week. His pants were starting to sag and not because he was going through some mid-life crisis and attempting to don the latest street fashion.

Her father was rapidly losing weight.

After one dinner consisting of hastily thrown-together soup and sandwiches, Amber decided to put her cooking skills to the test. She'd helped her father in the kitchen over the years, but hadn't planned and executed a meal on her own before. Determined, Amber went online and looked up recipes, then checked the refrigerator and pantry to assess their supplies.

One night, Amber prepared a roast chicken and Rice-A-Roni. The meal wasn't entirely homemade, but it wasn't bad, either. Her father smiled weakly and obligingly ate his dinner, but Amber was dismayed when he didn't converse. Her questions received only one-word answers. Her father's disengagement from their daily life was even more frightening than ceasing to serve as house chef.

After dinner, her father trudged off to his study. As Amber cleared the dishes, the feeling that she was drowning threatened to engulf her.

What was she going to do with him? She didn't know how to help him.

Instead, she went to her room to call Shelby. Talking to her oldest friend always calmed her down. Unfortunately, true to her father's warning when they'd first moved in, she was unable to get a Wi-Fi signal. Frustrated, Amber stared at her laptop before shifting gears to finish her schoolwork. When bedtime rolled around, Amber hoped she'd be able to shut off the fearful thoughts in her head and get some rest.

She fell almost immediately into a deep sleep, until music began playing from the intercom. Her eyes rapidly began moving back and forth, indicating the onset of a dream state.

Amber stood in a clearing at the bottom of the Twelve Apostles. A sliver of moon provided little illumination for the dark, stone cathedral spires that loomed overhead.

A flash of white atop the formation drew her attention. Without understanding why, Amber tried to call up to the figure far above. The Santa Anas roared up from nowhere in their fashion, drowning out her voice.

Amber watched helplessly as a woman in a long white dress stepped off the edge of the Twelve Apostles. Her garment fluttered rapidly as she plummeted.

Racing over, Amber found the battered, broken body of a forty-something year old Latina amid the rubble. Her head was completely turned around backward. Eyes open, they stared at Amber, the only witness to her suicide.

Claaaangggg!

The alarm clock noisily announced the start of another day. Her right hand automatically swatted it off as her left went over her sweat-drenched shirt, her chest pounding as hard as if she'd just run the mile in P.E. Ghastly dream still vivid in her memory, Amber shuddered despite the Southern California warmth and quickly moved to shower away the awful imagery.

Unfortunately, her efforts failed and Amber was preoccupied with the dream during breakfast. As she ate cold cereal, neither she nor her father spoke a word, each in their own purgatory of thought and Kibbles neglected with nary a pat upon his head.

An incoming message from Seth, announcing his arrival, broke into Amber's morbid thoughts. A thoughtful kiss goodbye earned a barely muttered response from her father.

Her dwelling upon the nightmare was quickly replaced with another matter:

"Tell her!" Ms. Lobata insisted.

A dismayed sounding Seth retorted, "Geez mom, I was *going to*, until you interrupted me."

"Tell me what?" Amber asked blearily, still suffering from the ill effects of nightmare-plagued sleep.

"It was all over the Internet last night. I'm surprised you didn't see it," Seth stalled, uncomfortable in the role of morbid messenger.

"What?" Amber's tone took on the distinct edge of redheaded exasperation.

"*Kick a Ginger Day*," Seth looked down at his hands, as if he were the one who invented this torture. "Some kids at Calabasas started it and now it's spreading to other schools. Today is the day."

Seth glanced at Amber and drew back slightly as the tiny yellow flecks surrounding her green eyes enlarged, momentarily transforming to the same sandstone shade as the Simi Hills.

Amber clenched her hands into fists, making a cracking noise. "Not *this* *ginger*." She was in no mood for this form of stupidity. If being a gawky teen wasn't enough, the plight of her mother's abandonment, the ghosts and the gnarly dreams would ensure that there'd be no 'soft target' to be had here. If some dumbass wanted to come and try to beat her up, bring it.

The agonizing crawl to Castle Peak High may as well as been a stint upon the medieval rack in the dungeon. Anticipating what was waiting twisted Amber's insides into knots.

When she burst from the car that morning at school, subtle eyes shifted in her direction. Seth leaped out after to stand bravely by her side. He was an odd defender, given his much smaller stature.

Sensing a shift and realizing it felt like that night upon the trail under the Twelve Apostles, Seth glanced over at his friend to find she had drawn herself up to her full height, head held proudly, chin out and eyes fierce. Amber was every inch the warrior princess battling zombies from his video game.

His usual grin returned as the crowd turned away and went back to whatever more important business now beckoned. "Let me know if you need me. I got your back," Seth offered, confident in the fact that no help would be required, whatsoever.

Perhaps it *was* the way that Amber carried herself that day, or maybe the glare she gave everyone except trusted friends who came within even a few feet of her. Whatever the reason, anyone and everyone stayed clear of her. She heard not one giggle as she passed. Indeed, talking seemed to cease as she stalked the halls from class to class.

Only one studied her from afar, with abject fascination, having never seen *any* girl carry herself with such confidence under complete duress. Smiling, George Salvia grasped his backpack and prepared to head off to class, unable to believe the remarkable transformation the girl had made since the day he and his brothers had teased her crossing Lake Manor's main drag.

"What's with you and the gringa?"[11] Someone making no effort to hide her annoyance spoke from behind him.

"Lourdes," George greeted his heavily made-up classmate with penciled-in eyebrows and a Bettie Page hairstyle. "Not your problem anymore, is it?"

"No need to be cruel, *Jorge*," she pronounced his name the Spanish way, Hor–hay. "What'd you want with that little kid, anyway?"

---

[11] Spanish for 'white girl'

George countered, "You should worry more about your grades, than some old boyfriend."

"You used to be one of us! What the hell happened to you?" Lourdes challenged.

George laughed bitterly, "We were done before we even got started! I don't wanna have a bunch of kids by the time I'm twenty-five. It's not my life."

"You can pretend all you want, but I know the real you," Lourdes Navarro snarled at his retreating form as George Salvia left her in the hallway.

Noelle and Amber walked across the student parking lot to the Metro bus stop near school. They had stayed late to work on a film project for class. Not being enrolled in film, Seth left right after school and her father was still at work.

It was one of those Southern California days plagued by Santa Ana winds, gusty blasts reaching up to sixty miles an hour in the canyons and mountain passes. As Amber walked with Noelle to the bus, she realized she had been so consumed by 'Kick a Ginger Day' that she had neglected to make plans for the evening. Shielding her face from the wind, she learned that Noelle would be tied up at Friday night prayers at her synagogue. As African Jews, the Mertens family often attended services. Amber was welcome to join, but she wasn't keen on sitting through any religious service.

Amber finally decided that a shower and a session binge watching TV was the way to go. The best Netflix options would reveal themselves after she was cleaned up.

"Hey *ginger!*"

Bristling, Amber and Noelle turned to confront the speaker. They spied an angry senior with heavily drawn-in eyebrows, standing near a grey Chevelle.

"Stay away from my boyfriend," she demanded.

"Boyfriend?" a puzzled Amber responded, "I don't know who you're talking about."

"That was weird," Noelle remarked as the orange accordion bus rolled up. "I guess you've got a mystery boyfriend!"

Castle Peak High was at the northern end of the San Fernando Valley line and Amber guessed her stop was last on the bus's route, given that the Simi Hills bordered the Ventura County Line. Her hunch was correct. Noelle departed within three stops, as did the rest of the remaining passengers, leaving her alone with the bus driver.

As the main road through Lake Manor was extremely narrow, with no shoulder or sidewalks, the only place wide enough for a bus to pull over and stop was the dog park's dirt parking lot.

For Amber, this meant that the bus had actually driven past her house to take her to this drop-off spot, but there was nothing to be done. There was nowhere wide enough for the bus to stop and the driver had actually laughed when she suggested that he pull into her driveway to let her off.

The bus finally groaned to a stop in front of the park, a quarter-mile from her house. The grassy area where dogs normally frolicked was empty. The little picnic area was unnaturally quiet and still. Many Angelinos were averse to *weather* of any kind.

The smile faded fast from her lips when the bus pulled away.

An old grey Chevelle pulled off the road and parked next to the nature preserve fence. Amber realized it must have followed the bus. The doors opened and the senior who'd confronted Amber at school emerged, with three friends.

They slowly strolled across the street, gracefully moving through the wind as if it were only a minor inconvenience. Stepping backward across the dirt parking lot to put distance between, Amber's eyes locked on theirs, unwilling to show fear.

The four looked to be around seventeen years old. Their exaggerated, heavily penciled eyebrows gave them an ominous look, accentuated by tattoos lining their muscled arms. Wavy dark hair tumbled down over their shoulders and the blunt cut of their bangs spoke of another era, but Amber didn't have time to question their fashion sensibility.

The girl who'd confronted Amber held up her hand when the group was about six feet away. When the trio behind her stopped, she lowered her hand.

"We need to talk about my boyfriend, *George Salvia.*"

Mind racing, Amber was baffled, retorting, "I don't even know him!"

Eyes blazing, the senior turned to her compatriots. "She's lying. Let's make her talk. After all, it's Kick a Ginger Day.'"

"Now wait a minute!" Amber was quickly going through all the self-defense moves she'd seen in the movies. Somehow, they all seemed inadequate at the moment, given her meager skill set.

As the girls advanced on Amber, her memory offered up a piece of advice from a Jason Bourne movie, in which the handsome actor Matt Damon had played the lead.

Everything is a weapon.

In one, smooth movement she grabbed a handful of sandy dirt off the parking lot floor and flung it outward into their faces. Amber saw the dirt leave her hand as if it were in slow motion, until it exploded into their eyes and they were left coughing and gasping for air on the ground.

The gusting wind had been her friend, in this one instance.

Amber fled.

She tossed her school bag into the first laurel sumac bush she passed, intending to return for it later. She then took the trail that cut straight across the park and up the hill to the private road where Kibbles had made his escape the day before school started. The topography of the dog park was open and exposed, leaving nowhere to hide for very long without being quickly found out. Her only hope was to outrun them until she could find help.

Dashing past thigh-high buckwheat bushes turned crispy rust by the sun; Amber consciously kept her breathing even to conserve her strength. She hoped that perhaps they were so out of shape she could lose them at some point.

Spying the cut-off to Seth's house, her spirits soared at the prospect of making a break across the open field and finding safety at the Lobata's. Quickening her pace, Amber was nearly to the turn-off when something large and dark swooped down to land in the middle of the trail juncture.

Stretching out its six-foot wingspan, *Cathartes Aures* the vulture blocked Amber's escape route.

Waves of anger surged through Amber as she envisioned herself thundering down the trail toward the turkey vulture and kicking its feathered ass out of her way. As she drew near the trail that would take her west to safety, it reached out and overwhelmed her consciousness.

Images of dead and dying creatures assailed her brain along with a pressing urge to flee *north. The way west would end in death. North* was her only chance. There was no time to reason out what she was experiencing, the urge was overpowering, compelling her to run for her life.

Amber fled north.

When she reached a higher vantage point, she briefly turned and saw to her great dismay that the teenagers had recovered and were rapidly advancing. She was clearly visible, vulnerable and quickly running out of options to avoid taking a serious beating.

Remembering the maze of trails in the state park on the other side of the hill, Amber realized she could lose them there. She began running again, keeping the private road at the top of the hill in her sights. Angry shouts and curses taunted her, borne on the wind.

Reaching the crest of the hill, Amber leapt onto and across the private road in three seamless bounds. Memory served up the location of one trail she'd spotted, a steep deer track over-hanging with foliage. She headed straight for it and soon disappeared into sage and chaparral. Although the scrubby trees and thick bushes obscured sounds of the hunt, she could still hear voices when her pursuers reached the private road moments later. Her progress had slowed considerably because of the dramatic decline, narrow path and giant boulders that appeared in the center of the path at odd intervals, forcing her to climb over or squeeze around. Running was out of the question at this point, but at least they couldn't see her.

"Where'd she go?" a rough voice growled.

"I've got sticky-things in my socks!" another whined.

"C'mon, she couldn't have gone far," George Salvia's supposed girlfriend silenced them.

It was impossible to see in front or behind for more than a few feet because of the low-hanging brush, nearly touching the trail in many places. Branches batted her in the face and chest, forcing Amber to keep one arm extended to protect her eyes from being poked out. Willing herself not to think about ticks dropping onto her head or down the back of her shirt, she painstakingly made her descent in something of a spiral pattern. She couldn't tell how close they were, but chose not to think about it. The only thing that mattered at the moment was her continual progress downward.

Suddenly, Amber broke through the brush and onto a tiny clearing atop a rock outcropping. The meadow was now within view, but still hundreds of feet below. To her deep dismay, patches of trail were also clearly visible the rest of the way down, meaning that she would be painfully exposed out in the open. The only bright spot in her dilemma was that the trail had widened and she could now move faster.

Brush tottered above, indicating that the older girls were still in hot pursuit.

Something scaly brushed Amber's leg. Yelping with surprise, she leapt aside. Gaping, she watched a rattlesnake slither obliviously past.

Readying to bolt past the rattler, she was stopped yet again by a furry wave of small rodents. Bushy-tailed tree squirrels and thin-tailed ground squirrels moved in unison with their sworn enemies, voles and weasels. Tiny field mice scampered astride bulky gophers. Unbelieving, she saw more snakes join the fray, as predator and prey descended side-by-side.

Desperate, Amber spied a ledge along the canyon side, higher than the rutted trail. Leaping up, she stumbled precariously through brush while trying to keep her balance.

Trying hard not to look down into the deep chasm, Amber made her way down to a gully. The streambed was deep, requiring her to scramble on all fours up the banks. She found her hands and knees sinking into the caramel sands of the trail rounding the meadow.

The entire hillside erupted in a cacophony. Quickly turning, she faced the path and simultaneously had to duck down low as a screeching flock of quail stormed over, grazing her as they went.

Before she could lift her head, a clowder of bobcats stampeded past with unearthly screeches. Whatever pursued the creatures had reduced them to blind terror, despite their fearsome pit bull size and Goblin ears.

Before she could stand, deer bounded down the hill and leapt over the streambed. One nearly kicked her in the head with its hind legs. The herd kept on going as if the devil himself was in pursuit.

Amber's nose twitched with the scent. Raising her head, she saw what was *really* coming for her.

Cascading in a tidal wave, a raging inferno stormed down the hill. Laurel sumac bushes caught fire as it came, flames coalescing around the maroon core and then exploding as the combustible oil of the chaparral reacted to the fuse. The sounds of cannon fire drowned out all other sound as the fire sucked oxygen, creating its own swirling wind.

Amber changed course and turned to run out the path by the cemetery. She had taken only a few strides when a tongue of flame shot across the trail, igniting a large grove of laurel sumac on the other side. Sparks sprayed from the brush like a Roman Candle on the fourth of July, igniting the open field behind the cemetery.

The only way out that Amber knew of was now blocked by a fast-moving wall of flame.

Close to panic, she stopped. Crazy images came to mind: red-haired women in homespun cloth running with young children in their arms as their village burned. Blond barbarians wielded battle axes indiscriminately, destroying everything in their path.

Three chilling words pierced her consciousness:

Burn the witch

In the midst of the chaotic vision, Amber witnessed one redheaded girl defiantly confronting the invaders as she called upon the wild creatures, wind and rain.

With renewed courage, Amber raced across the meadow, feet finding the way to a hill where she saw the animals stampeding. The fire mocked her, aided by the wind and burning along the eastern edge of the park as she ran. It was *following* her, blocking all chance of escape.

To the north were towering cliffs over which the birds had already flown the proverbial coop. Necessity stopped Amber momentarily. Thick smoke filled the air, every breath becoming more and more labored.

She had to keep moving and according to the vulture, north was the only way to safety. Out of options, she had no choice but to follow the direction in which the animals and birds had fled. Keeping her eyes on what bit of trail she was still able to see, Amber coaxed her limbs into a slow, painful jog. The soot-filled air trapped heat that pressed in upon her from all sides.

Before long, Amber was staggering, having no idea where she was, only understanding that she'd just come up yet another hill, flames burning bright to the south and the east, towering cliffs to the west blocking escape.

North, keep going north where the animals went...

Fire lit up an ancient oak like a torch in front of her, flames rocketing up over fifty feet in the air as the fire sucked oxygen in a whirling vortex. Nearby laurel sumac bushes exploded with resounding *boom* sounds against the backdrop of the now fully engulfed state park.

Amber was surrounded by the inferno.

I'm not going to die here! she thought defiantly.

The wind momentarily blew smoke away from the cliff face directly in front of her and she spied a cave, inset high up in the wall of stone. Recognition dawned. It was the cave at the grotto where she'd come with Marisol.

Here was her chance!

Amber half-staggered, half-stumbled, until her fingers touched stone. Finding purchase for one hand and foot, she lifted herself up.

The air was already uncomfortably hot, every breath a painful exchange containing less and less oxygen.

She had to hurry, but one misplaced hand or foot could send her plummeting. Drawing upon meticulousness inborn from her father, Amber's hands grew red with abrasions as she painstakingly scaled the sheer rock face.

She never looked down, or out to either side, and as much as she yearned to cling to the rock face, her body went into autopilot and followed the instructions given when she and Shelby took rock climbing. All new climbers are taught to resist the urge to hug the rock because gravity and friction work better with weight concentrated on fewer points rather than spread out across a body, and a climber's knees should never touch stone.

After what seemed like an eternity, her hand reached up and felt a broad expanse of flat, horizontal rock. Cool air touched her fingertips, bringing a burst of adrenaline that hauled the rest of her body in as she kicked up and over.

Amber rolled onto her stomach and roughly coughed, energy spent.

Weakly turning her head, Amber gazed out upon a sea of fire, a vision from the book she'd been reading in ninth grade honor's English, *Dante's Inferno* spread out in a masterful arc before her, from the murky depths of the grotto to the pinnacle of the mountains. As far as she could see, ragged orange and gold tongues licked furiously at the sky.

The roaring of this fire was of a different sort than the homey crackling of the campfire, or even the exciting *whoosh* of the initial combustion when one adventurous soul decides to squirt lighter fluid on the pile of stacked logs in order to awe the assembly. These guttural croaks were ancient and vengeful. Every shattered and broken thing wrenched forth another howl of rage for fuel consumed too quickly.

Far below in the amphitheater, the strange old oak was in flames. The tree stood alone; stripped white-hot in the center of hell, streams of sparks flying off in all directions, black smoke billowing from the burning canopy to join the already soot-filled air.

Amber dangled precariously between a narrow precipice where survival is questionable and sensing as much, she shakily raised herself onto her elbows and creepy-crawled combat-style further back into the cave. A tentative, incoming draw of breath brought welcome, not-so-baking air into her lungs. Beyond laid empty, unknown darkness.

Smoke billowed in through the cave opening, sending a signal to Amber's slowly dimming brain that further retreat was necessary. She wondered if the back of the cave opened up into a yawning pit that dropped several thousand feet down into the earth. With this image fixed in mind, she feebly outstretched her fingers and proceeded slowly, right into a wall of stone.

Literally stopped by solid rock, Amber weakly rolled over onto her back. She realized with a wry smile that, for all her mother's clucking that harm would come to her when she was a child, it was, indeed, when her mother was not hovering over Amber that she was now truly in danger.

Under normal circumstances, the thought of dying brings a fight or flight response. But smoke inhalation had nearly sucked all the air from Amber, depriving her of that essential ingredient humans' need in order to live. She was now under the Rule of Three:

Three days without water.

Three hours without warmth.

Three minutes without air.

In the swirling smoke, images returned, flashes of scenes remembered, to reveal what had happened with the Salvias. Effervescent light, haunting, intense eyes, the scent of sage and green apples, the gathering of shadows and *Amber* calling upon the birds for aid, help that had come readily when she'd become one with the inherent magic of the Simi Hills.

She saw an image of a flame-haired young woman in homespun cloth, gathering the elements.

Amber's head reeled as smoke continued to fill the cavern and Amber knew she was close to passing out.

The fire continued to rage outside, turning everything in its path into fuel, designed to feed the monster while the night sky was ablaze with demonic light.

II

METAMORPHOSIS

*Never underestimate your innate abilities, or those of your
enemies*
— James J. Kerst

CHAPTER 7

RECOVERY

Golden light cut through the smoke at the cavern's entrance.

Amber watched the lights dance and wondered if this was the light that people see when they are dying.

Do you think you're dead?

Amber tried to turn her head at the sound of the voice, but she couldn't move. Her limbs were stone. After a moment, she understood she hadn't actually heard someone speak. Rather, she'd 'heard' the words in her head.

Who are you? Amber questioned, without speaking.

I am known by many names. Brigid, Brigante, Astarte, Maria, Mary the Mother. The name is unimportant. We are the same. We are one.

What should I do? Amber thought.

Look for me on your path. Those who seek me, find me.

The handsome young vaquero[12] stood next to Cowboy Joe at the northern end of the Simi Hills where Larry's Stage Stop used to be in the late 1880's. As Cowboy Joe smoked a cigar, the two men watched the animals stampede up and over the old stagecoach route. They'd expected them, having seen flocks of birds screeching overhead minutes earlier.

Watching the animals flee to the safety of Simi Valley, the vaquero asked, "Think La Bruja helped them escape?"

"You know how girls feel about critters. Even witches love 'em," Cowboy Joe chuckled.

A nondescript rental car pulled to a stop in front of Castle Peak High School, where Lake Manor's residents had been evacuated from the fire. Michelle McBride flung open the door as she leapt out onto the sidewalk. Dr. McBride was already waiting at the curb.

"What...how..." he stammered, but his wife cut him off.

"Just drive, I'll tell you how to get there."

"Am I even listed as a driver? What if there's..."

"Shut up! There's no time! Get in the car!" his wife ordered as she pushed him toward the driver's side.

Dr. McBride was no wussy and he certainly wasn't about to be shoved

---

[12] Spanish for 'cowboy'

around by anyone, let alone his wife. Turning around, he refused to move and stated, "I'm not going anywhere until you tell me what's going on!"

Tears of frustration streamed down Mrs. McBride's face as she apologized to her husband, "Chris, I could only fly as far as San Francisco and I've been driving all night! I'm exhausted, but you have to believe me when I tell you, I know where Amber is! Please, please, let's go!"

"But go *where*?" Dr. McBride asked as he got in the car.

Mrs. McBride got into the passenger seat and wrung her hands together fretfully. "I'll know it when I see it," she informed her husband as she peered at passing landmarks, searching for what she'd seen in her mind's eye.

Dr. McBride felt physically ill. Amber had been gone since yesterday afternoon, and with every passing hour the chance of survival lessened. He'd not slept and was running on adrenaline. So when his wife called on route from Seattle, claiming she knew where Amber was, he feared for Michelle's sanity.

Losing his wife *and* daughter would destroy Dr. McBride. He'd have no reason to go on…

"Go this way," cutting off his descent into hopelessness, Mrs. McBride directed her husband around the Chatsworth Nature Preserve, past the House on Lizard Hill and through tiny Lake Manor, past the blackened dog park and to the end of town. Bidding him to turn left, she spied a private driveway winding up a steep hill.

"*Here*, turn here!" Mrs. McBride ordered.

An Eagle Scout stood in the center of the driveway, blocking their passage. Holding up his palm, he ordered them to stop.

Mrs. McBride rolled her window down and met his eyes. "Get out of my way," she ordered in a low, dangerous tone.

The Eagle Scout flinched as he watched her pupils enlarge, engulfing her eyes in darkness. Not wanting to find out what would happen if she stepped out of the car, the Eagle Scout scrambled to move aside as Dr. McBride proceeded up the narrow, twisting driveway.

They reached the top of the hill where, unbeknownst to the two, Cowboy Joe had returned Kibbles to Amber the day he'd gotten loose in the dog park. "Stop!" Mrs. McBride ordered, "This is it, we can't get any closer by car. You bring the binoculars?"

Disembarking, Dr. McBride retrieved the binoculars and handed them to his wife as she anxiously scanned the mountains.

"Where are they?" Mrs. McBride cried. Flinging the binoculars at her husband, she retrieved her cell phone and dialed 9-1-1. As soon as she got an operator on the phone, Mrs. McBride unleashed a verbal tirade, "What's wrong with you people? I'm here, right now and I can see her! Do I have to rescue her myself?...What's it going to take to get someone out here?...Oh, okay, well thank you! Finally!...No, I'm not giving you my name. It's none of your business…"

♪

Firefighters from Los Angeles and Ventura counties worked throughout the night to contain the monumental blaze in the northwest Simi Hills.

Officers Gutiérrez and Johnson had been flying all night for LAPD, surveying the damage and keeping watch to report the fire's spread.

The account from four terrified teenage witnesses stated that the inferno started out in the nature preserve and had nearly overtaken them in its lightning-like progression. The girls would've been burned alive, had it not been for the Rock Tower homeowner. He also saw the fast-moving fire heading towards his house and fled for his life in his car, taking nothing with him other than the clothes on his back. He reported tearing down the road and nearly swerving over a cliff when he slammed on his brakes to avoid the girls. They jumped in his car and escaped just in time, right as the flames raged across the dog park and jumped the road.

Gutiérrez and Johnson searched the ground carefully, as closely as they could while remaining above the smoldering remains of oak and brush. The officers were quite troubled by both accounts, but the report from the teenagers concerned them most, joining the ever-growing shit list that was Chatsworth-Lake Manor. LAPD was here today for one purpose. One of the youths, Lourdes Navarro, had been inconsolable about another girl who'd gotten lost in the state park: Amber McBride, a redheaded teenager who lived in the old house at the west end of the preserve.

Gutiérrez and Johnson knew that no one could've survived that inferno. In police parlance, this operation was no longer a search and rescue, it was a body recovery.

Johnson thought about the officer who had been sent over to evacuate Mr. McBride and to inform him that his daughter had been in the park when the fire broke out. Johnson's little daughter Tessa, safe at home, was just three years old, with a cherubic face, giant green eyes and gorgeous curls.

There is no pain like the ache a parent feels when their child is in danger. A child is a part of a parent's body. Asking a mother or a father if they can survive the loss of a child is akin to asking which arm or leg they prefer to lose. The loss would be palpable and a constant reminder that something is missing, the parent is not whole. He would do anything to save his little girl, because the alternative was unthinkable. He wondered what Mr. McBride was going through at that moment, not knowing if *his* daughter was alive or dead.

Meanwhile, Officer Gutiérrez recalled the first dead body he'd ever seen. Coincidentally, it was here in the Simi Hills. He'd been on a final training run with Commander Rodriguez a little more than three years ago, flying the chopper as Rodriguez rated his skills.

"Go towards that formation," Commander Rodriguez had instructed, sending them closer to the strange cathedral spires known locally as the Twelve Apostles. Inspecting the shard-strewn area at the bottom through his binoculars, Rodriguez took control of the helicopter as he bade Gutiérrez take a look.

A woman's broken body lay at the base of the cliffs.

After calling it in, they went back to the station to complete all of the necessary paperwork. It was there that Officer Gutiérrez learned the woman's name: *Daniela Salvia.*

In the time since, he'd seen other dead bodies and crimes too grisly to ever discuss outside the fellowship of officers. Nonsensically, the only one that stuck with him was the Salvia woman who *intentionally* took her life.

The helicopter reached the southern edge of the fire. Down below, on the hill with the strange stone circle, LA Fire Department officials were investigating. What would later be called the 'Chatsworth Lake Fire' had started *there*

Officer Gutiérrez gratefully turned away from the enigmatic hill and headed back north to make one last run over the park. "Ready to call it a night?" he asked his partner.

"You mean call it a day," Officer Johnson corrected him, as the sun had risen over an hour ago.

"Air Four," Dispatch hailed the duo, "I hate to bother you with this, but 9-1-1 insists we check this tip out."

Fatigue instantly fell away and Gutiérrez urged, "Yes, we're listening."

"Probably some crackhead, but the woman called several times, and was so specific about where you'll find the McBride girl, she sure convinced the 9-1-1 operator! Seeing as how you guys are already there, you may as well check it out." Dispatch proceeded to relay the instructions.

"Who's the tipster?" Gutiérrez asked.

"Wouldn't give her name," Dispatch responded.

Whirring rotors caught Dr. McBride's attention as a helicopter roared overhead. Gritting his teeth, he watched as the chopper slowed over a broad meadow on its approach toward towering cliffs.

Mrs. McBride's body began shuddering involuntarily from the strain, so Dr. McBride moved closer and put his arms about her waist. She allowed him to hold her, even leaning into him for support. If circumstances had been different, this little gesture would've flooded him with happiness. But facing the likelihood of their daughter's death, he simply looked over her shoulder at the helicopter hovering near the cliffs, the sick feeling now swelling from the pit of his stomach to tickle his throat.

"Can you see anything? What's happening?" he begged, yearning for any bit of information she'd gleaned.

"They're looking at something, but I can't see what!" Mrs. McBride snapped.

In that moment, Dr. McBride desperately wished for a deity he could bargain with. He'd bow on bended knee and offer his life in exchange for Amber's. Heart thumping in his chest, his mind raced through the possibilities. Was she clinging to the cliff? Lying atop it? Crumpled, at the bottom? The scenarios were horrible. The inferno had incinerated everything in its path.

Survival *wasn't* possible and he was completely helpless. There was nothing he could do to change any of this. Powerless, he had no ability to impact whatever had come to pass.

Sweat dripped off Mrs. McBride's fingers to stream dusty grime from the binoculars down the length of her arms. Under different circumstances, she would've handed them to her husband so he could also see what was going on. But she couldn't tear her eyes away from the scene unfolding in the strange stone amphitheater. The pilots obviously spotted something. Whether that 'something' was alive or dead was the most pressing question.

As soon as her husband called with the terrible news that Amber was missing and presumed lost in the fire, Michelle O'Donnell McBride hopped on a plane and headed for Los Angeles. In spite of her carefully orchestrated life in the ordinary world, that house now left her no choice but to reopen old wounds. Aunt Ester's prophetic words stung, "...*you'll all end up there whether you like it or not.*"

She'd denied her true nature for nearly two decades but now brought all of her inner resources to bear. Her reward was 'head pictures' showing her roughly where to go. However, Mrs. McBride was rusty, so she prayed her instincts would prove correct. Anything other than Amber's survival was unthinkable...

Adrenaline flowing, Gutiérrez and Johnson followed the directions and flew over an area that now looked like a moonscape, golden-brown sandstone turned ashy grey, chaparral blackened into skeletal remains. The officers soon found themselves hovering over strange rock formations in an area known locally as 'The Grotto.' The startling nature of the formation was made even more apparent by burning away all vegetation. Laid bare, the officers observed what resembled a concert venue on the planet Mars.

Movement in the cliff face off to the left caught their attention. They couldn't fly the helicopter too close because strong updrafts could smash the chopper into the cliff side before they'd have time to react.

As Gutiérrez cautiously hovered, Johnson pulled out his binoculars for a closer look. Johnson peered for a few minutes before motioning for Gutiérrez to check out the northern cliff face.

Placing the twin lenses to his eye sockets, Gutiérrez was shocked to see a pale white arm dangling from the mouth of a cave.

The hand twitched as a breeze briefly blew a length of flaming red hair up into the air, off the head of the owner.

Smiling broadly, Gutiérrez felt a rush of relief as he set the binoculars aside and hailed Dispatch with, "Ladies and Gentlemen, allow me to introduce you to Amber McBride."

∞

Dr. McBride squeezed his wife's waist as the LAPD helicopter retreated from the grotto to admit a red LAFD helicopter. "You've gotta tell me what's happening!" he begged his wife.

Mrs. McBride's words poured out in a rush as she relayed what she saw. When the LAPD helicopter pulled away, Mrs. McBride spied the small cave she'd seen in her 'head pictures', near the top of the cliff. Also revealed was the reason the officers couldn't land atop the cliff: power lines hung right in front of the cave's mouth and were being buffeted wildly about by the Santa Ana winds.

Mrs. McBride stamped her feet in frustration as she handed the binoculars to her husband. Ironically, the power lines ran across the State Park for the sole purpose of bringing electricity to Dr. McBride's employer, Boeing, up at the Santa Susana Field Lab.

Dr. McBride handed the binoculars back to his wife and placed a telephone call to one of Boeing's bigwigs, requesting an emergency call to DWP to cut the power. "They're taking care of it now," he sheepishly informed his wife after he hung up with Boeing.

After about fifteen minutes of hovering and waiting, the power was cut and the rescue operation resumed. An orange sled appeared at the red LAFD helicopter's door and was slowly lowered. Shuddering as the sled spun around in the high winds, Mrs. McBride watched LAFD lower it to the top of the cliff at a point far from the power lines. Relaying the information to her husband as he now paced nervously back and forth, peppering her for details, she tried not to hold her breath, reminding herself that greater forces were at work...

When the orange sled was safely upon the ground, Mrs. McBride watched a medic being lowered in a harness from the helicopter. Jumping off next to the sled, he secured it to a rappelling clamp and proceeded to lower it over the cliff. Giving the helicopter pilots the 'thumbs up' sign, the medic secured another rappelling rope and went over the edge towards the cave. When the medic's feet reached the cave's mouth, he guided the sled safely inside. Mrs. McBride watched medic and contraption disappear into the depths of the cave.

Dr. McBride tore the binoculars from his wife's hands as she danced in place, knowing in her heart she'd been *right*, yet refusing to allow herself to believe until she saw her daughter with her own eyes.

"I can't...how is this possible?" Dr. McBride stammered as the medic pulled the orange sled to the mouth of the cave.

Strapped securely in the contraption was an unconscious Amber.

Tears streamed down Dr. McBride's face, blurring his vision as he handed the binoculars back to his wife. Snatching them, she watched the medic gently guide Amber into an upright position against the cliff and pull on the rope. A second medic had descended to the belay pins and slowly pulled the sled up the pitted rock face, causing Amber's unconscious form to ascend in halting, jerky motions. When the sled neared the top, the Santa Anas picked up again, yanking the sled out of the medic's hands. Amber's sled arced away from the medic and was poised to overturn.

Throwing the binoculars aside, Mrs. McBride called upon the wind as she inhaled deeply. As she exhaled in a quick burst through an open mouth, the sled stopped mid-air and gently floated back down, coming to rest in the medic's strong hands.

Dr. McBride caught his wife as she collapsed, unconscious, to the ground.

AΩ

Amber stood upon the branch beneath the grotto oak, a light breeze rustling the profuse new growth of leaves overhead. Content, she placed her palm upon the silvery trunk, relieved to feel the slow, vibrating pulse as her old friend drank deeply from the earth.

Her nose crinkled as the breeze grew stronger and became the infamous Santa Ana winds, mercilessly battering the oak, causing it to bow, to bend and in doing so, revealing the wall of fire racing up the creek bed in its merciless quest to enjoin Amber in its deathly embrace.

A deep, sonorous voice resonated in her head as the oak twisted, transforming into a cloaked, skeletal form, white knuckled hands grasping at Amber.

Lose your way and the Lady of Shadows will claim you...

Amber opened her eyes to find her parents at the foot of a hospital bed. Before she had a chance to speak, her mother bent down tenderly to stroke her hair and kiss her cheeks. Tears streamed down her father's face, which he didn't seem to notice because he was kissing her and smiling so broadly. "I can't believe..." her father couldn't finish his sentence.

Her mother continued, giving her husband time to for composure, "You're alive! That's all that matters! *It* didn't get you!" Mrs. McBride hugged Amber tightly as her tears flowed freely into Amber's hair.

"It didn't get you…" Her mother's words sent a shiver down Amber's spine. She'd wondered if the girls who wanted to kick her ginger ass had started the fire, but her mother confirmed an insight she'd had in the cave: *Shadow Man* was after her, and he'd tried to burn her alive. But what did her mother know about it? How could her mother possibly know anything about this when she'd only just arrived?

A doctor entered the room and reassured the McBrides, "She's doing quite remarkably, considering what she's been through." After examining Amber's vital signs and studying her chart, the doctor suggested Amber should get some rest.

Mrs. McBride refused to move until her cell phone rang. Glancing at the screen, her features briefly screwed up in distaste before she deliberately smoothed them, nodding as she moved away to take the call. Dr. McBride kissed Amber once again, grasping both her shoulders as he reassured her, "We'll be right here."

Out in the hallway, Mrs. McBride informed Aunt Ester O'Donnell that Amber had been found alive and was unharmed. Of course, Aunt Ester already knew this, but she wanted a blow-by-blow account of the rescue from her niece. Forcing her to relive the harrowing experience was excruciating, but when Mrs. McBride reached the part of the story where she'd commanded the elements, she learned the *real reason* why her aunt had called: Aunt Ester asked Mrs. McBride to consider returning to her people. As a direct descendent of the Celtic Goddess Brigid's noble line, Amber and her mother belonged to a powerful band of high priestesses and druids. Aunt Ester ended the call with, "Just think about it. No need to make any decision right now. We're not going anywhere."

Amber felt dazed as blood was drawn, her throat was scoped and numerous other tests taken. Time had ceased to have any meaning when a nurse returned to inform her parents that Amber had to stay at the hospital overnight. Sunlight streamed in through windows directly facing the Twelve Apostles, setting Amber to wondering if she would ever escape their watchful eyes, now bearing witness to her being fussed over.

Dr. McBride took the chair next to the hospital bed. Puzzled, he watched his wife casually pass the chair next to him to seat herself at the foot of Amber's bed. Mrs. McBride had refused to be checked out at the hospital after fainting while watching Amber's daring rescue. She'd claimed it was caused by the extreme duress of not knowing whether their daughter was dead or alive.

After briefly studying his clasped hands, her father informed Amber of something she already knew, "Your tests are coming out fine, but they just want to keep you here overnight to be sure. The doctor says she's never seen anyone survive a fire like that without any damage from smoke inhalation. It must have been the Santa Ana winds! The guys at the lab told me they're really erratic up here. They must've kept the smoke from reaching you up in the cave."

"Dad, I'm alive! It's okay now." Amber willed her voice to convey confidence. This was a challenge because, in all likelihood, Shadow Man was still out there, and still wanted her dead.

"Why didn't you tell me about this Kick a Ginger Day?!! I would've kept you home from school!" Dr. McBride's eyes betrayed hurt that she hadn't sought fatherly protection.

Surprised, Amber asked, "How'd *you* find out about it?"

"It's all over the news, even in Seattle," her mother responded.

"A few redheads were roughed up at Calabasas High School because of it. More scared than hurt," her father added hastily, unwilling to upset Amber further after the trauma she'd suffered.

"Well, no one bothered me," Amber lied, stalling for time to make sense out of the strange, conflicting accounts she'd been given of her rescue.

∞

Officer Johnson stared at his reflection in the bathroom mirror, but he didn't recognize *this face* with its dark features and brown eyes. Deeply disturbed, Johnson reached a shaking hand atop his head, simultaneously relieved to feel its smooth baldness and totally freaked out to see a short, spiky mane of brown hair in the reflected image.

Closing his eyes as he rested his hands upon the counter, Officer Johnson tried to banish the crazy vision. He knew what'd happen if he reported any of the strange thoughts that intruded into his head ever since that night he'd lost consciousness over the Chatsworth Nature Preserve. Minimally, he'd be grounded. In the worst-case scenario, Johnson would be pensioned out on psych disability. He'd be finished at age thirty-eight.

That night over the preserve, after Officer Johnson regained consciousness, he'd begged his partner Gutiérrez not to report the incident to their superiors. Officer Gutiérrez agreed, but the shared secret introduced unease into their normally collegial relationship. Johnson now felt uncomfortable around his junior ranking officer and partner because he knew something that would end his career if word got out.

Even worse were the strange, alien images that intruded into his head. It was like having the contents of someone's hard drive containing all their personal videos downloaded into his brain. The first experience began innocuously. Officer Johnson recalled flying with Gutiérrez on a training run. But when they neared Twelve Apostles and Johnson spotted a woman's broken body at the base of the cliffs, a shiver went up his spine. She wore a long white dress, now spattered with blood from the brutal fall.

She had come to rest on her stomach, with her head turned unnaturally so that it almost faced him. Her unblinking eyes accused Johnson that *he'd* left something important unresolved. Now he bore some of the blame for this woman's death…

What in the hell was wrong with him? Gutiérrez and *Commander Jose Rodriguez* were the officers that spotted the woman! Because Chatsworth-Lake Manor was a small community, he'd heard all about Daniela Salvia's suicide, but why was he seeing her battered body in his head? What was with the crazy thinking? Johnson hadn't even known the Salvia woman…

Other less ominous visions had followed and Officer Johnson feared he was losing his mind. He'd briefly considered telling Gutiérrez about it. But common sense warned Johnson that Gutiérrez would think him insane, and therefore rat him out for sure.

Fearful of what he'd see, Officer Johnson glanced up at his reflection, relieved to find his face once again, and not *Commander Jose Rodriguez* staring back at him.

Having been medically cleared as suffering no after-effects from smoke inhalation, Amber was released from the hospital the next day. The McBride family ferried a carload of flowers, balloons and stuffed animals, including an enormous, colorful floral arrangement sent on behalf of Jonah, no doubt financed by his movie star father, Marcus Abernathy. A gigantic balloon arrangement filled with crazy animal shapes blocked the rear window, courtesy of Mr. Baccharis. The Garcia family dropped by the hospital when Amber was asleep and Marisol left a fragrant white sage plant, with instructions for Amber to plant it in the flowerbed outside her room.

Even better, Amber's confiscated cell phone was returned, putting an end to the strange, discomforting disconnect. After checking her mobile and reading the many warm wishes for her recovery, Amber posted a selfie with the caption: *Still here.*

She didn't know what else to say.

Numb, Amber felt somehow removed from what had happened to her. After the drug-induced sleep, memories of her frantic flight from death seemed foreign, as if the experience no longer belonged to her. It was almost like someone else had survived the fire, and Amber was watching it replayed on You Tube. Being separated from her emotions made Amber feel even more abnormal than usual.

A vibrant Mylar bird floated in front of her face, cutting off Amber's train of thought and bringing to mind the magician who had sent the enormous balloon bouquet. "Mr. Baccharis! He must be okay, right? I mean, he sent the balloons, did his house burn down?" Flames roared again in her mind's eye to race down the slopes of the skulking hill, toward Mr.

Baccharis' whimsical yard.

"I'm sure his house is fine," Dr. McBride tried to reassure his daughter.

"Who's Mr. Baccharis?" her mother asked.

"He's a retired special effects guy that Seth knows." Turning back to her father, Amber insisted, "How do you *know* he's okay, you haven't been there. How'd the fire get from the nature preserve to the dog park? It had to cross somewhere!"

Knitting now sweaty fingers together, Amber craned her neck to see if she could get a better look across the broad, burned meadow, but her line of sight to Mr. Baccharis' house was completely blocked, by none other than that blasted hill where the fire started! "I have to know, Dad!" Decided, Amber announced, "I'm walking over there, as soon as we get home!"

Sighing heavily, her father bypassed the twisting driveway to the House on Lizard Hill and continued on Lake Manor's main strip. "Where's this Baccharis live?"

Amber threw her arms around her father's neck in a grateful embrace, nearly causing him to veer off the narrow road. "Sort of around and behind the Log Cabin."

Selecting the most likely route, Dr. McBride turned right onto a one-lane road that wound in between houses jammed together cheek by jowl. "Which one is it?"

"There!" Amber pointed ahead to a long, ornately designed metal fence that stretched along the roadway for nearly a half a block. Strange sculptures of iron and other scrap metals adorned his quirky yard. As their car pulled up to the gate, she was relieved to see his funny little house intact.

"Well, well, I see you received my balloons?"

Amber shrank back from the windows in surprise. Recovering herself, she pressed the button to roll down her window and stuck out her head. Mr. Baccharis was standing right outside her car door, black top hat bobbing as he inclined his head. Despite the heat, today he was wearing a long magician's cape.

"Thanks! I'm so glad your house is okay."

"Me? No need to worry about me. *You*, on the other hand, you gave us all quite a fright. Especially your parents here, I imagine."

Dr. McBride rolled his window down and extended his hand in introduction. Mr. Baccharis' height made it necessary for Dr. McBride to crane his neck around in order to properly look him in the eye.

"Mrs. McBride," Baccharis tipped his hat down over his eyes in an oddly formal gesture of greeting.

Amber withdrew her head back into the car as Baccharis said, "I think I've taken up enough of your time. Welcome home, Amber."

His tall, lean form retreated back through the funky gate as they drove away.

"Odd fellow," Dr. McBride remarked.

"What do you think of Mr. Baccharis, Mom?"

Mrs. McBride didn't answer. Her delicate features appeared fixed in a frozen stare, red eyebrows furrowed in consternation.

"Mom?" Amber asked again.

No response.

"*Mom?*"

"*What*, Amber?"

"Why were you so rude to him? I know he's weird, but he's nice!"

Turning her head away from her husband and daughter to stare out the window, Mrs. McBride said nonchalantly, "I'm sure he's perfectly pleasant."

When they returned home, Kibbles greeted them exuberantly at the door. The dog seemed certain Amber had been gone for eons, and stayed at her side as her father helped carry the tokens of affection to her room.

Fingering the fragrant white leaves of the sage Marisol had left her, Amber noticed something white tucked in between the dirt and the container. Retrieving it, she found a note from Marisol:

I'm so happy you're okay! I looked online to see if your ancestors are Bruja, and guess what! Your family's name is connected to the Celtic Brigid. And she's related to Saint Brigid! Anyway, check it out when you get a chance. Maybe you'll find something.

As instructed, Amber typed in the name of her Celtic ancestor *Brigid* to see if Wikipedia had any insight to offer, and was confounded by the confusing array of information about what god Brigid was married to, who her father was and a lot of other things that Amber didn't give a rat's ass about. Scrolling down, she hoped to learn something that would actually be useful...*she had two oxen...invented a whistle used for night travel...*blah blah blah...Amber was growing increasingly disappointed. What good was any of this nonsense to her?

Moving to slam her laptop shut, her finger accidentally swiped another link on the Internet search, bringing up colorful, beautifully drawn images of a red-haired woman. Most had the same caption: *Celtic Goddess, a mother of pre-Christian Ireland. Associated with healing waters. Keeper of the sacred flame...*

Intense green eyes stared out from the screen. Between her palms, she cradled flames.

Brigid ruled fire.

Amber stared at the central image onscreen awhile longer, unsure about what any of this meant. If Brigid ruled fire, then why had the friggin' fire been after her? Had someone else started the fire and maybe Brigid rescued her? It all seemed a little fantastical.

Feeling overwhelmed, Amber picked up sage plant and headed outside. In an attempt to show her parents she was as healthy as the doctors claimed, Amber carefully dug a hole in her flowerbed and planted it. Kibbles sniffed at the small plant. The dog appeared to relish this new and exotic fragrance amidst the pervasive oily soot smell that permeated the air.

Amber heard a car pull away as her mother emerged from the larger of the two detached apartments. She called across the courtyard, "Where did dad go?"

"He ran to the store to pick up something to make for dinner. Are you sure you're well enough to go to school tomorrow?"

Amber groaned inwardly at the irony of this conversation. Normally she was the one trying to convince her mother to let her out of school when she didn't feel like going. "Really, I'm fine. I don't want to miss assignments and get behind."

"Are you ready to tell me the truth about what happened in the fire?" her mother pressed.

Rather than feeling relieved, Amber felt she was being treated like someone who'd done something wrong, chastised like a child! Her mother was always going to treat her like a little kid! In the hospital, her father had regaled Amber with the daring tale of her rescue. When Amber asked how they knew where she'd be and where to watch for her rescue, her mother's answer was noncommittal. Now that Amber knew about *Bruja* running in families, her suspicion grew and she demanded, "Is there something about our family you need to tell me, mom?"

"What are you asking, Amber?" Mrs. McBride answered her daughter's question with another question.

"C'mon, mom, I'm not a baby! I learned that our family name is related to a Celtic Goddess named Brigid! But I've never even met my grandparents in Ireland, how messed up is that? You and Aunt Cathy don't even talk to them? How bad can two old people be?"

"You wouldn't understand, Amber. I can't expect you to, not at your age. Maybe when you're older…"

Amber exploded, interrupting, "What, when I'm like, thirty? You have no idea what it's like! So much crazy stuff has happened and you've never, ever believed me! We're **Bruja** and you never told me anything about it!"

"*Bruja*? What's a Bruja?" Mrs. McBride asked as her nose crinkled, caught off-guard for once because she didn't know Spanish.

"A **witch**," Amber retorted.

Her mother's features smoothed as she looked overprotectively upon Amber, responding airily, "Don't be ridiculous! This isn't the dark ages. There's no such thing." Turning her back, her mother resolutely walked away in an attempt to end the conversation.

Amber was having none of it. Racing after her mother, she peppered her with questions, "Why won't you talk about our family? What are you so afraid of?"

When her mother quickened her pace and continued to ignore her, Amber thought of the most hurtful things she could possibly say to get her mother's attention. Wounded and feeling abandoned, Amber shouted, "I've been handling everything on my own since I was six because you were never there for me!!! You're the worst mother and *I hate you!*"

With these last words, Mrs. McBride whirled toward Amber, "How *dare* you! After everything I've sacrificed? You ungrateful little brat! You have no idea what you've gotten yourself into, Miss Know-It-All! You don't even know what you don't know. You'd never have been rescued if it wasn't for…" realizing she'd said too much, her mother broke off with a strangled cry as she escaped into the guest unit and slammed the door in a stunned Amber's face.

After a couple of seconds, Amber recovered her senses and pounded upon the door, shrieking at her mother to come out. When her demands were ignored, Amber threw the garden spade at the door in frustration and listened to it bounce off and clatter away down the brick path. Tears streamed down her face as she desperately searched the courtyard for a glimpse of her ancestral Celtic Goddess, but of course, no one was there and Amber was left, as usual, to deal with the unfolding nightmare on her own. Her mother's refusal to acknowledge Amber as a young woman, and one who could be trusted with whatever secrets the family kept, made Amber feel as lost as when she'd first glimpsed the contents of her dog's mind and her mother told her to stop making up stories.

Head spinning, Michelle/Aislinn O'Donnell McBride flopped wearily down upon the bed. All she wanted to do was protect her daughter, but if her instincts were correct, her task would be much more difficult than she could have ever imagined. Mrs. McBride suspected Amber would work against her at every turn because her daughter had always been headstrong. She'd anticipated this challenge, and she'd find a way to work with it. Although Amber's words hurt Mrs. McBride deeply, harsh words were the least of the trials she would face in the coming weeks.

It was the attempt on Amber's life, and the person she feared was behind this heinous crime that had Mrs. McBride reeling, as if she'd been sucker-punched.

She had followed Aunt Ester's instructions to the letter and carefully applied a spell of protection to Amber the night she slept in the hospital. She studied the lunar calendar and made certain she re-applied the spell on the appropriate nights, so that it wouldn't wear off. Aunt Ester assured Mrs. McBride that Amber would be able to return to school and go about living her life.

Mrs. McBride hadn't said one word to her aunt about her suspicions regarding the fire-starter. Surprisingly, Aunt Ester hadn't displayed her usual intuitiveness and given voice to Aislinn's fears. Indeed, Aunt Ester ascribed no supernatural motivation whatsoever to the Chatsworth Lake Fire. But Mrs. McBride knew better. Aunt Ester was like a spider, biding her time, waiting to use the information when it would best suit her purposes.

Mrs. McBride had then taken the next step. She paid a visit to the one she suspected was behind the attempted murder of her daughter.

During the drive over to his place, Mrs. McBride felt queasy. She hadn't seen him in over twenty years. Would she feel the same way about him after all this time? The passing of so many years bent and bowed many men, reducing them to shells of their former selves. And yet, the same could be said of *her*. Would he find her aged beyond recognition, transformed into a crone from the young girl he'd once known? Perhaps she would know his inner thoughts, betrayed by the look upon his face as soon as he laid eyes on her.

Her thoughts wandered to the way his hair strayed into his eyes, and how he would gently take her hand when she'd brush it back...

Mrs. McBride chided herself for allowing a lapse down memory lane, given that she suspected him of trying to kill her daughter in order to get back at her. After what had happened between them, he had every reason to want revenge. Additionally, he was the only person she knew who was capable of this heinous act.

As she pulled up to his house, her heart quickened. Getting out of the car, Mrs. McBride readied herself for the confrontation as she walked to the door.

He answered with a casual greeting of, "Hello Aislinn," acting as if only days had passed since they'd last seen each other.

SETH LOBATA

CHAPTER 8

DISCOVERY

Mrs. McBride was at a loss for words. She'd expected accusations and recriminations, but he simply waited to hear what she had to say.

Finally, she stammered, "Robert, were you responsible for the fire? Did you try to kill my daughter?"

Snorting derisively, he closed the door in her face.

Hope now flared at his wife's arrival and Dr. McBride laid aside rationality, giving way to superstition. He dared not jinx this incredible, horrendous and yet remarkable turn of events that brought her back to him.

Soft, romantic music played in the background. Candles were lit for added effect, avoiding all unnatural light. Dr. McBride slowly surveyed the room to ensure that all was in order.

Satisfied, he exited and checked back on the Bananas Foster, her favorite dessert, perfectly flambéed in its pan upon the stove. Their best china and silver had been set for two, in expectation of a communion of sorts, a shared housewarming.

She'd joined them in the new home and that was all that mattered now.

He smiled at the prospect of better days, of something to rejoice over: the fact that their daughter had survived the Chatsworth Lake Fire was a miracle. Dr. McBride did not believe in destiny, fate, or any such nonsense, but his wife's appearance suggested the possibility of recapturing happiness.

Amazing how quickly the human brain can process more than two decades of memories. His mind flashed lightning speed over their wedding: their theme song had been *Every Little Thing She Does is Magic* by The Police, to the birth of their daughter. How terrifying it had been to bring a life into the world, to be completely responsible, for however brief a period of time, for another person. Yet Michelle had taken all the worry and fear from him in her most capable parenting of Amber. She was motherhood epitomized: there for every slip, fall, and skip.

Dr. McBride recalled how lovely she looked in the backyard of their old Seattle home. Sometimes he'd arrive from work at the end of the day and sneak around the side of the house to peak over the fence into the yard, just to watch his wife gardening, her lovely porcelain arms deep in the Northwest's lush, loamy soil or laughing musically with Amber in the playhouse he'd built.

She'd enchanted him pure and simple. He was as love struck as the very

119

day he'd met her. Every day since had been exactly the same for him, even during fights about money, Michelle feeling fat and ugly when she was pregnant, hormonal after the baby was born and whatever else couples fought about, none of it mattered to him because he'd loved her just the same.

He could not have asked for more and had *no clue* about what to do if his wife Michelle no longer loved him.

Surveying the kitchen one last time to ensure all was perfection; he gathered his courage and walked to the guest unit where she was staying.

Pausing before her door, it felt weird to have to knock to see his wife. But these were strange times in his marriage, so he gathered his resolve and firmly knocked.

Amber was still a little girl in her mother's eyes, a child in need of protection. Opening up the Pandora's box of their ancestry would only lead to ruin, just as it'd nearly destroyed Mrs. McBride's life when she was young. She'd made a sacred vow to keep Amber in the dark until it was time; hopefully when she was an adult, and old enough to handle the responsibility of being a Celtic high priestess. Only initiates knew the sacred songs, rituals and ways of the clan. Those of her line kept their traditions close and the O'Donnells had successfully protected their secrets for generations.

Hearing someone knock upon the guest room door, Mrs. McBride opened it a crack to find her husband.

"Can you come to the kitchen?"

"Chris, I'm really tired right now. It's been a long day."

"This is really important," he insisted.

"Fine." Mrs. McBride huffed, locking the guest room door behind as she left.

Dr. McBride walked to the kitchen with increasing trepidation, but he'd started down a path. This had to be seen through, no matter what the outcome. Opening the door, he gestured for his wife to enter before him.

Taking two steps into the candlelit room, Mrs. McBride stopped short, "Chris, I'm not going to do this."

"It's just dessert," he tried to joke, moving around her to take the Bananas Foster off the stove. "Anyway, it's your favorite," he added.

"No, I mean *this*," Mrs. McBride stressed, as she began backing out of the kitchen.

Dr. McBride sat the dessert on the kitchen counter, inviting, "Sit down with me and we'll talk."

Exhaling heavily, Mrs. McBride finally revealed, "There's nothing to talk about. I'm not here for you."

Her indifference to his overtures hit Dr. McBride like body blows and he experienced a painful physical reaction to her rejection as she walked out of the kitchen and across the courtyard. In under a minute, he heard the sound of the rental car in the driveway as she drove off into the night.

He stood at the counter for a while, unsure of what to do, what to think, what to feel.

A scientist to the core, Dr. McBride had just been given irrefutable evidence that his marriage was over: his wife no longer loved him.

Amber knew she was in for trouble when she spotted the media vans across the street from her gate as she and her mother approached in the rental car, serenaded by angry honking from the morning's commuters'. Gripping the steering wheel, Mrs. McBride clicked the button to open the gate and floored the gas, gunning it onto the road in the opposite direction from the way that they would normally take to school. Turning to look back, Amber was amused to see reporters scrambling for their news vans to give chase. For the moment, her mother's clever maneuver had lost the throng.

Amber had refused to speak to her mother all morning. The atmosphere between the two was taut with tension as they passed the dirt parking lot where the bus had let Amber off the day of the fire. A scorched, blackened trail stretched from the nature preserve to the south, across the dog park and up the hill before disappearing over the other side. The debris field was littered with broken branches and the shards of once-noble oaks and things so damaged it was impossible to tell what they had once been. The fire's march appeared to have purpose. The swath of destruction looked more like pillaging from an invading army than the supposedly random act of nature.

What remained of Lourdes' grey Chevelle was a sunken lump of metal, charred beyond recognition.

Mrs. McBride decided to make the first move in calling a truce, "I read in the 'Chatsworth Patch' about a wild animal stampede that came through a neighborhood in Simi Valley during the fire. The reporter interviewed a wildlife biologist that tracks mountain lions, and a lioness that lives in the State Park was one of the animals that escaped with the others into Simi! It sounds like they all got out in the nick of time!"

Setting aside her anger, Amber peppered her mother with questions about the online article, like what kinds of animals escaped, where did they go, were any of them hurt? Incredibly relieved that animals and birds survived the inferno, Amber allowed herself to relax a little during the drive to school. However, anxiety flared again when her mother neared Castle

Peak High and Amber spotted the local media vans lining the streets. Embarrassed, Amber found that her hands were shaking. The noise and incoming stimuli were overwhelming and she wanted to turn around and go home.

"You okay?" Mrs. McBride asked, prompting Amber to remember that little girls hide behind their mothers. She was no longer a child.

"I brought you a scarf to hide your hair," Mrs. McBride removed a colorful, matronly head covering from her purse.

"No chance," Amber refused.

Though she'd declined the disguise, Amber was grateful her mother was by her side as they passed the gauntlet of reporters, for Mrs. McBride deflected all of their questions.

As the heavy front doors of Castle Peak High closed behind Amber, the noise on the street was definitively shut out.

Walking to class was a surreal experience. Amber was treated like a celebrity, or someone with the plague in equal measure, depending upon whom she passed in the hallway. Alternating between a gracious face and the stern mask of defiance worn on Kick a Ginger Day, she successfully reached her homeroom.

"Hey girl, I heard you're getting your own reality show: The Real Flame-Proof Gingers of Chatsworth," Slone teased.

The advisor called class to order and began by asking Amber to share a tip on surviving an extraordinary situation. Groaning, Amber reflected wearily that perhaps her mother was right after all. She should've just stayed home.

During lunch, she sat with her friends under one of the courtyard's large Eucalyptus trees, attempting to absorb the fleeting moments of fresh air before returning indoors for class. As the girls giggled and chatted, a shadow fell across the group from an approaching interloper.

Shading her eyes, Amber looked up, but couldn't make out the shadow caster because the sun was directly behind him. She was aware that it was a 'he' because the broad shoulders betrayed masculinity.

"Amber McBride," a deep voice spoke in a matter-of-fact manner, adding, "The Girl who Survived the Chatsworth Lake Fire." Moving into the shade, the dark, chiseled features of George Salvia became discernable. "Hard to believe anyone could've survived."

Amber looked about to ensure Lourdes wasn't lying in wait as she rose to stand. She had to get up on her tiptoes in order to come nose to nose with the tall boy. "Is your place okay?" she inquired, genuinely concerned as she shoved worries about his intentions aside.

George nodded, lowering his gaze as Amber came off her toes to settle back upon her heels. "No big deal, we watched it from our roof." He studied her face, waiting for her reaction.

"What? You didn't evacuate?" Amber asked.

George slyly grinned and answered, "We kicked back, had a few beers and watched the show."

Seizing him by the arm, Amber waved goodbye to her friends as she steered George Salvia away from the eucalyptus tree. "You saw what happened," she confirmed.

Clanging stirred the assembled teens back to reality from the lunch break as the school bell rang out the obligatory five-minute warning.

Leaning in, lips nearly grazing her ear, George whispered, "I'll be at the church at 4:00. We'll talk."

One of his friends had walked up from behind during the intense détente and hailed George for the next class. They moved off together, George whistling as he went.

Amber blinked hard following the surreal exchange and found her friends had vacated the tree to stand by her side, anxious to hear what had transpired.

Slone was the first to speak, "Amber McBride, I gotta hand it to you! You make all kinds of friends!"

"It's not funny," Marisol responded soberly, "stirring up the Salvia brothers is like poking a nest of rattlesnakes. This is my brother's fault! He dragged Amber into this mess!"

Slone Summers elbowed Amber in the ribs as they walked back to class after lunch. "Check it," she whispered.

Glancing out of the corner of her eye, Amber noticed what had caught Slone's attention. As they walked the hallway, students nudged each other and inclined their heads in Amber's direction. Slone expertly ignored the attention, yet soaked it in at the same time. Amber allowed the attention to wash over her. The resulting impact was immediate: she felt prettier, more interesting and less vulnerable. Amber dropped her combative look and smiled.

The rest of the day sailed by as Amber decided that she enjoyed the attention and had no interest in fading quietly into the gray tapestry of everyday school life.

∞

No sooner had her mother pulled the car into the driveway after school, Amber was disembarking with excuses of needing to meet briefly with Seth Lobata over a critical assignment due the following day. Despite her mother's insistence she be driven, Amber protested fiercely, accusing her mother of treating her like a baby, "We're just meeting at his house! There aren't any news vans around!"

Mrs. McBride studied her daughter, worry easing as she shook her head before finally giving in, "I'm sorry Amber, it's just that, after what happened…be right home as soon as you're done, okay?"

Leaving hastily, Amber hesitated when she reached the gate between her yard and the nature preserve. An oily, sooty smell pervaded the air and she'd ruin her shoes if she ventured into the ashy mess. Deciding to opt for the road, Amber turned to leave when the sickly scent of death tickled her senses.

Glancing back across the nature preserve, she spied the darkly clothed man atop the lumpy hill where the Chatsworth Lake Fire had started. His form blurred at the edges before retracting down into the stony hilltop.

Amber's heart pounded in her chest and she broke out into a cold sweat. Anxious to be away from Shadow Man, she dashed down her driveway. Shutting her creaky gate behind, she waited for it to lock into place before racing across the road.

"Hey."

Nearly leaping out of her tennis shoes with surprise, Amber whirled around to find George Salvia leaning casually against the large walnut tree by her front gate. Exhaling with relief, she offered, "Truce? Can we just forget about what happened at the Twelve Apostles?"

Laughing good naturedly, George disagreed, "It was pretty funny, so no, I'd rather not." Changing the subject, he asked, "How'd you end up trapped by the fire?"

"Why don't you ask your *girlfriend*?" Amber shot back impulsively, "None of this would've happened if it hadn't been for her!"

George's good humor vanished as he retorted, "I assume you're talking about Lourdes. She's *not* my girlfriend! What'd she do?"

Amber immediately regretted her angry outburst. What was she going to say to George? That Lourdes had accused her of something going on between the two of them when she and George had never met? As far as she was concerned, calling out to her from his car didn't quite count as being personally acquainted. He'd think Amber was the one who was crazy.

When they reached the clapboard church, George gestured for Amber to take a seat on one of the empty white chairs on the tiny patch of grass next to the front entrance. He put out no pressure to continue until she was ready.

Breathing deeply before continuing, Amber left out the real reason Lourdes pursued her, stating instead, "I guess she wanted to kick my ginger ass because of, well, you know."

Amber hoped George would fill in the rest.

Punching his thigh with his fist, his face flushed with anger, "You mean that crap about beating up a redhead? I'm really sorry about all this. She's gonna end up in jail!" Assessing Amber anew, he added, "You didn't tell the police."

Amber shook her head, "I'm no snitch."

Standing up, George towered over Amber as he revealed, "That day, the day of the fire, I saw you and something about you was…unusual. I can't really explain it. Sounds crazy, huh?

Staring at George Salvia with a mixture of fascination and surprise, Amber responded quietly, "Not so crazy."

Exhaling with relief that she hadn't questioned his sanity, he gently replied as he sat back down, "If you knew *half* of the shit that went on around here, you'd go back to wherever it is you came from."

Before Amber fully understood what she was doing, she poured out the story of what had happened to her in the fire. She was only able to stop herself when it came to the Celtic Goddess Brigid. As she recalled the experience in the cave, Amber found herself reimagining its walls encompassing her, protecting her from the flames.

Inwardly cringing, she stopped talking. Amber was horrified. She'd *never* shared so much personal information with a complete stranger. No doubt this lapse in judgment would come back and bite her in the butt…

George Salvia sat back in his chair, dark eyes thoughtful as he considered her words. "I watched the fire come across the preserve in seconds. I've never seen fire move like that." Running his hand through his short, dark hair, he continued, "It was through the dog park in no time."

His right hand strayed near a lock of her hair, nearly touching it before withdrawing his fingers and asking a question to which neither had the answer, "So how does a skinny white redhead cheat Santa Muerte?"

As George drove the Salvia's second shared vehicle home, a 1966 Stepside pickup, he considered how unlike him it was to show any interest in the redheaded ninth grader. His intentions were not amorous. There were no girlfriends in his senior year strategy. Since breaking up with Lourdes Navarro, he'd found life much simpler following the Salvia brothers' playbook: keep company with older women who were satisfied with the short-term companionship of a handsome younger man. George didn't want any entanglements before heading off to college.

Yet on Kick a Ginger Day he'd glimpsed what he could only describe as a different version of Amber McBride: not a fourteen-year-old girl, but a young woman, perhaps what she was destined to become in a few short years.

He'd heard the old stories, passed down through his family. When Amber miraculously survived the Chatsworth Lake Fire, his suspicions crystallized. If this kid was a Bruja - a witch - then she might have the mojo to help them lift the curse that had plagued the Salvia males for generations. After briefly considering sharing this wild theory with his brothers, George decided to keep it to himself, for now.

The following days were as strange and disjointed as the dreams Amber endured in the hospital's drug-induced sleep. She was arguably one of the most recognizable teens at school. Everyone knew who she was and almost everyone wanted to be her friend. But after the initial shock wore off, an uncomfortable jittery feeling began to take root. Amber nearly jumped out of her seat every time the bell or her cell phone rang; even the gentle vibration of a text message caused her to flinch as if she'd been struck. Even worse, she'd nearly punched Luis Garcia in the face when he snuck up behind her in the hallway. Only quick-thinking James Toshima saved Luis from a black eye by yanking him backward, pulling Luis out of harm's way as Amber's left jab went wild. Amber's reaction was totally instinctual and she'd not understood what she'd done until Luis backed away with an odd expression on his face, muttering, "What was that for?"

Every day when she'd emerge from school, Amber felt as if she was being watched. Every day she'd scan the sidewalks and streets for the perpetrator, only to find teenagers going about their business. Inevitably she'd turn back towards the school to find Castle Peak looming overhead, stone eyebrows darkly arched in disapproval.

The brightest spots in the day were, oddly, her interactions with George Salvia: the brief conversations in the hallway, followed by texting back and forth after she got home from school. Amber learned they had much in common: they were both solid A students, liked the same music, and played at the same warrior level in the virtual world decapitating zombies. George claimed he'd never met a girl that played at his level. They both snowboarded and George challenged Amber to make it down Mountain High's infamous 'Wall' without wiping out come winter. Perhaps most importantly, both teenagers shared the desire to get away from their dysfunctional families.

Amber even got up the nerve to ask him about the Salvia Senior Stunt and George joked, "I'm not saying that they did it, but supposing they did, they're gonna be hard to beat."

Yet despite the distraction George Salvia offered, Amber found herself increasingly isolated and lonely. She really missed having the irreverent Shelby by her side. Although never alone in her new school, none of Amber's new friends *really* knew her. They saw only the surface stuff, what she felt safe enough to reveal. Amber wore her mask naturally and deflected questions about her wellbeing away with such ease that no one noticed she never answered. Her inner self remained protected and hidden, cloaked just as Santa Muerte indicated:

We hide our true selves from the rest of the world...

At night, Amber found herself waking up around 3:00 AM, her heart pounding and her sweats soaked through to the skin. Her throat ached as if she had been screaming, the pervasive stench of soot still clinging to the inside of her nostrils.

Mrs. McBride expressed her concern about Amber's wellbeing when she picked her up one day from school, "Honey, I think what happened to you is affecting you more than you're willing to admit."

"*Mom*, I'm fine, really!"

"Well, your dad and I will feel much better if you talk to someone about it."

Amber eyed her suspiciously.

"You know, a *professional*."

"No way, mom! I'm not crazy! Why would you even think that?" Amber defiantly crossed her arms over her chest as she glowered over her mother's latest intrusion into her personal life.

"Too late, I already made the appointment. We're heading over there now," Mrs. McBride cut off her daughter's protestations. "Besides, she's not a psychiatrist, she's a psychologist."

"Like there's any difference. I'm not talking. So you're wasting your money." Amber sulked for the remainder of the drive, longingly gazing up her driveway when they passed her turnoff, wondering how much it would hurt to hit the dirt if she jumped out of the moving car and made a run for it.

Amber gave her mother the silent treatment as Mrs. McBride drove out to the highway and then onto a major thoroughfare. After driving but a few blocks past a saloon called the Cowboy Palace and other vacant low-slung buildings reminiscent of a Wild West community, Mrs. McBride turned left into the parking lot of a squat, square, black glass building. Beyond it spread a flat, dusty plain hosting the Chatsworth Train Depot, fashioned in the manner of the old west in its simple wooden one-story framing and construction. The last stop on the Los Angeles County route, the decaying facades in the eccentric burg of Chatsworth led many a naïve traveler to believe he or she had mistakenly arrived in a ghost town.

Amongst the many and varied travelers walking away from the depot in the direction of the Simi Hills was a man with flowing grey hair and a handlebar mustache, wearing a long black canvas duster and a western style string tie.

"No wonder they call this the land of fruits and nuts," Mrs. McBride remarked.

Stopping at a nondescript building, Mrs. McBride marched Amber to a door titled, "Dr. Betty Morton, Psychologist." Flipping a switch to notify the doctor, her mother sat in one of the comfy waiting room chairs and picked up a magazine, ignoring Amber's pointed, angry glare.

An inner door opened and a fashionably dressed, tall slender woman in her early sixties emerged. "You must be Amber?" Dr. Morton gently questioned.

Mrs. McBride shooed her forward with the magazine as if Amber were Kibbles being taken out for a whiz.

Dr. Morton quickly glanced between the two of them, quietly assessing the interaction before politely inviting Amber inside to a comfortable and decidedly non-threatening grandmotherly office. "So, I take it you don't want to be here?"

Amber nodded, some of the tension easing with the good doctor's acknowledgement of her predicament.

"And, we're just doing this to get your mom off your back?"

"Yes, Dr. Morton," Amber concurred.

Dr. Morton winked conspiratorially. "Call me Betty, will you? Dr. Morton is so…formal. I've never cared for titles."

Amber stared at her feet, unsure about what to do next.

"Well, this is your time, so we can spend it however you want. I should tell you a little bit about what I do. You've probably seen in movies where someone comes to see the psychologist and, over a period of weeks, the patient opens up little by little and learns to trust. We can dispense with all of that and cut straight to it. My specialty is treating Post-Traumatic Stress Disorder: PTSD. That's just a fancy term for the reaction normal people have to experiencing something *extraordinary,* something outside the range of everyday experience."

"Like almost being burned alive," Amber had lifted her head and now looked directly at Dr. Morton, "where maybe lots of animals died! I don't even know for sure if they all escaped."

"Definitely an extraordinary situation," Dr. Morton confirmed, voice absent any judgment or condescension. "You know," she added thoughtfully, "ground squirrels have been known to burrow deep underground. They're quite clever, that's how they can survive fire."

"Oh." Amber recalled the crazed flight of the animals and birds and felt a bit unbalanced, so she ventured to ask, "How do people react?"

"Well, when you have PTSD, you may be really jumpy, we call it hypersensitive. Because of the hypersensitivity, some report hearing things that may or may not be what they think. Nightmares are common and so are misinterpreting situations, like seeing a threat where none exists. It can certainly *feel* like you are going crazy, even though PTSD does *not* make you crazy. The good news is that there is effective treatment for it. You can be out of here in two months and you won't have to take any medication."

The color drained from Amber's already pale face.

"No worries here, psychologists don't prescribe. PTSD can be treated very effectively in young people without any drugs. I've no need to go into your personal life, talk about boyfriends, none of that because none of it is relevant. You're a normal teenager who experienced something out of the ordinary, easily treatable."

Dr. Morton reassured her in calm, measured tones that scraped over Amber's last nerve.

"That all sounds *great*," Amber remarked sarcastically, "but how would you know what it's like to be me? What would you know about it?"

Dr. Morton smiled thinly. "Normally psychologists don't go around sharing personal information, but in your case, I think you need to know a little bit about me, so you understand that there's a way out."

Slowly standing, knee joints cracking in the process, Dr. Morton strode over to the window looking out over the train depot. "I was fifteen when I lost my entire family in an accident at a train crossing. I should've been there too, but I was over at a friend's house that night." Dr. Morton looked at Amber and assessed her reaction before continuing, "We didn't have any other relations that could take me, so I bounced around between a few foster homes before I eventually ran away at sixteen. I've been on my own ever since."

As an only child, Amber couldn't imagine losing both her parents and being entirely on her own at her age. Why would Dr. Morton want to be reminded about the cruel turn of events that left her an orphan? The irony of Dr. Morton's office situated across from the train station puzzled Amber, so she asked, "Doesn't it bother you, you know, the trains running right outside the window?"

Dr. Morton paused, her elder's face framed by the waning sun streaming through the window. "I moved here *on purpose*, Amber. You see, I learned early on that we must confront horror directly. Whatever you're afraid of? Stare it down, without flinching." When Dr. Morton turned back toward Amber, her face was surprisingly at peace. "If we allow it, fear takes control of us. We spend our lives either running away or fighting it. We must make a friend of horror."

Ben Salvia sat back in his desk chair, still staring at the image of a redheaded girl onscreen, courtesy of the local online newspaper: the Chatsworth Patch. Amber McBride, the same redhead who'd been with those trespassing punks, and here she was yet again: the "Girl Who Survived the Chatsworth Lake Fire."

His childhood home atop the mountain, shared with his three brothers, had barely escaped being burned to the ground, bypassed by luck and a heroic stand by the LAFD. Had the inferno claimed the lives of the brothers, the ancient curse would've wiped out an entire generation of Salvias in one fell swoop. The curse was simple: there had never been a Salvia male who'd ever died peacefully or of old age. Down to every last man, they'd all expired in some calamitous manner.

As if the curse wasn't enough, virtually every bit of flora, from an emerging blade of grass to all but the mightiest oaks on the Salvia property had been knocked down by the fire. The entire Salvia Homestead was now laid bare, leaving their land exposed and vulnerable.

AΩ

Thursday saw a return to semi-normal: the news people had moved on to another story and the interest in the fire died down. During lunch, Amber sat at the eucalyptus tree with Slone Summers and her friends. The group laughed as a crowd of wanna-be's hung around wistfully, like minnows flitting about at the edge of a pod of dolphins, hoping to be admitted rather than eaten.

Marisol and Noelle emerged from the breezeway and into the ever-sunny courtyard. Marisol spied Amber and began walking towards the group, but then frowned and stopped before abruptly walking off in the opposite direction. Noelle shrugged to the group, indicating she didn't have a clue, and then followed Marisol out of the courtyard.

"What crawled up her butt and died?" Slone asked.

Within seconds, a text from Marisol came through on Amber's cell: *Need to talk, when you're alone.*

After school, she tried calling Marisol, but got no answer.

After dinner, Amber went to her room to finish her homework and got a text message:

Look out the window

Frowning, Amber looked out the window facing the preserve to find George Salvia. Grinning, she stashed her phone and slipped outside. Checking the courtyard to ensure no parental eyes were prying, she darted around the corner and down the stairs, taking the route leading away from her parents' rooms.

When she reached the gate, Amber asked, "What's up?"

"Thought I'd check out where the fire started. Want to come?"

Amber hesitated inwardly even as she nodded. What if Shadow Man was lurking about? She'd never faced a demon before. Amber had no idea what would happen, and didn't want to be responsible for someone else's safety. Yet instinctually, she knew George Salvia was no wussy.

Hands in his pockets, George whistled softly as he walked toward the misshapen lump opposite the House on Lizard Hill. Vibration in her pocket alerted Amber to an incoming message, which she ignored.

Suddenly tongue-tied, Amber wasn't sure how to tell George about what she'd seen on the hill and grew frustrated about her discomfort. Conversation flowed easily when the two connected in the virtual world, yet now she found herself struggling to find something to say that didn't make her sound like a complete idiot. Willing her brain to function properly, she breathed a sigh of relief when she found a coherent question to ask, "Did you decide where you want to go yet?"

Smiling, George considered her question before responding, "Depends on who comes through with a full ride. I'd be happy at UCLA or Berkeley."

Impressed, she asked, "So you won't have to pay for anything?"

George Salvia modestly looked away as he shook his head.

Amber would've known they'd reached the hill had her eyes been closed because of the palpable change: her skin tingled painfully and a ringing started in her ears. Looking to George, she realized from the pained expression on his face he'd experienced something. Boldly, Amber stated, "You feel it too."

Nodding, George started up the hill. With no visible trails in sight, Amber remarked, "I think the animals avoid this place."

Nodding again, he remarked, "Something's been *wrong* here for a long time." Stopping, George appraised her before adding, "Maybe we'll figure out what it is, because if we can't...we just need to get the hell out of here."

Eyeing the handsome boy as they resumed walking, Amber cautiously asked, "What do you mean?"

Avoiding her gaze, George admitted, "I'm not sure you'll believe me, but what the hell. As far back as anyone in my family knows, since even before the 1700's, we've only had boys. No girls. Maybe that's not so strange, but..." Here he paused, considering his words carefully, "everyone dies unexpectedly in what my grandfather called a calamity."

Trying to process this revelation, Amber asked in a rush, "Who died? What's a calamity?"

"Something tragic and unforeseen, like my father. He was going through an intersection when a tractor-trailer blew the red light and plowed into him. He was dead before the car stopped moving." Sensing that perhaps he'd revealed too much, George Salvia moved on to a less painful memory, "Or my great-uncle Shandor, what an idiot! Always wore his pants up to his chest! He thought he'd beat it by holing up in a bunker in the hills and never going outside. So get this! He gets bit by a mosquito and dies of an infection!" George smiled upon recollecting his eccentric relative.

"Maybe it's just a coincidence?" Amber suggested kindly, "I mean, two guys, it's horrible, especially your dad, but maybe just bad luck?"

Laughing bitterly, George continued, "There've been so many relatives that've died of lightning strikes over the years, I've lost count. Let's see, then there was Walter, he was a fighter pilot, decorated Korean War hero, came back with a fist full of medals! He's vacationing in Hawaii and gets hit on the head by a coconut and dies instantly. Then there was Juan, he did two tours in Vietnam and got the Purple Heart! I guess he ate some bad chicken in Barstow and never made it back to Simi. That Impala was a friggin' mess from what my dad said, white interior covered in shit..."

Upon seeing Amber blanch, George concluded, "Get the picture?"

"Wait a sec," Amber thought back to the infamous Senior Stunts in light of this information and wondered, "if your relatives all die in weird ways, why are you guys always doing crazy stuff that'll get you killed? It doesn't make any sense!"

Grinning, George revealed, "I don't think the curse was very well-thought out. We figured a way to cheat it. It's almost like a super-power: As long as we stare death down we survive. Our motto is: *Keep the Reaper in front of you.*"

Incredulous, Amber sputtered, "So if I put a gun to your head and pull the trigger, you won't die?"

Laughing, George nodded, "We play Russian Roulette all the time, there's always a misfire or some other crazy shit. You get a couple of Salvias together and it's on! Knife throwing, grenade juggling, whatever you can think of, we've done it! You should see our family reunions!"

Wide-eyed, visions of testosterone-fueled death defying stunts filled Amber's imagination. If George was telling the truth, how could any mother handle sons like the Salvias? Amber's mom would be a nervous wreck! "How'd you figure it out? I mean, how to beat the curse?"

"Who knows? Probably during some war, our family's filled with decorated vets going back to the Civil War. They volunteered for the worst possible missions and never got killed, although I had a second cousin who fell off a bunk bed and broke his neck"

"Who cursed your family? Who'd be so mean?" Amber struggled to figure out what possible act could inspire hatred worthy of condemning future generations to succumb in some untimely and painful manner.

As George shook his head, Amber had no idea what she could possibly say that would offer George encouragement of any kind in the face of an ancient curse.

In a more serious tone, George stated, "Interesting how you move here, and the biggest fire anyone can remember starts right outside your house."

Before Amber could question George's motives for making this statement, he hastily added, "Maybe bad things are drawn to people like you. Like a *curse*, just different from the Salvia curse."

Shocked, Amber stopped walking. Had George Salvia just called her out? How could he know her secrets? She felt vulnerable and exposed. Unsure, Amber didn't know how to respond. Yet hadn't the tall boy revealed painful truths about his personal life? George had told her about the death of his father, and about the Salvia family curse. She'd not heard any gossip around school about the curse, and therefore assumed it wasn't common knowledge.

Because Amber was so empathetic, she was used to her peers opening up to her and sharing their secrets. However, something about the manner in which George communicated was very different. Unspoken was the expectation of reciprocation.

Other than Shelby, when Amber's friends in Seattle talked, they were more than happy to go on and on about themselves and never ask one question about how Amber was doing or how Amber was feeling. This suited Amber just fine because no one asked uncomfortable questions that could lead to schoolmates questioning her mental health. Yet here was George Salvia, waiting for Amber to reveal something personal. A part of Amber wanted to bolt down the hill, yet years of practice had taught her to keep her secrets close. This time she was on guard after her previous blunder with George when she'd spilled her guts about the fire. Amber wasn't about to tell him about the *Ghostly Adventures of Shelby and Amber*, or her ability to communicate with wildlife.

Nonetheless, George's magnetism compelled Amber to share something in a goodwill gesture of friendship. Considering the Salvia family history in the Simi Hills, Amber wondered whether George knew something about the House on Lizard Hill. Deciding that it couldn't hurt to talk about Lucy Carpenter, Amber shared what she'd learned about the missing teenager: that she'd disappeared from a party at the House on Lizard Hill in 1982, and the homeowner was later arrested for pretending to be a doctor.

"That's messed up," George concluded when Amber finished the tale of Lucy's disappearance.

They'd crested the top of the hill and as Amber surveyed the scene before them, she wasn't sure if George Salvia was commenting on her story or the boulders arrayed in a perfect circle.

On the other side of the hill, a darkly clothed, hooded man stepped from behind one of the boulders.

"Welcome, Amber McBride" he hissed.

George moved to step through the stones.

Amber grasped for his arm to try and yank him back. Her fingertips grazed his skin.

Entering the druidic circle, George disappeared from her line of sight.

Luis Garcia

CHAPTER 9

BONDING

As Amber moved to follow George, she saw that she stood alone on the hilltop.

George found himself surrounded by thick mists. A jumbled cacophony of voices beseeched him. Although the words were not understandable, the underlying tone betrayed hopelessness and despair.

George reached out for the man in black, and found only empty air. Centuries of facing death daily brought an innate calm in the midst of crisis. George kept a level head, standing still until he could find his sense of direction.

George

The voice spoke in the softest whisper, but the speaker was clearly recognizable to him. He walked toward its source and called out, "Mom?"

You can't be here!

"Wait, mom, come home with me," George begged as he followed her voice. "Please, we need you."

Please, mijo, there's no time! [13]

"Why can't you come with me, why…" George stopped speaking as he found himself outside the stone circle. Night had fallen.

Amber found herself surrounded by the same murkiness as George. She called out to him, and was gratified to hear someone move toward her through the mists.

"Let's get out of…" Amber trailed off as she found herself face-to-face with the darkly clothed man.

Grabbing Amber in a chokehold, he let go just as suddenly, howling in pain.

"Witch! It burns, it burns!"

Amber ran. She had no idea where she was going; she only knew she had to be away from him.

Light feathers brushed her forehead. Amber could barely make out the dark form that flew past. Running to catch up, she stumbled out of the mists and into George Salvia.

Oblivious, he pushed her roughly aside on his way back into the stone

---

[13] Mijo is a Spanish term of endearment, which generally means "my little boy"

circle.

"George, wait!" she yelled as she ran after him.

No mists encircled the teenagers; anguished voices did not assail them. The dark hilltop was silent.

"Where is he?" George raged as he searched the hilltop. "This is a trick! There's got to be a fog machine stashed somewhere!"

Hearing something in the distance, Amber spotted the searchlights of incoming LAPD helicopter and warned George, "We need to leave, NOW!"

The teenagers scrambled down the hill, sending ashen debris skittering around their legs in sooty showers. Upon gaining the meadow, they dashed full speed across to the fence as the chopper cleared the ridgeline. In a flash, Amber had the gate unlocked and the two were through.

"What just happened up there?" she asked, hoping George would reveal what he had experienced.

"Someone's effing with us, *both* of us," George decided.

"But who?" Amber asked, "and why?"

AΩ

On Friday, Amber and Marisol walked out to the car, where Mrs. McBride was waiting. Amber had wanted to speak to Mari about what had happened, but needed to do so in person, and away from school.

Dinner was an uncomfortable affair because everyone had something they needed to say to somebody, yet no one said anything of importance. Attempts at small talk fell flat and the girls practically fled the table when the meal ended, anxious to escape parental oversight.

As soon as Amber, Mari and Kibbles were safely within the confines of her room, Amber poured out her story in a rush, leaving out no detail, including her belief that she'd called upon the birds for aid at the Twelve Apostles in order to get rid of Ben Salvia and his brothers. Amber concluded her revelation with what had transpired between her and George Salvia atop the hill.

Incredible relief overcame Amber upon finally sharing the truth with someone who not only seemed genuinely willing to listen, for no doubt George met that criteria, but also didn't want anything from her. Amber suspected that George Salvia *wanted* something; she just didn't know what the heck it was. Frankly, it frightened her.

When Amber finished, she waited on pins and needles for Marisol's reaction.

Mari spoke slowly, deliberately, "All this week, my grandmother keeps coming to me in my dreams, but for some reason, I can't hear her. It's so frustrating. She wants to tell me something!"

Finally, Amber knew what action must be taken. It was time to stop allowing things to *happen* to her and to actually *do* something for a change.

"I've been thinking," Amber began, "when I lived in Seattle, all we wanted to do was go to kickbacks and hang out at the mall. Why is it *we* keep going into the Simi Hills?"

"You're right," Marisol answered quickly. "I go there all the time and so do the guys. They always find excuses, like they're mountain biking or whatever, but *we all keep going back*. It's something about the mountains that draws us there!"

"We need to go back to the grotto," Amber decided. "That's where all of the animals and birds showed up and where I survived the fire."

"Magic," Marisol exhaled.

Max pulled up to the funky wrought iron gate and prepared to let the boys out at the old magician's place. Mr. Baccharis had kindly agreed to help them with their group science project and Jonah had asked to come along because he always learned some new trick from Baccharis during their impromptu get-togethers. About to pull away after the boys disembarked, the sight of two strangers on the property caught Max's attention. Parking the SUV along the narrow road, Max exited the vehicle after the teens, remarking casually in response to Jonah's quizzical look, "I make chat with Baccharis. See how he is after fire."

To the untrained eye, the old cowboy and the gentleman in the Wyatt Earp getup appeared eccentric. But Max had seen their kind before, long ago in his homeland. The question was, what were they doing here?

Smiling broadly, Max strode to the tall magician and greeted him with a hearty handshake. Without missing a beat, he turned to the two strangers, extending his hand.

"Well, I'll be, I think my cigar's gone out. Will you excuse me a minute?" Cowboy Joe turned his back and made motions of relighting his cigar.

The other gentleman in the long black duster and broad black hat merely nodded at Max, but did not extend his hand in greeting.

Laughing, Baccharis informed Max, "Fred Graves here is a direct descendent of Chatsworth's first sheriff! He gives the kids a treat at our Historical Society get-togethers by dressing up as his ancestor. We just came from an event this afternoon, in fact."

Nodding, Fred Graves resumed smoking his cigar as Max realized what was wrong. Although Max saw the tips of Graves' and Cowboy Joe's cigars redden as they inhaled, and he observed smoke as they exhaled, he couldn't catch the distinctive scent of tobacco leaves amidst the pervasive sooty remains of the Chatsworth Lake Fire. However, it was possible that the inferno's devastation overwhelmed all other scents, so Max decided to test his theory. He retrieved one of his own cigars from the inner pocket of his jacket. Inhaling along its length before clipping off the end, he said, "We all smoke. Nothing left here to burn."

"How long are you hanging out?" Jonah asked Max impatiently.

Inhaling deeply, Max blew a perfect smoke ring before responding, "Awhile."

"Nice to have you join us," Mr. Baccharis welcomed Max as the older magician began assisting the boys with their science project. "Good turnout today at the Historical Society," he remarked to Fred Graves and Cowboy Joe.

"You bet." Cowboy Joe's eyes crinkled as he chuckled, "Not one time goes by where some yahoo don't ask where the treasure is."

Seth perked up and came over to ask, "Treasure? What treasure?"

Chuckling, Fred Graves informed him, "Just an old story about a stagecoach robbery on the Devil's Slide in the Santa Susana Pass. Supposedly, it was Fernando Salvia that made off with the gold. Got shot in the back as he fled, but to this day, the gold's never been found."

Luis, James and Jonah had joined the circle during Fred Graves' treasure tale and excitedly asked questions.

Jonah asked, "If he got shot in the back, how'd he get away with the treasure?"

Seth wanted to know, "Did he bury it?"

Whereas Luis sputtered, "Shoulda known those Salvias were bad from way back! Did they hang him?"

Prompting Jonah to retort, "What'da mean, dumbass? Sheriff Graves said he got shot in the back!"

Laughing, Cowboy Joe held up his weathered hands for silence and explained, "As the story goes, Salvia was mortally wounded, but got away far enough to hide the treasure. Where it's hid, no one knows."

"Why'd he do it?" James Toshima asked quietly, "Why'd he rob the Stagecoach?"

Fred Graves and Cowboy Joe looked to Mr. Baccharis, who solemnly concluded the tale, "He did it for love."

Tingling with anticipation as the evening passed, every hour seemed like an eternity as the teens at the House on Lizard Hill waited for the McBride parents to go to sleep. Amber's father obliged by turning out the lights in the master bedroom at around 11:00, yet the lamp in her mother's room shone stubbornly through the cracks in the wooden blinds on the windows. Amber felt like she was going to explode as she paced back and forth across the wooden floor of her room.

Finally, at midnight, darkness enveloped the House on Lizard Hill. Ready to bolt out the door, Marisol placed a cautious hand on Amber's arm and made her wait an additional agonizing fifteen minutes after the lights went out, to ensure that her mother was really asleep.

Slightly pulling back the brown curtain over the French door leading from her room to the courtyard, Amber stealthily peeped out, gratified when no reflected light shone from any room in the house. "We're good," she confirmed and quietly exited. The elderly Kibbles was too tuckered out to rise in an attempt to follow.

Dressed in dark clothing, the girls moved silently down the stairs by the laundry room. Pausing briefly at the bottom, Marisol insisted on one final check as to whether they had been detected. They were rewarded for their caution, as nothing stirred from the dark angles above their heads.

Amber and Marisol dashed along the northern arm of her U-shaped home, grateful that Amber's parents' rooms were both on the opposite side. The lock on the nature preserve gate was quickly opened, aided by the light of a nearly full moon.

"What if he's out there now?" Amber asked. "Shadow Man could be waiting for us."

A pungent, oily smell permeated the nature preserve. Ash floated up with their footfalls, pale ghosts of the inferno. The former occupants: crickets, mice, snakes and coyotes, had either fled entirely, or were silent as the grave. The dead quiet was unnerving.

When Marisol didn't respond, Amber followed her friend's gaze to the lumpy, misshapen hill opposite the House on Lizard Hill.

An image appeared in Amber's head: a hooded figure bending over and lighting a match, then running away as flames engulfed the dry brush atop the hill.

She was seeing what the animals witnessed, the day of the fire.

"He started the fire *on purpose!*" Amber whistled, immediately grasping the meaning of the vision. When Marisol asked what she meant, Amber explained, "I just 'saw' what the birds and animals saw!"

Realization dawning, Amber grimly concluded, "It's the same guy that lured me and George into that black hole! It's *me* he's after."

Horrified, Marisol asked, "Do you think Shadow Man possessed someone? Why would anyone be out to get you? You just moved here!"

"You're right," Amber shuddered.

"An evil spirit," Marisol Garcia hissed. Turning from Amber, she spoke a few words in Spanish.

A breeze picked up from nowhere, disturbing ashen debris in its wake. A small twister formed. Fascinated, Amber watched it whirl around the length of the nature preserve before vanishing across the road and into the dog park.

Amber heard an elder's voice state, "He is not here; you have safe passage."

✝

Officer Johnson quietly made his way to the kitchen, taking care not to wake his wife and little daughter Tessa. Absent-mindedly searching the refrigerator for a late-night snack, he pondered the real reason he'd woken in the middle of the night. Johnson hadn't been able to shake the feeling that he knew the "Girl that Survived the Chatsworth Lake Fire." Intellectually, he knew this wasn't possible. The kid was only fourteen and had just moved to Chatsworth within the last month. But his cop instincts were on fire, and when it became clear his gut wasn't going to leave him alone, Officer Johnson drove on his day off over to LAPD's cold case division and asked for the files Commander Jose Rodriguez had worked on over the course of his career.

The officer in charge of records was initially skeptical about giving Johnson access because he wasn't a detective assigned to the unit, but Johnson managed to bluff his way in with an invented story of how a fresh set of eyes might help. Ultimately it was Officer Johnson's warm personality that won the cold case clerk over. Figuring no harm could come by getting extra assistance, copies of Commander Jose Rodriguez' files were provided.

Officer Johnson signed out three boxes of material related to unsolved murders and missing persons.

Marisol wobbled and would have collapsed, had Amber not steadied her.

"What just happened?" Marisol asked.

As Amber attempted to explain what she'd witnessed, Marisol became increasingly anxious.

"If my grandmother is trying to speak *through me*, we're both in danger! We have to get to the grotto!"

Resolute, the two friends forged across the nature preserve, through the dog park and into the state park. Because the foliage had been burned away, they were able to quickly descend the trail Amber had used to flee from Lourdes Navarro and her friends.

Reaching the far side of the sooty meadow, Marisol led Amber up a low hill before turning off toward the cliffs.

They progressed down an animal track, unable to escape the sickly, charred smell. Mari motioned for Amber to follow her around what must have once been a grove of laurel sumac. Stripped bare by the fire, huddled clusters of dry, bony branches reached skyward in the moonscape.

Darkness receded to shades of grey as they neared the cliffs. What was left of the laurel sumac lined both sides of the path, the wild chaparral forming a natural arbor. Sharp, thin fingers intertwined overhead, plunging the girls into shadows when they entered.

The brittle, dry prairie grass that normally would have scratched their legs along the path in late summer was gone. Broken twigs crumpled and then shattered beneath their feet as they continued their trek upward. Branches caught in their hair with tendril-like stickiness, snapping off with a souvenir of dusty residue. The trail inclined steeply into a rock face, summiting into darkness where the arbor and path appeared to join.

Mari scrambled up the hill on all fours, grasping at holds in the rocks, and disappeared over the top.

Heart suddenly racing, Amber looked frantically around for a way out of the arbor tunnel, this experience bearing all of the elements of Déjà vu: the return to the grotto as the inferno pursued her, scrambling up a rock face to the unknown…

The scent of green apples overwhelmed her senses, tickling her memory of when they had first encountered one another. Laurel Sumac in full bloom, defying the withering heat of summer, when she and the guys hid behind the giant grove on their mountain bikes waiting for the Salvia brothers to depart. The memory dissolved to reveal a picture in her head of flocks of birds flying over the hills into the safety of Simi Valley beyond, followed within minutes by a cavalcade of deer, mice, squirrels, raccoons, and possums. Two men wearing cowboy hats stood with their backs to Amber as they watched the animals charge past.

The vision faded and Amber spied Mari's beckoning hand extending down over the top of the rock wall.

Amber deftly climbed to the top to join Marisol, practically tackling her as she ascended. Hugging her friend, she proclaimed, "The animals and birds, they're safe! I saw it! I mean, I must've seen what one of the animals saw when they escaped!!! My mom was right, they made it into Simi before the fire got them!"

Marisol hugged Amber back fiercely as joyous tears streamed down her face. After another round of high-fives for the miraculous wildlife escape, Marisol asked, "You think maybe *you* told them to head north, and that's why they got out in time?"

"Oh." Amber grinned sheepishly as she kicked at the dirt. She'd not considered the possibility that she'd subconsciously connected with the animals and birds and passed along the turkey vulture's warning to flee north.

Suddenly uncomfortable, Amber looked around to see where they'd emerged from the arbor. She and Marisol stood upon a narrow stone ledge in between a towering cliff face and a small, secret meadow, not visible from any other location in the park. A dark depression high in the cliffs to the north marked Amber's salvation. The route taken by the girls brought them in from the south, above the natural rows descending into the basin. Columns of boulders lined the trail, leaving only the grey cliff walls visible.

The teens began a cautious descent, carefully picking their way in between rocks and around enormous obstacles that challenged the outsider to simply climb over, only to lead to a sheer drop-off or a confusing boulder maze on the other side. Marisol kept the cliffs to the west and steered the two onto what Amber knew was the correct path. The revelation of the hidden meadow had her considering how many other secret canyons and caves the wayward traveler might find himself in after following an innocuous-looking path, only to become lost despite the view of the San Fernando Valley promising a way home.

The downslope grew particularly steep, causing the girls to edge sideways around a single cottage-sized sandstone boulder. Upon rounding the stone, the grotto was revealed in ghostly moonlit splendor.

Mari and Amber stopped, briefly uncertain, before bolting down the remainder of the path. Eyes meeting in growing alarm, their attention shifted simultaneously to the oak. The once-enormous canopy was stripped bare of leaves and most of the smaller, outer branches in the crown were gone in choppy chunks, leaving a frayed knot in place of the sheltering umbrella. As they ran forward, moonlight clearly illuminated the burnt core in the center of the once hardy trunk.

Collapsing in an exhausted heap at the base, Amber privately felt the fool. Everything was rapidly changing around her: she'd moved away from her best friend she'd known since childhood, a school where she'd been well liked and a home where her parents had seemed happy. Now she was in completely unfamiliar territory where her life was spiraling out of control. Her mother could barely tolerate being in the same room with her father and her dog was close to the end of his life. Kids at school wanted to do her bodily injury just because of her hair color! Her guy friends would shun her if they knew about the boy she was consorting with. Despite his terrible reputation and contrary to common sense, she feared she had a crush on George Salvia, thereby setting herself up for bitter rejection at some point in the near future. Worst of all, she was receiving a hero's attention for accidentally not dying!

Now, some nefarious man in black was after her. She had no idea what to do; how to protect herself. If she really was a witch, she must be the worst one on the planet.

Sniffling, Amber checked her cell: 2:00 AM. What a frigging waste of time!

During Amber's inner rant, Marisol's eyes were transfixed on the oak. Tentatively, Marisol placed her palm inside the burnt shell. Eyes widening, she grasped Amber's palm with her other hand and placed it next to hers.

Thrum, thrum, thrum. Pulsating vibrations emanated from deep within the blackened shell of a trunk. The ancient tree had survived and was still drinking water. Amber quickly withdrew her palm, sitting back against the oak in a thoroughly bewildered state.

142

Marisol clapped her hands, marveling, "Wow!"

Nodding slowly, Amber considered the fact that the oak had made it out alive, just as she had. Yet in this strange and unfamiliar land, she felt alone, small and vulnerable as images of the flames licked up inside her head.

"What's wrong?" Marisol asked, concerned about her friend's shaking hands and faraway eyes.

Tears spilled down Amber's cheeks as she struggled to find the words, "Nothing. Everything! I don't know what to believe anymore."

Marisol's brow furrowed as she contemplated their situation. Decided, she placed her palm on the oak for silent guidance. After a few moments, she replied, "Whenever I was confused, I used to go to my grandmother. She always had the answers I needed. Maybe she can help?"

"No offense, but how do we ask your dead grandmother?" Amber inquired skeptically.

"I only saw Grandma Graciela do this once, and my mom would kill me if she knew about it. But I never forgot how the women reacted to what my grandmother saw. We just need to find the right place to put the water. Do you have any left?"

Producing a plastic bottle with a few ounces left in the bottom, Amber handed it to Mari, who used a branch to scrape away ash until she found a small circular depression at the base of the oak. Straggly dark shadows interlaced over the stone basin as moonlight streamed down through skeletal branches.

"What do we do now?" Amber asked.

"It's called *screeing*. We use the water to see into the past, present, or future. If there's something my grandma wants us to know, this is how we'll find out." Mari poured the meager contents of the water bottle into the little basin, adding, "And you're right, I don't know how to call up the dead." Shuddering at her ghastly thought, Marisol pondered, "I don't know that I want to do that." Inclining her head in the direction of the graveyard, she concluded, "there's hundreds of them not too far from here."

Sitting cross-legged on either side of the circular formation, the girls joined hands.

"Breathe with me and stare at the water. Then repeat after me," Marisol Garcia instructed. She began inhaling and exhaling in a slow, rhythmic manner that matched the *thrum, thrum, thrum* of the oak's underground water intake. Amber joined in the soulful chant of breath. Although neither of them touched the tree, the thrumming sound amplified with every breath until it united with them, a trio aligned in purpose. Moonlight streamed down in shards and flickered off the water like candlelight. Everything else faded away as they became an island in space and time.

Marisol spoke her grandmother's name: *Graciela Hernandez,* and then solemnly intoned a few words in Spanish, which Amber, trancelike, repeated.

The water shimmered briefly, light jarring and blurring to become one white, round image of the moon. The cold orb elongated and then disappeared to leave behind a dark, empty space.

Marisol's house burbled up onto the surface of the little pool. Everything looked the same as present day, including the horse paddocks, riding ring and the dirt driveway. It was night in the vision, and as there are no streetlights on Mari's road, the only feeble illumination came from the lighting at the house and barn.

The scene pulled back like a camera would to reveal the dirt road leading to the house. Here they received their first clue as to whether they were viewing past, present, or future.

A 1960's Chevy Stepside pickup truck was parked near the entrance, inside the property line. Its vibrant orange color was clearly visible, even in the darkness. It was not a vehicle Amber had ever seen at Marisol's house before and it looked new.

Snickering reached their ears, indicating some private joke being shared. Amber and Marisol twitched uncomfortably and the water in the little pool rippled slightly. Howling wailed from somewhere on the dirt road but it sounded...wrong, like someone trying to imitate a coyote.

Furtive, dark forms stealthily loped along the fence line, ten in all. Marisol and Amber were now able to remain still as the images played out in their mind's eye.

Sinewy figures gathered at the entrance to Mari's driveway. Weak light from the ranchero's entrance sign revealed faces: the invaders were a group of teenagers. Some of them were young men, but the majority were young women. Their faces were innocent, pretty and somehow familiar to both Amber and Mari.

The view shifted back to the house. At the open window stood a small girl with long, dark braided hair: Susanna Hernandez Garcia: *Marisol's mother.*

The thrumming of the oak as it drank deeply helped keep Marisol and Amber's breathing in time and the vision steady. Strangely detached from emotion, they continued to watch the events unfold.

The image inside the pool of water revealed a thin teenager with crazy eyes. When she spotted young Susanna Hernandez, she cocked her head to the side at an unnatural angle.

The strange movement caused little Susanna to withdraw slightly from the window.

The eerie teenager straightened her neck, cracking vertebrae, never taking her eyes off the youngster.

Susanna froze with her hand on the curtain, eyes wide with disbelief. The teenager with the wild eyes placed a finger to her lips and motioned for the group to advance toward the house, leading her pack to the edge of a circle of light cast off by the front porch lamp.

Just as the intruders neared the front porch steps, the door swung open to reveal a diminutive Latina: *Graciela Hernandez*. She appeared to have been interrupted while doing the dishes. Mrs. Hernandez casually dried her hands on a cheerily patterned apron.

The assembly began tittering with laughter as the wild-eyed teen spoke, "What did you tell Spahn? You shoulda stayed outta our business." Unsheathing a knife at her belt, her eyes grew foxy, lips frothy with desire for the hunt.

Susanna Hernandez remained at the window in a terrified stasis, little hands trembling as her fingers played unconsciously with the edge of the curtain.

"I told him you were bad people and that nothing good will come out of you being there," Graciela Hernandez sounded as if she were discussing plans for Sunday's after-service church luncheon. "It'd be best for you if you leave, *now*."

At first the group of young people looked incredulous at the demand, until a titter of laughter burst forth into outright guffaws.

"What'd ya do, did you go to the police?" the teen with the crazy eyes accused, menacing Graciela Hernandez with her knife.

The Latina on the porch did not respond; a slight twitch in her upper lip was the only indication she'd perhaps been listening.

From Marisol and Amber's perspective, something shifted in the scene, like when a computer reboots itself. When the scene righted itself, Graciela Hernandez looked *directly at them*.

Light streamed out through her eyes and chest. Her stature appeared to increase until her head nearly touched the rafters of the porch. Dark, luxurious braids framed the noble features of an Aztec warrior queen and tumbled down over strong shoulders. A wreath of wild cucumber vine adorned her hair. Her clothing was garlanded in native cordage decorated with Humboldt Lilies.

Graciela Hernandez was revealed as *La Bruja*, a powerful witch.

The pack gasped in unison and involuntarily threw their bodies on the ground before *La Bruja*. Only the teenage girl with the crazy eyes and a barrel-chested bearded man who's glazed appearance suggested he was under chemical influence remained standing.

The booming voice of La Bruja echoed from the hills, "Go back to wherever it is you are from."

Everyone covered his or her ears in response to excruciating pain. Despite a trickle of blood that ran from her right ear, the wild-eyed teenager's face remained stubborn.

"I offer amnesty to anyone who wants to leave this path to hell that *your master* is leading you down," La Bruja intoned. "If you abandon him now, you will get out in time."

Panic crossed the young leader's face as she turned the knife toward her companions. "Anyone who runs gets what's coming to them!" Her eyes were wild in desperation, thin line of spittle trailing from the corner of her mouth.

The others were hastily crawling backward in retreat, eyes downcast, limbs quivering, all save the crazy-eyed teen.

A child's high-pitched scream turned everyone's head away from the scene upon the porch. The fierce-looking, bearded man had torn the screen off the open window and yanked little Susanna Hernandez out into the yard.

"Enough talk!" he ordered as he jerked little Susanna roughly by the neck, forcing her to stand in the dirt next to the crazy-eyed leader.

JAMES TOSHIMA

CHAPTER 10

EMERGENCE

La Bruja turned toward the man holding Susanna Hernandez, her clothes subtly morphing from natural, native plants and materials to a long, dark, flowing cloak. As she shifted, a stark, skeletal form was revealed.

She smiled broadly, white skull gleaming from beneath her lovely mask. *La Bruja* had become Santa Muerte: Lady of Shadows.

Flames ignited from the back of her cloak, framing the skull, now wreathed with blood red Manzanita. One long, bony finger pointed in his direction and then flipped unnaturally backward.

The rushing beat of oncoming wings filled the air.

Eyes widening in horror, he looked up disbelievingly as a black vulture with a wingspan the size of two grown men swooped down and snatched shirt, belt, skin and bone in its claws and seized him up into the air. Flames were reflected against that terrible, blood red head.

A horrendous screech tore through the night air, mingled with the desperate screams of the man, borne away, on the wind.

Within moments, he was gone.

Another cry of pain erupted as the wild-eyed teen's knife arm was twisted and the weapon deftly snatched from her hand. A well-placed foot to her backside sent her sprawling in the dirt before Santa Muerte.

A tall boy of about twelve years old gently picked up Susanna Hernandez and placed her at the feet of Santa Muerte. Kneeling, he vowed, "I am now and forever, your servant."

The handsome boy then turned and looked directly at Marisol and Amber. As he deliberately caught and held their gaze, a deep shiver passed through each girl as the image in the booking photograph provided by Max became superimposed in their minds. With his shoulder-length blond hair, high cheekbones and aquiline Roman nose, they locked eyes with none other than a young *Robert Hugo Franklin*.

He only turned away after it appeared he was *certain* they'd recognized him.

Eyes mere slits and breathing labored, the teen with the crazy eyes spit dirt out of her mouth before she lifted herself, lizard-like, on all fours. In a flash, she was on her feet and bolting out of the yard, disappearing into the brush on the other side of the road.

The shared scene in their mind's eye and the water started to break apart, just as Marisol and Amber witnessed the pack running down the road.

Graciela Hernandez returned to herself and collapsed onto the porch, unconscious. Robert Hugo Franklin was at her side in an instant.

Before the image dissolved completely, little Susanna stood up and defiantly shouted to the retreating pack, "Tell your master he knows nothing about being *witchy*."

"Holy shit!" was all Amber could manage to stammer when the scene dissolved completely.

Marisol remained still, her young brow furrowed in concern before exhaling heavily, "Madre Maria!" She shook her head in disbelief, clearly having difficulty processing the horrific, long-ago events that she had just witnessed.

Cramped, the girls stiffly rose.

"We need to talk to my mom!" Mari concluded. "I don't even know what to think about all of this. What's up with Robert Franklin? In my house? Why did he want us to know? You saw how he looked at us!"

"What do you think he wants?" Amber asked.

"I don't know," Marisol contemplated the possibilities. "Grandma would've never let him in the house if he was bad! But no one's ever mentioned him!"

"I wonder when he left? I mean, he said he'd stay with her forever! But then he ends up at *my house*, then jail!"

Marisol shook her head in frustration. "Amber, this can't be a coincidence, you, a Bruja moving here, then finding out about a missing girl, who just happened to go missing because of this guy! I think maybe he betrayed grandma, and now she's trying to warn us! Otherwise I woulda heard about him!"

"So that redhead's a witch?" a disbelieving Louis Garcia shook his head, unable to make sense of what his sister and her new friend were up to in the middle of the night out in the Simi Hills.

"Will you shut up?" Jonah Abernathy hushed him from their hiding place behind some boulders, "They're gonna hear us!"

The guys had been checking out the old Stagecoach Trail for likely escape routes that Fernando Salvia may have taken after the gold heist. The task was proving more daunting than they'd initially thought. Atop the Santa Susana Pass lay half a dozen escape routes. One likely possibility included disappearing into the vastness of nearby Simi Valley. As it was late and they had snuck out after dark, they descended the Stagecoach Trail and decided to explore a southerly branch near the bottom. They'd been checking it out when they heard voices and decided to investigate.

When the retreating forms of the girls were no longer visible, James Toshima remarked, "I knew she was holding back!" Deciding it was time to share what he witnessed at the Twelve Apostles, James revealed his suspicions that Amber McBride *ordered* the birds to attack Ben Salvia.

Seth chimed in, "Yea, it happened pretty much like Jimbo said." Turning to Luis, he asked, "So, you had Malfoy living with your granny?"

"Don't even," Luis menaced, "we don't know what's what. My sister's right, no one's ever mentioned this asswipe!"

The boys argued the entire way back about the meaning of Luis' grandmother taking Robert Hugo Franklin into her home. As they walked, the conversation quickly turned to the possible applications of this newly discovered talent called *screeing*, particularly in relation to finding the fabled Salvia treasure.

Mrs. Susanna Hernandez Garcia awoke early, unable to sleep again following the recurring childhood nightmare that forced her to relieve the evening when everything changed between her and her mother. Mrs. Garcia was a "change of life" baby and ten years younger than the sibling nearest her in age, so she'd been the only one home with her mother the night the cult invaded the Hernandez Ranch. Her father was away with her older brothers at the rodeo.

Mrs. Garcia had witnessed firsthand the lack of interest by her brothers in the craft. Like their father, their calling lay with the rodeo. Even though Susana had been very young, her mother hadn't been able to hide her disappointment.

As the youngest and last best chance to carry on the great Las Brujas tradition, Graciela Hernandez provided little Susana with patient instruction. Initially, it appeared that Susana had natural abilities and progressed in her studies. Her confidence grew and family gossipers reported she had the makings of a great Bruja.

Thinking of that horrid Robert Hugo Franklin made Mrs. Susana Garcia want to smash something, preferably his smug, arrogant face. The moment he showed up, it was as if her power started draining away. The more she thought about it in retrospect, she was sure he'd connived a way to steal her talents. Mrs. Garcia morphed from promising student into abject failure. When she'd sought help from her mother, she was politely rebuffed. The message was quite clear, however: Graciela Hernandez was enamored with her star pupil Robert Franklin and had no time for disappointment. The rejection drove a wedge between Mrs. Garcia and her mother that was never subsequently bridged.

Mrs. Garcia thought about the fact that Robert Hugo Franklin eventually abandoned the Hernandez home, only to end up at the House on Lizard Hill. Now Amber McBride lived at the same house; another outsider appearing on the scene to wreak havoc on the Garcia-Hernandez Family.

∞

Afternoon sun streamed through the glass, casting bright rays into Amber's eyes as she awoke. Grasping for her missing body part, her mobile phone informed her that it was 1:00 in the afternoon. "Mari, wake up, it's after lunch!"

"After the night we had, I'm not surprised," Marisol grumbled.

Pushing back the sheets, Amber exclaimed, "No way can my mom see us like this."

The bed sheets were black with soot and filth from the evening's adventure, as were their legs and feet. Amber gathered up the sheets and stuffed them into the bottom of her hamper, intending to launder them later when she could be certain her mother wasn't around. The mere act of Amber doing her own laundry would send up warning flags to her mother that something was afoot.

As she showered, Amber thought about the force Marisol's grandmother had wielded. The idea of being so powerful was both tantalizing and terrifying. Toweling dry, she put on clean clothes and rejoined Marisol. Her friend had already confirmed with the Garcia's that Amber was allowed to come over and spend Saturday night. After Marisol showered, the girls walked with Kibbles across the courtyard to the kitchen.

"I bet we can scree to solve the mystery of Lucy's disappearance!" Mari realized.

"Yea, you're right!" Amber agreed as they entered the kitchen. "After we talk to your mom. I want to know what happened with that Robert Hugo Franklin. It's all just too weird." Amber called out, "Hey, anybody home?"

A half-grunt, half "yes" sounded from her father's office. Amber motioned for Mari to stay behind as she rounded the corner to find her father at his computer, appearing uncharacteristically disheveled.

"Dad, are you okay?"

"I didn't sleep well last night," he responded groggily.

"Where's mom?"

"She went out," he responded in a flat monotone.

Unsure what to do, Amber asked, "Mind if I go to Mari's?"

Her father waved her away, so Amber vacated the room feeling like her father had sucked the life out of her day. She friggin' hated pitying a grown man! If Marisol's grandmother knew how to transform into the Lady of Shadows, maybe she and Mari could acquire similar abilities, like how to make her father man up?

Hastily gathering energy bars and water bottles from the pantry, they headed to Marisol's. Mindful of the harrowing vision, the girls paused at the ranchero driveway. Rather than appearing ominous, in the full light of day the house looked cheerful with its deep russet Spanish tiles and bright adornments around the windows and doors.

"Hey there, mija,[14] where's the love?" A compact, muscular man wearing a cowboy hat and dusty boots hailed Marisol as he walked from the barn. A toothy grin greeted Amber as he hugged his daughter. "Jorge Garcia, nice to meet you!" Unlike George Salvia, Marisol's father's name was pronounced, "*hor-hay.*"

"Dad, I gotta talk to mom, it's important!" Mari squeaked as she dislodged herself from his grasp.

"Okay, okay, always in a hurry." Mr. Garcia shook his head good-naturedly as the girls bolted for the house.

Unnoticed by Mr. Garcia or the girls, Luis and his friends snuck out from the barn and circled behind the house to enter through the back door.

Bursting through the front door, Marisol sent it slamming into the opposite wall as she hollered for her mother.

"Lo que?"[15] Mrs. Garcia rushed out to greet the girls in the entryway, wondering what teenage calamity had befallen Lake Manor.

"Um..." Mari paused, unsure how to begin.

"Start with your dreams, all week," Amber encouraged her.

Ushering the girls into the living room to be seated, Mrs. Garcia bade Marisol continue. None of them heard the four boys silently creep into the hallway from the backyard. Marisol proceeded to relate how she had dreamed of her grandmother and how they had gone to the grotto oak last night. She eyed her mother cautiously before diving into the story of the strange band of teenagers threatening the Hernandez-Garcia Ranch.

Throughout the tale, Mrs. Garcia remained stone-faced.

Mari concluded with, "Mom, we were so scared for you!"

When Mrs. Garcia finally spoke, her voice was condescending; "Nice story, but it never happened."

Δ

After Amber left and Luis' friends had been sent home, Mrs. Garcia confronted her daughter with, "Mija, I know you've been running around at night."

"Mom!" Marisol protested, but her mother cut her off.

"I expect that of your brother, but you? You're a good girl. It's that *Amber*, she's a bad influence..."

Luis walked into the kitchen as his mother was lecturing, interrupting, "What'd ya mean, expect it of me? What'd I do?"

"Be quiet, this isn't about you!" Mrs. Garcia ordered as Marisol simultanesouly told him to shut up and get out.

Turning back to her mother, Marisol accused, "You're not being fair,

---

[14] Spanish for 'little girl'
[15] Spanish for 'what's wrong?'

mom! And you won't let us talk about grandma! It's like she never even existed!"

Luis chimed in, "That redhead's weird! She's got Marisol talking smack about Bruja this and Bruja that…"

As Marisol stared at her brother, wondering how he knew this, he realized he'd revealed too much and shut up. Glaring at Luis, Marisol's features hardened. For a moment, he thought he glimpsed a skull beneath her angry face.

Shuddering, Luis was reminded of the one woman and witch he truly feared: Graciela Hernandez. His mother was right to ban all mention of his grandmother. Whereas others saw a kindly old woman, Luis believed he and his mother were the only two people to see through the mask to the monster beneath. To Luis, Graciela Hernandez was Santa Muerte 24/7. He'd only been able to sleep without nightmares after she died.

Mrs. Garcia's face grew taut as she threatened, "Enough! Your father and I have talked about how Castle Peak High School may not be the best place for you. You keep getting into trouble, we'll pull you out and send you to St. Bea's. Comprende?"[16]

Marisol bit her lip as she sadly nodded.

Seth invited the guys over to watch an Indonesian martial arts movie called *Raid Redemption*. Upon seeing the main character, Rama, a diminutive, unassuming Asian law enforcement officer, Luis scoffed, "C'mon, dude! What is this, a comedy?"

Luis was quickly silenced, however, when Rama fought his way, at times bare-handed, through several levels of a nefarious apartment building housing evil doers that'd be at home in the deepest of Dante's seven levels of hell.

Completely forgetting his earlier pronouncement, Luis announced, "THAT WAS AWESOME!" when the motion picture concluded. "Where'd you find this movie?"

"I didn't find it," Seth responded, "*it* found me!"

"My kinda guy," James Toshima concluded, happy to see a tough Asian star that really knew his stuff. "Imagine Rama and your dad in a movie, together!" he suggested to Jonah.

Fired up, Jonah insisted, "Imagine us being tough like Rama and doing something to help the girls!"

"You heard my mom!" Luis countered for the umpteenth time, "She said it never happened!"

"Bullshit!" James countered. "I think the girls need our help!"

---

[16] Spanish for 'understand?'

"How're we going to ask them for help finding the treasure if we aren't gonna help them?" Seth pondered. "Amber had our backs when the Salvia brothers were after us at the Twelve Apostles!"

"What they need to do is listen to my mom and stay away from each other!" Luis fumed.

"Wait a sec," Jonah countered, "if nothing happened, then why'd your mom tell Mari to stay away from Amber?"

"Because she's bad luck!" Luis retorted, causing Jonah to snort and accuse, "When did you lose your 'nads?"

Luis paused in shock before contorting with rage as he dove across Seth's living room floor in an attempt to take down the tall boy.

Hearing the scuffle, Ms. Tammy Lobata appeared in the doorway. "Boys! Knock it off or y'all can go home right now!"

"This is a waste of time," James muttered as he walked out.

ΑΩ

Amber eagerly awaited the arrival of Noelle, Marisol and Slone for a sleepover at her house. As Marisol's mother banned her from the McBride's, Noelle had cleverly orchestrated the ruse that Marisol would be staying at the Mertens house.

They hoisted their bags and headed off to Amber's room. Slone's hand touched the doorknob from the kitchen to the living room when Amber stopped her, "Not that way, let's cut across the courtyard."

Depositing their overnight bags, the friends decamped with the dog to the den for a movie. Slone immediately hopped behind the bar and made motions of pouring drinks, including pretending to chug a bottle of tequila.

Amber pointed out the sliding door in the direction of the master bedroom and informed her guests that her parents could see right into the den, thereby knowing exactly what they were up to.

Fulfilling her hostess obligations, Amber also pointed out the location of the hall bathroom. She was relieved to see the door in between the hallway and the living room firmly shut.

After midnight, four heads began to droop.

Around 3:00 in the morning, Slone awoke in need of the bathroom. The light from the courtyard lamps had gone off automatically after midnight. Pale moonlight spilled in through the sliding glass doors and across the hardwood floor, guiding her passage to the Chinese guest bathroom in the hallway.

Finishing quickly, Slone washed her hands and shut off the faucet's tap as sounds of music and laughter reached her ears. Poking her head out into the hallway, intent on shutting off the TV, her eyes met a blank screen. Slone slowly turned her head in the direction of the noise, whispering to herself, "No friggin' way!"

Sprinting over to her friends, she batted them about the head with throw pillows.

A few coarse phrases were hurled in her direction, but she persisted until the girls were sitting up, rubbing the sleep out of their eyes.

Amber instantly woke up when she spotted Kibbles standing near the door, throat rumbling in a low growl, also alerting Marisol that something was gravely amiss.

"What the hell..." Noelle began and then stopped, as she, too, heard the dog's menacing growl, overlaid by loud talking, laughing and music. Leaping up, Noelle stated, "What are you waiting for? There's a party in your living room!" Looking around in dismay at her compatriots when she realized that she was the only one enthusiastically headed toward the door, she entreated, "What's wrong with the rest of you?"

"Are you nuts?!!" Slone stammered. "We don't know who's in there!"

"Join hands!" Amber commanded, her take-charge manner shutting everyone up immediately, "Whatever happens, *do not let go!*" For added security, she placed herself on one end and Marisol at the other. Only Noelle had an eager, Girl-Scout ready look.

"Ready?" Marisol queried the four.

Slone shook her head, but Noelle exclaimed, "Let's do this!"

Slowly placing her hand over the knob, Amber turned and pushed open the door in between the hallway and the formal, old-fashioned living room, just as Tears for Fears lamented in lusciously haunting tenor from *Working Hour* about the paralyzing effect of fear...

The now brightly lit room was filled with young people, dressed in vibrant colors of hot pink, neon green and pumped-up blue. Mullets abounded on the men and the girls wore hairstyles alternating between sporty and enormously poufy.

Everyone fell silent. The music screeched to a stop when the four entered and all heads swiveled toward the newcomers. No one noticed when the dog immediately bolted over to the fireplace.

Noelle inclined her head toward an intense, raven-haired Latina. Blue eyeliner accented haunting, dark eyes. Ignoring Noelle, her eyes swept over to Amber in one, jerky motion and locked on her face. The Latina remarked bitterly, "After all these years! What do you have to say for yourself?"

Amber was taken aback. She had no idea what to say. She didn't know the teenager. How could she? She hadn't been born until 1997!

The mannequin-like partygoers did not appear to be breathing. Chests did not rise and fall with each intake of breath. Stiff arms were bent at angles to balance drinks and cigarettes mid-air in macabre display.

No one twitched or even blinked as both sides stared at the other in frozen silence.

Only Slone noticed Marisol's features harden. When she spoke, her voice sounded older than the sophomore Slone knew.

To Amber's ears, she heard a voice that sounded much like Marisol's grandmother command, "Step forward, you who has summoned us."

"Hola *Senora Hernandez.*" A deep, sonorous voice responded to Marisol in Spanish, booming from across the room.

In the general pandemonium that ensued, many things happened at once.

The ghostly assembly turned in robotic unison toward the back of the room, in the direction of the speaker.

Slone shrieked, "Hell no!" Roughly shaking off her friends' hands, she bolted out of the room in a panic.

In the split second that Noelle, Mari and Amber regrouped to join hands again, they spied a man near the nature preserve fence. Dark shadows gathered around him; he appeared to unfold.

The ghostly partygoers scattered, disappearing into walls and the floor.

A young blond woman, who the girls took to be Lucy, stood vulnerably alone at the fireplace. Kibbles stood protectively in front of her. Bizarrely, Lucy's legs disappeared *into* the slate bench in front of the fireplace. She stared at the shadowy figure in the nature preserve. Then, Lucy Carpenter crumpled and vanished.

The doorway from the kitchen burst open and Dr. McBride charged in, red hair sticking up crazily at all angles. He sent the door crashing into the built-in bookcase and knocked books off the shelves. The ruckus brought Kibbles around with a start, right before he was readying to leap through the window in an effort to bring down Shadow Man.

Blinking hard from the glare, every light was ablaze in the living room, assaulting his eyes just roused from sleep. Dr. McBride shouted, "What on *God's green earth* is going on in here?!"

"We heard someone outside!" quick-thinking Noelle pointed out the window.

Amber's father peered out, then looked closely at the corner of the bay window, jaw setting into a tight line as he bent down for a better look. The girls crowded around to see what it was that had caught his attention.

The corner square pane of glass had been shattered, pointy shards littering the window seat.

Turning forcefully on his heel, Dr. McBride grabbed a Maglite and marched out the door, girls trailing behind. "Stay inside!" he ordered in no uncertain terms, leaving Kibbles behind to stand guard.

No one wanted to remain in the living room other than Noelle, so the teens rushed to the sliding glass door in the den, trying to get a glimpse of what Dr. McBride was doing.

"Um, where's Slone?" Amber asked. The three looked frantically around, wildly hoping she would somehow materialize out from behind a couch. Quickly realizing how silly this was, Amber grabbed her friends' hands and they ran en masse to her room. Amber frantically wracked her brain, trying to remember if she'd locked the outer door after they'd come in from the party.

Amber's room lay empty. Her door was wide-open.

Racing to the den's sliding glass door, she collided with her father, returning from his investigation outside.

"I found footprints in the dirt, from a man's shoe, under the window. It was broken from the outside," he informed them, simultaneously pulling out his cell phone to call the police.

Grasping her father's arm, Amber inadvertently yanked the cell from his ear as she shrieked, "Slone's gone!"

Remaining calm, her father advised, "See if you can get her on her cell."

All three friends tried to reach Slone on her mobile, to no avail.

Dr. McBride strode down the hall to Amber's room, where he shut and locked her door. On his return, he secured the door from the hallway to the courtyard. The French-style doors were pathetically flimsy and inadequate to the task of keeping intruders out.

"I'm going out to look for Slone. Come with me," Dr. McBride ordered.

The teen trio and dog followed Amber's father back through the living room as he called 9-1-1.

"Holy shit!" Amber exclaimed.

Covering the phone, her father chastised, "Language, Amber!"

"Where's mom?!" The stress in his daughter's voice indicated she was on the verge of panic.

Completing the emergency call, Dr. McBride ushered the three into the master closet, ignoring Amber's question, "Lock the door behind you. Don't open it for anyone but me. Call me on your cell if you need me."

Amber hugged him fiercely.

"I mean it. Don't open this door for anyone but me."

She watched her father walk out the hallway door leading to the courtyard as she shut the closet door, bolting it with a click.

The three slumped down upon the carpet. Kibbles instinctually situated his body protectively in between the girls and the doorway, remaining at the ready upon his haunches.

Noelle exhaled heavily and demanded, "Start talking. I want to know EVERYTHING!"

Mari looked to Amber, who stared at the door through which her father had exited moments earlier.

"How is my dad going to take on Shadow Man?" Amber worried, "He needs us! We can't just sit around in here and do nothing!"

"Wait a sec, you mean that guy by the fence?" Noelle asked. "I don't think he can get near *your house*, Amber! It looked like an invisible wall stopped him when he got to the edge of your yard!"

"What?" Marisol asked, "Are you sure?"

"It looked like he ran into a sliding glass door! That's all I saw. But you haven't told me anything! Marisol, how could you hold back from me? You and I have been best friends since elementary school!" Noelle accused, causing an exchange of guilty glances between Mari and Amber.

"Noelle," Amber began, "you'll just think we're crazy."

Noelle laughed outright. "You're shitting me! After what we just saw?"

Looking anxiously to Marisol, silent agreement passed between the two. Neither had been able to make sense of what Brigid or Senora de la Sombras meant to them. The full telling of these incidents would have to come at another time. Perhaps it was best just to tell a short-end Graphic Comic Book version of the story for now.

"It started when Mari and I went to this place called the grotto in the state park and all these animals showed up," Amber began…

∞

Under the shadowed eaves, Dr. McBride stayed close to the wall as he moved. The funk of depression instantly shaken off, his senses were sharper than they'd been in a long while.

His wife's room had been empty when he'd gone to check on her. The smaller of the two guest rooms was empty as well. Yet their two vehicles were side-by-side in the driveway.

Mrs. McBride was not in the house, so where the hell was she?

Dr. McBride quickly checked the garage and his adjoining man cave, knowing, even as he did so, that both would be empty.

Scanning the driveway for any sign of movement, he skirted across the front of the garage and back up the stairs to the front door. Crouching down, he slunk along the southern, outer arm of the house's U shape, under the windows of the two guest rooms and down and around the lip of the pool jutting out into the skyline above his head.

Tiny insects skittered off into corners when Dr. McBride shone his Maglite onto their spiny bodies in the women's changing room. The light reflected blearily from the marred vanity mirror over the once-grand dressing table, now sagged and bowed with age and neglect.

He clicked off the light and kept his back to the wall, moving along to what was once the outer bathroom, listening intently for any sign of life before closing in.

Empty.

Only the men's changing room remained. Breathing deeply of the night air that still stank of soot, he pressed on. Steadying the bat in his right hand before breaching the entrance, the flashlight revealed dirty corners in the dank little hideaway. Cobwebs fluttered gracefully in the dilapidated changing stalls. The stained yellow tiles in the shower reflected a shine of light here and there, reminders of the luxury that once was.

Immediately an unforgettable smell registered in sensory memory, something he had only smelled once and hoped to never smell again: *death*. Dr. McBride had been asked to do a six-week stint abroad after Kuwait's liberation by allied forces from Iraq. It was the only time, until recently, that he'd been separated from his wife Michelle. On a road connecting the two countries that would later become known as the Highway of Death, he'd seen horrors etched indelibly into his brain. Worst of all was the horrific and unforgettable smell of burning flesh that filled his nostrils, gagging and choking him.

Crickets chirped loudly, their tinny little calls echoing off the stone beneath the pool.

Dr. McBride found himself now facing the nature preserve, the source of the putrid scent.

Out in the meadow, a young, blond woman stood vulnerably alone. Her head hung down and her shoulders were slumped.

"Slone?"

Her back to Dr. McBride, she ignored him, instead slowly raising her head in the direction of the large, stony hill overlooking the house.

"Slone! Come out of there!" Dr. McBride demanded as he ran down to the gate and began unlocking it, flabbergasted at how she had managed to get out beyond the fence.

Poppin' bottles and f----- models... rudely pierced the night air, causing Dr. McBride to drop the lock and bang his elbow painfully into the gate, adding a curse word of his own to the refrain.

"Slone, where are you?"

Another male voice yelled out to Slone from far away, clearly perturbed at being disturbed in the middle of the night.

Rustling, crunching and snapping sounds were the answer.

"What the *hell* are you doing in the bushes? Get in the car!"

An angry dad voice floated over the hill from the end of their driveway, too far from where Dr. McBride stood to see what was happening.

"Dad! Thank God you're here!" Slone Summers sobbed hysterically, followed by the slam of a car door as it screeched away.

Turning back to where the *other* blonde girl had stood in the meadow, Dr. McBride found only the burnt, stubbly remains of the blaze's leavings.

The ghastly stench of burnt flesh had dissipated.

A loud siren's blare was next to rent the silence. Sprinting down the driveway and around the hill to the gate, Dr. McBride opened it for the police car.

"Evening Dr. McBride." Officer Gutiérrez greeted him from the backseat. Officer Johnson sat next to a young Asian officer in the driver's seat. "We were just clocking out when we heard the call come in and thought we'd tag along with Officer Huang here."

✝

Officer Gutiérrez beckoned for Dr. McBride to hop in the back next to him as Officer Johnson pleasantly bade him good evening, strange under the circumstances. Explaining their predicament during the brief drive back to the house, Dr. McBride was rewarded with Gutiérrez' confirmation, "You did the right thing. Show us where the girls are. Let's make sure they're safe and then we'll search the house."

Leading the officers up the long set of stairs to the front door, Huang waved him aside, hand resting on his holster. Motioning Dr. McBride back behind him, Huang placed his hand upon the knob.

It swung open before he could turn the brass handle, to reveal Mrs. McBride. "The girls are right here. I'll show you," she informed LAPD. Knocking upon the closet door, Mrs. McBride called to the girls.

"Is dad with you?" Amber anxiously inquired.

Confirming his presence, the door was thrown open as Amber hurtled into her parents' arms. "Slone?" she pressed.

"Her dad picked her out up front," Dr. McBride reassured the teenagers.

"Why don't all you folks stay in here while we search the place?" Officer Huang suggested. "Keep the door locked, we'll be back when we're done."

Dr. McBride nodded and ushered his wife, Amber and the girls back inside.

The officers proceeded to search the house and grounds thoroughly, confirming that a male suspect had been spying from outside the living room and that the windowpane had been broken from the outside in.

"Think it's a peeping Tom?" Officer Johnson soberly pondered.

"Maybe, could be some local perv who wanted a look at the girls," Officer Gutiérrez remarked.

"It doesn't look like a typical break-in. Maybe McBride scared him off," Officer Huang concluded.

As they continued around the backside of the pool and checked the old changing rooms, Officer Huang remarked, "I know I'm pretty new to LAPD, but have you guys ever had to go out on call like this? I mean, I know my partner's probably not coming back; he'll be out on permanent disability, but why weren't there any officers around tonight to take this call?"

"You ever think that maybe it's you?" Officer Johnson joked.

Seeing the crestfallen look on the young Asian officer's face, Gutiérrez countered, "You're right, it *is* strange. I've never heard of helicopter pilots being called out in a squad car, but we're happy to do it." Grinning, he slapped Huang on the back for reassurance.

"Dang, this place is big! I can't believe I didn't know this was here, seeing as how *we Johnsons* founded Chatsworth. I bet this was something, back in the day," Johnson marveled.

"Yeah, yeah, California belonged to La Raza before you Johnsons invaded Chatsworth, so who was *really* here first?" Gutiérrez kidded, on the square.

The officers circled to the stables, but found them empty, leaving the garage and adjoining workspace. Entering through the back door, Officer Huang pressed the garage door button in an attempt to both open it and trigger the interior light, but was rewarded with only a sick whirring sound.

When no one tried to bolt past them for the door, strong flashlights illuminated the interior, revealing piles of moving boxes atop wooden tables and dust motes disturbed by their intrusion.

A dark, gaping opening in the wall near the floor to the left caught Officer Huang's attention. "What do we have here?" Crouching down to take a closer look, he motioned for Gutiérrez to angle his flashlight over.

White wooden doors opened inward into a darkened cavern. Hanging onto the left side of the opening for balance, Officer Huang leaned in and reached into the darkness with his right flashlight-hand.

One minute, Gutiérrez witnessed Huang balanced precariously at the edge of crawl space, his back to him as his thin frame partially blocked the entrance. Light flared briefly and then flashed into Gutiérrez' eyes as Officer Huang folded over and was *flung* backwards, sprawling onto the garage floor.

Gutiérrez and Johnson drew their guns and pointed their flashlights down into the darkness of the crawl space. Looking between the strange storage area and Huang, Gutiérrez quickly checked the officer for injuries.

Relieved to find none, the officers carefully helped a pale, sweaty, shaky Officer Huang to his feet and walked him outside to gently sit back against a young oak tree.

"What's the matter, man? What happened?"

"Uh, um, I think I must have food poisoning from that BBQ joint I ate at earlier. Bad cramps, you know?" Face flushed, he averted their eyes.

Gutiérrez was mystified. Huang's body had *recoiled*, as if he had been struck. Clearing his throat, Gutiérrez said, "Hey don't worry about it. You want me to call you in sick?"

"Nah, let's just finish this thing and get out of here." Cradling his head between clammy palms, Huang waved them off.

"Okay, we're going to clear that crawl space and the man cave next to the garage." As the officers stood, Gutiérrez thought he saw momentary panic in Huang's eyes. Aiming for levity, he joked, "I'll be right back. Holler if you need someone to stand guard when you use the bathroom."

Gutiérrez propped the garage door open with a large sandstone rock lying nearby. The moon didn't provide much light, but it was better than the alternative. Illuminating the entrance to the crawl space with his flashlight, he found a narrow built-in ladder leading down to an earthen floor below ground level. Although the entrance was small and required hunching over to get in, the room appeared large enough to stand once you reached the bottom. The ceiling was the underside of the house, kept in place by thick, dark wooden beams. Concrete block walls lined three sides, except for the wall facing the nature preserve, which was brick.

The strange space was filled with jumbled junk: piles of broken furniture, doors and twisted metal all haphazardly strewn about: lots of places to hide.

The beam of the flashlight came to rest on a footprint in the dirt that appeared to be the same size and shape as the prints found outside.

Officer Gutiérrez sat back on his heels for a moment, weighing his options. Descending that ladder would leave him completely exposed, with his back to whomever might be lying in wait. Decided, Gutiérrez asked Johnson to hold the flashlight and light up as much of the strange space as possible. Facing the entrance, he jumped, gun drawn, in one leap, to the bottom.

His legs shuddered upon impact, given the drop of over five feet to the dirt floor. But even beyond the impact of the jump, something *changed* perceptibly when he crossed the threshold. It began quietly, niggling at the edge of his consciousness. Unintelligible at first, it increased in volume until his ears identified the sound and provided a label: *whispering*.

Gun in hand, he spun around and tried to locate the source. Pacing around trash piles, no one jumped out to attack him.

"You okay down there?" a worried Officer Johnson asked from above, sounding very far away.

The whispering grew more insistent. Gutiérrez was able to catch snippets.

Juliana

Bumping his shin painfully on a ragged piece of outstretched metal, Gutiérrez caused the entire heap to shift and groan. Spinning around, he backed against the brick wall, right where the footprints ended.

Juliana was his wife's name.

Whispering echoed around the room from all sides, rising to a crescendo.

She's going to burn

Unreasonable, crazy, overwhelming panic flooded Gutiérrez, urging him to flee, to escape this dank hole in the ground as quickly as possible. Racing back across the dirt floor, he scampered up the ladder and threw his body over the top and into the garage.

Officer Johnson was at his side immediately, helping him to his feet and out the door. "What happened down there?" Johnson asked.

"Not here," Gutiérrez whispered to Johnson. Exiting the garage, Gutiérrez leaned against the open door for support and asked, "Hey Huang, you sure you didn't see or hear anything in that crawl space?"

Looking up at the flyboys, Officer Huang's pale face glistened with sweat. "What, you guys start believing in ghosts or something? Let's get outta here, I feel like shit."

Officer Gutiérrez' suspicion was confirmed. Huang clearly experienced something similar to what he had, but didn't want to talk about it for fear of having his sanity questioned. He needed time to think, to try and make sense of what he'd experienced, before speaking to Johnson about it.

Having checked the property and finding no perpetrators, the officers liberated the McBride family, pup and guests from the master bedroom.

"How about I take you girls home?" Mrs. McBride suggested.

Marisol looked anxiously to Noelle, who countered, "The Garcia's are out of town this weekend and were going to pick Mari up at my house on Sunday anyway. We can just go back to my place."

To their great relief, Mrs. McBride agreed and the teenagers walked back with Amber to her room to gather their belongings.

A now-recovered Officer Huang informed Dr. McBride, "Call us if anything else happens, if you see anyone, or anything else suspicious occurs." He handed Dr. McBride a business card with his contact information.

Officer Gutiérrez found himself clearing his throat again before saying, "By the way, that crawl space in the garage…"

"You got the door open?" Dr. McBride scratched his head. "How'd you manage that? I couldn't get it to budge."

Gutiérrez eyes narrowed, but then widened as Johnson asked, "Dr. McBride, do you happen to have the plans for this house?"

Dr. McBride sighed, "I wish I did. I got absolutely no information about this place when I bought it. Nothing." Curious about the officers' interest, he queried, "Why do you ask?"

Gutiérrez gave Dr. McBride a greatly truncated version of events: of finding the doors open, footprints crossing the floor and improbably, disappearing into a wall.

Dr. McBride shuddered, stating, "There's a lot of weirdness here. I just wish it wasn't every day."

"Got a way to bolt that thing shut from the outside?" Officer Huang offered.

"Yeah, I think I do. Do you guys mind sticking around while I take care of this?" Dr. McBride asked. Spying his wife emerging from the larger guestroom he added, "Can we keep this just between us, for now? I don't want to frighten the girls."

Nodding in unison, the officers waited patiently as Mrs. McBride departed with Noelle and Marisol. Amber, not wanting to be left alone, asked if she could sleep on the window seat in her father's room with Kibbles, to which he readily consented. "I'll be back in a sec, honey. I'm going to see the officers to the door." Kissing Amber on the forehead, he covered her with a blanket, her hazel eyes wearily closing as the first, pinkish strands of sunlight peeped over the horizon. Dr. McBride checked the time: 5:00 A.M. Not since his stint abroad had he been up all night and in the midst of such turmoil.

Fatigued, Dr. McBride retrieved his drill from his man cave and set it down upon the garage floor. The officers watched carefully as Dr. McBride reached into the dark to pull the doors shut.

Dr. McBride didn't flinch.

Pacing back and forth inside Castle Peak's hidden cavern, Shane questioned, "Why is this so hard? She's a kid! This should've been done already!" Looking at his arms, he felt only slightly reassured to find his burns healed, thanks to the elixir of life within the stone basin.

A sibilant voice hissed, "Patience. She has powerful allies. You are growing stronger. Soon, she shall be yours."

KENDRICK SALVIA

CHAPTER 11

SYNTHESIS

Amber, Noelle and Marisol agreed that they needed to get a handle on the insanity. The question was: what, exactly, to do?

Because Mrs. Susanna Garcia had frowned on any discussion of what she considered the old ways in her home, Marisol had little to no knowledge of what must have been formidable skills from Graciela Hernandez. Her experience with ghosts, to date, had been with the likes of Director John Ford: those that chose to stay on in the Simi Hills because, to them, *it was heaven.*

Amber's experience prior to moving to SoCal had been with a different type of ghost: the lost. In particular, she and Shelby had only encountered lost children. Amber was especially puzzled as to why the Latina from the '80's had reacted so angrily to her when they had never met before.

Desperate for answers, Amber went online to try to find out how to vanquish Shadow Man. She encountered dead end after dead end. One website for a man claiming to be a wiccan elder suggested sitting cross-legged in the center of the room and meditating in an attempt to communicate with the dead, in order to find out the deceased' intent.

However, he offered no advice for what to do, whereupon walking into the center of an entire roomful of ghosts, all of who resolutely refused to speak to you. The useless crackpot had nothing to say on the subject of tackling a potential demon hanging around outside one's living room window. Amber smirked as she envisioned flashing Shadow Man the peace sign. Maybe if she'd started chanting *ohm,* one of the 80's partygoers would have put out a cigarette on her head?

This was, by far, the stupidest thing she had read all day. Clearly, none of these people had ever actually encountered a ghost, let alone a demon! Like all wannabe's and grifters, the symbols sold had nothing to do with the reality. They were simply purveyors of empty promises and useless trinkets, potions, sage bundles and salt lamps designed to relieve the gullible of their money.

Buzzing indicated an incoming message. Amber picked up her cell phone and read a text from Marisol, who'd also included Noelle:

We must ask my grandmother

Noelle had already responded: *When? Where?*

Saturday at the grotto

Feeling much more optimistic now that a plan was in place, Amber realized that they were following the ghost playbook she'd developed with Shelby over the years by seeking assistance from the elders.

The girls fashioned the most reliable and oldest teen disappearing gambit: Marisol would be spending the night at Noelle's house and Noelle at Amber's house. The plan was to meet at Amber's at 6:00 and then head over to the grotto. It would be dusk by the time they reached the oak and any park visitors, not that they ever saw any, would have cleared out by then.

Opening her laptop, Amber dialed Shelby. They'd not spoken 'virtually' face to face in nearly two weeks, a record for the best friends. She answered and to Amber's surprise, a handsome boy squeezed onto the chair next to her.

"Hey Anton, how goes it?" Amber greeted an old friend, a boy she and Shelby had known since middle school.

"Hi Amber. Liking it down in SoCal?"

"Yeah, um, it's great. So, uh, you two? How long?"

"A couple of weeks," Shelby beamed, answering Amber's question as to why the two best friends hadn't connected during this time.

Amber had always been honest with Shelby, but couldn't put words to the mixed emotions she currently experienced. Instead, she said cheerily, "You two make a really cute couple. When's homecoming? Are you going?"

Shelby answered yes, and proudly informed Amber that Anton had made first string on the JV football team.

"Wow. Do some damage in the Homecoming game!" Amber was unaware that the JV team doesn't play in the Homecoming game.

Crackling sounds from the intercom interrupted the conversation and Mrs. McBride's voice cut through the static with, "Amber, dinner."

"Gotta go," Amber bid her friends goodbye. Walking down the hallway to the den with Kibbles, she thought about this latest development. A boyfriend! Shelby looked happier than usual and Anton was certainly a nice, hot guy. Yet Amber felt queasy, uncomfortable with her initial reaction:

Jealousy

On the way to the kitchen, Amber sat down on the arm of the couch for a moment as the dog gently licked her hand, instinctually understanding the need to provide comfort.

OMG, did Amber want a boyfriend? Was that what this was about? Had the trauma she'd suffered reduced her to the role of fairytale princess in need of rescue?

But wasn't it normal to have a boyfriend at her age, go to football games, the homecoming dance…

Amber realized the ridiculousness of this line of thinking. She'd never been *normal*. The appearance of the Celtic Goddess Brigid reinforced the fact that she'd always be at the fringes, different and apart from the rest of humanity. *Normal* boys sought out girls that conformed to social expectation. Possession of extraordinary power would make most boys feel

167

insecure and inferior.

Thoughts of George Salvia simultaneously invaded Amber's musing, causing her to wonder if this feeling of jealousy had something to do with the charismatic young man. Yet, what would a graduating senior want with an awkward ninth grader? Lanky and lean, Amber looked nothing like the womanly, voluptuous Lourdes Navarro. She hated the conflicting feelings of attraction for George, coupled with the wish that she could keep him at a distance due to distrust about his motives.

At least Amber wasn't entirely alone in being abnormal: Marisol Garcia had inherited her grandmother's powers, so they'd have each other for company. And Noelle? Other than being outrageously courageous, Amber didn't know where Noelle's talents lay. She hoped their combined strength would be enough to take on Shadow Man.

Amber felt sad when she realized that she didn't have the luxury of worrying about the things normal teens think about. She and her friends were under attack from something very dangerous, and they didn't have a clue about what to do.

"C'mon in!" Seth shouted to his friend James Toshima, who he'd been expecting.

"Hey, what'd Luis say he wants to talk about?" James asked as he walked in.

"Dunno, Jimbo, guess we'll find out," Seth replied.

Luis Garcia arrived within a few minutes. James hadn't spoken to him since they'd argued about Amber McBride, which distressed Luis. He'd enjoyed the relative peace and calm that had characterized his life since the passing of his grandmother Graciela. The distraction provided by his friends was what got Luis through living with a witch that practiced the dark arts. He wouldn't tolerate major disruption to the fearless foursome.

"Truce, okay?" Luis held up his hands in a peaceful gesture as he met James' glare.

"At ease," Seth tried to joke, but James' body language remained tense.

Luis remained standing as he retrieved some papers he'd gotten from the local historical society. "You'll wanna hear this!" he announced, and began to read, "Treasure Tales from the Simi Hills: The Stagecoach Robbery."

"We already checked their website!" Seth interrupted. "How'd you get this?"

"Muy suave!"[17] Luis joked. "I went over to the museum and asked one of the old ladies if they had anything else about the Salvia stagecoach robbery. They liked me so much, they gave me cookies, iced tea, and this!"

[17] Spanish for 'very charming'

"Nice work!" Seth congratulated his friend as he snatched the article from Luis. Seth hastily scanned its contents before handing it off to James, who did the same.

"This changes nothing," James stated flatly.

"Here's the deal," Luis countered. "We help the girls, but first, we go for the treasure on our own. We've got clues right here, in the article!"

"What about Jonah?" Seth asked.

"Abernathy doesn't need the money, we do!" Luis insisted.

"Normally there's no way I'd leave him out," Seth countered, "But if he get caught, his dad will freak."

"Yea," James agreed, "his dad might send him to military school, like that time when we rigged that dumpster with explosives."

Seth snorted at the memory of the metal trash bin blasting five feet off the ground from the explosion's force. The boom rattled windows throughout Lake Manor as the boys fled the scene of the crime. Seth hadn't gotten away fast enough, and lost the hearing in his right ear for an entire month!

Unfortunately, Max caught a whiff of sulfur from the explosives. He began his interrogation with, "I hear of great explosion in Lake Manor. I know you boys did it. Confess to me, or to the police." The truth was out within minutes.

Marcus Abernathy found nothing funny about the prank and tried to convince the parents to ship the lot of them off to military school. The main thing that prevented the boys from being sent away was that they were all too young, being only 11 years old at the time of the crime. Few facilities took in children of such tender age. The mothers in particular balked at the harshness of Marcus Abernathy's recommended punishment, and vowed to keep the boys under tighter supervision.

For their part, the boys learned to plan a better getaway and not get caught next time.

"Dude! Don't put the horns on our mission!" Luis begged.

"We do this once," James acquiesced, "but no matter what happens, we help the girls next."

"Works for me," Seth said.

"We got a deal!" Luis summarized.

Δ

Dr. McBride did his best to reassure Amber that in the full light of day, what seemed ominous in the middle of the night likely presented little danger. "Maybe it was some local boy. You know, up to some mischief, spying on the girls."

Amber wished it were so simple, rather than the very disturbing possibility that Shadow Man was lurking about, waiting for the right moment to attack.

"Listen Amber, I don't want you to worry about this. We're getting a new security system installed tomorrow." Turning to his wife, he added, "Remember Todd Harris, that guy from DARPA I met in Kuwait?"

Mrs. McBride raised an eyebrow, asking, "DARPA?"

"Military black ops, but non-lethal stuff," Dr. McBride enthusiastically explained, "apps like sound waves that'll bring you to your knees, effectively disabling the enemy, but no permanent damage. Anyway, Harris owed me a favor, so I got hold of a new app DARPA's beta testing."

Curious, Amber asked, "What does it do?"

"It picks up cell signals, so we can see anyone with a cell phone that comes on the property. I sent you an email with the link." He handed her a slip of paper with the password. "You can install it right now."

Amber pulled out her cell, clicked on the link, input the password and installed the app. When the Beta app finished downloading, Amber opened it and, true to her father's word, a small circle representing Amber appeared right where the kitchen counter should be, as viewed from the air. Two circles appeared next to her, representing her parents, and another circle appeared a short distance away, representing Kibbles.

"Put in our cell numbers so our names appear under our dots," her father explained as he showed how to input data into the app. "Isn't it *cool*?" Dr. McBride always sounded distinctly *uncool* whenever he tried to talk street.

Staring at four circles with names underneath as her father avoided his wife's gaze, Amber wondered if the app had the dual purpose of keeping tabs on her mother's whereabouts.

"Wait, Kibbles doesn't have a cell phone. How come we can see him?" Amber asked.

Dr. McBride whistled and the elderly dog padded over. Tugging on Kibbles' new collar, her father explained, "This collar has an RFID chip in it."

"What happens if somebody else is here?" she asked.

"Unless it's a friend of yours and you put in their cell number, it'll say UNKNOWN," Her father responded.

Sensing her mother's discomfort, Amber leapt up from the kitchen counter and began clearing dishes. Amber pulled the plate from under her mother while her fork was still in hand, anxious to be free of them both before any fireworks erupted. Cleanup was completed in record time and Amber walked back with Kibbles to her room to finish her homework before school the next day.

"Amber McBride. The action never stops at Lizard Hill, does it?" George Salvia, from Amber's laptop, was presently addressing her.

"How'd you get on without me answering?" she asked, to which he shrugged. Continuing, Amber asked, "So, you heard?"

Nodding, he studied her face before adding, "There's more. How about telling me everything?"

Spinning around once in her chair, Amber asked a question that had been bothering her since the strangeness on the hilltop, "Why do you want to get mixed up in any of this? After what happened up on the hill, anyone else would be outta here."

"Salvias don't run," George countered, "and what's been hanging over my family started way before you were even born, Amber. I'm just trying to find some answers. I think we've got a better shot if we work together. We're on the same side."

Seeing the concerned look on his face, Amber conceded, "I understand."

George added, "I've been thinking, what if that prick we saw on the hill is the same guy that murdered Lucy Carpenter?"

Thinking of Lucy, Amber proceeded to tell George about interrupting the ghostly gathering from the 1980's in her living room.

George did not appear shocked by Amber's revelation, nor did he question her sanity. Instead, he asked, "You weren't scared?"

"No, only Slone ran away."

"Weren't you afraid that they, you know, might hurt you?"

In a rush of pride, Amber retorted, "The big hair and mullets were freaky, but I wasn't afraid."

George responded, "Maybe ghosts can't hurt you, but men can." Eyes narrowing, he insisted, "You think anyone's outside your house again, you *call me* and I'll be right over. Promise me."

The outrageous intrusion onto the property at the House on Lizard Hill signaled to Mrs. Michelle McBride that drastic measures needed to be taken. After engaging in a long-distance shouting match with Aunt Ester, Michelle O'Donnell McBride finally got what she needed: agreement to seal Amber with the sign of the O'Donnell clan. The family sigil carried centuries of protection and bore the combined power of the O'Donnell women throughout the ages. It would provide Amber the added layer of security urgently needed in these uncertain times.

But help from the Old Country came at a price: Aunt Ester extracted agreement from her niece that she'd come to Donegal County, Ireland for a visit when the battle was over and Amber was out of harm's way.

Watching her daughter sleep, Mrs. McBride glanced out the window in the direction of the Twelve Apostles. Aunt Ester was right: she'd not been able to avoid the past and this reminder was particularly painful. The forbidding stone cathedrals were the place where her childhood friend Daniela Cervantes Salvia leapt to her death. Michelle O'Donnell and

Daniela Cervantes had written to one another since first grade in a now outdated custom called 'pen pals.'

Daniela Cervantes Salvia had moved atop the Twelve Apostles after she'd married, only to commit suicide on the first anniversary of her husband's untimely passing. Mrs. McBride knew these facts only because she kept abreast of Lake Manor events via local online news.

Daniela Salvia had ceased speaking to Michelle McBride a long time ago. Nonetheless, Mrs. McBride wished she could change the past and return to the light-hearted days of their youth. She'd savor every moment with Daniela, take nothing for granted...

Chiding herself for letting her thoughts wander from the task at hand, Mrs. McBride lit the last of the four candles. One had been placed at each corner of Amber's room. Seating herself in the center of the floor, Mrs. McBride cut her left index finger, drawing blood. She then began carefully drawing the O'Donnell sigil with her blood. Mrs. McBride placed her right hand on the floor and carefully traced the outline. When she was finished, Amber's mother sat back and invoked 'Brigid' in the Celtic tongue.

Candlelight flickered and then flared sharply as the outline of her open hand upon the floor began to bleed from the fingers. Rivulets oozed out from the thumb and pinkie at a ninety-degree angle before veering sharply away in opposite directions. Red lines turned sharply once again and flowed toward Mrs. McBride as they curved together and joined at the bottom. The outline of a soldier's shield had been formed. The pace of blood etching sped up as a five-pointed star was drawn at the bottom, then two fierce, standing lions clawing at one another with two stars hovering over their heads.

The candlelight suddenly snuffed out. The O'Donnell family crest appeared in white light, absorbing all evidence of Mrs. McBride's blood etched upon the floor. Luminous lions threw back their heads and roared silently. The hand, appearing like a three-dimensional hologram, floated up off the floor and pointed its index finger at Amber.

The O'Donnell family shield rose into the air, lions and hand balanced atop it like a flying carpet. The shield slowly started to spin as the three stars floated upward to hover over the lions' heads and whirl in the opposite direction. With the joining of stars, the sigil began to spin faster. Whirling toward Amber, the family crest slowed its rotation as it hovered above her. Now the size of a fist, it floated gently down to rest upon her chest.

Brilliant white light flared from the O'Donnell family crest, illuminating the entire room and causing Amber's mother to cover her eyes.

When the light faded enough for Mrs. McBride to take a peek, she found the still-sleeping Amber bathed in a halo of gauzy light.

As she dreamed, Amber hazily perceived an illuminated room and unnatural light reflected in Kibbles' eyes. Her enchanted dog watched as a golden shield spun midair, trailing sparks in its wake. As the O'Donnell sigil drew near, Amber heard gentle whispers:

We're here, child.

You're one of us.

Welcome, sister.

Amber realized she wasn't alone as she floated out of her body. Hovering above the bed, she saw female ancestors of all ages surrounding her in a semi-circle. She'd never met any of her mother's relatives other than Aunt Cathy, and hadn't understood until now what she was missing until the combined strength from generations of O'Donnell women enveloped her. Amber hungrily absorbed the nurturing vibes. The protection spell culminated in waves of golden light that streamed from their outstretched arms and into Amber's chest. Her body was wreathed in a golden bridal veil of light.

Floating back down into her body, Amber's eyes met those of a teenager standing at the foot of her bed. It was the flame-haired girl she'd seen in the inferno vision: the Celtic priestess that called upon the elements to defend her small village from Viking raiders.

∞

Flopping down on Dr. Morton's couch, Amber tried to make herself comfortable.

Dr. Morton asked, "So, what do you think about tackling some of the recurring images that have been bothering you?"

Dr. Morton had explained in a previous session how PTSD treatment works. It sounded straightforward. A body cannot be relaxed and anxious at the same time. They first worked on the relaxation part, involving flexing and relaxing each body part, until every bit of tension was gone.

The time had come to introduce images from the traumatic experience, starting with the least anxiety provoking, while keeping Amber relaxed when seeing those images. The goal, Dr. Morton noted, was to gain control over the symptoms of PTSD. By learning to relax, the images would eventually no longer have the power to paralyze her.

"Promise, we have to stop if it gets too intense?" she asked nervously.

"I promise. You just show me the signal we agreed to and we'll come right back to a happy place," the psychologist Dr. Betty Morton reassured her.

Dr. Morton took Amber through the progressive muscle relaxation exercise again. "I'm standing right next to you," Dr. Morton's voice sounded far away from Amber's dreamy state of semi-awareness. "You're viewing this like it's on TV. You're holding the remote control. You can pause or stop what you're seeing at any time."

Amber had decided to begin with the bus pulling away to reveal Lourdes and company lying in wait across the road.

Dr. Morton instructed, "Let's examine Lourdes again, with fresh eyes."

Amber floated along in a blissful state as she studied Lourdes Navarro. She no longer saw an imposing, tough Latina. Revealed beneath the tattooed, painted veneer was a sad, pathetic girl. Abandoned by the one she loved, she desperately sought to make sense of why George Salvia no longer cared for her.

Lourdes Navarro no longer frightened her.

Dr. Morton took note before moving on to the next image.

Standing atop the hill overlooking the State Park, Amber heard angry shouts echoing up from the hillside behind her before making a break for the narrow, brushy deer path representing her best chance of escape. The rocky hills and plants were vividly colorful, particularly the laurel sumac with its maroon limbs …

Amber took all of this in with the dispassionate objectivity of the scientist.

Studying her closely, Dr. Betty Morton took additional notes. Normally at this point in re-experiencing a traumatic event the patient twitches or moves around in discomfort.

The alabaster face upon the couch was serene and childlike.

Uttering reassuring words, Dr. Morton decided it was time to bring Amber back to conscious awareness. She had made remarkable progress during tonight's session.

A voice thick with an Irish accent hailed Dr. Morton. Amber's mouth moved, but it was *not* her voice saying, "Betty, it's so good to see you again."

Dr. Morton dropped her tablet into her lap, letting it fall away to the floor. She had not heard this voice in nearly half a century, yet it was one she could *never* forget.

The Celtic Goddess *Brigid* greeted her with a luminous smile.

Mrs. McBride banged on the door to Dr. Morton's office, demanding to be let in. When the psychologist opened the door, Mrs. McBride found her daughter lying on the couch.

"What's going on? Why is she like this?" Mrs. McBride grilled.

Dr. Morton lied, explaining that it was an effect of the relaxation procedure and nothing to be concerned about.

Mrs. McBride's eyes narrowed as she helped her groggy daughter to her feet. "Right," Amber's mother snapped, "I'm sure that's all it is."

Dr. Morton's face showed no reaction as Amber and Mrs. McBride departed. She changed her clothing much more quickly tonight and rapidly descended the stairwell steps to the parking lot. Starting up her old Jaguar, Betty Morton found herself uncharacteristically impatient as she waited the necessary three minutes for the old girl to warm up before pulling out, lest she risk stalling in the middle of the intersection. From her office building, the drive to the Santa Susana Pass State Historic Park was accomplished within minutes.

Clicking the button to lock her car, she rounded the trunk to enter the park through the skeletal oak-lined trail next to the cemetery, but paused as she spied furtive movement near the graveyard.

She watched a young man climb up from within and drop quietly over the locked wrought iron gate, slipping down gracefully to the street side.

Upon landing, he felt someone watching and said, "Dr. Morton."

"Ben, it's been quite some time."

Nodding stiffly, Ben Salvia backed away into the shadows of enormous eucalyptus trees growing along the edge of the cemetery.

"You know, my door is always open, as I told you when we last spoke."

Waving her off, he pulled a motorcycle out from under the brush and started it up. Nearby horses whinnied piteously at chainsaw revving sounds as Ben Salvia sped away.

Dr. Betty Morton remained standing at the entrance for a few more moments.

Lake Manor had always been an interesting place to live, but things were about to get a whole lot livelier in the coming weeks, even by the kooky standards of her eccentric community. Shaking her head, Dr. Morton hiked into the twilight of the state park.

Δ

It had taken Officer Johnson a lot of time to comb through the material in Commander Rodriguez' cold case files. With what little time he had on his days off, he'd begun with the most recent files and meticulously read, then re-read each one before setting it aside. Officer Johnson wasn't sure what he was looking for, but he was certain he'd know it when he saw it.

Johnson had worked his way through nearly all of the cases and was on the last box, containing cold cases from the mid-1980's, when Rodriguez was a rookie officer. He'd been reading for hours and groaned aloud as he shifted uncomfortably in his seat. Chiding himself for going off the deep end since losing consciousness over the nature preserve, Officer Johnson contemplated giving up on what was turning out to be a fool's errand.

Deciding to read just one more file before calling it quits, Officer Johnson's eyes widened as he read Rodriguez' notes pertaining to interviews conducted after the disappearance of a local teenager, eighteen-year-old *Lucy Carpenter*. The girl had last been seen in Lake Manor at a party place known locally as the House on Lizard Hill.

Amber McBride's house!

Re-energized, Officer Johnson quickly scanned the notes, reading an interview with the homeowner, *Robert Hugo Franklin*. He'd reported last seeing Miss Carpenter leaving on a motorcycle with a young man. Rodriguez noted that he believed Franklin was lying, but a thorough search of the house and grounds revealed no clues to tie him to Lucy Carpenter's disappearance.

Officer Johnson knew he was on to something as he read a post-script about the search. Rodriguez reported that, though nothing of import had been found, the officer that searched the crawl space under the garage had a rather 'unusual' reaction. Rodriguez then proceeded to describe a situation almost exactly like the one Johnson witnessed when Officers Huang and Gutiérrez tried to clear the storage area.

Frowning. Johnson thought back to the most recent search of the creepy crawl space, and was troubled that whatever weirdness Gutiérrez had experienced, he'd chosen to keep the information to himself. Johnson pushed his chair back from the table, sadly reflecting that he'd not trusted his partner enough to share what happened to him over the nature preserve. Hell, Rodriguez was a good friend and if the situation demanded, Johnson would give his life for his partner. Yet now there was mutual unease and distrust between the two, and Johnson suspected the source of their troubles was the House on Lizard Hill.

Returning to the files, Officer Johnson read Rodriguez' next account: he'd documented an interview with a teenager who had her parents and a lawyer by her side the entire time. The lawyer answered all of the questions while the girl sobbed hysterically, clearly fearful for her friend Lucy Carpenter's safety. Rodriguez didn't consider this teenager a suspect. Her name was *Daniela Cervantes*.

Incredulous, Johnson shook his head. He didn't believe in coincidence. He knew that Cervantes was the maiden name of *Daniela Salvia*. So somehow, the Salvias were connected to this mess!

What Officer Johnson read in the third interview sent a chill up his spine.

BEN SALVIA

CHAPTER 12

PURGATORY

Rodriguez wrote that this particular interviewee was poised, polished and answered every question with the 'right' answer. He noted that he'd never seen *anyone* so calm during a police interrogation. Rodriguez' final entry about this interview read, "She's the coolest, most calculated liar I've ever met."

The interviewee, an eighteen-year-old visiting from Vancouver, Canada was named *Aislinn O'Donnell.*

Although the name didn't ring a bell, Officer Johnson clearly saw a 'head picture' of an older, more sophisticated *Amber McBride* sitting across from him in a police interrogation room. Figuring he'd come this far and found a connection to not only the Salvias but also Amber through the House on Lizard Hill, Johnson conducted a cross-state DMV search and hit the jackpot:

Aislinn O'Donnell was the given name of Amber's mother, *Michelle McBride.*

Amber awoke around noon and headed to the kitchen, where her mother sat alone at the counter; Dr. McBride was nowhere in sight. Before Amber could speak, her mother informed her, "Your father got called into work. Some sort of emergency up at the field lab."

Before Amber could ask about the emergency, Mrs. McBride's phone chirruped loudly. Her normally pale face greyed as she read the incoming message.

Increasingly worried about her father, Amber asked, "Is dad okay? What's going on?"

Her mother looked dazed as she slowly raised her head. "It's…he's fine. It's got nothing to do with him. I need to step out for a while." Looking around as if perhaps she needed to take something with her, but finding nothing, she slowly stood, and then quickly left the kitchen.

Rapidly moving into action, Amber messaged Jonah Abernathy, followed by urgent missives to Las Brujas regarding reconnoitering at her house.

As soon as Jonah confirmed he would be over shortly, Amber flew to the shower, officially launching the daily feminine ritual of getting ready. Just as she finished towel drying her hair; Jonah texted to announce his arrival. Racing across the courtyard to the double doors, she found Kibbles waiting under the buzzer that opened the front gates.

"You planning on lending a paw and letting Jonah in?" she asked, to which vigorous tail wagging and uplifted snout were received in answer. "Right, no thumbs," Amber quipped, depressing the button.

Amber ran down the stairs to meet Jonah. Finding him walking down the driveway, she decided to go for it. "So, I'm guessing you hate your school because it's no place for the truly *fabulous*."

Jonah stopped walking and stared, unsure about how to respond to the bombshell she'd just dropped.

"C'mon Jonah, if I figured it out, you *must* know."

Jonah opened and closed his mouth, shook his head and resumed walking. "No one knows!" he hissed ominously.

"Hey, dude, chill, I get it: 'Don't Ask, Don't Tell.' It's your business."

"So how'd you figure it out?" he asked, surprised by her intuition.

She shrugged, "I've got a great *gaydar*." Giving Jonah a quick hug, she reassured him, "It's no big deal."

The forlorn look on her friend's face gave way to a chuckle as they ascended her front steps. "Listen, I'm going to 'out' myself eventually, probably soon."

Chuckling along with Jonah, Amber nodded, "I understand. I honestly don't think it'll be a big deal, but I get it."

Changing the subject, Jonah asked, "So, do you think it was the Salvias spying on your place?"

Thinking of George, she chose her words carefully, "The police don't know who it was."

"Well, did you go out and look at the footprints under the window for yourself?"

"D'oh", Amber chided herself as she led Jonah around the outer curve of the U where the kitchen lay and on over to the northern side where the living room windows faced the omnipresent Twelve Apostles rock formation.

The broken glass pane had been fixed and the shards removed, but the telltale footprints of the intruder were clearly visible in the grass, courtesy of her father watering the lawn in order to will it back to life after being neglected for so long.

Jonah knelt down and placed the length of his long hand into one of the prints. The outline of the footprint extended well beyond his fingertips. Frowning deeply, he shook his head, dusted off his hands and stood up.

"Amber, maybe it *was* George! These are, like, a size thirteen! George is the only one tall enough to have feet that big."

"How do you know?" Amber asked.

"I'm a size eleven. Look how much bigger these are compared to my feet." Jonah placed his foot right next to the muddy imprint, which extended an inch beyond his shoes.

Amber was pensive as her eyes narrowed to slits, considering the awful truth of Jonah's discovery.

"So, that's good, right? Now you know who it is!"

But nothing could be further from the truth. Although George had appeared outside her window that day he'd asked her to come check out the enigmatic hill inside the nature preserve, Amber knew he'd not been the middle-of the night intruder.

Demons didn't have bodies and therefore couldn't leave footprints, so Amber now felt certain that Robert Hugo Franklin was her stalker. Even worse, she suspected Franklin might be possessed by Shadow Man. Why else would the two of them show up, together, outside her living room window?

On a whim, she pulled out her cell and opened up the app her father had installed. It showed her house as if she were viewing it from above, with two dots labeled 'Amber' and 'Jonah' where they currently stood outside the living room window.

"What's that?" Jonah asked.

Amber turned her screen so he could see.

"Cool!" Jonah took the phone from Amber and studied it, entranced by the latest Beta app. Suddenly his grin faded into astonishment before settling upon a fretful grimace. Jonah pulled her to the ground as he ducked down underneath the windows, hunching his body close as possible against the house, pressing Amber back against the brick façade with his right arm.

He turned the cell phone's screen back to Amber for inspection.

Three dots had joined theirs onscreen, in the women's dressing room underneath the pool. The one perfect circle was named 'Kibbles.' The other two appeared as fuzzy blobs. Despite what her father had told her, neither was labeled UNKNOWN. Indeed, no words appeared underneath the two gauzy dabs.

"What's with these two?" Jonah pointed to the two anomalies. "You sure the app's working?"

On edge, Amber informed her friend, "I don't want to drag you into this, so bug outta here."

Eyes narrowing, he asked, "Drag me into *what*, Amber?"

Glancing eastward in the direction of the women's changing room, she admitted, "You're not the only one with a secret."

Eyebrows arching, Jonah inclined his head slightly, encouraging his friend to continue.

Amber whispered, "Remember that stuff Max found about Robert Franklin and that girl that disappeared from a party here back in the 80's?"

Grimacing as he pointed toward the dots on her cell, Jonah hissed, "What if one of those is Robert Franklin? What if *he's come back*?"

"Jonah, my dad says if it's someone we don't know, it's supposed to say

UNKNOWN. Did you see any of those dots move in from somewhere else, like someone walking in?"

Eyes widening considerably, Jonah revealed, "Only Kibbles, he came in from your room. The other two just popped up."

"Let's go see," Amber decided.

Sneaking to the edge of the house, the two friends crept around the backside of the pool. When Amber gave the signal, they darted around the curving concrete belly.

Through the dank opening, they observed two teenagers. One was Lucy, long blond hair tumbling down her back, alternately opaque and solid. Amber could see pristine upholstered chairs and a newly tiled shower through her clothing. The other was the same haunted-looking Latina that Amber had come face-to-face with in her living room the night of the ghostly '80's gathering. Kibbles stood protectively in between the two. His butt was toward the opening where a door once hung. His ears laid back and his ruff stood up as he growled menacingly at the darkness beyond the two teenaged girls.

The intense dark-haired young woman was gesturing expressively, as if she was having an argument with someone standing in the recessed shadows.

Suddenly, Lucy's body shook and jerked unnaturally as she collapsed to the ground, causing the now alarmed Latina to rush to her side and the dog to whine piteously.

The inside of the changing room suddenly resumed its present-day state of decay as the wind roared to life around Amber and Jonah, spiraling acorns down upon them from the nearby oaks in a stinging assault. A great *whoosh* sounded as they were blown backward and nearly knocked off their feet.

Regaining their balance, the ferocious winds ceased as an incoming furry missile barreled through the sagging doorframe, leaping upon Amber's chest in adrenaline-fueled joy, knocking her backward into Jonah as the trio collapsed upon the path in a heap. Disentangling herself from slobbery kisses, Amber and Jonah leaned back against the wall to catch their breath as an exhausted Kibbles sprawled out upon the path.

Jonah slowly turned to his friend, face ashen and grim, and asked, "Lucy?"

Amber solemnly nodded.

"Who was that other chick?"

"Who're you talking about?" Noelle called from above their heads.

Yelping, Jonah bumped into Amber, sending the two of them tumbling over the prone Kibbles. Peals of laughter rang out as Mari and Noelle watched their friends collapse in startled sprawl.

Springing to her feet, Amber disentangled her long legs from Jonah's and helped him up as her giggling friends descended the stairs. Upon observing the serious expressions and still panting dog, Noelle eyed Jonah briefly before inquiring, "Someone want to tell us what's going on?"

Jonah glanced anxiously to Amber, unwilling to be the first to speak due to uncertainty about how much the others knew.

"Lucy," Amber informed them as she peered into the now empty changing room, relaying the wild scene she and Jonah had just witnessed. "She was with that same Mexican girl we saw in the living room!"

Jonah watched Noelle and Marisol closely, and when they showed neither shock nor surprise, he demanded, "What else aren't you telling me?"

Awkward silence ensued as the assembly searched each other's eyes, no one willing to dive in with an explanation that would most certainly fall flat.

Jonah demanded, "Listen, I didn't ask to be part of this! This shit just drew me in! So, out with it!"

Everyone looked to Amber, who proceeded to fill Jonah in on almost everything that had happened since moving to Chatsworth-Lake Manor. A quick, private glance exchanged with Marisol assured her that Graciela Hernandez' as-of-yet unclear relationship with Robert Hugo Franklin, and Amber's equally confusing relationship with her ancestral Celtic Goddess Brigid would remain secret, for the time being.

After Amber finished, she bowed her head, shoulders slumped from the retelling, stating, "There's more, but let's get moving to the grotto. I don't want to be here when I talk about it."

Jonah figured Amber was referring to sharing what she and Marisol learned when he and the guys had been spying, thereby saving him the discomfort of confronting her, so he kept quiet for the time being. Marisol hugged Amber in sisterly solidarity as Amber led the group to the kitchen in order to pack supplies.

Noelle wagged an accusatory finger, "Wait a minute, why is there a guy in our group now? This is a chick thing!"

Amber returned from the pantry with plastic water bottles and busied herself with tucking them into a backpack, offering no response or insight to what was, in actuality, a legitimate question.

"Um, well...I fit with you all better than you think," Jonah shyly responded.

Noelle's eyes widened as she absorbed the news. Composing herself, she patted his shoulder in reassurance, "Well, it was probably time."

Marisol remained completely confused, asking, "What are you guys talking about? If Jonah's with us, that means my brother's going to want in too and there's no way I want that pendejo[18] being a part of our group!"

The three friends were speechless for a moment until Jonah revealed,

---

[18] Spanish for 'dumbass'

"Mari, I'm gay."

Marisol appeared momentarily stunned, prompting Jonah to ask, "So, I'm in?"

"You're in," Marisol deadpanned. "We just have to keep this on the down-low, so my brother doesn't find out."

"Marisol, you're so street!" Noelle joked as the foursome headed out.

As soon as the coast was clear, the teens dashed across the country lane to the opposite side. Someone had placed a scarecrow upon a pole at the crossroads. Surveying the odd man, Amber found his form all-too-human. Scarecrow appeared shriveled and skeletal, like something that had been left out in the sun too long. His blanched face and head, covered by an old fedora rather than the traditional straw hat, gave the illusion of petrified skin. Instead of the button eyes borne by the straw men of the field, this raggedy man had two deep, dark pits with X's sewn across where eyes should have been, reminding Amber of something she'd heard once about a custom of threading eyelids shut after death. A gash was slashed across the face instead of cheery red mouth. Stumps stuck out from each sleeve, extended straight out from his sides in a Christ-like pose.

"I hate that thing," Marisol glared at the scarecrow.

"I wonder what the hell is wrong with whoever made it?" Noelle made a face at the ghastly creature as she passed.

Despite their bravado, the group unconsciously picked up their pace.

"Wait!" Jonah cautioned, "We can't pass Seth's house! What if he sees us?"

Motioning for the girls to follow him, he bypassed the main intersection, continuing along Lake Manor Drive, until the assembly reached the edge of the dog park.

Pointing to a nearby rock formation, Jonah declared, "We're just going to have to make a run for it and hope they're not hanging out in Seth's backyard. Or else we can walk all the way around and come in by the cemetery, but that's going to take twice as long!"

"You're right," Amber agreed, by now quite keen to reach the grotto and conduct their business. Peering around the drooping tendrils of a Coastal Live Oak that survived the fire, she was relieved to see no activity in Seth's backyard.

"What are they were doing today?" she asked.

"Mountain biking," Jonah hung his head at the prospect of being discovered. "Which means we could run into them at any time. They think I'm grounded, by the way," he added.

"Ready?" Amber asked, scanning the meadow beyond for movement, but other than a lone hiker with an exuberant dog leaping about far off in the distance, no one else could be seen.

"Let's go!" Jonah confirmed, sending the four racing across the stubbly, ashen field to the shelter of the rock formation.

Leaning into the sandstone, four faces alighted with smiles as they realized they had gained the dog park undetected.

Jonah pointed out a trail Amber hadn't seen before, one that appeared to wind along the eastern edge of the park. She glimpsed it here and there along the hillside, in between giant, stacked sandstone.

"Follow me; no one will see us on this one." Jonah commanded as he led the way.

The teens lapsed into silence as they walked across the top of the ridgeline. Amber scanned the skies for birds and found none. She understood that the landscape would need to recover a bit before the animals would return, but complete absence of the birds was puzzling. "Something's really wrong," Amber shared her concern.

"Tell us something we don't know," Jonah grumbled.

"I'm serious! Have you seen squirrels and birds around your house?"

"Yea, sure," Jonah answered.

"Have you seen even one bird since you've been in Lake Manor today?"

Jonah, Noelle and Marisol searched the skies as they reached the private road and crossed over to the other side.

"I don't even know why I'm looking!" Marisol fumed. "I haven't seen or heard any birds at my house since the fire. Amber's right, this isn't normal!"

"Uh, this is gonna sound weird because I don't live in Lake Manor, but now that I think about it, I haven't seen any animals or birds in Bell Canyon since the fire," Noelle observed. "But that doesn't make any sense, the fire didn't even come anywhere near my house, and I'm like, two minutes from Jonah!"

"One more question for Marisol's granny," Jonah concluded, "Oh, speaking of uncomfortable situations, let's keep a lid on me being gay. The guys don't know. I'll tell them sometime…soon."

Marisol nodded sagely, "I wonder how Luis would react, him and his Latin machismo."[19]

"I think Seth and James won't think twice about it," Noelle pondered, "That is, if they haven't figured it out already."

Noelle suggested, "Maybe someone's trying to tell us something. Think about it. These things could have happened *anytime*. Why when Mari and I were over? Why *today*, when Jonah was there? I hate to say it, but maybe even Slone was supposed to be part of this, if she hadn't run away."

Everyone was attentive, listening closely as they passed one of the trail's elbowed switchbacks, this one containing a rock fall of trailside grey, weathered sentinels surrounding a charred oak, indicating that this particular crease amongst the mountain range's many folds became a

---

[19] A Spanish term that roughly equates to 'masculine persona and attitude'

185

torrential waterway during the winter rains.

"So we just put it out there: whatever it is we're supposed to know next, we'll find out," Noelle concluded.

"That makes it a lot easier," Amber said as the feeling of being overwhelmed receded a bit.

The four youths handily descended the remaining switchbacks, reaching the bottom of the hill to continue across the burnt, silent meadow eerily absent the rabbits and sundry fauna that would normally be hopping about and popping up out of the ground.

Marisol was the first to clear the natural tunnel and extended a hand to help the others up and out of the spiny chaparral. Clambering over rocks, Marisol led the little group to the narrow rock ledge that she and Amber stood upon the fateful night when they learned about Robert Hugo Franklin's connection to Graciela Hernandez.

The others proceeded along the narrow pathway but Noelle stopped suddenly as she looked out over the valley, unable to believe her eyes.

Echoing against the giant sandstone rocks for Noelle's ears only sang a prayer from a broad assembly arrayed before her. African women raised their outstretched arms in rapture. No men were present in a colorfully vivid landscape.

Turning to find the others, she saw their retreating forms.

She'd been the only one to experience a glimpse into an ancient African temple, run not by men, but by *women*.

♀

Minutes later, Noelle caught up with the others. Gaping at the natural stone amphitheater, she accused, "This place is crazy! How come you never took me here before?"

"I…uh…I'm sorry," Marisol apologized.

Jonah was gob-smacked. "I've actually been here before," he admitted, "but it's like I'm seeing it for the first time!"

Waning rays left a soft haze around the northern cliff face. Shadows cast from the eastern cliffs intersected with brilliant sunbeams, alternating between light and dim, clarity and obscurity.

Leading the group to the ancient oak, Amber and Marisol seated themselves cross-legged around the small stone basin at the foot of the charred, hollowed out oak. The wind picked up, rustling bare, burned branches overhead as Jonah and Noelle joined in.

Uncapping one of the plastic bottles of water from the backpack, Marisol poured the contents into the natural depression, filling the small stone basin entirely. "Join hands," she commanded in an unusually forceful manner.

Four pairs of hands obeyed and clasped tightly, fingers squeezing in fretful anticipation.

Jonah looked expectantly to his three feminine companions. "Well? Aren't you supposed to, you know, chant a spell or something?"

Amber skeptically raised one red eyebrow at him. "If you know so much, *Harry Potter*, why don't you show us what you've got!"

Jonah shifted uncomfortably, fidgeting frog-like in his cross-legged position as the girls sat like stones.

Noelle groaned aloud before finally snapping, "Stop dicking around! We're supposed to be concentrating!"

Soft strains of guitar chords floated down from the hillside beyond.

"Cowboy Joe!" Jonah remarked.

The haunting lyrics were disturbing, and yet lulled them into a peaceful, dreamy state as they stared at the water. Amber thought she should get up and see if the old cowboy was headed their way, but found that she had no desire to move. As she drifted into peaceful, formless nothingness, Amber subconsciously recognized the song Cowboy Joe played, the *Streets of Laredo*. He sang mournfully about the death of a young man. The cowboy knew he deserved to die and, resigned, gave instructions for the disposition of his corpse.

As Cowboy Joe soulfully strummed, the surface of the small pool shifted slightly. At first only a brief ripple appeared, followed by a wave that ran the depth and breadth of the basin. When the pool stilled, an image had formed on the surface of the water, causing the four friends to immediately drop their handholds in shock.

Three mountain bikes and a metal detector lay in a heap atop the Twelve Apostles. Luis Garcia and Seth Lobata lay slumped next to the bikes, dusty and bruised. Ken Salvia held James Toshima's arms behind his back. Although his face was bloodied, the short Japanese boy looked as fierce as Rama from Raid Redemption as he bravely looked Ben Salvia in the eye and spat in his face.

The pool began to dissipate as the four alarmed teenagers leapt to their feet, but not before Amber caught a glimpse of an impassive Ben Salvia cocking his fist and punching James in the stomach.

The grotto erupted as the three girls began shouting. Only Jonah was momentarily silent, as his reaction was to immediately pull out his mobile and hail Max for assistance. He joined the chorus of cursing, however, as soon as he realized they were in a dead zone.

"We've got to go help them!" Amber raged, her conscious mind registering the fact that only three Salvias appeared in the vision. *George had been nowhere in sight.*

"We need Max!" Jonah insisted. "Maybe Cowboy Joe can go get help!" He ran up the hill to the trailhead. Searching about frantically, Jonah shouted for the old man several times. Hearing no response, he ran back down to the girls. "I don't know where Cowboy Joe went! I don't see him anywhere!"

"We can't waste time trying to find him! What's the fastest way to get to the guys?" Noelle demanded.

Pointing up to a narrow crevice high above, Marisol indicated the distant point where, were it raining, the water would pool at the top and then cascade down the stark, sheer cliff face.

"There's a road to the Twelve Apostles at the top?" Amber asked, earning a nod from Jonah as she began crossing the circular amphitheater floor, calling back over her shoulder, "Any houses?"

"Yea, but..."

Cutting him off, Amber declared, "You'll get cell service up there. Let's go!" Jumping as gracefully as a mountain lioness, she cleared the first layer of natural stone seating, moved across in one bound and was up and over the next layer within seconds. The third ring in the formation was much higher and flanked by rock columns at odd intervals.

Turning back to her friends, she saw that they were close on her heels. Spying a narrow deer trail winding upward to the northeast, Amber made her way to it. Her eyes followed the thin line until it disappeared in a tangled stone maze. Forging ahead, her calf muscles protested as she encountered a steep incline. Unlike the hard-packed caramel-colored earth that characterized many of the trails traversed thus far, this path was little used and the soil, covered in ash and soot, was dark, loose and slippery.

Amber was forced by necessity to slow down and walk sideways. She carefully picked her way in order to avoid being pitched headlong down into a boulder-lined creek bed. The deer trail naturally followed the seasonal stream, small branches veering off at intervals in order for the animals to find water. Soil and small pebbles dislodged by her passing skimmed down the hill and over the soles of her companion's shoes.

"Sorry!" Amber apologized to Noelle, nearest her on the steep hillside as she released another thin veil of debris upon her.

"I can't believe they took my metal detector and went without me!" Jonah grumbled.

"What'd they need your metal detector for?" Marisol asked.

Amber silenced her friends as she scanned the cliff walls towering above them. The feeling was unmistakable and it wasn't the warm fuzzies of the First Peoples she had tuned into.

Someone was watching them.

The teens neared the cliff face, where a break in the wall became visible. Ancient geological activity had caused part of the mountain to buckle backward, wrenching a portion of the hillside off and leaving a natural stone arch under which they must pass. Scrambling on hands and knees up the last several yards, Amber reached the archway and paused.

The cliff face beyond didn't look quite the same as it had from down below in the grotto. Alternating light and dark bands of stone lined the wall horizontally in snake-like pattern.

Noelle came up short behind Amber and whispered, "What's up?"

Amber ventured no further as she assessed the waterfall. Ridges were clearly visible in the cliff face, about two stories in height. The ascent would be risky, but doable.

"Well?" Noelle prodded impatiently.

Turning to her companions, Amber's face was solemn as she said, "Once we go over, there's no turning back. You up for this?" She may as well have been asking them to sign up for a stint with the Navy Seals. Amber's heart was racing so fast she could hear thrumming in her eardrums. Instinct screamed that crossing the threshold would *change* things. Nothing would ever be the same.

All heads nodded vigorously.

The decision made, Amber turned back to the archway and resolutely strode through. As she passed underneath, rising anxiety informed her that the unseen eyes would not go unchallenged. Risking a glance up, she spotted the yawning maw of another cave about twenty-five feet above her head. It was invisible, unless you stood directly underneath.

There was nothing she could do. Now was not the time for a side trip to investigate the unwelcome peeper. Glaring up at the cave, she treated whoever was up there to her most unpleasant face before she was forced to flatten herself against the stone and move sideways as the crevice narrowed in an L shape, funneling the would-be rescuers to the waterfall.

Reaching the elbow of the L first, she assessed the now-dry waterfall they must ascend. As the crow flies, it was the most direct route to a dirt road that should lead them to the Twelve Apostles and their imperiled friends. The trail dropped away into a deep, shard-strewn gully a few feet from the tips of her shoes. Negotiating their way to the top of the cliff meant inching out over a sheer drop-off and then free climbing two stories up, without the assistance of a safety rope or any other climbing gear she didn't know the names of.

The others inched as near as they could, but were unable to see around the corner, penned in as tightly as cattle in the chute.

Amber checked her shoes to make sure her laces were securely tied and thought, *Brigid, if you're there, I'd really like to make it to the top in one piece.*

Reaching out, her fingers found a handhold. The right leg followed, her foot toeing onto a narrow ledge. Finding a hold for her left hand, Amber eased her foot off the ground and hung over the dry, deep pool. Rocks split from the mountain's face had been brought low by the inevitability of gravity, their sharp, jagged edges a testament to separation under extreme protest.

Noelle stoically watched Amber's progress as she moved forward to take position as the next in line. Slowly and steadily, Amber crept up the cliff face in crab-like fashion, the stone gritty and sandpaper rough beneath her fingers. Dirt flaked off the top of narrow ledges as she reached for handholds, jamming under her fingernails, which were quickly becoming jagged from scraping around in her best efforts to grab hold of something unyielding and keep moving up.

Feeling buoyed by her progress, Amber easily scrambled the rest of the way up the cliff. Upon clearing the top, she rolled away from the edge and onto her back, appreciating the feel of solid ground.

Turning onto her stomach, Amber saw Noelle had already made her way up, her friend moving gracefully to join her.

Mari was the next to climb, tentatively, slowly, stopping several times to get her bearing. Words of encouragement were whispered, Amber in particular taking care to avoid urgency creeping into her voice. The sun was reaching the westerly part of its zenith and would soon be down. She was anxious that they all be up and over the cliff and well on the road before dark.

Scaling the cliff was not yet the greatest challenge they would face.

Nearing the top, Marisol over-estimated the distance to the next foothold and instead found her right foot toeing open air. Panic coursed through nerve endings in sharp bursts as her foot sought in vain for something, *anything* to get a hold in. Finding none, her left foot slipped as well, leaving her hanging by her hands, dangling out in the open air over the angular rocks thrusting up from below.

"DON'T flatten against the cliff! Push AWAY from it!" Jonah yelled as he stamped his feet in frustration.

Mari's body flailed and her grip began to slip from the sweat that now dripped from her fingers.

With speed Amber didn't think possible, Noelle was back over the side of the cliff and hanging next to Marisol.

"Marisol," Noelle ordered. Further words were whispered that Amber and Jonah could not hear.

The ringing in Marisol's ears silenced as a peaceful calm enveloped her. Pushing away from the cliff face, Mari's left foot regained its toehold. Inching her right big toe against the wall, she found an indentation in the rock face and dug in. After taking a few moments to catch her breath, she began climbing again until she was close enough for Amber to grasp her arms and haul her to the top.

"I don't know about the rest of you, but this feeling of being watched is creeping me out!" Jonah had left the ledge when he was certain Marisol had regained her position. He hastily ascended the wall to join the girls.

The three girls fell into a horizontal row as they trotted next to Jonah across a short flood plain and then up a low hill as he pulled out his cell phone. As promised, a dusty dirt road awaited them atop the hill.

"Thank God! Reception! We're saved!" Nearly weeping with the rush of relief, Jonah dialed Max.

"Oh yea, I'm sure everything's gonna be just fine now!" Noelle quipped.

Amber motioned toward the south in the direction of the Twelve Apostles, breaking into a slow jog. Marisol and Noelle trotted after Amber. Jonah hastened to keep up with the now fast-moving girls, attempting to inform Max about their dilemma in between gasping for air. When he finally finished, he shouted, "Stop! We don't even have a plan! You're going to get us killed!"

This last accusation brought Amber up short, memories of the fire leaping anew into the forefront of her mind. It was one thing to risk her own safety, but quite another to put the lives of her friends in jeopardy.

"You're right. We have to have a plan."

"We're wasting time!" Marisol cried. "You saw what I saw! Luis was unconscious, or maybe even…"

"Hey, girl! He was breathing, I saw! Didn't the rest of you?" Noelle insisted; Amber and Jonah quickly agreed.

"Plus, we don't know if what we saw happened in the past, right now, or a little ways in the future! Maybe we're going to get there just in time," Amber added.

"Then what are they doing up there with a metal detector?" Marisol accused Jonah. "It doesn't make sense that the Salvia's beat them up just for trespassing. What's going on?!!" she demanded.

Jonah admitted sheepishly, "Uh, er, there's a legend about a Salvia outlaw that robbed the stagecoach and buried the treasure, so they're looking for it."

"Those dumbasses!" Noelle said, "If there was gold, someone would've found it by now!"

"The Salvia's must believe it too! We've got to go, the guys are in danger!" Marisol begged.

Turning to Jonah, Amber asked, "How far away is Max?"

"He's maybe a half hour away."

Amber brightened, "Then he'll be there not long after us!"

The little band grew silent, unsure how to proceed as the Santa Ana winds kicked up dust and debris from the dirt road. The wind whirled faster, faster, up and into a loud funnel, pulling their hair in crazy directions, stinging their eyes.

Amber used the momentary distraction to wrack her brain for ideas, *anything* that could help them.

The merciless wind howled in her ears, bringing back the memories of Native American stories of…coyote! The Simi Hills were full of coyotes and Amber could call upon the animals to come to her aid…

They were saved!

191

Her companions sensed the change in Amber's body language. Seeing the smile on her face, they waited, expectantly. The songs she'd learned with Shelby came to mind and Amber opened her mouth to give them voice.

Nothing came out.

Damn it! The songs were there, in her head! Why couldn't she sing? Why had she been temporarily struck mute?

Jonah gently touched her arm. "Amber, what is it? What's wrong?"

Amber opened her mouth to speak, relieved to find she still had her voice. "*Coyote*, Coyote the Trickster. I wanted to call on him to help us by singing the song I learned from Shelby's tribe, but when I try to sing, I can't!"

Mari was anxiously knitting her hands together and looked as if she wanted to bolt down the road at any second toward Luis, but her face suddenly softened as she offered, "Maybe because they're not *your* songs. That's why you can't sing them. You're not supposed to. They don't belong to you." Her face fell into worry again when she realized the alternative. "I don't suppose you know any Celtic songs?"

Frustrated, Amber recalled when she'd been beneath the laurel sumac, how she'd become *one* with the hills. "Give me a sec," she held up her index finger to the others and turned her back, breathing in deeply of the mountain air. Her vision swam as the edges blurred, bringing a sensation that she and the hilltop were joining as her breathing took on the rhythm of the mountain itself. Extending her arms to either side, palms facing outward, she called out with her mind's eye to coyote.

Amber expected something like the gentle pulsations experienced when she connected with small animals, or the wispy brush of feather-light consciousness from the birds, or even the intriguing sensations from the vulture. But what answered Amber's call was foreign, strange, and discomfiting. Something latched onto Amber and *pulled*, separating her from her body in bizarre schism. Terrified, she tried to break off.

Time began to lose meaning as she was swept toward the chasm that opened up in the stone beneath her feet.

Seth's mother wrung her hands together nervously. It had been one of those days where she'd been jumpy and had a bad case of the 'drops', most recently shattering a vase at a house she'd shown to a prospective buyer.

Unsure as to the cause of her disastrous day, she decided a stiff drink was in order and made arrangements to meet her friend Rose Novak, owner of Lake Manor's Log Cabin Curiosity Shop, at the Hillbilly Haven for Happy Hour.

Greeting her old friend with a warm hug, Ms. Lobata settled onto her bar stool with relief as the sounds of pool cues clacked around the dimly lit room.

Concerned, Rose inquired, "What's up?"

Taking a sip from her drink, Ms. Lobata plunged in, "I don't know why, but I can't stop thinking about that house."

Rose Novak asked, "Is it the strange old house on Lizard Hill, where Seth's friend Amber lives?"

Ms. Lobata nodded as she gripped her drink tighter. "I told you about how weird the whole thing was. I've never had so many obstacles thrown in my way when trying to broker a deal! I figured everything went catty-wampus because of that moron manicurist handling the listing. But I don't think so anymore." Meeting Rose's eyes, she found her rapt with attention.

"As soon as I got the call from McBride, everything fell into place. Funny how he just happened to see the online photos the night before his interview at the Santa Susana Field Lab. That bumbling idiot manicurist manages to show up right when McBride is at the front gate on his way back from the interview! His house miraculously sells, right after he's offered the job. McBride puts in a lowball offer and Blank Jr. takes it, and we close in a record three days! I've never closed escrow that fast! I mean, inspections completed lickety-split and no problems? When does *that* ever happen? Suddenly the universe aligns in my favor...it's too much to be a coincidence."

Pale and shaking, she took a gulp of whiskey for fortification, clutched her friend's hand and revealed, "As much as I want to believe the universe aligned for me, that's not what happened. I think that house sent everyone else packing and rigged the deck for the McBrides because it wanted them."

✝

Raising outstretched arms to the sky, Marisol cried aloud, "Madre María, líbrame en mi tiempo de necesidad!"[20]

The howling wind stopped.

In a rush, Amber came back to herself as skeletal fingers retracted.

To the north a lone coyote howled. As the mournful wail faded away, the shadowy hills around the four teenagers erupted into a raucous chorus of coyote yowling and yipping.

Staring at each other in alarm, no one said a word.

Movement in the dimming light drew their attention up the road to the north where the dusky outline of a creature slowly and deliberately walked in their direction. Breathless, everyone waited in anticipation. Out of nowhere, a brilliant ray of sunshine illuminated a patch of earth several hundred feet away and into the light walked an enormous coyote the size of a German Shepard. Golden-furred, he was more wolf-like than the scrappy

---

[20] Spanish for 'Mother Mary, deliver me in my time of need'

grey animals Amber had seen scurrying around in the Pacific Northwest.

Ears perked up, he stopped and surveyed Amber.

Inwardly sending up a rude gesture to whatever loathsome bony-fingered creature had tried to hijack her, Amber took command, urging, "Get to the Twelve Apostles as fast as we can!" She broke into a sprint, her friends by her side. Risking a quick glance behind, Amber found the golden-furred coyote following at a low lope.

Jonah realized with a sinking feeling that Amber was absolutely correct: *There was no turning back now.*

They swiftly moved ahead through what was now a barren moonscape, and soon reached the large stand of laurel sumac, behind which Max had previously hidden the SUV for their mountain bike outing, the day Amber had first encountered the Salvia brothers.

There was no sign of the Russian.

Refusing to think about what could happen, Amber took the lead down the narrow trail. Keeping a steady pace, the collapsing remains of the once lively Zorro's cabin soon came into view. Coming to a stop, Amber held up her hand for silence as her friends gathered around. In unison, the teenagers turned back to the north to see what sort of help Amber had conjured.

The golden coyote was sitting ten feet away. Arrayed around him in a semi-circle were at least a dozen coyotes, eyes shining craftily, ears twitching. Some sat, others paced back and forth as if to tell the four to *get on with it.*

A nagging voice reminded Amber of the Native American legends warning '*Coyote was the Trickster,*' but it was shut up by a human wail that faintly floated from the direction of the Twelve Apostles. "We need to do this now!" Amber announced, "We can't wait for Max."

Slipping in between the narrow boulders leading to the Twelve Apostles, she led the way, her companions following silently behind. Where running down the dirt road had seemed to occur in the blink of an eye, traversing the narrow path blanketed by stifling, heavy air seemed like a damnable eternity.

What if the vision had been of the past and they were too late to save their friends?

A cool breeze informed her that the Twelve Apostles lay near and she held up one finger behind her in warning.

Now what? Leaping out like an action hero hollering a battle cry seemed ridiculous.

Unsure, Amber stopped.

A chorus of yelps erupted behind her, to which she soon added her own when something furry brushed past her thighs. Realizing what was happening, she threw caution to the wind and raced out from the opening in the stone maze, a wild battle cry in a language she didn't know raging from her lips.

As she emerged from the split in the rock, coyotes streamed by her sides as fierce winds blew her long red hair in crazy flame-like angles.

Ben Salvia had just punched one of the boys in the stomach when the top of the Twelve Apostles exploded into a howling, shrieking circus as a fire-haired Goddess emerged from the stone, surrounded by wild animals. It took his brain several seconds to process the image before recognizing it was none other than *Amber McBride.*

The shrieking wind was filled with snarls and growls as his brothers were surrounded by coyotes.

Ben Salvia dropped James Toshima and ran to help his brothers. He skidded to a stop when an enormous golden-furred coyote leaped in his way, fangs bared.

Ken and Martin put their backs to each other in formation, baseball bats outstretched, angrily swiping at the feral creatures as they drew near.

Racing to the prone boys, Amber and her friends cradled their heads, desperately trying to revive them.

The coyotes appeared to be toying with the brothers. Clearly, the Salvias were outnumbered, as the coyotes could overwhelm them at any moment. Yet the pack teased and taunted them, first moving in as if to bite and then quickly withdrawing when a weapon swiped too close to a furred head.

Slowly but surely, the coyote pack herded the Salvia brothers in the direction of the cliff.

Kendrick Salvia was the first to recognize the horror of what lay in store should he do nothing. Grabbing Martin's shirt, Ken swung his bat wildly and broke through the line of coyotes. Kendrick made a break for the crevice, dragging a flailing Martin close behind. Yipping and howling at their heels, the coyotes gave chase.

The golden coyote continued to stare down Ben Salvia.

Ben never took his stark eyes off the coyote as he jerked a handgun from his waistband.

Suddenly, the coyote was gone in a flash, sensing something far more dangerous than Ben Salvia. Sensing it as well, Ben slowly raised his eyes to the stone maze.

Atop one of the large rocks was a mountain lioness, sitting patiently, watching the entire scene unfold, lazily licking a paw when Ben Salvia spotted her.

When Amber saw the head coyote run, she followed Ben Salvia's eyes to what had captured his attention. Horrified, she realized that seated atop one of the cottage-sized boulders was the mountain lioness she'd met her first night in Lake Manor!

When the mountain lioness felt Ben Salvia's eyes upon her, she gave a low growl, ears flattening menacingly atop her head.

195

Ben raised his handgun in her direction.

"*No!*" Amber screamed, her rage borne away into the surging wind. Leaping up from James's side, Amber bounded to Ben and dove headfirst into his midsection, causing his shot to go wild.

It was with immense gratification that Amber witnessed the lioness turn and flick her tail at Ben Salvia in haughty dismissal as she leaped away, unharmed.

Right before Amber and Ben hurtled headlong over the cliff.

III

BRUJA

According to the law of three, whatever harm you do to another will come back upon you and yours threefold

CHAPTER 13

ILLUSION

The black SUV skidded to a stop by the Laurel Sumac grove. Max stepped from the vehicle. The strength of the gusting wind would have caused a lesser man to adjust his suit jacket, but the Russian was indifferent.

LAPD had not yet managed to find the location and Max was not inclined to wait. Sticking to the brush-line, he moved quickly, silently, avoiding the path but keeping to the general direction of the Twelve Apostles. When he reached the sagging doorway of Zorro's cabin, the Russian unsheathed his 9mm Sig Sauer pistol. Max held the pistol close to his side, with his finger across the safety as he cautiously made his way to the back of the decrepit building.

Upon gaining the corner, guttural growls caught his attention, spurring him to retract slightly as he waited.

A large golden-furred coyote came trotting from around the back, yellow eyes warily regarding Max. Sniffing lightly, the coyote turned and moved away in the opposite direction.

Extending his weapon hand, Max slid around the corner.

Unexpectedly, Ken and Martin Salvia raced from the boulder maze as if the devil himself were in hot pursuit, coyotes streaming behind, biting and snapping for purchase.

"Ostanovit!"[21] Max ordered loudly in his deep, heavily accented voice.

Kendrick stopped short, causing Martin to crash into him from behind. Acknowledging Max, the coyotes didn't slow their pace but distinctly avoided him, following the same path off into the hills as the golden-furred one had taken.

Max ordered, "You two Salvias, put hands behind back, you know drill."

Incredulous, Kendrick stuttered, "What are you doing? Get the hell off our land!" as Martin lunged forward, only to be brought down by a blow from Max.

"You want next?" Max asked Ken as he weighed his options.

"No Salvia ever goes quietly," Kendrick spat as he tried to disable the Russian, but was soon rendered unconscious like his brother.

"No time for chat. I must help Jonah," Max said as he quickly took out handcuffs and secured the two Salvias around a scrub oak, then headed into the boulder maze.

---

[21] Russian for 'Stop'

The call came into LAPD that there was an assault atop the Twelve Apostles rock formation, and a patrol car had been sent out to deal with the latest lunacy in Lake Manor.

Within twenty minutes of dispatch, Officers Johnson and Gutiérrez received a call in their helicopter from Officer Huang and his new partner, hopelessly lost. Apparently, LAPD tactical maps showed a confusing maze of dirt roads and deer trails, all of which looked the same and some of which led over sheer cliffs.

"I've bottomed out five times already!" Officer Huang complained "The motor pool guys are gonna want a piece of me when they see this car! What we need is a jeep."

"There's a lot of wind. It's really bad," Officer Gutiérrez replied.

"Well, the hits keep on coming! One of the teenagers involved is that redhead from the creepy old house on the nature preserve."

Perking up at the controls, Officer Johnson immediately turned in the direction of the Simi Hills as Officer Gutiérrez confirmed in a resigned tone, "All right, we'll come check it out."

Johnson quipped, "I'm starting to see a pattern here…"

Gutiérrez nodded, adding, "Hold onto your ass, it's gonna get rough."

☯

Amber experienced a sickening feeling of freefalling, but the powerful strength of a giant warm hand shoved her backwards, slamming her body painfully into the side of the cliff. Without thinking, her hands scrabbled for something to hold onto. Finding a partially exposed oak root, the end winding back into the cliff a few feet away, she clutched it firmly. Kicking furiously for the rock face, her frantic feet found a toehold.

Blowing furiously, the wind continued to batter her. A short distance away, Ben Salvia clung to the cliff face in much the same manner as she. Although it was now past twilight, she could make out his startling dark eyes, staring directly at her. For once, his face actually showed emotion.

He shouted something to her, but in the wind's ceaseless howling, it was lost.

The darkness underneath opened up into a yawning maw with pointed teeth that awaited her, should she lose her grip. One misplaced hand or foot and a painful, merciless death waited, for the second time in her short span of moving to Lake Manor.

Her fingers were becoming stiff and cramped in the rapidly cooling evening.

∞

Max emerged from the stone channel and onto the open plain atop the rock formation as Jonah hurtled into him, tears streaming down his face.

Patting his shoulder reassuringly, Max urged, "Tell me what in hell is

199

going on out there?"

With a quivering finger, Jonah pointed in the direction of the cliff. "Amber!"

Max motioned for Jonah to step back with his friends. Seth, Luis and James were now groggily conscious as Marisol and Noelle anxiously hovered over them. Holstering his weapon, Max stepped fearlessly to the edge. Removing a flashlight from a pocket, he hunkered down and looked out.

About twenty-five feet down, pressed against the cliff, a flash of red hair was illuminated.

Pulling out his mobile, Max called LAPD back.

"Amber, don't look down!" This time, Ben's voice cut through the blustering Santa Anas.

Shocked, Amber looked away from the hazy bottom, hundreds of feet below and met his stark eyes.

Brilliant light illuminated the two of them and their predicament: the narrow split in the cliff's face into which their feet were jammed. The spotlight was soon joined by another and yet another.

Ben remained resolute, ordering, "Look at me."

The wind continued to roar and shriek. A line of rope was flung down. It hung in front of her face for a second before it blew wildly around and out of reach. Amber was in a state of complete confusion. Why was he trying to help her? Didn't he want to finish what he started?

"Amber, grab it!" Ben shouted over the din.

Amber shook her head. *No way.*

Pressing his forehead against the cliff face for a moment, Ben then lifted his eyes, searching. Reaching his left hand over towards Amber, he grasped an exposed oak root, gradually moving his body closer towards her, toes inching along the narrow, horizontal split in the rock.

"Are you nuts?" she screamed.

Seeing the panic on her face, Ben insisted, "Easy Red, I'm trying to help you."

"Don't touch me!" she snapped back.

The rope fluttered tantalizingly close to Ben Salvia as he reached out, fingers momentarily brushing against it before it flew away in the tumultuous wind. Spying another length of exposed branch near Amber, Ben suddenly reached for it, pitching himself in her direction. The oak root, strong though it was, could no longer take such abuse. With a fleshy wrench, it began to tear free of the cliff.

Thrown headlong into Amber by the root's release from the cliff side, Ben Salvia grabbed her around the waist with one arm. He grasped the oak root with the other hand as it began to rip free, starting from the top of the rock formation and moving down with a mulching sound as it separated from earth and stone. Screaming helplessly, Amber nearly busted Ben's eardrum as they were once again thrown out into the open air.

Cursing as he observed the disaster unfolding before his eyes, Officer Johnson angled the helicopter dangerously close to the Twelve Apostles.

Underneath the LAPD helicopter, Officer Gutiérrez' subconscious registered the strong updraft moments before it hit them. "Hold tight!" he managed to blurt out before the wind shear ripped vertically through the air.

Officer Johnson's tenuous control was lost when the wind shear hit his rotors, sending the helicopter rocketing right over the Twelve Apostles. The blades whirred dangerously close to the gigantic rocks rimming the top, nearly nicking the one atop which the mountain lioness had stood not long before.

Luis, Seth and James were fully awake now and running with Noelle, Jonah and Marisol to the split in the rock. Max shoved the teenagers through when they reached the entrance. Marisol was the last to make it, blades chopping overhead, nearly decapitating her, had it not been for Max, who dove into her, torpedoing them both into the safety of the boulder maze. As Max made the relative safety of the stone, he hoped the rope he'd secured was still intact and dangling over the side of the cliff.

Down below, the length of rope slapped against the side of Ben Salvia's face when he and Amber slammed back against the cliff. Thinking quickly, he grasped it, found a foothold, and rapidly tied it about Amber's waist. "You've got to climb!" he shouted to Amber, who grasped the rock face and began working her way up, leaving Ben clinging to the cliff.

She'd climbed no more than a few feet when she felt herself being lifted. Taking advantage of momentum, she used her feet to propel rapidly upward, gaining the edge within a matter of minutes to find Max. After the helicopter cleared the Twelve Apostles, he'd immediately left the boulder maze and returned to help her. Thanking him profusely as her fingers worked frantically, Amber untied the rope and threw it back over the edge before Max could ask any questions.

Looking upward in shock, Ben ignored the rope and instead began to climb, unaided.

"You okay?" the Russian asked Amber.

Amber nodded as she watched Ben Salvia acrobatically ascend.

Moving back to make room for Ben as he neared the top, she found him staring intently at her before two LAPD officers roughly hauled him up by his arms.

"You're lucky nothing happened to her, or you'd be looking at a murder charge," Officer Huang informed him.

"Officer, I would like to invoke my right to remain silent." The stoic, emotionless mask Amber was used to seeing returned to Ben Salvia's face.

"You okay, Amber?" Officer Huang asked.

"What about my friends?" she inquired anxiously.

"They'll be fine. We've got them now," Officer Huang reassured her.

Adrenaline spent in the flight for their lives from the wayward LAPD helicopter, Luis, James and Seth had to be assisted as they wobbly-walked out through the stone maze. They were immensely gratified upon reaching Zorro's cabin, however, to find Ken and Martin Salvia handcuffed where Max had left them.

Head tilted and gesturing gangster style, Luis Garcia threw down his best taunt, "How's it feel, *maricon*?"[22] Behind him, noticed by only Noelle and Marisol, Jonah blanched.

Martin Salvia smirked as he answered Luis, in Spanish, "Diga a su madre que no vengo esta noche, pendejo!" Which means in English, "Tell your mother not to come over tonight, stupid!"

"Mi madre! A patear el culo!" Which means in English, "My mother! I'll kick your ass!" Luis roared as he lunged for Martin Salvia, seemingly healed by the gravity of the insult and the need to extract serious vengeance. Grabbing him about the waist, Max deftly swung him away from his quarry as the Salvia brothers chuckled.

"O.K. Machete, you can make revenge tomorrow," Max admonished. Depositing the boys in front of Zorro's cabin, Max smiled slightly as Seth extracted a promise from Jonah that he, under Max's protection, would return to retrieve the metal detector and mountain bikes. His smile broadened as he observed Ben Salvia being frog-marched out of the rock maze. Gesturing to the remaining two Salvia brothers, Max quipped, "I have also this trash, which should be taken with other bad man."

Max whispered low, so that only the Salvias could hear, "Please understand, if you have any trouble for these children, I will shoot many bullets into you, then kill you again, *Amigo*."

The color drained from Martin's face. He quickened his step, gratefully accepting being taken into custody by the LAPD and away from the menacing Russian.

Chuckling, Max quipped, "Kids!" as he clapped Jonah upon the back good-naturedly.

Observing the Salvias being taken away by LAPD, Seth teased Luis, "So, your mother and Martin Salvia? Didn't see that coming!"

---

[22] A Spanish insult on par with being called 'queer' or 'fag'

Luis lunged for Seth but missed the fast-moving boy. In his haste to tackle him, Luis tripped over a ground squirrel hole in the trail.

"Geez dude, did the Salvias knock your sense of humor out of you?" Seth taunted.

"Cut it out!" Marisol scolded Luis. Her voice cracked as she ordered, "Enough violence!"

Startled by the change in her voice, Luis looked up at his sister from his prone position upon the ground. Slender frame quaking with anxiety and anger, Marisol's face looked just like granny's did when she lost her temper over one of the many pranks Luis had pulled over the years. Her severe expression unnerved Luis and he retorted childishly, "I don't need your help, go bother someone else."

Just as quickly, the lines on her face smoothed. "Butthead!" Marisol shot back as she stormed away, looking very much like his sister again.

Luis reassured himself that his head wasn't right, given what he'd just been through. Although the Salvias were a menace, no one was more frightening to Luis than Graciela Hernandez. No wonder their rumble on the rocks inflamed memories of his formidable grandmother!

Seth Lobata stopped suddenly as he gingerly touched his head. His over-exuberant return to good humor caused tendrils of pain to shoot down into his neck. Noelle raced to Seth's side, throwing her arm about his shoulders as she looked him over anxiously. "That was quite a beating you took, huh?"

"Nah, it was nothing," he smiled, attempting to wave her off. Noelle ignored Seth's protests as she aided him in what now seemed like an agonizingly long journey back to the SUV.

Despite his insistence that he was fine, Max assisted Luis to his feet, helping him traverse the narrow path back.

"How about it, James?" Marisol grinned in relief that the nightmare was over, sparking a deep flush upon James' face from embarrassment over the need to be rescued. He wanted to die of shame at that very moment, but accepted her small hand as she helped him to his feet.

Jonah hung back with Amber, the last two upon the trail as they walked in fretful silence, both lost in their thoughts.

After what seemed a very long walk, the small band was grateful for the sight of the black SUV. Max drove cautiously, despite the boys' protests that they were fine and could handle the usual bouncing and jostling.

After a couple minutes, James Toshima spoke up, his voice distinctly and unnaturally loud, "I *can't believe* you four risked your lives for us like that. What were you thinking?" His dark eyes blazed with unnatural fire.

"Normally you say 'thanks' when you 'borrow' my metal detector and I have to come and save your ass," Jonah retorted.

Turning on Jonah in a fury, James raged, "How could you drag the girls into this! You nearly got Amber killed! The Salvias were *our* problem and you just made it *everybody's* problem!"

The youths were stunned into silence. Knowing James since elementary school, they had seen him angry only once, when he was seven and a boy at school had teased that James looked like the creepy Asian kid from the horror film *The Grudge*.

"I think they are done hurting you," Max's smooth, reassuring voice broke the tension. "I make nice chat with them."

Clenching his fists, James defensively crossed his arms over his chest. The disagreeable look that had settled in upon his face made no signs of departing as his brow remained deeply furrowed.

Max explained, "I know you have suffered, so we first must go to hospital, then police station. Is necessary, to keep animals in jail."

Seth, Luis, and James nodded, but Noelle, Marisol, Amber and Jonah exchanged nervous glances. What the hell were they going to say and how were they going to get their stories straight with Max in the SUV?

Taking charge, Noelle spoke in rapid-fire fashion, "You guys were unconscious, right? You didn't wake up until Amber and Ben went over the cliff?"

The three boys nodded, eying Noelle as to what she was getting at.

"You have to hear what happened, then!" she paused, presumably for air, but actually to collect her thoughts. Noelle *really* had to reach. How to explain that they knew the guys were even there?

Everyone waited, the atmosphere pregnant with expectation. Max registered the tense silence and invited, "Please continue. I very much would like hear."

"Ah...um...I wanted to see Zorro's Cabin!" Noelle announced a little too loudly. "I'd never seen it, so Amber and Marisol said they'd take me. We get to the cabin, and there's this rabid coyote! He chases us and before we know it, the entire pack is after us! We ran through the rocks and right into the Salvia brothers!"

Jonah rolled his eyes and tried not to groan aloud. *This was their story? No way the police were going to buy this crock of bullshit!*

Max did not look up, offering only, "Rabid animals, hmm? Nice story, Noelle."

Noelle glanced anxiously at the rear view mirror, but Max continued to look ahead. She knew that he didn't buy her story for one minute.

James cleared his throat and asked, "Why was Jonah with you?"

"Uh, he was at my house," Amber answered, trying to buy him time to craft a suitable answer.

The three boys turned to him, suspicious looks upon their faces.

Jonah decided the best defense was a good offense, and shot back, "How could you guys take my metal detector and sneak out behind my back?"

"Yes, please make tell me," Max added.

Luis sputtered, "So now you're a *snitch*, Abernathy?"

Max stopped the SUV and turned around in his seat, "I am waiting." When silence was the response, Max stated, "You remember dumpster that exploded? I find out truth in five minutes."

Seth confessed, "We found out more about the Salvia Stagecoach Robbery. The loot was never found, so we thought maybe the treasure was buried on top of the Twelve Apostles. Sorry Jonah, we didn't want your dad to ship you out to boarding school if we got caught."

"You've gotta be kidding me!" Noelle snorted, "I can't believe you guys got beat up over a stupid, made up story for little kids!"

In the wake of Noelle's outburst, Jonah asked sheepishly, "So, er, did you find it?" When she glared at him, he added quickly, "The treasure?"

"No," Seth admitted, "It's not there." Turning to Noelle, he insisted, "But bet your ass *the Salvias* believe the story, 'cuz they came out after us madder than I've ever seen them!"

"This is not good to tell police," Max responded. "The best way to tell lie is make *mostly* truth.

∞

At LAPD, Johnson and Gutiérrez completed the requisite paperwork. Officer Johnson remarked casually, "You're not gonna believe what I found out. Did you know Commander Rodriguez was working a cold case related to a girl who disappeared from a party at Amber McBride's house in the '80s?"

"That's strange," Officer Gutiérrez whistled. "How'd you find that out?"

"I went through his old files. It gets even weirder. Rodriguez interviewed three possible witnesses. One of them was the homeowner, Robert Hugo Franklin. This Franklin later goes to jail for quackery. Evidently, he got someone killed. He gets out and that's the last anybody's heard of him. The second witness was *Daniela Salvia*."

"No shit!" Gutiérrez thought back to the broken body of the Salvia boys' mother at the bottom of Twelve Apostles, where she'd leapt to her death three years ago.

"It gets better," Officer Johnson continued, "The third witness was Amber McBride's *mother*."

Officer Gutiérrez was stunned. Everyone they'd encountered recently was interconnected in some way to the past! Gutiérrez wondered if he should reveal Johnson's remarkable transformation into Commander Rodriguez that night above the nature preserve. Or did Johnson already know? Unsure of what to say, Gutiérrez instead asked, "Think Dr. McBride knows about it, maybe he bought the house to help cover his wife's tracks?

You know, if she had anything to do with the girl's disappearance?"

"I don't know," Officer Johnson frowned. "It seems like a stretch. I mean, why wait so long? If he was part of some cover-up, seems like he would've taken action sooner, maybe tried to make a move here earlier." A bit sheepish, Johnson admitted, "I asked Detective Karras to make some discreet inquiries at Boeing, and Dr. McBride has level fourteen NSA clearance. He's as squeaky clean as they come. I got a hunch he doesn't know anything about this."

Under normal circumstances, Officer Gutiérrez would've confronted his partner about holding out on him, but his hands were dirty because he was keeping secrets of his own. Deciding to reveal a little of what he knew in order to see how Johnson reacted, Gutiérrez said, "That night at the McBride's, in the crawl space, something's not right down there." Officer Gutiérrez went on to explain his spooky experience, and his suspicion that Officer Huang had experienced something similar. He concluded, "That house is *muy malo*."[23]

"Hey, I'm not gonna hold it against you," Officer Johnson responded reassuringly. "Rodriguez wrote that the same thing happened when they searched the place, and his notes said no one would even talk about it! I wouldn't believe it if I hadn't been there and seen what happened."

Relieved, Gutiérrez said, "Wow, so it's true! It wasn't just me."

"I don't even know where to go with all of this!" Johnson said. "But I have to find out what happened to that Lucy Carpenter, and something tells me that Amber McBride's mother is somehow the key."

Social media was ablaze with stories of the Rumble on the Rocks. By Sunday morning, in no small part due to Luis Garcia's influence over the tale, the three boys had been transformed from victims to heroes of the mountain biking constituency. The three friends gave a young, earnest face to the noble cause of seeing the wilds from two wheels and damn those self-centered property owners who thought they had any right to stop them!

Equally vociferous was the other side: the Salvias became unwitting poster boys for property owners sick of having their fences torn down, gates smashed open, livestock set free and lands trampled over, all in the name of 'public access.'

Their story was playing particularly well because of their Latino heritage. Property owners in the area, long portrayed as curmudgeonly old white men, had been delivered the perfect poster boys for their cause.

The Salvia brothers photographed surprisingly well, particularly Ben. He had been transformed into a dashing hero. The footage of his dramatic

---

[23] Spanish for "very bad"

efforts to rescue Amber from the cliff face were played and replayed countless times by the local media. It was at that crucial moment, when Ben Salvia made the decision to leave the safety of his ledge and inch over to Amber that the news crews arrived.

Of course, none of the viewers had the benefit of seeing the chain of events that landed Amber and Ben dangling, several stories up, precariously perched on the side of an extraordinary rock formation oddly named the Twelve Apostles.

LAPD offered no comment, not that it would have mattered. The story had taken on a life of its own.

Following the insane tale's trajectory evoked an exasperated groan from Amber. Like Ben, she was currently on lockdown, albeit in much more comfortable surroundings and minus the orange jumpsuit. She was grounded indefinitely, which may as well have been forever because her parents refused to set an end date.

The next headline was sent to Amber by Noelle with an *OMG!* The tagline provoked a reaction no less violent than kicking one of her schoolbooks across the room as Amber let out a ferocious rebel yell, earning a quizzical look from the dog.

ZORRO IS BACK!

Dashing owner of "Zorro's Cabin" risks life to save beautiful trespasser!

Locals say: "Adrenaline junkies have gone too far!" In the battle between property owners and mountain bikers...

Amber snatched up her cell and dialed Noelle, smashing her fingers into the screen in the process. "Your parents are lawyers! Now I'm a criminal? They were beating the guys! Who knows what they'd have done if we hadn't gotten there..." she sputtered, unable to even find words for what she wanted to say. Whirling around in her desk chair, she continued, "If my parents see that, I'll never be able to leave the house again!"

Noelle responded soberly, "I'm on it. Let me see what my parents can do. Back atcha as soon as I have news."

No good deed goes unpunished. Jonah and the guys would be heroes on Monday. To her dismay, Amber realized she'd been unwittingly cast as the old-school fairytale princess that required rescuing, and none other than the infamous Ben Salvia had stepped into the role of handsome prince. Argh! She wanted to scream!

Amber's bedroom door opened, without benefit of her father knocking. "Amber, we need to talk." The lines around his eyes had deepened, shadows underneath a testament to sleepless nights. Motioning for her to follow, he left her room and headed toward what she presumed would be her sentencing in the kitchen. With slumped shoulders she trudged after him, dreading the inevitable parental pronouncement.

Opening the kitchen door, Amber spied her equally grim mother seated at the kitchen counter. Padding by her side, Kibbles drew near to provide whatever moral support an elderly canine can offer. Looking from one parent to the other, Amber waited. For once, she did not want to be the first to speak.

Her father cleared his throat and announced, "I think you should go back to Seattle with your mother." The light drained from his eyes as he spoke these hated words that reeked of failure to make a new life for his family.

Absorbing the enormity of what the announcement meant, Amber was taken aback by her lack of immediate reaction. Shouldn't she be happy? This was her ticket out of this mess! Finally, the chance to go home, to return to her best friend Shelby and the life she knew! She would never have to deal with the Salvia brothers again...

Her mother spoke up, breaking off Amber's inward struggle.

"No."

Amber and her father were too stunned to react, so Mrs. McBride continued, "We're staying put for now. Amber's psychologist is here and she's making so much progress. It would be too disruptive for her to leave now."

In utter disbelief, Dr. McBride asked, "Are either of you living on the same planet I am?" Slamming his fist down on the counter, he no longer made any effort to control his temper. "Amber, we're pressing charges against these guys! If there's more we need to know, we need to know it now!"

Eyes flashing, Amber retorted, "How can you claim to be my father and believe there's something going on with me and the Salvia brothers?!" Angry tears began to flow as she bolted from the room.

Mrs. McBride shook her head as she stood to abandon the room, when her husband grabbed her arm.

Glaring at him, she met his gaze with equal measure.

"You're not concerned about this, not at all?" Dr. McBride accused.

His wife's eyes darkened, her pupils momentarily engulfing her irises in blackness. Dr. McBride drew back involuntarily at the change but didn't let go.

Shaking him off, Mrs. McBride left the room.

Silently seething for a moment, fists clenching and unclenching, his body shuddered as his veins coursed with rage. With an animal roar, Dr. McBride punched a hole in the door to the living room.

Amber watched the footage of her astounding rescue for the umpteenth time. It irritated her that Ben Salvia was being played up as her savior, like she was some helpless idiot frozen by fear and incapable of grasping the rope on her own.

Shelby appeared onscreen and teased, "Adrenaline junky?"

"Don't *even*," Amber menaced as she closed her eyes and covered her face with her hands.

"What do you think about this treasure business?" her oldest friend asked.

Amber uncovered her eyes, pulling down her cheeks and lower lip in the process. "I dunno. If it was a made-up story, why'd the Salvia's go all psycho on the guys?"

In LA County jail, the Salvias were also dealing with the realities of newfound celebrity. A few young gang members, seeing as it was their first time in stir, wanted to prove their mettle to the old gangsters by taking down the newcomers. The brothers Salvia sat at a table, hunched over trays, elbows out to defend from those who might take a notion to swoop in, and finished eating what passed for dinner.

No strangers to incarceration, the brothers knew to watch each other's backs at all times.

Ben was the first to sense that something was different from the usual menace: uniformed guards were conveniently absent from the room, only cameras to monitor the goings-on. Unobtrusively nodding to his brothers, they nonchalantly picked up their trays and left the table as a group. Their breathing joined and became unison as they dumped their trays at the end of the room and exited.

Others followed into the hallway, blocking the view of any guards that might be watching the feed from the video camera somewhere within the labyrinth.

The would-be attackers, three young men with shaved, tattooed heads thought they were getting the jump on the Salvias. They tried to corner them in an alcove, but instead found themselves quickly and viciously brought down by synchronized, simultaneous blows with cupped hands to the ears, followed up with knees to their groins. As the Cholos[24] silently fell to the ground, Ken looked over and commented, almost without any excitement, "I never noticed you're left knee-ed."

To which Martin replied, "Actually, I'm switch-knee-ed: left or right"

---

[24] Spanish for 'gang member'

"Niiiiiice!" Ken complimented his brother's hand-to-knee combat skills.

The chest pumping and posturing of the newbies were no match for the quiet precision and unified combat skills of the Salvias. The Salvias had been fighting for centuries, and took to the martial arts like artists experimenting with clays and oils: they really knew how to tailor a beating to suit any situation.

Before the guards knew what had gone down, the losers had been quickly dragged away. The point had been made: the newcomers weren't fresh meat. They had earned respect and space.

Ken and Martin discussed the aftermath of the fight with each other as they left the scene of their triumph. Ben had moved on ahead of them and offered not one word on anything that had happened, not about the fight, or any of the events leading to their arrest.

Ken caught up with his older brother as he stalked down the hall. "You trust George to guard the property while we're in stir?"

"He's a Salvia," Ben growled. "Family first."

"Think those little shits will come back?" Ken called after Ben, but he kept walking, leaving behind his perplexed brother.

ΑΩ

"Slone?"

The blond ninth grader looked up from her homework to find her mother standing at the door of her room.

"What's up, mom?"

Leaning against the door, her mother hesitated as she subconsciously twisted her wedding band back and forth.

"Mom? What do you want?" Slone asked again.

Decided, her mother entered Slone's room and sat on her bed. Clearing her throat, she stated, "We need to talk about your brother."

Slone turned around in her chair to face her mother. She did not respond.

"I, uh, we want to do an intervention, but we don't know where he is."

Slone waited. She knew this day would come, but she needed to hear someone say the words that would reassure her she really was unique and not some carnival freak.

"We haven't talked about this before, but I…you have a secret talent, Slone. You know things that regular people can't possibly know," her mother's words poured out in a rush now. "Use your God-given gift, please, help us find your brother. Help us find Shane before it's too late."

GEORGE SALVIA

CHAPTER 14

UNBOUND

Slone watched helplessly as her father and two burly men subdued her brother.

As her "head pictures" predicted, they found him sitting atop Castle Peak. He was mumbling unintelligibly to himself and seemed unaware of their initial approach.

When the two men from the treatment center were nearly upon him, Shane sprang from his seated position and attacked. Caught off-guard, Shane landed a disabling kidney blow to one of the men. The second man tased Shane, yet he kept on fighting. At that point, Slone's father jumped into the fight and pinned Shane's arms behind his back.

Her mother was crying hysterically, begging them not to hurt her son.

Through the din, Slone understood two words amidst the gibberish uttered by her brother:

Amber McBride

A tap on Amber's shoulder on Monday at school brought her face-to-face with Slone.

"I'm sorry I freaked out. I want back in on whatever *this* is."

Opening her mouth to speak, Amber couldn't find words at first. Sputtering, she finally managed, "I'm not sure what you think this is!"

"I know I was supposed to be there with you guys! You have to believe me!" Raising her voice in frustration, Slone's urgency caused Jonah and the others to stop talking. In a strange turn of events, Amber now fled from Slone.

Despite the frantic texts that streamed in throughout the day from Slone, Amber ignored them. What good was someone who freaked out in front of a group of ridiculously dressed ghosts from the 1980s? How would Slone have reacted to the mayhem atop the Twelve Apostles? Amber envisioned Slone squeaking in fright at the appearance of the golden coyote, shrieking at the sight of the guys and their bloodied faces...it was too annoying to consider any more possibilities.

Shutting her locker door, Amber jumped back in surprise when she found George Salvia leaning casually into the wall.

"Sorry, I didn't mean to sneak up on you like that. You sure you're ok?" His deep voice was kind.

"Yeah." Looking down, Amber was uncertain about what else to say.

After all, his brothers were in jail right now because of her and her friends.

Reading her body language, he asked, "You want to talk?"

"Where?"

"How about my car?" Noticing her uplifted eyebrow, George held out his palms and laughed, "Okay, it's not my car. We all share it, but seeing as how you landed my brothers in jail..."

"I don't think it's funny," Amber fumed. "Aren't you worried about them?"

George laughed out loud. "My brothers? Yeah, I'm worried for the poor saps that have to bunk with them. Shit, the Salvias practically have a wing named after us in county lock-up!"

"It's still not funny," Amber grumbled.

"Truce, okay? I don't think it was right of them to beat up your friends and I don't blame you. I just want to talk." George sounded perfectly reasonable, not at all angry, so why was she so uncomfortable?

Acquiescing, Amber followed the tall boy out to the overflowing student parking lot where the strange Franken-Bronco without a top or front doors sat conveniently parked in the so-called *Kojak* spot near the entrance. This was in reference to the '70's cop show where the bald detective always magically parked in front of whatever crowded place he was going to. What Amber didn't know was that that spot had always been the Salvia's private reserve. Even a first year Math teacher ran out and moved his car when he was quietly told of the mysterious injuries that befell the last teacher who repeatedly took that spot.

Gesturing toward the passenger side in gentlemanly fashion, George bade her enter before he settled into the driver's side. Sensing her discomfort, he dove in, "I didn't want any part of it, so I stayed home. Maybe I should've done something to stop it..."

"No, they're your brothers," Amber finally spoke up, staring at her hands before continuing, "I'm glad nobody was hurt." Looking directly at George, she asked, "Do you really believe that story about the treasure?"

Sighing, George grasped the steering wheel and said, "My brothers do. Our ancestors searched our property, but no one's ever found it, so if it even exists, it must be somewhere else."

"Aren't you curious?" Amber asked, "Don't you want to find it?"

"I don't have any idea where it is," George responded. Changing the subject, he asked, "How'd you know your friends were at the Twelve Apostles?" His dark eyes were as intense in that moment as his eldest brother's.

"Amber!" A high-pitched voice caused her to jerk about. Searching, Amber found Slone standing upon the pavement, hands clenched into fists.

The blond accused, "You're avoiding me!"

"Shit Slone, not now!" Amber hissed back, at the same time spying

Noelle and Marisol rounding the corner and heading in their direction.

Apologizing, she hastily exited the Franken-Bronco, but not before her friends spotted her rather undignified departure.

Amused, George remarked, "I'll see you around, Amber McBride."

Δ

After school, a somber Dr. and Mrs. McBride were waiting in the car for Amber as she emerged, hot and sweaty, from the gym. Noelle looked up from her cell phone and hopped into the back seat with Amber, flashing the message from her mother Belinda onscreen:

Meeting at our house. Much you didn't tell us. VERY DISAPPOINTED!

Gulping, Amber anxiously wove her fingers together on the silent, brief drive over to the gates of Bell Canyon. After being cleared by the guard, they wound their way up through scenic streets lined with spectacular homes boasting even more amazing views of the San Fernando Valley, none of which Amber noticed as her mind ran wild. Neither the Salvias nor the boys had spoken to the police about the treasure, so the parents wouldn't know about that. Nobody knew about Las Brujas. So what *did* they know?

Her dismay only increased when she saw Max's black SUV and vehicles belonging to Tammy Lobata and the Garcia Family in front of the Mertens' modern marvel. A new Lexus was parked on the street behind the Garcia's Prius, and Amber assumed it must belong to the Toshima family.

The gig was up. Hanging their heads, Amber and Noelle slunk out of the car with the enthusiasm of prisoners walking down death row's green mile.

"Admit to nothing," Noelle managed to whisper before Mrs. McBride was at Amber's side, ushering her into the house.

A grim-faced assembly awaited in the vast, cold living room with floor to ceiling windows and an expansive view of the San Fernando Valley. Amber briefly envisioned making a break for it, crashing through the glass and escaping to freedom. Sighing heavily, she risked a quick glance over at James, seated between his disappointed-looking parents.

Recalling something Seth told her about James' father directing a non-profit, and his mother curating LA's Japanese American National Museum, Amber sat down in between her parents, awaiting the inevitable.

Max alone stood, off in the corner of the room, his face unreadable as usual.

Attorney Belinda Mertens was the first to take the stand, rising from her seat after she waved Noelle's younger brother Nick back to his room. "The Salvias were released today. As all of you were trespassing on their property *and this isn't the first time*, they agreed to drop all charges, provided we drop charges as well." She stared pointedly at the boys with her prosecutor's glare. "Their attorney informed us today that you boys had been warned, *repeatedly,* during the summer to stay off their land." The tone of her voice grew dangerously low. "We also learned that the last time this happened, Amber was there and when the Salvias asked you to leave, you rode away from them down a deer trail that runs along the side of the Twelve Apostles!"

At this last revelation, everyone began talking at once and when no one could be heard over the din, they began shouting, until Attorney Steven Mertens stood in the middle of the assembly and yelled, "Enough! Let her finish!"

Luis opened his mouth to speak, provoking the evil eye from Max. Quickly sealing his lips, he sat back into the couch in an attempt to make himself smaller.

With a wife who stood close to six feet tall and Steven Mertens at over six feet, they made a formidable pair in the courtroom. Lowering his voice, Steven Mertens continued, "Given what we now know, it's a reasonable deal. We can argue about who was at fault all day, but that's best left to each of the parents. Belinda and I are not here to judge."

Luis could contain himself no longer over the outrageous injustice of it all. Turning to his father, he pleaded, "They had baseball bats and Ben had a gun! So they just get away with beating us up…er…trying to give us a beating?"

Mr. Jorge Garcia's normally sunny face was dark as he witnessed the tears that rolled down his wife's drawn, worn face. Reaching over to comfort his wife, he smacked Luis hard in the back of the head. "You're lucky I don't give you a beating myself! Endangering your sister like that?"

"None of the boys' injuries was consistent with use of any weapon. The Salvias will argue they keep weapons nearby for self-defense, given their remote location. Even if they used them to scare the boys, no matter, no weapons were used and no one was seriously injured," Attorney Steven Mertens confirmed.

Mr. Garcia's accent grew thicker as he became angrier. Standing abruptly, he pronounced, "Thank you for your wise counsel. We're in complete agreement." Helping his wife to her feet, this appeared to be a sensible course of action, given her overall shakiness and the tears that now flowed freely. Mrs. Garcia attempted to cover her face, unaccustomed to such public display of emotion. Marisol hugged her mother tightly as they walked out, Luis trailing dejectedly behind.

Mr. Toshima quickly exchanged a glance with his wife, a silent conversation taking place between the two before he spoke on their behalf, "We'll deal with our son. Thank you so much for your help." After formally shaking both attorneys' hands, the Toshima family departed.

"Yes, thanks, really. I'm so sorry for any trouble Seth caused you," Ms. Lobata added as she and her son hastily retreated.

Mrs. Emily Abernathy, a lovely, pin-thin woman with long, dark hair and exotic eyes inclined her head to Max, signaling it was time to leave. Thanking the Mertens for their assistance, she inquired as to the cost, but was waved away with a polite refusal and words of friendship.

After likewise thanking the Mertens, the McBride family took their leave. No sooner than they were in the car, her father launched into Amber, making no pains to conceal the betrayal he felt in response to her actions. "You *lied* to me about how you got a concussion."

Opening her mouth to speak in her defense, Dr. McBride cut her off by holding up one hand as he pulled away from the Mertens' house. He refused to look at Amber in the rear view mirror. "I know everything now. Nothing you say is going to change anything." Despite his anger, his voice was sad and spoke of yet another knife in the back from a female he loved and trusted.

Mrs. McBride turned around in her seat to confront Amber directly. The dark circles underneath her eyes were a testament to worry and lack of sleep. "We were right to ground you! You're not going anywhere other than school, and to see Dr. Morton."

"Mom! You're not being fair!" Amber protested.

Normally at this point in one of their many arguments, her father would step in as the voice of reason. Instead, Dr. McBride ordered, "You heard your mother, Amber. End of discussion."

When the McBride Family reached the House on Lizard Hill, everyone went their separate ways. No further words exchanged. Each was dispirited, exhausted, and unable to answer the bell to a new round of emotional boxing.

In the middle of the night, Amber awoke awash in sweat from a lingering bad dream in which she'd caught George Salvia and his friends laughing at her, the truth finally revealed. His time with her was nothing more than a dalliance; some bet he'd made with a friend about bagging a ginger. She meant nothing to him. Shame enveloped her as Amber came awake and rose to use the bathroom. As she slouched down the hall in the dark, she swore an oath to herself that she'd be nobody's fool: George Salvia would be kept at arm's length, as he himself had put it, a friend, for all intents and purposes.

∞

During his time in stir, Ben was informed about Max taking down Ken and Martin, and the dire threats to the Salvia brothers should they tangle with the trespassers again. Death threats were nothing new to the Salvias and were usually treated with great humor in light of the family curse. Considering their dalliances with so many unavailable women, a good number of men wanted to inflict grievous bodily injury upon the infamous Salvia brothers. As Martin succinctly summarized, "It's the cost of doing business."

Unprecedented was any man taking down one of the legendary Salvias. As a result, his brothers were completely rattled by this 'Max' character. Neither Kendrick nor Martin could explain how and why the menacing Russian posed a genuine threat to the Salvias, but there it was: he was a definite danger, different from any man they had ever encountered before.

Proactively, Ben asked Kendrick to reach out to an ex-girlfriend who worked for one of the online gossip mags. Though to be precise, 'ex' was sort of a misnomer, because most of the Salvia's girlfriends may have accepted the break-up on the face of it, but invariably stayed available in some form. Excited by the renewed interest of her former flame, she returned Max's last name and a fairly complete dossier on his activities since arriving from the former Soviet Union within the span of twenty-four hours.

Next, Ben placed a phone call to one of his cousins, Rico Salvia. Rico was one of the many decorated war veterans in the Salvia family tree. He had done several forward operational tours in the danger zones of Iraq and Afghanistan and, although never rising above the rank of gunny sergeant, he had the ear and respect of many higher-ups, including several Intelligence officers.

Ben chose his words carefully when describing the encounter with the Russian to his cousin Rico Salvia, "It's not about Ken and Martin turning into little bitches. You know nothing rattles them. But somehow, this guy took them down. I'd like to learn some more about him. Who knows if *Maksim Kiselev* is even his real name?" Ben mused.

His cousin Rico agreed wholeheartedly, "I'm on it. An enemy of one of us is an enemy to all of us."

Amber's lockdown and her mother's non-stop checking in made for an atmosphere so cloistered and smothering that school actually felt liberating. Amber stubbornly refused to discuss the Salvia brothers, despite her mother's non-stop badgering. When bullying didn't work, her mother tried a kinder, gentler approach. It, too, went over like a lead balloon.

"Honey, I remember what it was like at your age. When I liked a boy, I thought I was going to die if we couldn't be together."

Groaning inwardly, Amber mounted her defense, "Is this about the Salvias again? Just because you were boy-crazy doesn't mean I am!"

"You say that, but then you keep getting mixed up with them. Why don't you tell me what's happening?" her mother pleaded, "You can trust me!"

Furious, Amber struggled momentarily to find the right words of retort. A part of her wanted to believe her mother, but history had shown otherwise. With a tone of voice that sounded like a child to her ears, Amber accused, "Trust you? Every time I've ever needed you, you tell me to stop making things up! Now you want me to *trust you*?!!"

Wringing her hangs together, Mrs. McBride appeared close to panic because she was failing to get through to her daughter. She begged, "Amber, you're still young, there's so much you don't know. Someday I'll explain it all. But please, listen when I tell you those boys are dangerous! That *Ben* is in his twenties! They're too old for you to be running around with! You've got to stay away from them or you're going to get hurt!"

Dangerously close to tears, Amber fired one last retort as she fled the room, "I don't give a rat's ass about the Salvias! They can *drop dead*, for all I care!"

Because Las Brujas were grounded, the only way they could speak away from gossipy snoops was online. One night after school, the teens reviewed the Rumble on the Rocks again, and reached two critical conclusions:

#1: Although the coyotes had come to their aid, none of them was willing to take one for the team. The coyote was and would always be 'the trickster.' The main evidence in support of this conclusion was the fact that coyote had set up his enemy, the mountain lioness, to take a bullet. Had it not been for Amber, coyote's plan would have been literally 'executed.'

#2: Marisol's prayer to Madre Maria kept everyone safe. No one had been badly hurt that night, not even after the vertical wind shear hit the LAPD helicopter.

Jonah asked, "We know about Amber's ability to ask the birds and animals for help. What about you, Marisol? Did anything tip you off that you might be, you know, *different?*"

Marisol answered, "Since middle school, little kids and really old people stare at me, in a weird way. One time at church this old lady wouldn't stop. It was totally freaking me out! When we were leaving she's suddenly there next to me, telling me she sees light all around me, that I'm blessed with the saints." Thoughtful, Marisol added, "I never saw her again after that. When I asked the priest about her, he told me she died the week after I saw her."

"Wow," Amber responded. "How about you, Noelle?"

Noelle's memory flashed back upon her Kendo sparring sessions and subsequent matches at tournaments. She'd handily defeated her opponents, not unusual. What stood out in her mind was *the look* upon their faces as she charged, yelling forth the traditional warrior's battle cry and wielding the wooden staff. In Kendo, the warrior dons a uniform similar in many respects to Darth Vader, complete with a dark helmet, which made her opponents' reaction all the more unnerving because they could never clearly see her face behind the mesh wiring of the mask.

Down to every girl and boy she ever competed against, the overwhelming reaction to Noelle in the heat of competition was sheer *terror*.

"No, nothing unusual," she replied a little too quickly. "How about you, Jonah?"

Now appearing as if he regretted bringing up the subject, he responded sheepishly, "My mom's family lives in Louisiana, so we'd go out and visit when Jeremy and me were little. One time I must've wandered off because I ended up down by a swamp, talking to some strange old dude whose face was deformed. When they found me, I wasn't scared, just hanging out with him. I was only five but I remember my aunties and mom smiling, saying, *"That boy sees beyond the flesh."* They thanked the old man before they took me home. It was so weird." He shuddered. "When I was older I found out that most of the locals were terrified of this guy. I guess he practiced *voodoo*. But I knew he was all right. And I've always been that way. I just know who's good and who's bad."

The teens grew quiet as they considered the implications of Jonah's revelation. Jonah hadn't thought about this event since he was very small. Re-examination of the memory, in light of recent events, suggested his mother and female relations might be keeping a few secrets themselves.

"So…George?" Amber queried.

"George what?" Jonah snapped, knowing full well what she was asking.

"Good or bad?"

Groaning, Jonah turned away from his laptop camera before admitting, "Why do you think I ran around all summer with the guys trespassing on their property? I always knew none of the Salvias would *really* hurt us. Act like assholes and try to scare us, yeah. But they're not murderers."

Thinking back to the frightening excursion down the side of the Twelve Apostles, Amber accused, "Woulda been nice to know when we were running for our lives!"

"Right! Like you would have believed me!" Adopting a more scholarly look than usual, Jonah lectured nasally, "Excuse me Amber, but there's no need to run. The Salvia brothers are really like blow pops: hard and crunchy on the outside but soft and gooey on the inside."

"That just sounds so wrong." Marisol pulled a wry face, concluding, "Your definition of good is messed up. Luke Skywalker saw good in his father, but before Darth Vader switched teams he blew up a planet and murdered hundreds of Ewoks!"

Snorting, an insulted Jonah retorted, "I would've put Darth Vader on Team Evil. It's what you do that makes you good or bad."

"Wait a sec! Then why did you panic like the rest of us when we saw the vision at the grotto?" Noelle accused.

Shyly, Jonah admitted, "That night, for the first time, I really doubted my ability. I started to wonder if maybe I'd been imagining it all these years, or just been lucky. Knowing what I know now, I'm really sorry. If I'd spoken up maybe none of us would've freaked out. We'd have waited for Max and let him handle it."

Marisol stated emphatically, "I don't think letting them get beat up would've been the right thing to do. I still think we did the right thing."

Jonah asked Amber, "Hey, haven't you ever tried talking to your dog?"

Flushing, Amber turned around in her desk chair, so she faced away from her laptop camera. Shelby and her aunties understood because they'd known Amber since she was a little girl. Marisol knew a little about her ability because she'd witnessed a gathering of 'first peoples' at the grotto. But how to explain what it was *really* like without sounding insane?

Looking down to find Kibbles at her feet, she had an idea. Amber took the laptop down to Kibbles' level, so her friends would see things from his perspective. She explained, "I didn't understand what was happening at first. Think about how an animal sees things. They're down here and we're way high up from how they see it. I can see what animals see, like through their eyes. So I was with Shelby when we found Kibbles. I'm holding him and I see what looks like a giant salmon coming down from the sky. It was his first owner feeding him but I didn't know that, I was six! The salmon looked like it was floating down from heaven! It was so freaky because I felt like I wanted to eat that nasty fish head, mushy eyeballs and all! The smells were awesome, there aren't even words to describe them…"

Amber trailed off as she recalled the elder Native American owner, lying motionless upon the floor, and Kibbles desperately trying to revive him by licking his face. She decided not to share this painful memory.

"Do your parents know?" Noelle asked with obvious interest.

"My mom told me not to talk about it. She was no help! It was Shelby's aunties that showed me I wasn't a freak. They explained that I had a gift, but not everyone would understand it, so not to talk about it outside of our circle. If it wasn't for them I don't know what would've happened to me. I mean, what the heck was I supposed to think when I saw *butts*? Up close dog butts, people butts…I don't *even* want to talk about those smells."

"Wait a sec, if you're Snow White, and you got the coyotes to attack the Salvias, then that means you can make animals do stuff!" Jonah realized.

"The coyotes are the first animals that ever answered when I called," Amber responded quietly. "I've been trying my whole life just to talk to animals and birds. I could only listen and see things that just happened to them. I don't know what happened up on the mountain, but *something changed.*"

The bell rang, signaling the end of one sentence and the beginning of another period of incarceration. As Amber gathered her books, Slone lightly touched her arm, "We need to talk."

"There's nothing to talk about."

"There's something about the Bat Cave *you need to know*, so I think you'll want to talk to me. Meet me for lunch."

Whirling around to leave, Slone Summer's long blond hair whipped about to make her point clear, turning Amber's stomach sour as she digested this latest news.

Detective Karras asked Officer Johnson what he'd been up to over the weekend. Grinning, Officer Johnson informed Detective Karras that he and the wife had managed to find a reliable babysitter and gone out on a date, the first one in some time.

"My friend, it was an evening of *mucho amor.*"

Officer Gutiérrez' ears perked up immediately at the unusual lack of a white man's accent in Johnson's voice. His partner's Spanish had always been laughable at best, and yet he'd just now fluently spoke two words effortlessly, as if he'd been born in Mexico! Officer Johnson had even rolled his "R's," a feat he'd *never* managed during his previous pitiful attempts at conversing in Spanish.

Slone Summers was seated in her usual spot beneath a large Eucalyptus tree in the center courtyard intently studying a book. Catching Amber's glance, she waved her over and patted the concrete next to her as she bade Amber to sit.

Amber was slightly annoyed at being 'summoned' and refused to speak first as Slone simply turned a book in her direction. The photo of Munits's Cave she'd been studying was from a book, Susan Suntree's *Sacred Sites: The Secret History of Southern California.*

Intrigued, Amber read the author's vivid, poetic narrative retelling of the ancient Native American legend:

Munits liked to rest just beyond his cave on Castle Peak, a place where people observe the passage of the stars, sun and moon.

"Munits was an evil wizard," Slone concluded. "It's all there, in the book. I know I joke around a lot, but I've been to that cave and it's got a bad vibe. Like everything's dead or dying." Lowering her voice, Slone confided, "I'm scared, Amber, it's true, but I can also help. There's *more* but we need to be in a protected place to talk about it. And I know you know somewhere!"

"I need to talk to the others," Amber responded as she searched for the right words. "A lot has happened since you left."

A familiar shadow fell across the two girls, broad-shouldered and masculine.

"Got a minute?" George Salvia asked Amber, ignoring Slone completely.

"I'll just get going, see you guys later," Slone hastily moved off in order to give the two teens privacy.

"I think I figured out a way we can see each other," George informed Amber.

Curious about what George had in mind, Amber asked, "What've you come up with?"

"Come with me to Homecoming. Tell your parents that you're going with your girlfriends. They won't make you miss the dance. But go with me."

George Salvia's words so completely caught her off-guard that Amber was rendered speechless. She opened her mouth to speak and no words came out. Her brain was trying to make sense of what she'd just heard. Had he really asked her out? On a date?

Finally, despite her internal vows of keeping him at arms' length, Amber managed to croak, "Okay, sure."

"It's in two weeks, so I'll pick you up in the church parking lot at 7:00."

Upon seeing that Amber remained fairly frozen in place, George grasped her shoulder, asking, "What's the matter?"

Giving voice to her doubts, Amber said, "What are we doing? Maybe this isn't such a good idea."

"It's just a dance. What, you worried you're going to get me killed?"

Favoring her with a smile indicating they shared a secret conspiracy, George moved off as a friend came up from behind to hail him for class.

Just when her life seemed to be coming back under her control, everything was poised to descend into chaos again. Amber frowned as she wondered if she'd walked right into a trap. He'd spoken of friendship and now he was asking her out?

If George was indeed setting her up for something, why did this enigmatic guy draw her closer, instead of pushing her away? Given everything she knew about him, she should be running in the other direction. Yet here she was, offering herself up like a mumbling schoolgirl. When Amber tried to look at her situation logically, her reaction to George felt less like a friendship and more like being under a spell.

During film class, Amber discretely explained both predicaments to Noelle.

Laughing heartily, Noelle reassured her friend, "You're not the first person to feel like you're going insane! That's what it feels like when you really like someone."

"Well, I don't like it," Amber grumbled. Feeling out of control was not an emotion that suited her, not in the least.

"We'll all be there at Homecoming anyway, I mean we girls will. We got your back."

Amber hugged her friend, "You don't think it's a bad idea?"

"Live on the edge, girl! He's the cutest Salvia, and the only one that's never been arrested!"

"What about Slone?" Amber asked.

"I have to hear what she's got to say," Noelle confirmed.

"*What?*" Jonah yelled into Amber's room from her laptop that evening.

"Um, don't you think you're overreacting just a little? I mean, Munits the Sorcerer is only a legend. Let's hear what Slone has to say before we start freaking out."

"I don't like this Amber, not one bit! What if that's a black hole on that hill outside your window? Now we find out that the Bat Cave behind the school is Satan's last known address? And you're telling me not to panic? And now I hear you're going to homecoming with George Salvia? What the eff is going on?"

"Argh!" Amber scrunched up her hair, "We sure suck at keeping secrets! I told you, we're just friends!"

After signing off, Amber connected to Marisol on her computer. Her friend's kind face appeared onscreen as Amber informed her, "We need to talk."

"I know, Noelle told me. George Salvia asked you to homecoming!"

Fighting back the desire to put her fist through the screen, Amber clenched her teeth, snapping, "That's *not* what we need to talk about!"

"Well, I haven't learned how to read minds yet," Mari giggled.

Taking a deep breath, Amber shared Jonah's concerns, concluding with, "Maybe we should hear Slone out."

Thoughtful, Marisol answered, "Yeah, but we should also get help from my grandmother."

"Okay, now we just have to figure out how to get away from our parents," Amber moaned, thinking about the latest obstacle to overcome.

"I'm sure Noelle will think of something," Mari responded.

Sitting back in her desk chair, Amber remarked, "When did this get to be so much work?"

George and Martin entreated Ben to come with them on their way out the door to the Hillbilly Haven. For George, having Ben along would provide him with an excuse to sneak away for a little bit and perhaps go over to Amber McBride's house. Her consenting to go out had emboldened him. George Salvia believed Amber was very close to sharing the truth about what she *really* was. An hour with the redheaded Bruja would be infinitely more productive than being bored out of his mind playing pool at the local watering hole.

C'mon, man, it'll be good to get out," Martin encouraged Ben.

Without answering, Ben continued staring out the windows of their modest home.

"Leave him be," Ken shooed his brothers out the door. "Be out in a sec."

Ken walked around and stood directly in front of his brother, blocking his view.

"You mind?" Ben ran his hand through his dirty hair.

"Yes! You know mom wouldn't want this, not even today."

Ben turned away as he waved his brother off.

Pacing back and forth in front of the windows, Ken's tone took on increasing urgency, "I'm worried about you! You think I want to find you at the bottom of the Twelve Apostles?"

"What the hell are you talking about?" Ben snarled, "*I'm* the one that found her! Stop whining and leave me the hell alone."

Kendrick stopped pacing and met his brother's eyes, "You're sick, man. Get help before you drag us all down with you." Frustrated, Ken slammed the door as he left the house.

Sighing, Ben lifted his chin toward the ceiling, and then resumed staring out the window.

Officer Johnson had been able to talk Detective Karras into revisiting Lucy Carpenter's cold case. Although he really hadn't uncovered any new evidence, Detective Karras was a fan of the old *Zorro* TV series, and wanted to go check out the film set. He'd then agreed to interview the Salvia brothers, to see if their mother kept a diary.

"Thanks for taking me here." Detective Karras said to Officers Gutiérrez and Johnson as he took off his jacket and threw it across the back seat of their vehicle, his shirt stained with sweat. "How the hell did you guys know how to get here? On the tactical maps, it looks like a bunch of deer trails!"

They'd been given permission to take one of LAPD's huge suburbans, a vehicle much more suited for the primitive dirt roads upon which they now traveled.

Officer Gutiérrez turned the vehicle to the south and slowly followed the thin line of red dust that passed for a road as he bumped over deep potholes. He wondered what happened if a car came down from the Salvia place? One of them would obviously have to back up, or they would be at an impasse.

The rough road gained in elevation as it climbed alongside the cliff at an impossibly steep angle.

"I'd sure hate to try and get down outta here in a fire," Officer Johnson remarked.

"No shit, Sherlock," Detective Karras added as he peered out the window and over a sheer drop off that fell away into a dark chasm, adding, "It's not the fall, it's the landing!"

The SUV neared the top of pinnacle Salvia. Their small, white, one-story house sat at the very edge of a triangular rock jutting northeast of the Twelve Apostles.

Pulling the SUV next to an old pickup truck, the officers disembarked.

Martin Salvia saw a telltale cloud of dust above the road as he turned towards home. Ken had asked him to go back and check on Ben and now he wondered, who was headed up to their house?

Unconsciously and expertly he navigated the familiar long, narrow climb to the top.

Skidding to a stop, Martin honked the Bronco's horn.

In the middle of the road stood a huge coyote, as large as a German shepherd, with robust, thick golden-hued fur.

Lazily staring back at him, the coyote ignored the horn's blaring.

Martin wasn't about to get out of the Ford, not after the run-in his brothers had with that pack of rabid animals. For all he knew, this vermin was infected as well.

Instead, he revved the engine in warning.

The golden coyote lightly skipped out of the way to reveal a pile of rags in the road.

The bundle twitched, then shifted as a bony hand reached up from the center, the rags rising in jerky motion as something appeared to *unfold*.

Not waiting to see what might come next, Martin floored the gas on the Bronco to send it skidding backwards down the hill, away from the gruesome creature.

Sputtering, the powerful engine died as Martin Salvia frantically tried to restart the truck.

With long strides, Shadow Man walked over to the open cab with the golden coyote by his side. The rest of the pack loped silently up the roadway to join their master.

Amber snuck out to make the impromptu meeting with George Salvia at the church parking lot, figuring she was already grounded. What else would her parents do, if she got caught?

As usual, she felt a certain amount of butterflies in her stomach whenever she anticipated seeing George. Amber found him by the little chapel door, whistling softly as he rocked back and forth on his heels.

George asked, "So, homecoming, can you swing it?"

Flushing, Amber nodded.

George looked pleased. "Cool. What're you doing for Halloween?"

"Probably hanging out with Marisol and Noelle. I've got a witch costume, in case we decide to go Trick-or-Treating."

"La Bruja," George responded.

"You know about Bruja?" she asked, certain she was onto something of interest to George when she caught a momentary gleam in his eyes.

Answering with deliberate casualness, not unnoticed by Amber, George said, "I've heard the stories, from my great-aunts. Most are healers; a few are something more." He waited patiently to hear what she'd say next.

"So maybe *I'm something more*," Amber admitted.

Ben Salvia opened the door to find LAPD on his doorstep.

A blaring horn honking from down the road turned everyone's head.

Officer Gutiérrez asked, "Expecting someone?"

An ear-splitting scream caught Ben's attention before he could answer Gutiérrez' question. Instantly, Ben was off the porch and bolting down the road.

Officer Gutiérrez was instantly transported in his mind to the night over the nature preserve when he'd nearly crashed. The blood-curdling shriek was identical to the one he and Johnson had heard. Without saying a word, the officers drew their guns and followed Ben Salvia.

Something fast and running low to the ground was headed up the road in their direction, but in the waning light, it was difficult to make out until it was only a few feet away.

The huge golden-furred coyote slowed when it encountered the men. Perhaps it was wary, but he trotted closer, closer, until Ben Salvia saw what it had in its mouth.

The policemen were all jaded veterans of crime scenes and horrific reactions from victims, families of victims and people being told their loved ones were injured, dying or dead. None of them had ever heard the sound that came from Ben Salvia. When they recognized the object that Ben had seen in the coyote's mouth, they understood its relevance.

A human hand…a hand, tattooed with a rattlesnake.

Ben Salvia shouted as he leapt toward the coyote. The vermin took off.

Giving chase, Ben outran the officers, reaching the Bronco first. Frantically, he searched the truck and found nothing as the officers caught up and moved to each side of the vehicle, looking for anything that might betray the driver's location.

Officer Gutiérrez was the first to spot the trail of blood behind the vehicle, leading back down the road.

Cautiously, he now took the lead, motioning the others to silently follow and had descended only a few feet when he spied movement on the plateau atop the Twelve Apostles.

The final rays of the setting sun shone over a circle of feeding coyotes. In the center was Martin Salvia, still alive but in the throes of a death rattle.

Spotting the officers far above on the road, Martin gurgled something unintelligible.

Moving into position, the officers began firing into the air in the desperate attempt to scatter the coyotes. They knew that their pitiful efforts were futile. They were simply too far away.

Of one mind, the pack firmly latched onto whatever body part they could get hold of.

Snarling, they wrenched off in different directions, taking pieces of Martin Saliva with them.

MARTIN SALVIA

CHAPTER 15

REVEALED

Officer Gutiérrez wearily waited at the portable trailer that served as LAPD's Chatsworth Division. Detective Karras put out a call to the group of teens that had witnessed first-hand the Rumble on the Rocks rabid coyote attack in hopes of learning something that could help them make sense of the insanity they'd just witnessed.

It would be all out war on coyotes after news of this attack got out. A terrified public would demand that every one of them be exterminated in an effort to protect the community from the menace.

Except Officer Gutiérrez was having a serious problem with what he'd seen. Their actions were not behaviors representative of animals crazed by illness, but had been thoughtful and deliberate, as if the coyotes had wanted them, particularly Ben, to *bear witness.*

The officers waited until everyone arrived before bringing the families into the makeshift briefing room.

"I'm afraid there's been an *incident*," Detective Karras began as gently as possible before informing the assembled parents and youths about Martin Salvia's murder at the fangs of a pack of rabid coyotes. He kept his story as matter of fact as possible, as if there were such a way to discuss someone being torn to pieces in a calm, detached manner.

Surprisingly, Jonah's mother Emily Abernathy was the first to speak. Everyone else was stunned into silence.

"The same pack that attacked the night the kids were at the Twelve Apostles?"

Detective Karras responded, "I'd like to find out. That's why we're all here."

Amber was unable to speak as a horrendous thought occurred to her. What if, in bringing the *Trickster* to their aid, she'd unwittingly unleashed a monster? Hadn't she screamed in rage, *"The Salvia brothers can drop dead, for all I care?"*

Was Martin Salvia dead because of *her?*

"I don't know how you'd tell one pack from another," Noelle finally spoke up. "Except for this one coyote. He was really big with yellowy-gold fur."

Jonah was a study in petrified horror and Marisol had joined Amber in crying. None of them had anything to add and they were therefore dismissed with a request to contact LAPD if anything else even remotely relevant occurred to them.

After the families left, Officers Johnson and Gutiérrez were in complete agreement about two things:

Fact Number One: The four teenagers knew more than they were telling. But what could they possibly know that would shed light on Martin Salvia's bizarre death? Fact Number Two: Life in Chatsworth-Lake Manor had always been odd, but it was about to get a whole lot weirder before things settled down to the quirkiness that passed for normal in Los Angeles' most eccentric outpost.

ΑΩ

Shelby's eyes grew moist as Amber related the details of Martin Salvia's horrific demise. Swallowing heavily, she could barely contain her anger, "It bothers me that your mom doesn't want to send you back to Seattle. That's so messed up!" Clenching her fists, she struggled to reconcile the Mrs. McBride she'd known over the years with this alien being now inhabiting her body. "I mean, why aren't you on a plane right now? This is so whacked! I just can't figure it!"

"Maybe because it's my fault!" Amber broke down and sobbed openly, confessing her deepest fear. "*I* brought the coyotes, and when I asked for help, something really bad answered! If it hadn't been for Marisol's prayer, I'd be dead too! Now Martin's dead because of me!"

It was well after midnight before the crime scene investigators and the coroner left, taking the harsh spotlights, cameras, duffel bags and the black body bag containing what remained of Martin Salvia. The coyote that had taunted Ben and the officers with Martin's right hand had not been found.

Ben Salvia sat atop the single column of the Twelve Apostles that jutted out from the others; a contrary triangular formation where the remaining companions presented sheer faces to the valley, the Judas of the group. Dangling his legs over the edge, he agonized over the thought of Martin's hand out atop the mountain somewhere, separated from the rest of his body.

Ben

The suggestion of his name on the wind was insufficient to rouse Ben from his misery.

I've got something for you, Ben

Leaping to his feet, Ben clearly heard her this time and searched the darkness for his mother. His eyes followed the long dirt driveway up to his house. Seeing nothing, he continued to scan the hillside, until his eyes reached the scrub oak astride the house, at the edge of the cliff.

Movement at the base caught his eye.

Breaking into a run, Ben traversed the boulder maze as quickly as possible, the air inside stifling in stark contrast to the blustery winds outside. Within minutes he cleared the stone tunnel and loped in long strides through the brush, taking a shortcut and moving directly toward the road to their house. Star-thistle weed dug into his socks and clung stubbornly to his shirt as he passed, but he ignored it and gained the road in short order. Without pausing, he sprinted up, huffing air as he ran. When his calves felt like they were on fire, he ran faster.

As he neared the top of the hill, his lungs burned and his face flushed. Collapsing over his knees, he placed his palms atop them to steady himself, heart feeling as if it would pound right out of his chest.

Leaning in, his eyes focused on something at the base of the scrub oak:

Martin's hand

Collapsing onto the ground as he swept up the hand between his own, Ben clutched it to his chest. Recalling all the times they'd wrestled, he half-expected Martin's hand to be warm, but it felt cold, stiff and heavy.

A normal person would probably burst into tears in such a situation, but Ben simply sat there, holding his brother's hand. At age twenty-four, he was spent. Any tears that might have been shed had been done away with a long time ago.

Ben Salvia felt dead inside, as icy as his brother's hand.

Δ

As Jonah got into the car and clicked his seatbelt into place, he found that he wasn't surprised by his mother's unnerving calm when discussing the particulars of Martin Salvia's demise with LAPD. He had a feeling the conversation he'd been avoiding since realizing his mom and his aunties were more than they seemed was now about to happen.

"So, are you ready to talk now?" his mother asked kindly as she started the car.

"About what?" Jonah responded evasively.

Grasping her son's shoulder with her right hand and giving it a gentle squeeze, Mrs. Emily Abernathy stated, "You being gay or a voodooist?"

Surprised, Jonah asked, "A what?"

"Honey, we come from a long line of voodoo practitioners. It's been an ancient tradition with our family, all the way back to when our people lived in Haiti. Sometimes it skips a generation, but I knew you'd come to it someday, ever since you were drawn to Robie."

"You mean that old man you found me with when I got lost?" Jonah asked, recalling the disfigured man he'd instinctually sought out in the Louisiana swamp when he was five years old.

His mother laughed, explaining, "Everyone looks old when you're a child! Robie Roubideaux must've only been in his forties when you met him. He's one of our most powerful practitioners, and a good friend to my family." Pausing, she smiled fondly at the mention of her old friend before adding, "Robie foresaw Max coming to join our family. Max has kept watch over you, you know, until you were ready. Dark things are attracted to the talented, to people like *you and me.*"

Sputtering, Jonah managed to gasp, "You, *and me*, you're Bruja!"

The delicate veneer his mother wore to mask her true nature was dropped momentarily as she inclined her head slightly in confirmation.

"*And* you know I'm gay?"

"I'm your mother, I know everything."

Open-mouthed, Jonah slumped into his seat as his mother demanded, "I need to hear *everything* that happened leading up to this so-called Rumble on the Rocks."

Acquiescing, he told his mother about seeing the guys in peril in the grotto vision, sneaking past the peeper in the cave by the waterfall, Amber calling upon the coyotes and then nearly being sucked into an invisible chasm had it not been for Marisol's prayer. Due to the media, his mother knew all about their adventure's culmination in the 'rabid coyote attack.' Unwilling to give in completely, he left out the treasure tale.

When Jonah finished, Mrs. Abernathy told him about their family's ancestral spiritual protector: *Ma'Man Brigit*: known badass voodoo Goddess and relative of the Celtic Goddess *Brigid*. She concluded with, "It's no coincidence that your friends are all coming of age at the same time. Robie told of this, too."

Jonah sat bolt upright in his seat, asking, "You mean Amber, Marisol and Noelle, right?"

"And Slone," his mother insisted.

Pensive, Jonah mused, "Slone told Amber about an ancient sorcerer named Munits that lived in the Bat Cave behind our school." Pausing, he delivered the bombshell, "Munits was also a *cannibal.* Is *that* what's after us?"

Inhaling deeply, his mother slowly responded, "I wish I knew for sure, but whenever I try to pierce the veil, all I see is blackness. Whatever it is, it's *powerful*, very old and acts like the devil."

Unnerved, Jonah worried, "How are we supposed to defend ourselves? It's living right next door to Amber! That hill outside her house must be some kind of gateway!"

His mother tried to reassure him, "You've got powerful friends of your own, what with *Ma'Man Brigit* looking out for you. And Ma'Man has an old Irish cousin named Brigid. She's got Amber's back."

Desperate, Jonah pressed, "But I still don't know what to do! What happens next?"

Mrs. Abernathy's forehead creased and her lips tightened momentarily before she revealed, "You'll all be tested in the coming months. Even Robie didn't know who will pass and who will…" her sentence trailed off. Catching herself, she concluded, "There are greater forces that have to be played out."

Dispirited, Jonah remarked, "Sounds just like what Amber's Native American friends told her, when she asked for their help. What about Noelle? That legend says Munits also lived in the Bat Cave at Castle Peak. That's right by Bell Canyon! Can't I at least use some voodoo to protect her?"

His mother responded, "Whatever you want to learn, I'll teach you, on one condition: our traditions are our own. You don't share our secrets, our spells, *nothing*, you understand me?"

✝

After Marisol spent time crying in her room, her father had quietly entered, crossed over to her dresser and lit the candle she always kept at the base of the little statue of the Virgin Mary.

"Madre Maria is there for you, mija. Lay your troubles at her feet. She has suffered many troubles herself, you know. Yet she always watches out for us."

He kissed his daughter's head and hugged her close before leaving.

Through her tears, the truth of what her father said resonated to her core:

The mother of her personal savior would *never* betray her in this way.

What had happened to Martin Salvia was someone else's doing.

Mari quickly got her girlfriends online and explained her reasoning to them, "I was very specific in my prayer! I asked Mother Mary to protect us. All of us! Think about it! Other than getting banged up, none of us were hurt, including the Salvias!"

"She has a point," Noelle conceded. "You and Ben should've been killed when you went over the cliff. I mean, I know the Santa Anas are, like, insane, but *really*? Who'd you include in your prayer?"

Marisol responded, "I thought of all of us, including the Salvias! Even George! I didn't know he wasn't there. I didn't want anyone to get hurt!"

Jonah joined the online conversation at this point and informed his friends about the bombshell conversation he'd had with his mother. He concluded, "Amber, it's not your fault! She says this Shadow Man's been stalking us!"

Amber had been very quiet, thinking over what had been said. With Jonah's revelation, she agreed, "You're right. LAPD probably should've crashed when their helicopter got blown over the Twelve Apostles. Mari's protection spell worked that night. Spells must be time-limited or something, because otherwise, Martin would still be alive!"

Noelle chimed in, "It makes sense to me. In Kendo, we have to practice every day before a match, or our skills are off. It's not like we go to one practice and then expect to win. Why would magic be any different? Especially if someone is working against us."

Solemnly, Jonah said, "I'm starting to think Slone's onto something. My mom says it's not Satan, so who's out to get us? Maybe it really *is* Munits. He was a cannibal, and look what happened to Martin!"

"Then why the Salvias?" Amber mused, "What've they got to do with any of this?"

"I'm going to ask my grandmother," Marisol decided.

"How're we gonna get away from our parents now?" Noelle wondered.

"I'm gonna try from here," Marisol responded, sounding a bit uncertain about the undertaking without the help of Las Brujas.

"I'll learn whatever badass voodoo I can and get to work," Jonah attempted to infuse confidence into his statement, but came off as goofily unsure.

Amber summarized, "We've got homework to do. Let's report back tomorrow and see what we've got."

Signing off, she searched online. Typing in "protection spell" yielded many hits:

One was a You Tube video of a man chanting, "I use the powers of the universe and my own urine to create a protection spell."

Wrinkling her nose in disgust, she moved onto the next site: AsktheDruid.com. Figuring she had nothing to lose at this point, she typed in her question.

The email response was immediate: a photograph of a pale, chubby forty-something man in a banana-yellow Speedo, and nothing else. For all her joking, a horrified Amber was now viewing a nut sack.

Hastily closing the terrible image, she decided to give one more link a try.

Images appeared of a beguiling interlaced trefoil knot. In some depictions it stood alone: simple in design, and in others it was intricately wrought. Some pictures showed the triple knot surrounded by a circle, others by a circle and a triangle. Reading the wiki entry, Amber learned that the trefoil knot was Irish in origin, named the Celtic Triquetra, and symbolized various aspects of trinity such as the three phases of a woman's life: maid, mother and crone. Christians later adopted the symbol as their own to represent the trinity of The Father, The Son and Holy Spirit.

The circle represented protection, particularly for wiccans. Launching a new search using the term "wiccan protection circle," Amber found a You Tube video by someone named *morgainelefay*, a wiccan who boldly stated she "could care less about tradition" and cast a protective circle "in a way that made sense to her."

Amber recalled what she'd learned about her ancestral Celtic Goddess:

Brigid ruled fire.

Through a fiery baptismal in the Simi Hills, Amber learned the truth about her Bruja background. In the mists atop the misshapen peak outside her house, she'd fought off Shadow Man's minion by *burning him* with her hands.

A plan began to take shape in Amber's imagination, involving a gathering of Las Brujas. It was time to take the fight to Shadow Man.

No rules: we make the rules.

THE AMERICAN BRUJA SERIES

CONTINUES WITH

DAY OF THE DEAD

IN 2017!

AMERICAN BRUJA: THE LOS ANGELES CAULDRON
CAST OF CHARACTERS

In order of appearance

1. <u>Amber McBride</u>: Incoming freshman from Seattle, relocated to Lake Manor in Los Angeles County. She has the unique ability to see through the eyes of animals and birds and is a ghost magnet. Amber is a redhead, like her parents.
2. <u>Dr. Christopher McBride</u>: Amber's father, rocket scientist and also a redhead (owing to his Irish ancestry)
3. <u>Kibbles</u>: The McBride family dog, found on an Indian Reservation in the Pacific Northwest
4. <u>The Turkey Vulture</u>: His name in Latin is Cathartes Aura, which means 'purifier.' Vultures have an uncanny ability to detect odors from decaying corpses.
5. <u>The Mountain Lioness</u>: She is a real mountain lioness (not a spirit animal). They live in the Simi Hills
6. <u>Shelby Pierce</u>: She is Native American with a 'larger than life' personality. Amber's move is the first time the best friends have been separated since Kindergarten.
7. <u>Mrs. Michelle (Aislinn) O'Donnell McBride</u>: Amber's mother has kept secret from her the fact that she is descended from a long line of Celtic priestesses. Pronounced 'Ash-ling', she goes by the mainstream name Michelle. She emigrated from Ireland to America with her older sister when she was just a baby.
8. <u>Mrs. Susan Pierce</u>: Shelby's mother and one of four sisters
9. <u>Aunt Merri</u>: One of Shelby's aunts and the first woman Amber and Shelby watched where she allowed a ghost to inhabit her body (in this particular instance, the ghost of Aunt Merri's grandmother Eleanor)
10. <u>Aunt Fawn</u>: Another of Shelby's aunts and the head of their Tribal casino
11. <u>Aunt Flora</u>: Rounding out the four sisters is Aunt Flora. Each of the sisters is powerful in her own right. Together, the women make a formidable team.
12. <u>Officer Johnson</u>: Los Angeles Police Department (LAPD) helicopter pilot in his thirties. His sunny disposition makes him a sought-after partner in what can sometimes be a grim business.

13. <u>Officer Antonio Gutiérrez</u>: Junior-ranking officer to Johnson and one of the first Latinos to make LAPD helicopter pilot. Mentored by the very first, Officer Jose Rodriguez.
14. <u>Seth Lobata</u>: Ringleader and chief mischief-maker among his friends in Lake Manor and the first new friend that Amber makes when she arrives. Also an incoming ninth grader at Castle Peak High
15. <u>Martin Salvia</u>: Third of the four Salvia brothers. Martin has had a rattlesnake tattooed on his right hand since he was twelve. Creative, he typically thinks up death-defying acts for the brothers to try out
16. <u>Mr. Baccharis</u>: Elderly magician and local eccentric. Retired special effects man
17. <u>La Luz</u>: Mr. Baccharis' cat. Her name means 'Lucy' in Spanish
18. <u>Jonah Abernathy</u>: Friend of Seth's. Jonah's father is an action-hero movie star and he attends private school (which he hates). His family on his mother's side comes from Haiti, so he prefers to be called 'black' rather than the politically correct (but in his case, inaccurate) 'African American.'
19. <u>James Toshima</u>: Another friend of Seth's, 'Jimbo' (as he is known to his friends) is very shy. He only speaks when there is something important to be said.
20. <u>Luis Garcia</u>: Rounding out Seth's posse is Luis, gregarious and outspoken in contrast to the quiet James. Longs for adventure and wishes he could be a modern-day Mexican superhero like Zorro
21. <u>Maxim Kislev</u>: Max is a thirty-something Russian bodyguard that works for the Abernathy family. The boys all want to be him and the girls wish he would stop bossing them around.
22. <u>Shane Summers</u>: His addiction to heroin renders him susceptible to the demon's influence.
23. <u>Ben Salvia</u>: Eldest of the Salvia brothers. Ben is missing the 'filter' that most people have that stops them from saying the first thing that comes to mind and, as a result, ends up pissing most people off.
24. <u>Kendrick Salvia</u>: Next in line among the Salvias, Ken usually acts as the peacemaker when the brothers get into one of their frequent fights. Also serves as the house cook since the passing of their mother
25. <u>Marisol Garcia</u>: Luis' elder sister and a sophomore at Castle Peak High. Favorite granddaughter of her mother's mother (now deceased), Graciela Hernandez
26. <u>Mrs. Susanna Hernandez Garcia</u>: Marisol and Luis' mother. The only girl among the Hernandez clan and the only one to show promise as a Bruja.
27. <u>Mr. Jorge Garcia</u>: Marisol and Luis' father, his name is pronounced 'Hor-hay'

28. <u>Noelle Mertens</u>: Marisol's friend and also a sophomore at Castle Peak High. An African Jew

29. <u>Slone Summers</u>: Like Amber, Slone is an incoming freshman. Unlike Amber and the others, she is mainly concerned about being popular.

30. <u>Aunt Ester O'Donnell</u>: Matriarch of the O'Donnell clan back in Ireland, she knows far more than she lets on and is intent on Mrs. McBride returning home one day

31. <u>Detective Bert Karras</u>: The fiftyish LAPD detective finds himself entangled in a cold case that takes a very strange turn.

32. <u>Officer Ernie Huang</u>: A twenty-something Chinese-American LAPD patrol officer assigned to the Chatsworth/Lake Manor area

33. <u>Ms. Tammy Lobata</u>: Seth's mother is a large-size lady and proud of it. Pretty and blond, her outgoing personality easily makes her Lake Manor's most-sought after realtor.

34. <u>Rose Novak</u>: Owner of the Lake Manor Log Cabin Curiosity Shop and good friend to Tammy Lobata

35. <u>Charles Graymer</u>: Mean, bitter octogenarian intent upon buying the House on Lizard Hill. The House had other plans.

36. <u>Cowboy Joe</u>: This Simi Hills original strolls around strumming old school country songs on his guitar; if you come to Chatsworth Oaks Park and walk the trails, you will find him serenading the Simi Hills.

37. <u>George Salvia</u>: A high school senior, the youngest Salvia is determined to resolve the curse that has plagued his family for centuries. He believes newcomer Amber McBride holds the key.

38. <u>Lourdes Navarro</u>: George's ex-girlfriend, this jealous senior is not ready to let go

39. <u>Robert Hugo Franklin</u>: Former owner of the House on Lizard Hill, and somehow connected to the disappearance of teenager Lucy Carpenter

40. <u>Dr. Betty Morton</u>: Psychologist working with Amber to treat her Post-Traumatic Stress Disorder, she is interconnected with the Hernandez/Garcia family in ways that none of the teenagers could have guessed

41. <u>Fred Graves</u>: Chatsworth's first lawman; some say he is still on the job

42. <u>Graciela Hernandez</u>: Marisol and Luis' grandmother, now deceased. One badass Bruja

43. <u>Nick Mertens</u>: Noelle's annoying younger brother

44. <u>Belinda and Stephen Mertens</u>: Noelle and Nick's mother and father. Because the Mertens are African Jews, they encounter their fair share of ignorance: "I didn't know there were Black Jews!" is the most common. They both stand over six feet tall and are attorneys. The ignoramus is usually fixed with a prosecutor's glare, whereupon one of the Merten's will respond, "There are Jews in every country in the world. Why do you think Mossad is so effective? We speak every language and we're

everywhere. Of course you can't tell what a Jew looks like, because we look like no one and everyone."

45. <u>Marcus Abernathy</u>: Action hero of the big screen, he is perpetually disappointed in his youngest son Jonah

46. <u>Emily Abernathy</u>: Jonah's mother and a model by profession, her people come from Haiti and brought their traditions to Louisiana when they immigrated

47. <u>Mr. and Mrs. Toshima</u>: James' parents live atop a large hill inside a gated community at the southeastern end of the nature preserve. His father is the Executive Director of a non-profit and his mother curates the Japanese-American Museum in downtown Los Angeles.

AMERICAN BRUJA: THE LOS ANGELES CAULDRON
GUIDE TO SYMBOLS

In order of appearance

AΩ Alpha and Omega: The first and last letters of the Greek alphabet, symbolizing the beginning and the end.

∞ Infinity: Mathematical symbol that represents that which continues on endlessly.

Oak Tree: Sacred to the priests and priestesses of pre-Christian Ireland, oaks grow in abundance in the Simi Hills. Oak trees are protected in Los Angeles. No one is allowed to cut one down without a special permit.

Δ Delta: Greek letter and mathematical symbol representing change.

Celtic Triad: This three-pointed symbol represents the three phases of womanhood: maid (youth), mother and crone (elder). When Christianity came to Ireland, the Celtic Triad was co-opted and adapted to represent the Father, Son and Holy Spirit.

Lizard: The little lizards are known as Skinks and are common in San Fernando Valley backyards. Medium-sized lizards are called Western Fence Lizards. The biggest ones are called Alligator Lizards. If you ever see one, you will understand why they were given such a fearsome name (Hint: some have tails so long, they are often mistaken for rattlesnakes).

Evil Eye: This symbol is common in many cultures. The unifying theme is that wearing this talisman wards off evil. Affixing the evil eye to one's door serves the same purpose.

Yin and Yang: A common Taoist (pronounced "dao-ist") symbol representing two parts of the whole. Some interpret the two aspects to be in conflict (e.g., dark and light, male and female), but the Taoist views yin and yang as complementary to one another. Both are necessary to be in balance.

241

<u>Dharma Wheel</u>: It is sometimes shown with eight spokes to represent the paths of Buddhism. However, the concept of dharma originates in Hinduism and signifies living in accordance with universal law and order.

♀ <u>Ankh</u>: Egyptian symbol of the eternally divine female.

✝ <u>Christian Cross</u>: A popular method of execution during the time of Roman dominion over Europe and the Middle East was crucifixion. It is therefore a great irony that Caesar's symbol of death was later adopted by Emperor Constantine to represent rebirth and renewal (when Christianity became the official religion of Rome).

<u>Spider</u>: Tarantulas and Black Widows are common in the Simi Hills.

AUTHOR NOTES

I approached this work of historical fiction as I do my work as a Community Psychologist. I publish nothing without consideration of community context and input from cultural insiders. As a result, we have had a lot of fun in this creative endeavor; collaborating with others beats working alone any day.

The male characters in American Bruja are authentic because they speak with my husband's voice (I asked, but he refused to accept co-author credit). Most everything that makes you laugh in American Bruja belongs to Dodd Harris. His review comments were hysterical (and completely accurate). My favorite was "too much tree talk." I could have filled the entire book with loving descriptions of the "First Peoples." Perhaps ten people here locally would have wanted to read such a book.

My daughter, Piper Harris, provided key insights on teenage life and dialogue. Rather than reading it by herself, she insisted that we read the book aloud, together. This method proved to be quite enjoyable as well as valuable because a lot of material wound up discarded as a result of her feedback. It probably wasn't easy reading what will be the first in a series of books about her fictional counterpart, but she handled this adventure with good humor (and saved George Salvia in the process, but that's a story for another time).

Many thanks to my brave Beta readers; dear friends and family members that endured early drafts of American Bruja and returned valid critiques that greatly improved the final version. They are (in alphabetical order): Dr. Candace DePuy, Shelley Joiner, Dr. Jacob Kerst, Linnea Luker, Jennifer Lovell McCracken, Cherokee O'Dea and Agnes Weaskus. Walking the line between telling the known "Simi Hills Stories" while taking care to not inadvertently out anyone from the broom closet was a tricky business. My Beta readers helped me immeasurably in this regard.

Lake Manor, the Simi Hills, Castle Peak and the House on Lizard Hill are all real places. You can visit the Santa Susana Pass State Historic Park anytime (admission is free). If you see a singing cowboy when you are out on the trail, please tell him "hello" from me.

Elizabeth Harris
December 18, 2015
Chatsworth, California

Made in the USA
Lexington, KY
04 October 2016